The Cruel Sea

OTHER BOOKS BY

Nicholas Monsarrat

THIS IS THE SCHOOLROOM

(1940)

H. M. CORVETTE

(1943)

LEAVE CANCELLED

(1945)

DEPENDS WHAT YOU MEAN BY LOVE

(1948)

MY BROTHER DENYS

(1949)

Nicholas Monsarrat

THE
CRUEL
SEA

ALFRED · A · KNOPF

New York: 1951

This is a BORZOI BOOK, *published by* ALFRED A. KNOPF, *Inc.*

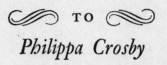

TO

Philippa Crosby

Note: *All the characters in this book are wholly fictitious. If I have inadvertently used the names of men who did in fact serve in the Atlantic during the war, I apologize to them for so doing. Where I have mentioned actual war-appointments, such as Flag-Officer-in-Charge at Liverpool or Glasgow, the characters who are portrayed in such appointments have no connection whatsoever with the actual incumbents; and if there was a W.R.N.S. officer holding the job of S.O.O.2 on the Clyde in 1943, then she is not my "Second Officer Hallam." In particular, my Admiral in charge of the working-up base at "Ardnacraish" is not intended as a portrait of the energetic and distinguished officer who discharged with such efficiency a similar task in the Western Approaches Command.*

Contents

The Cruel Sea

THE CRUEL SEA

Before the Curtain

This is the story—the long and true story—of one ocean, two ships, and about a hundred and fifty men. It is a long story because it deals with a long and brutal battle, the worst of any war. It has two ships because one was sunk and had to be replaced. It has a hundred and fifty men because that is a manageable number of people to tell a story about. Above all, it is a true story because that is the only kind worth telling.

First, the ocean, the steep Atlantic stream. The map will tell you what that looks like: three-cornered, three thousand miles across and a thousand fathoms deep, bounded by the European coastline and half of Africa, and the vast American continent on the other side: open at the top like a champagne glass, and at the bottom like a municipal rubbish-dumper. What the map will not tell you is the strength and fury of that ocean, its moods, its violence, its gentle balm, its treachery: what men can do with it, and what it can do with men. But this story will tell you all that.

Then the ship, the first of the two, the doomed one. At the moment she seems far from doomed: she is new, untried, lying in a river that lacks the tang of salt water, waiting for the men to man her. She is a corvette, a new type of escort ship, an experiment designed to meet a desperate situation still over the horizon. She is brand-new; the time is November 1939: her name is H.M.S. *Compass Rose*.

3

Lastly, the men, the hundred and fifty men. They come on to the stage in twos and threes: some are early, some are late, some, like this pretty ship, are doomed. When they are all assembled, they are a company of sailors. They have women, at least a hundred and fifty women, loving them, or tied to them, or glad to see the last of them as they go to war.

But the men are the stars of this story. The only heroines are the ships: and the only villain the cruel sea itself.

PART ONE

1939: *Learning*

[*1*]

Lieutenant-Commander George Eastwood Ericson, R.N.R., sat in a stone cold, draughty, corrugated-iron hut beside the fitting-out dock of Fleming's Shipyard on the River Clyde. Ericson was a big man, broad and tough: a man to depend on, a man to remember: about forty-two or -three, fair hair going grey, blue eyes as level as a foot rule, with wrinkles at the corners—the product of humour and of twenty years' staring at a thousand horizons. At the moment the wrinkles were complicated by a frown. It was not a worried frown—if Ericson was susceptible to worry he did not show it to the world; it was simply a frown of concentration, a tribute to a problem.

On the desk in front of him was a grubby, thumbed-over file labelled *Job No. 2891: Movable Stores*. Through the window and across the dock, right under his competent eye, was a ship: an untidy grey ship, mottled with red lead, noisy with riveting, dirty with an accumulation of wood shavings, cotton waste, and empty paint-drums.

The file and the ship were connected, bound together by the frown on his face. For the ship was his: he was to commission and to command H.M.S. *Compass Rose*, and at this moment he did not wholly like the idea.

It was a dislike, a doubt, compounded of a lot of things that ordinarily he would have taken in his stride, if indeed he had noticed them at all. Certainly it had nothing to do with

5

the ship's name: one could not spend twenty years at sea, first in the Royal Navy and then in the Merchant Service, without coming across some of the most singular names in the world. (The clumsiest he remembered had been a French tramp called the *Marie-Josephe Brinomar de la Tour du Pin;* and the oddest an East Coast collier called *Jolly Nights*.) *Compass Rose* was nothing out of the ordinary; it had to be a flower name because she was one of the new Flower Class corvettes, and (Ericson smiled to himself) by the time they got down to *Pansy* and *Stinkwort* and *Love-in-the-Mist*, no one would think anything of *Compass Rose*.

Those were trivialities, anyway. Perhaps the real trouble had to do with this precise moment of history, the start of a war. Ericson had been just too young to be closely involved in World War I: now he was secretly wondering if he were not too old to play a worth-while part in the second round of the same struggle. At the moment he had, as his novel responsibility, a new job, a new ship, and a new crew. In theory he was proud of them all; in practice, he was unsure of the ordeal and concerned about his fitness for it.

He felt remarkably out of practice. . . . Ericson had been axed from the Navy in 1927, after ten years' service: he had been on the beach for two hard years, and then spent the next ten with the Far East Line, feeling himself lucky all the time (what with the depression and Britain's maritime decay) to have a sea-going job at all. He loved the sea, though not blindly: it was the cynical, self-contemptuous love of a man for a mistress whom he distrusts profoundly but cannot do without. Far East Line had been a tough crowd: progress was slow, with the threat of dismissal always poised: in ten years he had only had command of one ship, an old two-thousand-ton freighter slowly pounding herself to bits on the Dutch East Indies run.

It was not a good introduction to responsibility in war. And now here he was, almost masquerading as Lieutenant-Commander G. E. Ericson, with one of His Majesty's ships of war to commission, a crew of eighty-eight to command, and a hundred things in the realm of naval routine to relearn, quite apart from having a fighting ship to manœuvre and to use as a weapon.

A fighting ship. . . . He raised his eyes from the interminable office-boy job of checking stores, and looked at *Compass Rose* again. She was odd, definitely odd, even making allowances for her present unfinished state. She was two hundred feet long, broad, chunky, and graceless: designed purely for anti-submarine work, and not much more than a floating platform for depth charges, she was the prototype of a class of ship that could be produced quickly and cheaply in the future to meet the urgent demands of convoy escort. Her mast, contrary to Naval practice, was planted right in front of the bridge, and the squat funnel behind it: she had a high fo'c's'le armed with a single four-inch gun, which the senior gunnery rating was at that moment elevating and training. The depth-charge rails aft led over a whaler-type stern—aesthetically deplorable, but effective enough at sea. Ericson knew ships, and he could guess how this one was going to behave. She would be hot in summer—there was no forced-draught ventilation, and no refrigerator—and cold, wet, and uncomfortable at most other times. She would be a natural bastard in any kind of seaway, and in a full Atlantic gale she would be thrown about like a chip of wood. And that was really all you could say about her—except that she was his, and that, whatever her drawbacks and imperfections, he had to get her going and make her work.

The crew he was less worried about. Both the discipline and the habit of command instilled by the Royal Navy died very hard: Ericson knew that he had them still. All things being equal, he could handle those men, he could make them do what he wanted—if he knew himself. The flaw might be in the material he would have to work on: in a rapidly expanding navy, a new ship's company was likely to be a scratch lot. The advance guard of a dozen key ratings had already arrived, to take charge in their various departments—gunnery, depth charges, asdic, telegraphy, signalling, engine room. As a nucleus they were satisfactory: but the numbers might be made up, and the gaps filled, by anything from professional hard-cases just out of Detention Barracks to green "hostilities only" ratings fresh from the farmyard. And his officers—a First Lieutenant and two subs—could make a hash of anything he might want to do with the ship. . . .

Ericson frowned again, and then stopped frowning. Whatever his doubts, they were not to show: that was a cardinal rule. He was a seaman: this was a seaman's job, though it didn't feel like it at the moment. He bent to his desk again, wishing he could develop some sort of a taste for paper work: wishing also that his First Lieutenant, whose work incidentally should have included the file in front of him, were a slightly more reassuring character.

[2]

Lieutenant James Bennett, R.A.N.V.R. (the "A" for Australia), First Lieutenant of H.M.S. *Compass Rose*, strode round the cluttered upper deck as if he owned every rivet of it, with Petty Officer Tallow, the coxswain, following him at a disrespectful distance. Bennett looked tough, and knew it, and liked it: everything about him—the red face, the stocky figure, the cap worn at an unusual angle—all proclaimed the homespun sailorman with no frills and no nonsense. That was the picture he had of himself, and with luck it was going to carry him through the war: certainly it had got him his present job, aided by fast talking and a selection board preoccupied with more important things than sifting claims about past exploits.

Chance had found him in England at the outbreak of war, instead of clerking in a shipping office in Sydney: his commission in the Volunteer Reserve was undeniable: the rest had been easy—an anti-submarine course, an interview in London, and the job of First Lieutenant in *Compass Rose*. It wasn't *all* that he wanted—too much paper work, for a start, though the subs could take care of that as soon as they arrived; but it would do until something better turned up. And meanwhile he was First Lieutenant of this little crap-barge, and he was going to act the part.

"Coxs'n!"

"Sir?"

Standing by the four-inch gun, Bennett waited for Tallow to catch up. It took a little time, for Petty Officer Tallow (seventeen years in the Navy, three stripes, due for Chief P.O. any moment now) was feeling disgruntled. This certainly wasn't what he had volunteered for—a fiddling bloody little gash-boat instead of a proper ship (his last ship had been *Repulse*), a First Lieutenant like something out of the films, and Christ knows what sort of a ship's company due to join next week. But Tallow, like the Captain, was a product of the Navy, which meant, above all, acceptance of the current job and the current circumstances: only in the subtlest ways (and none of them destructive) would he indicate that this sort of thing was *not* what he was used to.

As Tallow came up: "This man," said Bennett heavily, pointing to the rating who was working on the four-inch gun, "is smoking during working hours."

Tallow restrained a sigh. "Yes, sir. Not working proper routine yet, sir."

"Who says not?"

The seaman under discussion surreptitiously disposed of his cigarette, and bent to his task with extraordinary concentration. Tallow tried again.

"I was going to leave it until we had the full ship's company aboard, sir."

"That makes no difference," said Bennett briskly. "No smoking except during Stand-Easy. Understand?"

"Aye, aye, sir."

"And don't you forget it."

Jesus, thought Tallow, what sort of a country is Australia . . . ? Following once more in the First Lieutenant's wake, he sank a little deeper into resignation. This bastard was all wind, and the only other officers were two green subs (he'd had a glance at the scheme of complement).

Barring the Captain, who was O.K., it looked as if he'd have to carry the bloody ship himself.

[3]

The door of the dockside hut flapped open, letting in a ferocious draught. The Captain looked up, and then turned in his chair.

"Come in," he said. "And shut the door very firmly."

The two young men who stood before him were physically in strong contrast with each other, though their uniforms, with the single thin wavy stripe on the arm, gave them a surface similarity. One of them, the elder one, was tall, black-haired, thin-faced: he had a watchful air, as though feeling his way in a situation that only needed a little time to fall into its proper category, alongside hundreds of other situations that he had dealt with competently and effectively in the past. The other one was a simpler edition altogether: short, fair, immature—a very young man in a proud uniform, and not yet sure that he deserved the distinction. Looking at them, Ericson suddenly thought: they're more like father and son, though there can't be more than five or six years between them. . . . He waited for one of them to speak, knowing well which of them it would be.

The elder one saluted and said: "Reporting for *Compass Rose*, sir." He proffered a slip of paper, and Ericson glanced at it.

"You're Lockhart?"

"Yes, sir."

"And you're Ferraby?"

"Yes, sir."

"First ship?"

"Yes, sir," Lockhart answered, as the natural spokesman. "We've just come up from *King Alfred*."

"How long were you training there?"

10

"Five weeks."

"And now you know it all?"

Lockhart grinned. "No, sir."

"Well, that's something, anyway."

Ericson looked at them more closely. They were both very smart: number one doeskin jackets, gloves, gas masks—they might have stepped straight out of the Manual of Training. They had talked of this question of dress, on the long journey up from the South Coast to the Clyde: their orders had been endorsed: "Report to Admiral Superintending Contract-Built Ships," and it had seemed politic to dress the part. . . . The Captain, in his old serge working jacket with the faded gold lace, seemed theatrically shabby by comparison.

After a pause, Ericson asked: "What was your job in peacetime?"

"Journalist, sir," said Lockhart.

The Captain smiled, and waved his hand round the room. "What's the connection?"

"I've done a lot of sailing, sir."

"M'm. . . ." He looked at Ferraby. "What about you?"

"I was working in a bank, sir."

"Ever been to sea?"

"Only across to France, sir."

"We might find that useful. . . . All right—take a look at the ship, and report to the First Lieutenant—he's somewhere aboard. Where's all your gear?"

"At the hotel, sir."

"It'll have to stay there for a bit—we won't be sleeping on board for a week or so."

With a nod, Ericson turned back to his desk. The two young men saluted, somewhat uncertainly, and made for the door. As Ferraby opened it, the Captain said, over his shoulder:

"And by the way, don't salute me indoors when I haven't got a cap on. I can't return it. The proper drill is for you to take your cap off when you come in."

"Sorry, sir," said Lockhart.

"It's not vital," said Ericson. They could hear the friendliness in his voice. "But you might as well get it right."

When they had gone, he paused for a moment before returning to work. Journalist . . . bank clerk . . . trips to France . . . sailing. . . . It didn't sound very professional. But they seemed willing, and the older one, Lockhart, had some common sense, by the look of him. You could do a lot with common sense, at sea. And you could do precious little without it. . . . He picked up his pencil again.

[4]

Lockhart and Ferraby walked across the dock and then paused, looking up at the ship. They saw her with different eyes. Lockhart could, to a certain extent, appraise her lines and her design: to Ferraby she was entirely novel, in every detail, and this, like a lot of other things, worried him. He had been married only six weeks: saying good-bye to his wife two nights previously, he had confided once more his uncertainty, his doubt about what he had taken on. "But darling," she had said, with that loving smile that he found so moving and so beautiful, "you can do *anything*. You know you can. Look how happy you've made *me*." It was illogical, but it was very comforting all the same. Everything about their marriage was like that. They were just getting over their shyness together, and finding the process singularly sweet.

Ferraby had said good-bye to a new wife: Lockhart had said good-bye to nothing. He had answered: "Journalist" to the Captain, but he was not at all sure he deserved the title. He was twenty-seven: for six years he had scratched a living, free-lancing in and around Fleet Street: it had taught him a lot, but it had not given him an ounce of security or a moment's freedom from worry. He was not even sure that was what he wanted, in any case. He had no parents living, he had no ties: the only woman he had taken leave of had said: "Why ever didn't we do this before?" as he climbed out of bed and into his uniform, in the cold London dawn. That had been symptomatic of his whole life: uncertain, impermanent, shifting in emphasis and intensity. He had joined up because there was a war: he had joined the Navy because he knew about ships—small ships, anyway—and could navigate. Now he felt happy, and free, and confident; and he liked the change.

Ferraby, pointing, said: "What's that wire thing tacked onto the mast?"

"Some radio gadget, I suppose. . . . Let's go aboard."

They crossed the rough plank that served as a gangway, and jumped down onto the deck. Here and there it was still rimed with frost, and a hundred things were lying about it—oil drums, tool boxes, welding gear, oddments of equipment. There was loud hammering from a dozen places, and somewhere up in the bows a riveting machine was making a prodigious racket. Lockhart led the way aft, and they looked at the depth-charge gear—a replica of what they had worked on at the training establishment: then they went below, and presently found themselves in the cabin-space. There were only two cabins, one with a single berth labelled "First Lieutenant," and a tiny wardroom: the whole thing was cramped and full of awkward corners.

"This is going to be damned crowded," said Lockhart presently. "You and I share a cabin, I suppose."

"I wonder what the First Lieutenant's like," said Ferraby, looking at the label on the door.

"Whatever he's like, we'll have to put up with him. He can make or break this ship, as far as we're concerned."

"How?"

"Just by being bloody, or the reverse, as the fancy takes him."

"Oh. . . . I liked the Captain."

"He *loved* you. . . . Yes, he's all right. The good R.N.R.'s are really good."

"A lot of them don't like us."

13

"Us?"

"The R.N.V.R."

Lockhart smiled. "Two years from now, *we'll* do the picking and choosing. . . . Don't you worry about the V.R., my lad. It's going to be *our* war, in the end. That's the only way they'll be able to man the ships."

"You mean, we'll actually get commands?"

Lockhart nodded, abstractedly. He was examining the wardroom pantry, which was inordinately small.

A raucous voice over their heads shouted: "Below!" The noise rang round the empty wardroom.

"What a rough man," said Lockhart.

After a pause the shout was repeated, on a higher note.

"Is that us?" asked Ferraby uncertainly.

"I fear so." Lockhart walked to the foot of the ladder, and peered upwards. "Yes?"

The red face framed in the companionway was not reassuring. Bennett was glaring down at him.

"What the hell are you hiding down there for?"

"I'm not," said Lockhart.

"Weren't you told to report to me?"

"After looking round the ship, yes."

"Sir," prompted Bennett unpleasantly.

"Sir," said Lockhart. He could almost feel Ferraby's harassed expression behind him.

"Is the other sub down there too?"

"Yes—sir. We didn't know you were aboard."

"Don't wear a green coat with me," said Bennett obscurely. "Come up here—and double up."

Confronting the two of them at the top of the ladder, Bennett looked at them closely. He was frowning, and the rough Australian accent was prominent when he spoke.

"It's your job to find out where I am," he began sourly. "Names?"

"Lockhart," said Lockhart.

"Ferraby," said Ferraby.

"How long since you were commissioned?"

"A week," said Lockhart. And added: "Temporary Probationary."

"I can see that," said Bennett disagreeably. "It sticks out like a ——." He produced a colourful simile. "Ever been to sea before?"

"In small boats," said Lockhart.

"I don't mean ——ing about in yachts."

"Then, no."

Bennett turned to Ferraby. "You?"

"No, sir."

"Wonderful. . . . Which of you is senior?"

"We passed out together," said Lockhart.

"Jesus Christ, I know that! But one of you is senior, one of you is ahead of the other in the Navy List."

"We're not in the Navy List yet."

Bennett saw Lockhart staring at him, sizing him up, and he did not like it.

"You're not out of the egg yet, by the sound of it."

Lockhart said nothing.

"Well, we'd better find out what you *can* do," said Bennett after a pause. "Have you been round the ship?"

"Yes."

"How many fire-hose points are there?"

"Fourteen," answered Lockhart promptly. He had no idea what the right answer was, but he was quite sure that Bennett didn't know either. Later, if Bennett checked up, he would climb out of it somehow.

"Very clever," said Bennett. He turned to Ferraby. "What sort of a gun have we got?"

"Four-inch," said Ferraby after a pause.

"Four-inch what?" asked Bennett roughly. "Breech-loading? Quick-firing? Mark IV? Mark VI? Fixed ammunition?"

"Four-inch—I don't know," said Ferraby miserably.

"Find out," snapped Bennett. "I'll ask you next time I see you. And now both of you go back to the hut, and start checking C.B.'s."

15

"Yes, sir," said Lockhart. He turned to go, as did Ferraby.
"Salute," said Bennett.
They saluted.
"I'm the First Lieutenant around here," said Bennett.
"Don't you forget it."

"An engaging character," said Lockhart on the way back.
"I can see we're going to get on like a house on fire—and I
hope the bastard fries."
"What are C.B.'s?" asked Ferraby in a forlorn tone.
"Confidential books."
"Why couldn't he say so?"
"He had a reason."
"What reason?"
Lockhart smiled. "It's a process of *impressement*."
"French?"
"The French do it better. . . . Vulgarly speaking, the
motto is 'Bull-dust baffles brains.' I must say he's quite a
performer."
"It's not what I expected," said Ferraby.
"You're the sub-lieutenant around here," said Lockhart,
mimicking brilliantly. "Don't you forget it."
"But which of us *is* senior?"
"I think I'd better be."

[5]

With nightfall, a grateful quiet returned to *Compass Rose*.
The noise of hammering died, the bustle subsided: the last
workman hurried across the gangway toward the waiting
tram—this was before the unending urgency of night shifts:
the single watchman who remained, huddled under his canvas
shelter on the quarterdeck, cursed the cold breeze that blew
the charcoal fumes from his brazier directly into his eyes.

16

The ship rocked gently to the stirring of the river: queer shadows fell on the deck, and moved, and were still again.

Now the huge activity of the Clydeside ebbed to nothing: the river, lined with silent half-finished ships, deserted ship-yards, and cranes stationary against a spectral sky, resolved itself into a backwash of the war. It was the end of one day—no better, no worse than other days: the ships a little nearer completion, the jobs advanced a single stage toward their end—and toward other jobs, in an unending series that would test patience more than skill, and endurance more than both of them. The Clyde had done this sort of thing before: now, in 1939, it was going to do it again, as a matter of course, without heroics. But this moment was only the beginning; poised on the verge of a six-years' effort, there was still space to relax, and time to sleep at night.

The night-watchman, an old pensioner, grumbled and scratched and fell into a doze. He'd had his war—the last one: it was someone else's turn now. Good luck to them: but they mustn't expect miracles from everyone. Miracles were for young chaps: for the old, a decent rest, a decent sleep, were nothing to be ashamed of.

In a public house in the noisy part of Argyll Street, near the railway station, Petty Officer Tallow and the senior engine-room rating, Chief E.R.A. Watts, were drinking up before going off to their lodgings. They had been there since eight o'clock that evening: they had drunk seven pints of beer apiece: it had made not an atom of difference to either their diction or their bearing, save that Tallow was now inclined to perspire and Watts's eyes were a trifle bloodshot. They were there partly because there was nothing else for them to do—they didn't care for cinemas, and their lodgings were dirty and uncomfortable—and partly because they liked the place, and could not have felt more at home anywhere. There was a great deal of noise in the bar, and near by the dart players were going to work with quick frenzy, anxious to finish their game before closing time. Now and then Tallow and Watts looked up and watched one of the shots, but mostly they drank and talked in low grumbling tones. They had been grumbling, as well as drinking, since eight o'clock, and had mellowed very little in the process.

"She'll not be a happy ship, I can tell you straight." Watts was a Scotsman, grey-headed, bald, nearly through with his time in the Navy: his accent and Tallow's, broad Scots and full-flavoured Lancashire, blended in rough harmony. "There's not the makings of it. I'm not saying the skipper's not O.K., but that Jimmy's a bastard. He was round my engine room tonight, blethering about a watchkeeping bill—and me with the bloody main shaft still opened up. Sooner I get my ticket, and settle down on the pension, the better."

"There'll be no tickets while the war lasts," said Tallow. He took a pull at his glass tankard, and wiped his mouth. "If you're warm, you're in—for the duration."

"Well, there'll be shore-billets," insisted Watts. "Something easy, back in barracks—that'll just suit me. The ship's too small for my liking."

"She'll be lively enough," agreed Tallow. "By God, you could hoist the whole outfit aboard *Repulse*, and not feel the difference."

Watts laughed. "I hope yon *Repulse* will be handy, if we run into trouble."

"We're likely to do that, by the way they're talking. Beats me how they can expect ships of that size to put up any sort of protection for a convoy. It took destroyers all their time, last war."

"There'll be tactics," said Watts vaguely.

"They'll need a sight more than tactics, to come out on the right side. What've we got in the way of armament? One bloody little four-inch pop-gun, and a couple of rows of depth-charges. They'll make rings round us."

"What gets me is the accommodation," broke in Watts, reverting to an earlier complaint. "We're all mixed up together, *and* there's not enough room anyway. There's stokers messing alongside seamen—you know well enough they don't like that, either of them. The fo'c's'le's about six feet by four, there's no canteen, no refrigeration, no forced draught. You can't go from the mess-decks to the bridge without getting wet through, and the galley's right aft so that everything will be stone cold by the time we eat it. Whoever designed that ship must have been piss-arse drunk."

"Wish the bastard had to sail in her." Morosely Tallow took a final swig at his tankard, and then looked across to the bar as "time" was called. "What about it? One for the road?"

"Not for me. I've got to work tomorrow."

Outside, Argyll Street was noisy with people coming out of the pubs and stumbling about in the blackout. It was very cold: at the street corner a raw wind made them turn up their coat collars and put their hands deep in their pockets. As they made their way to their tram stop:

"Heaven help sailors," said Watts piously. "Man, it'll be bitter at sea tonight."

"We'll know that soon enough," said Tallow. "A couple of weeks from now we'll be crying our eyes out for Argyll Street, wet or fine. You just wait."

Lockhart and Ferraby were both tired. They had spent most of the day in the dockside hut, checking lists of stores and charts and confidential books, with periodic, maddening directives from Bennett to break off and do something quite different. The list of stores was interminable: the charts covered every ocean in the world, and there was at the bottom of the box a chart of the Black Sea. Lockhart, contem-templating this, had murmured: "What a long war it's going to be," and Bennett, overhearing, had countered: "It'll be a bloody sight longer unless you stop nattering and get on with it. . . ." Later they had been sent back on board *Compass Rose*, to start on the accommodation plan—unde-niably the First Lieutenant's job: the working day had finished at six, with a sharp order from Bennett to be back in the hut by half past eight next morning. As they had an hour's tram ride from their hotel to the shipyard, it would mean a very early start to the day.

Now, after a late dinner, they were both lying in bed in the hotel room they shared on Sauchiehall Street: Ferraby staring at the ceiling, hands clasped behind his head, Lockhart smoking and thumbing through the *Manual of Seamanship*. Outside, the crude noises of Glasgow at night gradually diminished.

Presently Ferraby stirred and, leaning over on one elbow, asked: "What are you reading?"

"The bible—our bible," answered Lockhart. "There's a lot in it which has to be squared with the actual facts."

"You mean, the First Lieutenant?"

Lockhart laughed. "Oh—him. . . . He's feeling his way, the same as we are, only he's making more noise about it."

"He's certainly doing that." Ferraby lay back again. "I wonder if I could get my wife up here?"

"Good idea. We won't be living on board for some time. Why not ask about it?"

"Ask who?"

"Bennett, I suppose. Or the Captain."

"Bennett would say 'no'. . . . I was just getting used to being married."

"It must be very satisfactory," said Lockhart, without irony.

"It's more than that." Shyly enthusiastic, Ferraby could not disguise the true focus of his thoughts. "It's meant everything to me, the last few weeks. I don't know how I could have got through otherwise. She's so—when you marry a person—" he floundered, and then made an effort. "Haven't you ever felt as if you must have someone you can trust absolutely—someone you can tell everything to, without—without ever feeling ashamed? Someone who's the other half of yourself."

"No," said Lockhart after a pause. "I don't think I've ever needed that."

"That's what it's been like for me. For both of us, I think. That's why it's so rotten to be separated."

"Well, see if you can get her up here." Lockhart closed

his book, and stubbed out his cigarette. "There's no harm in asking, anyway. After all, the Captain's wife is here."

"That's different."

"Not necessarily. Try it, and see what happens." Lockhart switched out the light, and lay back. "Oh God, why do we have to get up so early?"

"There's a terrific lot to do."

"Yes, I suppose so. . . . Good night."

"Good night."

"And don't let it get you down."

"It's all so different from what I expected."

"It'd be damned funny if it weren't."

Downstairs, in the lounge of the same hotel, Bennett was withholding his custom from a grim-looking tart he had picked up at the bar. He couldn't *quite* make up his mind—and, in the meantime, he felt like a nice chat. . . . The room was crowded, noisy, and very hot. Above Bennett's sweaty red face, his cap still maintained its informal angle.

For the fifth or sixth time the woman tipped her glass and said: "Here's fun, dear!" She had a face like a ruined skull, white and lined: her tight black skirt strained at its seams, overdoing the candour of the flesh, repellent in its allure.

"Cheerio!" said Bennett, as before. He drank, and stared at his glass. "Ever been in Australia?"

"No," said the woman. "Can't say I have. Long way from here, you know."

"Too right, it's a long way! Might be the other side of hell, for all the chance I have of seeing it."

"You'll get back all right. Soon as the war's over."

"Can't be too soon for me." He sipped his beer moodily.

"Don't you like Scotland? . . . Bonny Scotland," she added as an afterthought. She was clearly a Cockney, and the Scottish inflection, borrowed from the music halls, had a grotesque unreality. "Glasgie belongs to me—you know what the song says." She drank elegantly, finger crooked, and set down her glass as if ashamed of using so crude an instrument.

"Oh, Scotland's all right," said Bennett after a pause. "But you know how it is—" He waved his hand round the bar, knocked over a tankard, and drenched his coat and trousers with beer.

"Oh, bugger it!" he exclaimed loudly.

"Naughty!" said the woman mechanically.

Bennett mopped himself vigorously. "Waste of a good drink," he said. And then: "Scotland's all right. But it's not Sydney, by a long way."

"I suppose not," said the woman. She crossed her legs delicately. "Have you got a girl, back in Australia?"

"Sure," said Bennett, "rafts of them."

"The girls I left behind me, eh?"

"Something like that."

"Well," said the woman, a trifle edgily, "tonight's my busy night." She picked up her bag from the counter.

"Don't go," said Bennett, making up his mind. "Have another drink."

"No, thanks."

"I'll see you home, then."

"It's a long way," said the woman. "Fourpence in the trams."

"We'll get a taxi."

"My! Going the pace, aren't you?" She got down from her stool at the bar and stood looking at him, judging his mood. "What happens when we get there?"

"I'll see you're all right."

"I've met sailors before," said the woman.

"Not Australians."

"No," she admitted. "You're the first Australian I've met, socially speaking."

"It'll be a treat for you." Bennett heaved himself off his stool, and took her arm. "Well, here we go."

The woman nodded to the barman. "So long, Fred."

"See you again," said the barman. "Good night."

"I'll see to the good night myself," said Bennett, with a singular leer. "That's my little bit of the job." He crammed his cap over one eye at a jauntier angle still.

"Are you really an officer?" asked the woman on the way out.

The Captain sat in the lounge of the stuffy hotel on Kelvin-side reading a bad thriller picked up from the bookshelf: opposite him, Mrs. Ericson was knitting. She was a plump, placid-faced woman of about forty: she always knitted during the evening—pullovers and mufflers for her husband, cardigans for herself, odd garments for odd relatives and their new babies. It sometimes seemed to Ericson that she had been sitting opposite him and knitting, without a break, for nineteen years on end. This was the picture of her he always visualized, when he thought of her at sea or when he was coming home on leave: he warmed to it readily, but its reality often made him impatient and irritated by the time his leave was up and he was due to go to sea again.

They were quietly happy together: they never quarrelled. He was, he supposed, a good husband and father, and she was the female counterpart: certainly he had never looked more than twice at any other woman. But now, as so often before, he was conscious of the familiar impatience as they sat in silence together. He must have been long enough ashore. . . . Grace was a dear girl, but this time his leave had lasted over two months, and the ship and the sea were beginning, as always, to pull him away from her and everything she stood for. It was not unfaithfulness to her: it was faithfulness to the other love, the tough professional one that was stronger than any human tie.

They had never talked of this, save laughingly when they were newly married. She had come to accept the order of priority, and, being a sensible woman, she had ceased to worry about its deeper implications. For a few days of each leave she gave him all that he wanted—the warm welcome, the tenderness, the occasional shaft of passion, the softness after hard ordeal; then, matching his mood, she faded into the placid background of their lives and, perhaps symbolically, picked up her knitting again. She counted herself happy, and, as a sailor's daughter herself, she was proud of her husband's professional skill and standing. Sea-going was indeed a family matter. Their only son, now seventeen, was apprenticed to the Holt Line of Liverpool and was at sea, somewhere in the Atlantic, at that moment.

It was of their son that she presently spoke, while the clock ticked towards eleven and the shoddy lounge gradually emptied of visitors.

"George," she began.

Ericson laid down his book, without regret. "Yes, dear?"

"I've been thinking about John."

"He'll be all right," said the Captain after a moment.

"Oh, I don't mean *that*." Rarely did they talk of the chances of life and death at sea, and since the beginning of the war they had not mentioned the subject at all. They knew that they both had much to lose, and Grace Ericson most of all. "But," she went on, "with both of you away nearly all the time, the house is going to seem lonely."

"He'll get his leave, the same as I do, dear."

"That may be a long time coming, and in the meantime I'll be all alone."

"Well. . . ." The Captain shifted in his chair, to cover a faint embarrassment. He had a picture of Grace knitting, alone in an empty house, for weeks on end, and it did not worry him as much as it should have done. To make up for this lack of feeling, he added with special warmth: "You really ought to get someone to live with you. Some sort of companion."

"There's Mother," said Grace thoughtfully.

The Captain paused. There certainly was Mother, and Mother was a different matter altogether: a grim quarrelsome old lady who, on her infrequent visits to the little house on the outskirts of Birkenhead, had done nothing but complain the whole time and had spoilt her only grandson outrageously into the bargain. The nearest he had ever come to a clash with Grace was when her mother had taken it on herself to rearrange all the furniture in their sitting-room, and he had called it "damned cheek" and put it all back again. That had been a wonderful scene. But he did not want it re-

24

peated. And certainly he did not want Grace's mother as a permanent part of the household, when he came home on leave.

He temporized. "It's an idea," he said, "but I don't know whether it would really suit you. Two women living together all the time. . . . It's your house, you know," he concluded rather lamely, feeling her eye on him. "You don't want to forget that."

"Why should I forget it?"

"Your mother likes her own way a bit, doesn't she?"

"She's the same as most of us," said Grace equably. "She'd be company for me, I *do* know, own way or not. But of course if you don't want me to have her, I'll say no more about it."

"You must please yourself," he said, without enthusiasm. He realized that, compared with her, it would affect him very little—perhaps for a week or so every three or four months: he still could not bring himself to welcome the idea. "It's likely to be a long time till I see Birkenhead again, and John the same, I shouldn't wonder. You know I don't want you to be alone all that time."

"I'll see about it," she answered vaguely. She was gathering up her knitting preparatory to going to bed: it was a serious business—patterns, spare needles, wool, spectacles, and the square of silk in which she wrapped the current piece of work. "We don't want to decide in a hurry. You've plenty to think about already, haven't you?"

"Yes," said the Captain.

"Are you pleased with the ship, George?" she asked as they rose.

"Yes," he said. "The ship'll be all right."

[*6*]

They were a fortnight camping out in the crowded dock-side hut before they moved into the ship, and another three weeks before she was ready to sail; altogether, five weeks of concentrated work and preparation. It sometimes seemed to Ericson that there would never be any end to the new problems and questions that cropped up every day. He had to handle them all himself, or at least to decide how they were to be handled: the two subs were willing enough, but green as grass, and Bennett, he found, had less experience than his manner led one to expect, as well as a great deal less energy. . . . Everything connected with the ship seemed to be the Captain's province: ordering stores and ammunition, interviewing dockyard and Admiralty officials, settling the last of the alterations and additions with the contractors, mastering technical details about the hull and the machinery, arranging the accommodation on board, answering signals, checking lists, reporting the progress and state of the ship. He had to make two or three trips to the Naval Headquarters in Glasgow before he found that Ferraby, quiet and conscientious, could be counted on to relay any message accurately and to come back with the right answer. But this did little to dispose of the work that piled up, day after day, in the hut alongside *Compass Rose*.

Gradually, however, he had his reward: gradually there came to be less noise on board, less space cluttered up with tools and dockyard equipment, less untidiness, less oil and dirt. The workmen thinned out, until only a thin trickle of them mounted the gangway every morning: stores were stowed, cabins carpeted, the mess-decks fitted with their cots and lockers. *Compass Rose* took on, at last, the shape and feeling of a ship; it was time to transfer aboard her, and they were all glad to do it.

But when the main draft of the crew—sixty-odd men—arrived from Devonport Barracks, they lost little time in echoing, with choice variations, Petty Officer Tallow's strictures on their accommodation. The mess-decks were small, and intolerably crowded: the hands were all lumped together—seamen, stokers, signalmen, telegraphists: they had to take their meals in the sleeping-spaces, and read or write letters with other men jammed up against them on either side. And if it was like this in harbour, what was it

26

going to be like at sea, with the ship rolling her guts out and everything wet through as well. . . . Lower-deck wit, which flourishes (in the true English tradition) on discomfort and adversity, had plenty to play with; the first few days in *Compass Rose*, before the hands were acclimatized, produced as crisp a crop of invective and blasphemy as was ever crammed into a space two hundred feet long and thirty-three broad.

Ericson was conscious of this feeling of discontent as he surveyed the muster of hands at the commissioning ceremony. It was not that they looked sullen or mutinous: simply uninterested and perhaps a little cynical, not seeing the point of dressing up so smartly (and being ticked off for wearing a dirty jumper) just to commission a funny little sod of a ship like this. It must be his first care, he realized, to alleviate the discomfort on board: he had thought already of improvements in ventilation and in the cooking arrangements, and an energetic captain could do a lot with a new ship at the experimental stage, as long as the shoreside co-operated. And the job itself, with its prospect of a tough ordeal, might do much more than alleviate, by giving the crew a conscious pride in hard living and fighting. That was the thought that struck him most strongly, as the bosun's pipes sounded the Still, and the spotless ensign and the commissioning-pendant were broken out. *Compass Rose*, with a new coat of paint, looked clean and workmanlike: she had her numbers painted on her bows, she was nearly ready to move. . . . As he started to read the Articles of War a moment later, his firm clear voice matched the first stirring of his pride in the ship. She might be "only a corvette," not much better than a deep-sea trawler, but she could make a reputation at any level, and that was going to be his target from now on.

Meals in the cramped wardroom never seemed to progress beyond the sort of constrained artificiality that marks a public banquet attended by people who are complete strangers to one another. The Captain was usually preoccupied with the last job or the next one: he sat in silence at the head of the table, staring straight ahead or occasionally jotting down a note. Ferraby, naturally shy, was still feeling his way and never volunteered either a direct statement or a direct question: and Lockhart, who was the most articulate of the four, struggled through successive monologues that only rarely inspired any kind of answer. Bennett's contribution lay in the realm of eating. . . . He had formed an attachment for the crudest item in the wardroom store-cupboard, tinned sausages, which he knew colloquially as "snorkers": they made an almost daily appearance on the menu, either at lunch or dinner, and the recurrent exclamation—"Snorkers! Good-oh!"—with which he greeted them sounded the knell of appetite. Then he would sit down, rub his hands, help himself liberally to Worcester sauce, and go to with a will. In fishing circles he would have been described as a coarse feeder.

The leading steward, a morose man named Carslake, watched this performance with a sardonic eye. Clearly he had been used to better things. He was not alone in that.

Ferraby's congenital shyness had not been aided by a personal encounter he had had with Bennett. A few days earlier, since it seemed likely that *Compass Rose* would not be sailing for at least a fortnight, he had asked permission to send for his wife: she could stay at an hotel in Glasgow and he could see her on alternate evenings, when he was not Officer-of-the-Day. It would involve no sort of complication and he would not be dodging his fair share of the work. Bennett, however, had turned the request down, in a particularly offensive exchange.

"Wife?" he said, when Ferraby approached him in his cabin. "Didn't know you had one. How long have you been married?"

"Six weeks," said Ferraby.

Bennett smirked. "Time you gave it a rest, then."

Ferraby said nothing. Bennett affected to consider the matter, frowning down at his desk. Then he shook his head. "No, sub," he said, "I don't like the idea. There's too much work to do."

"But when the work's over—" began Ferraby.

"You've got to concentrate," said Bennett crisply. "What's the good of you slipping off for a honeymoon every time the bell strikes? It'll take your mind off the ship."

Ferraby swallowed. He hated the conversation, but he persisted bravely. "All I want to do—" he began again.

"I know bloody well what you want to do." The crude leer on Bennett's face was sufficient commentary, but he clinched it more crudely still. "You've quite enough to do without sleeping ashore every other night, and coming back clapped out. You'd better forget it."

It was something that Ferraby did not forget. . . . When he told Lockhart about it he was pitifully distressed.

"I don't mind so much having it turned down," he said. "But to talk like that about it. . . . It's—it's beastly!"

Lockhart shook his head. "You might have guessed it. He's that sort of man."

"I hate him!"

Lockhart tried to steer him away from the emotional aspect. "You know," he said, "I don't believe it's even necessary for you to get permission for this sort of thing. They can't possibly stop your wife coming up here. Ask the Captain about it."

"But even if she were here, Bennett could stop me going to Glasgow to see her."

"Not on your days off duty."

"I bet he could."

Lockhart nodded. "Yes, I bet he could too. He'd find some way, especially if you asked the Captain after being refused permission." He smiled at Ferraby across the wardroom table. "Better forget it, as that bastard said. There'll be other chances later."

The coxswain's particular responsibility, the rounding up of defaulters, was already under way, beginning with an odd breach of decorum that caused Ferraby, who happened to be Officer-of-the-Day, a good deal of embarrassment. He was routed out of the wardroom at nine o'clock one evening, after noises from the upper deck had warned him that one of the returning libertymen was making a considerable disturbance. At the top of the ladder he found Petty Officer Tallow, and by his side a sullen-looking stoker swaying slightly on his feet.

"Stoker Grey, sir," began Tallow grimly: and then, to the culprit: " 'Tenshun! Off caps! Stoker Grey, sir. Urinating on the upper deck."

"What!" exclaimed Ferraby, genuinely shocked.

"Urinating on the upper deck, sir," repeated Tallow. "Just came back on board. The quartermaster reported him."

Ferraby swallowed. He was somewhat out of his depth, and it was his first defaulter as well.

"What have you got to say?" he asked after a moment.

Stoker Grey swayed forward, and back again, and muttered something.

"Speak up!" barked Tallow.

Grey tried again. "Must have had a few drinks, sir."

"It's absolutely disgusting," said Ferraby. "I never heard of—"

"Sorry, sir," muttered Grey.

"Keep silence!" said Tallow.

"It's disgusting," repeated Ferraby weakly. "You ought to be ashamed of yourself. First Lieutenant's report, coxswain."

"First Lieutenant's report," echoed Tallow. "On caps! About turn! Quick march!"

The man shambled off. Presently a heavy thud resounded along the iron deck.

"Better keep an eye on him," said Ferraby.

"I'll do that, sir," said Tallow bleakly.

"I hope there won't be too much of this sort of thing."

"You know what beer is, sir."

"But still—" began Ferraby. Then he left it at that. War, it was clear, was not for the squeamish.

Two days before Christmas, the Captain went up to Glasgow for a final visit to headquarters: he returned with a fresh sheaf of papers, which he studied for some time in his cabin. Then he went down to the wardroom, where the others were assembled.

"Sailing orders," he said briefly as he sat down. "We go down river the day after tomorrow—and in case you've forgotten, the date will be December the twenty-fifth."

"A nice present," said Lockhart in the pause that followed.

"I hope so. . . . Here's the rough program, anyway." He consulted a sheet of paper in his hand. "We'll be towed down to the oiling berth, about five miles down river. We'll oil there, and then steam the rest of the way down to Greenock. There we stay at anchor for about a fortnight, taking on stores and ammunition, and adjusting compasses. Then we go out on our full-power trials, probably down to Ailsa Craig and back: we'll test the guns and the depth-charge gear on the way. That takes us to—" he looked at the program again, "to January 12th. Then if everything's all right we go north to Ardnacraish for our working-up exercises."

"How long will they take, sir?" asked Bennett.

"The program says three weeks. It won't be less, and if we don't put up a good show they can keep us there as long as they like. So it's up to us."

"Do you hear that, subs?" interjected Bennett unnecessarily. "We don't want any mistakes from either of you."

Ericson frowned slightly. "We don't want any mistakes from anyone, whether it's me or a second-class stoker." It was the first time the Captain had been heard to correct anything Bennett said: momentarily Lockhart found himself wondering if it had happened before, in private, and whether the Captain were actually as blind to the situation in the wardroom, and elsewhere, as he seemed to be. If he really had a critical eye on Bennett, then there was hope for the future. . . . "Well, there it is," Ericson continued: "we have to be ready to move in forty-eight hours from now." He raised his voice and called: "Pantry!"

Leading Steward Carslake, who had been listening attentively outside, waited a decent interval before appearing in the doorway: "Yes, sir?"

31

"Gin, please—and whatever anyone else wants." And later, over the second round of drinks, he said: "I think we'd better have a wardroom party tomorrow night. We may not get another chance for some time."

[7]

At ten o'clock on Christmas morning, waiting on the cold windswept fo'c's'le for steam to come to the windlass, Lockhart was conscious of a slight headache. He had drunk more than usual at the previous night's party: it would scarcely have been tolerable otherwise. Mrs. Ericson had presided, and rather well; but the rest of the company had been comparative strangers to one another—some officers off another corvette, a couple of dockyard officials, a friend of the Captain's from Naval Headquarters; and Bennett, coming in at about ten o'clock with a bedraggled-looking woman clearly picked up in the nearest hotel, had struck an unfortunate note. The sense of well-being, and the accompanying slight haze, induced by a dozen pink gins, had come as an essential relief; but Lockhart felt he was paying for it now. A biting wind, varied by an occasional drift of snow, was no cure for a hangover.

In the apportioning of jobs and stations on board, the fo'c's'le had been allotted to him as the senior sub-lieutenant, together with the two most interesting assignments—gunnery, and chart-correcting. Ferraby, with the second choice of everything, was put in charge aft: he was responsible for the depth charges, and in harbour he would have to deal with correspondence, the crew's pay, and the wardroom accounts as well. Certainly, thought Lockhart, he himself had come off best: it couldn't be helped, but it was bad luck on Ferraby having all the finnicking little oddments while everyone else had the glamour. Stamping up and down the fo'c's'le, wishing that his job (of which he had only the vaguest outline) were not so directly under the eye of the bridge, he found himself wondering once again how Ferraby—shy, inexperienced, defenceless—was going to meet the trials that lay in the future. He could be helped to a certain extent, but in the last analysis it depended on his own resources, and they were patently meagre.

The leading stoker in charge of the windlass turned a valve, and there was a heartening hiss of steam followed by a clanking noise. "Ready, sir," he called out.

"Right." Lockhart walked to the bows and, trying to disguise the fact that it was largely a process of trial and error, set to work on the task of casting off the spare mooring-wires and reeling them in. From the tug alongside, a man with a large red reassuring face watched him; ready, he felt, to correct any mistakes and deal with any crisis. He might well be needed.

When "hands to stations for leaving harbour" was piped, Ferraby walked disconsolately aft to the quarterdeck, prepared to execute as best he could an order he barely understood. "Single-up to the stern-wire," Bennett had said, and left it at that—though not forgetting to add, by way of farewell: "And if you get a wire round the screw, Christ help you!" To "single-up" presumably meant to cast off all their mooring lines except the last one needed to hold them to the quay; but only a process of elimination would tell him which one was the stern-wire, and he hardly felt equal to the effort of concentration.

He felt, in fact, confused and wretched. All that he had read about the Navy, all that he had learned at the training establishment, all the eagerness that had driven him to enlist on the day war broke out—all these were being destroyed or poisoned by his present circumstances. He had been immensely proud of getting a commission: he had been ready to accept without question, as an unbreakable bond, the whole of the rigid discipline and the tradition of service that he had read or learnt about: but there had been no one like Bennett in the textbooks, and Bennett, it seemed, was the reality behind the fine phrases. . . . He had known per-

33

fectly well, also, that he would be miserable as soon as he was separated from his wife: that was another thing he had been prepared to endure with a good heart; but the ache of separation was a high price—almost an impossible price—to pay for submitting to the present oafish tyranny. If the Navy were really Bennett, and Bennett's manners and methods, then he had been cheated and betrayed from the beginning.

He had slipped out of last night's party to telephone his wife in London. Waiting in the draughty dock-office for the call to come through, the eagerness of anticipation had almost choked him; but as soon as he heard her voice, with its soft hesitant inflection, the eagerness had ebbed away and he was conscious only of the miles between them and the weeks and months that might still keep them apart. This moment was their good-bye: there was nothing else in prospect. And it was for this that he was treated like a backward child or ordered about like a convict. . . .

But for her sake, and for his own, he had done his best.

"Hallo," he started. "Hallo, darling! Can you hear me?"

"Yes," she said. "Oh, how wonderful! Where are you?"

"Same place. I wanted to wish you a happy Christmas."

"And to you. . . . What are you doing?"

"Having a party."

"Oh. . . ."

"Not a very good one. A horrid one, really. I wish I could be with you. Are you taking care of yourself?"

"Yes, darling. Are you?"

"Yes."

"Are you in the ship?"

"No. In the dock-office. What are you wearing?"

"The striped housecoat. . . . Oh darling, I wish you were here. Is there any chance?"

"I don't think so. I'm afraid not."

"Can't I come up, then?"

"It's too late."

"Why? What's happening?"

34

"I . . ." Some phrase about careless talk pricked him, and he hesitated. "I can't really tell you."

"Is the ship ready?"

"Yes."

"Oh. . . ."

The wires hummed between them. They were not doing well. He said again: "This is just to wish you a happy Christmas," and then suddenly he could not endure it any more and he said: "I must go, I'm afraid. . . . Good-bye. . . . Take care of yourself," and rang off. He had stood in the dock-office, utterly defeated, for at least five minutes before he could bear to go back to the ship; and once on board he had slipped into his cabin, without a word to anyone, and lain down on his bunk, and felt the successive waves of wretchedness flood in, with nothing to check them and no hope to drive them out.

Now, on this queer Christmas morning, Ferraby stepped onto the quarterdeck repeating "Single-up to the stern-wire" as if it were some pagan incantation. The six hands of the after-party, under their leading hand—Leading Seaman Tonbridge—were fallen in by the depth-charge rails, waiting for his orders.

As he came up, Leading Seaman Tonbridge saluted and said:

"Take off the breast-rope, sir?"

"Just a minute." Ferraby looked at the moorings. There were four separate ropes—two leading aft, one leading forward, and one, a short one, going out at right angles to the ship's side. He hesitated, while Tonbridge, a tough self-reliant young man who knew it all by heart, adjusted the thick leather gauntlets that all the mooring parties wore. Then Ferraby had a sudden idea, a purely Bennett-idea that he was almost ashamed to use. He nodded to Tonbridge, and said, simply:

"Single-up to the stern-wire."

Tonbridge said: "Aye, aye, sir," and then, to the nearest seamen: "Take off those wrappings," and then, to the hands

35

waiting on the jetty: "Cast off breast-rope and spring."
Men moved: the wires splashed in the water, and were hauled
in: the moorings quickly simplified themselves to one single
rope running aft. It was as easy as that.

With a sudden surprised flicker of confidence, Ferraby
turned to the voice-pipe that led to the bridge. His ring was
answered by the signalman. He said: "Singled up aft. Tell
the First Lieutenant."

He felt humbly pleased with himself. He had cheated, but
now, as far as moorings were concerned, he knew the right
answer and he need not cheat again.

Down in the Captain's cabin, Watts, the Chief Engine-
Room Artificer, was reporting to the Captain about the
engines under his charge. There could be no mistaking Watts,
or the job he was busy on—his white overalls were stained
and splashed with grease, and his hands incredibly grimy.
After working most of the night on a refractory valve, he
was tired, and his face grey and lined.

"She's ready to move, sir," he said, without much enthusiasm. "As ready as I can make her, that is, with twenty
dockyard-mateys climbing all over her. I've had her turning
over at ten revs for the past hour. She's a little rough yet, but
it'll settle itself."

"What about the steering engine?" asked Ericson. Earlier,
there had been trouble over this, and they had been waiting
for replacements.

"Seems all right now, sir." Watts scratched his bald head,
leaving a smear of grease like a painted quiff on his forehead.
"There's a lot of loose stuff in the steering compartment—
wires and dry provisions and such—it'll have to be secured
when we're properly at sea. But I've tried the engine out a
dozen times, hard a-port to hard a-starboard, and she's
smooth as you could wish. And if we want to steer by hand,
it's simple enough—too simple, mebbe." He sniffed. He had
no very high opinion of the machinery in his charge, which
had few refinements of any sort and was scarcely more complicated than the stationary steam engine, run on methylated-
spirits, that had been his first real toy. Corvettes, it was clear,

were going to be turned out simply and economically, like pins or plastic ash-trays: as such, they hardly deserved a Chief E.R.A. to look after them.

"All right, Chief," said Ericson. "We'll leave it at that. You know the program: we'll be towed down to the oiler and then steam the rest of the way. I've allowed two hours for oiling: the tide's flooding all the afternoon so there's no hurry."

"Two hours should do us, sir. What about the revs, then?"

"That's something we can only settle finally when we've been running for some time." Ericson looked at one of the many slips of paper on his desk. "I see the builders' recommendations are: Slow Ahead, 35 revs: Half Ahead, 100 revs. We'd better try that, to start with. If it's too fast, or too slow, I'll give you the alterations on the voice-pipe."

"Aye, aye, sir." Watts, preparing to leave, summoned the vague and rare outlines of a smile. "Funny sort of Christmas morning," he commented. "Makes you think a bit."

"It won't be the last, Chief."

"D'you think it'll be as long as the other war, sir?"

"Longer, probably." Ericson stretched out his hand and rang the bell to the bridge. "That's what we've got to be ready for, anyway."

Watts, leaving the cabin, shook his head in doubt. His favourite Sunday paper had said that the war would be over in a year, and, on this Christmas morning, he wanted very much to believe it.

The rating who answered the Captain's bell and presently stood before him was Leading Signalman Wells, the senior of the three signalmen who made up *Compass Rose's* communications complement. He was rather older than his rank suggested; and Ericson, looking over his Conduct Sheet a few days previously, had discovered why. Wells had been a full Yeoman of Signals up to two months previously: then he had been disrated, and sentenced to eighteen days' detention, for (in the bleak words of King's Regulations & Admiralty Instructions) "conduct prejudicial to good order and naval discipline in that he (a) was absent over leave 76 hours and

37

The Cruel Sea

35 minutes, (b) did return on board drunk, (c) did resist the duty Petty Officer detailed to supervise him, and (d) did destroy by fire nine signal-flags, value 27/-." Reading between the lines, it must have been a lively occasion. But the implications were not encouraging, however much allowance one made for extenuating circumstances that could only be guessed at—a birthday party that got out of hand, a woman too acquiescent, a wife unfaithful: the odd part was that Wells looked the least likely candidate for this sort of escapade.

He was small, with a quick decisive manner and an air of competence: he kept a firm hand on his department, and Ericson had already found him helpful with suggestions, as well as absolutely dependable. Now, as he stood waiting in the cabin, cap neatly tucked under his arm, signal-pad ready, pencil poised, he was a heartening picture of a highly trained, wide-awake signalman—the sort of man worth his weight in gold to any ship. Ericson hoped that this picture would prove to be the true one: the other story—the one in the Conduct Sheet—would mean, in a ship the size of *Compass Rose*, endless trouble and endless waste of energy, before it was brought under control.

"I want to send a signal about our leaving," Ericson began. "Take this down, and send it off by telephone from the dock-office."

"Yes, sir," said Wells. He prepared to write.

" 'To Flag-Officer-in-Charge, Glasgow,' " the Captain dictated, " 'from *Compass Rose*. Sailed in accordance with your 0945 stroke twenty-three stroke twelve. Estimated time of arrival at Greenock, sixteen hundred hours.' "

Wells read the signal back when he had written it down, and then said: "Should we repeat it to Flag-Officer, Greenock, sir? They'll have to give us an anchor berth as soon as we arrive."

"Yes," agreed Ericson, conscious, as happened quite often nowadays, that his memory of naval procedure was rusty and needed constant prodding. "You'd better do that. . . . We'll fly our pendant numbers going down river, of course."

38

"Yes, sir," said Wells. "Pendant numbers, pilot flag, and Under Tow signal. I'll see to all that, sir."

When the Leading Signalman withdrew, Ericson sat on in his cabin, waiting for the First Lieutenant. By the normal routine, Bennett should report the ship "ready to proceed," just as the Chief E.R.A. had reported that his engines were ready to move; but though it was already past their sailing time, Ericson did not want to issue a reminder until it was absolutely necessary. He was by now aware that in Bennett he had got a bad bargain, a lazy and largely ignorant young man who should never have been given his present appointment; but he had not yet made up his mind whether to ask for a replacement, or whether Bennett could be trained to do his job properly, and he wished to give him every chance. The added complication—that Bennett bullied Ferraby constantly, and was in a state of imminent collision with Lockhart—was another thing that time might or might not solve. He did not want to step in unless the efficiency and well-being of the ship were seriously threatened; and it had not got to that point yet.

At ten minutes past their appointed sailing time, he pressed the bridge bell, and was answered by the signalman of the watch.

"Bridge, sir!"

"Is the First Lieutenant there?"

"He's on the fo'c's'le, sir, talking to Mr. Lockhart."

"Ask him to come to my cabin."

"Aye, aye, sir."

Presently Bennett knocked on the door, and came in. He was wearing a bridge-coat, with the collar turned up in a vaguely dramatic manner.

"You wanted me, sir?"

"Yes," said Ericson. "Are we ready to move, Number One?"

"Yes, sir," said Bennett cheerfully. "Any time you like."

"You should come and tell me. I can't guess at it, you know."

"Oh. . . . Sorry, sir."

39

"Are all hands on board?"

"Er—I reckon so, sir."

A singularly cold blue eye regarded him. "Well, are they or aren't they? Didn't you have it reported to you?"

"There was only the postman, sir. I know he's aboard."

"What about the mess-caterers? What about the leading steward?—he went shopping for me. What about the berthing party?"

Bennett looked as nearly crestfallen as Ericson had yet seen him. It was a cheering sight. "I'll check up, sir."

Ericson rose, and reached for his cap and binoculars. "Find out, and come and tell me on the bridge. And next time, remember that you report to me that the ship's ready to sail, with all the crew on board, at the proper time. That's part of your job."

Bennett recovered swiftly. "I'd better detail Ferraby to—"

"You won't detail anybody," said Ericson, as brusquely as he had ever spoken so far, "unless you want to change jobs with them."

He left the cabin without another word, leaving Bennett to make what he liked of this substantial warning for the future. It might be what was needed to pull him up short; in any case, it was a move in the right direction. Then, as Ericson mounted the ladder towards the bridge, the small annoying scene faded from his mind and was swiftly replaced: he was aware only of an intense personal satisfaction that all the months of waiting, all the worry of fitting-out and commissioning, and all the loose ends of departure, had now been disposed of, and that *Compass Rose*—his own responsibility, almost his own invention—was ready at last for her maiden trip.

It was not particularly impressive, that first tow down river to the oiler, save for one odd accompaniment to it that Ericson, like many other people on board, found moving. As *Compass Rose* edged outwards from the quay and gathered way, with a tug at either end, Petty Officer Tallow at the wheel, and Lockhart with his fo'c's'le party neatly fallen in by the windlass, a small cheer broke out from the knot of dockyard workers lining the quayside. It was ragged, it was unco-ordinated and unrehearsed: it was all the more impressive for this rough spontaneity. Other men from other yards left their work to wave to *Compass Rose* as she passed down river—men who had built ships, were building them now, and would build countless others, pausing in their jobs to speed on her way the latest product of the Clyde. The moment of farewell was not prolonged: it was too cold to stand about, and the dusting of snow that overlay the quays and docks and berthing slips lining the river was a sharp reminder of the wintry day. But the gesture, repeated many times on their way toward the open sea, remained in the memory: the last message from the fraternity of men who built the ship, to the sailors who would live and work and fight aboard her.

Five hours later *Compass Rose*, under her own power, left the last narrow section of the river and nosed her way down stream towards the Tail-of-the-Bank, the naval anchorage off Greenock. The early winter dusk was beginning to close in, hiding the far reaches of one of the loveliest harbours in Britain: the line of hills surrounding it turned from purple to black shadow, the lit buoys and the shore lights came up blinking to challenge the twilight. It was now very cold, though the wind had died earlier that afternoon. Their berth had been signalled to them, and identified on the chart; they still had a few hundred yards to go before they dropped anchor, and the Captain, with leisure to look about him, was studying the other ships that crowded the broad sweep of the Clyde estuary.

There were many of them—a battleship, a smart new cruiser, half a dozen destroyers, an aircraft carrier, scores of minesweepers; beyond them, in the merchant-ship anchorage, was line upon line of ships collecting for a convoy, dominated by two huge liners in the grey wartime dress of troopships. At the back of the bridge, Ericson could hear Leading Signalman Wells giving a running commentary on the ships in company—a commentary that revealed, as could nothing else, the sense of family that informs the Royal Navy. ("The battleship's the *Royal Sovereign*—we were at Gib with her, last spring cruise—there's the old *Argus*, one of the first carriers ever built—that must be the Sixth Destroyer Flotilla—wonder what they're doing here—that's one of the new Town Class cruisers—didn't know they were in commission yet. . . .") The pilot, a bluff Clydesider in a bowler hat, said suddenly: "Just coming on the bearing now, Captain!" and Ericson returned to the business of anchoring. The telegraph clanged for Stop Engines, and then for Slow Astern: he called out: "Stand by!" to Lockhart on the fo'c's'le; and a minute later, as the ship gathered gentle sternway, his shout of "Let go!" was answered by the thunderous roar of the cable running out. *Compass Rose* lay at anchor, her first journey accomplished. The time, he was pleased to note, was three minutes past four: the dividing dusk was now upon them, and the air had a bitter edge to it, but the ring of shore lights and the scores of craft in company seemed to be bidding him and his ship welcome.

[8]

Now came a further pause in their progress, easier to endure with patience because it was more directly geared to their sea-going preparation. They were fourteen days at Greenock, some of them spent at anchor, ammunitioning and storing and doing harbour exercises, others devoted to their sea trials and the preliminary gunnery and depth-charge tests designed to prove their weapons. They could hardly have had lovelier surroundings in which to try out their ship: in the grip of a hard winter that whitened even the foot-hills with snow and gave to the higher peaks a serene, unassailable purity, the Firth of Clyde, especially when approached from seaward, had a breathtaking beauty.

But they had not a great deal of leisure for looking about

them, nor inclination either, however attractive were their surroundings: their eyes were now turning inward, toward the ship and their task in her. It was astonishing how, isolated at her anchorage or slipping in and out on her various trials, *Compass Rose* was already coming alive as a ship, a separate unit with a developing personality. The process of eighty-odd men shaking down together was well advanced, and now it was moving toward the next stage—the welding together of these men into a working crew, the tuning up for action. This was not true only of the wardroom, though here it was strongest since the wardroom supplied the directive influence: it was true of all of them—they were beginning to concentrate, beginning to feel that they and the ship had work to do, and that it was worth doing.

Wishful thinking might exaggerate this process, and fo'c's'le backchat, designed to show that *Compass Rose* was the worst abortion of a ship that ever put to sea, might seem to deny it; but it was there all the same—a strong and subtle feeling of dedication. It was being helped, from outside, by the first convoy reports and rumours—some true, some exaggerated—and by the landing of Merchant Navy survivors at near-by Gourock, from which it was clear that there must have been a number of U-boats already at sea, in full operational trim, on the day that war was declared. This, then, was going to be *Compass Rose's* battle: it really existed, it was worth taking on, it had to be won, and the sooner they were ready for it the better.

Lockhart was specially conscious of the beginning of this feeling when they went out on their gun trials, at the end of their first week at Greenock. The trials were simple enough: they fired a few rounds from the four-inch gun on the fo'c's'le, and tested the two-pounder aft, and the light machine guns on the bridge, which completed an armament modest enough by any standard. ("God help us if we run into the *Scharnhorst*," said an imaginative seaman. "We'll just have to creep up behind and —— her. . . .") But among the guns' crews he had been working up in harbour, and especially in a leading seaman called Phillips who was the gun-

43

ner's mate—the rating responsible for the cleanliness of the guns and the storage of ammunition—Lockhart was aware of an encouraging interest. Most of these guns' crews were amateurs, of course—the "hostilities only" ratings who survived the derision of the regulars to become a huge majority in the Navy—but they learnt fast, and here and there an obvious instance of intelligence and enthusiasm marked one of them down for a higher rating, as soon as the necessary training had been completed. Phillips, who was also in charge of the fo'c's'le party, was big and slow-moving, a two-badge leading seaman with considerable influence in the mess-decks: it was clear that he would be, for Lockhart, an ally worth close cultivation.

Ferraby, isolated aft among his depth charges, was having less success in working up to the necessary standard of competence. His key ratings were all right—Wainwright, the torpedoman, who saw to the settings and actually dropped the charges, and Leading Seaman Tonbridge, who was in general charge of the depth-charge crews, were both energetic and dependable; but most of the rest of his men fell far below this standard. Much of the work aft consisted of reloading the depth-charge throwers at high speed—a heavy job involving skillful teamwork; and for it he had a motley collection of off-watch stokers and telegraphists, who did not take kindly to working on a windswept upper deck, like any common seaman, when their natural lair was a warm boiler-room or a cosy W/T office. . . . Many of them, too, were undeniably stupid, of the calibre of that Stoker Grey who had been the ship's first and (so far) most unconventional defaulter; and Ferraby, none too sure of himself at the best of times, was hardly the person either to drill them into efficiency or to take a tough line when they were wilfully slack.

The result was what might have been expected. There were mistakes, delays, failures: there was surprise when things went right, and a disgruntled indifference when they went wrong. Left to himself, Ferraby might have gained confidence and gradually worked his department into a going concern; but Bennett, sensing the weak point and welcoming an easier target than Lockhart, was continually wandering aft and, leaning over the rail above the quarterdeck, destroying by a stream of comment and counter-orders whatever self-sufficiency Ferraby might have built up. Ferraby grew to dread the daily depth-charge practices that were the rule when they were in harbour: it seemed hardly worth while giving preliminary instruction, and then setting the drill in motion, when at any moment the hated red face would top the rail above him and the raucous voice call out: "Ferrabee! The settings should be put on *before* the lashings are taken off!" or, more simply: "Ferrabee! That's no bloody good at all—start it again!" He had no one to complain to, nor, in the last analysis, any solid ground for complaint: he *did* make mistakes, and the depth-charge crews *were* slack and inefficient, and so, it seemed, it was going to continue, until he himself was superseded or *Compass Rose* was sunk.

For all this zest for supervision, Bennett was not enjoying himself nearly as much as he had expected. Riding a dumb kid like Ferraby was all very fine, he found, but it was about the only compensation in a job that was steadily proving a bit too serious altogether. . . . He had managed to farm out nearly every piece of work that should normally fall to the First Lieutenant, but still the inescapable oddments remained, and he found them irksome—particularly things like keeping up-to-date the watch bill, as various ratings changed their jobs or acquired fresh experience. Added to his failure to make any sort of impression on Lockhart (though he hadn't finished there yet, by a long way), and a suspicion that the Captain was a good deal less impressionable than he had seemed at the beginning, these awkward factors were in process of spoiling what had looked like an agreeable billet. Bennett couldn't make up his mind whether to chuck it now, and get something better—there were scores of soft jobs going begging, and snug niches to be filled, at this formative stage of the war—or to hang on a little longer and see if things improved. That would be one way of qualifying for a command, and a command was clearly the only thing to have,

45

if you wanted to enjoy yourself at sea; but sweating out a year or so as First Lieutenant might be too high a price to pay for it. Soon he would have to make his choice: in the meantime, there was Lockhart to be kept in view as a long-range target, and Ferraby to supply the essential comic relief.

Of them all, the Captain, with most to worry or distract him, was the least unsure of himself and of the future. He was beginning to like the ship, simply for her "feel" and her performance, quite apart from the proprietary pride that was always in the background: she had shown herself easy to handle, and though she was ludicrously slow in comparison with a destroyer—or indeed with any other warship he had ever heard of—she was highly manœuvrable and could turn the corners adroitly. That speed of hers, of course, might rank as much more of a handicap in the future: the bare fifteen knots that was the most the Chief E.R.A. could coax out of her was slower than a good many merchant ships, and only a knot or so above the general speed in convoy—when, supposedly, she ought to be whistling round performing the prodigies of valour and skill set out in the Fleet Signal Book. At fifteen knots, she was liable to qualify as a Pekinese of the ocean rather than as a greyhound.

The other major snag, from his own point of view, had already shown itself: that was, her behaviour at sea. In any kind of seaway at all, *Compass Rose* rolled abominably: she had given an appalling demonstration of it on one of their first trips outside harbour, when, running down to the Isle of Arran in a very moderate sea that should not have bothered her at all, she had achieved a forty-degree roll and, apart from other damage sustained to movable gear below decks, had put one of her boats under water and nearly lost it altogether. High up on the bridge, hanging on grimly while *Compass Rose* swung through a drunken eighty-degree arc, Ericson had found himself wondering what it was going to be like when they met real Atlantic weather and had, perhaps, to hold their course and speed through it. . . . This light-hearted frolic was not the best augury for that future.

But that was a test which need not yet be met: and on the

day when *Compass Rose* turned homeward after her final
trials and began the smooth run up the sheltered Firth of
Clyde, Ericson was conscious only of an exhilarating satisfaction. The ship went forward at an easy ten knots, with
the flood tide adding a couple more: the winter sunset, a
lovely red and orange, made the bracken on the surrounding
hillsides glow like fire. Moving through the still evening,
parting the cold keen air with a steady thrust, the ship
seemed to have a living purpose of her own, a quality of
strength and competence, and Ericson found it hard to ex-
clude from his voice, as he gave the helm-orders that would
lay a course through the defence boom, the eagerness that
possessed him. For *Compass Rose* was clear: her engines
and her armament were all in order: in a few days they would
go north for their final working-up, and then she would be
ready.

That evening, in his cabin, Ericson signed for the ship and
formally took her over from the builders. He was well content: there had been a good many flaws to start with, as was
natural with a new ship of a new design, ranging from navigation lights that could not be seen, to the usual crop of weep-
ing rivets; but one by one they had all been set right, and he
could find no more to complain of. Now it was his responsibility to say so, in unmistakable terms.

The shipyard representative, a small brisk man whose
badge of office—a bowler hat—he was reluctant to part with
for more than a few seconds at a time, laid the printed form
of release in front of him, and after reading it through Ericson
put his signature at the bottom. Then he sat back.

"That's that," he said. "And I'd like to thank you for all
you've done for us. It's been a great help."

"Glad to hear it, Captain." The small man snatched up the
paper, folded it, and thrust it in an inner pocket, all in one
swift movement, as though he feared Ericson would change
his mind. "I hope she'll no' disappoint you, and you'll have
good luck in her."

Ericson nodded. "Thanks. . . . How about a drink?"

The small man shook his head and then, rather surprisingly, said: "Aye." When the drinks had been poured he raised his glass formally and said: "Not too late to wish you a Happy New Year, Captain."

Ericson drank to it in silence. So much depended on *Compass Rose:* in fact everything depended on her—perhaps even the bare fact of their survival through 1940. But that evening, when the ship at last was his, he did not want to share this thought with anyone.

[9]

On her way north to Ardnacraish, *Compass Rose* spent her first night at sea.

She was lucky in her weather: when she slipped through the boom during the late afternoon it was raining heavily, with the promise of a hard blow as well; but by the time they had passed the odd, conical mass of Ailsa Craig, and turned northward again, the sky had cleared and the wind gradually dropped to nothing. Later still, the bright moonlight gave them a visibility of several miles, and by midnight they were ploughing along at a steady twelve knots, with the mass of land to starboard as clearly discernible as if it had been full daylight. *Compass Rose*, with no sea to bother her and only a long gentle swell to surmount, had an easy motion: the pulse of the engine, and an occasional vibration from forward, served as reminders that she was now on passage instead of swinging round her anchor in harbour, but apart from that the night was as peaceful and as free from stress as any they had yet spent.

Lockhart, muffled against the keen air in a kapok suit and sea boots, shared the middle watch—from midnight to four a.m.—with Bennett: it passed without incident or interest save that at two o'clock they met a southbound convoy and were fiercely challenged by one of the wing escorts, and that Bennett spent most of the watch dozing inside the asdic hut, leaving Lockhart to keep the look-out and write up the deck-log every hour. He did not mind: indeed, he would have taken it as a compliment if he had not known that it sprang from pure laziness and not from any particular confidence in his ability. But the brief period of authority, when the ship was handed over to him as his personal charge, was helpful to his self-confidence, apart from its value as a first experience of watchkeeping. He had been wondering just how sure of himself he would be, when the moment came for him to handle *Compass Rose:* now he knew, and the answer was reassuring.

Ferraby and the Captain came up together at four o'clock, to take over the morning watch: Lockhart was amused to note that Bennett handed things over with an air of weighty responsibility, as if he had been on tiptoe throughout the entire four hours and would, even now, hardly dare to close his eyes. . . . For the first couple of hours Ericson dealt with everything there was to be done, leaving Ferraby to watch him, or stare at the horizon, and occasionally to check a buoy or a lighthouse on the chart inside the asdic compartment: but towards six o'clock, when they were set on a straight, trouble-free course that would need no alteration for thirty miles or so, he decided that he'd had enough of it. He had been on the bridge from dusk until midnight—about eight hours altogether—the previous evening, and he needed sleep badly.

He yawned, and stretched, and called Ferraby, who had wandered to the wing of the bridge.

"Think you can take her now, sub?" he asked. "This is our course for the rest of the watch, and there's nothing in the way. How about it?"

"All right, sir. I—I'd like to."

"You can get me on the voice-pipe if anything turns up. Just watch out for those fishing boats, and if you have to alter course, go to seaward of them rather than inshore. But you'd better call me if there are a lot of them about."

"Aye, aye, sir."

"All right, then. . . ." He stayed for a few moments,

watching the hills still looming clear to starboard, and the flashing light, which had been their mark for changing onto a new course, now just past the beam, and then he said: "She's yours, sub," and turned to go. His sea boots rang on the bridge ladder, and died away, and Ferraby was left to himself.

He had never known such a moment in his life, and he found it difficult to accept without a twinge of near-panic. The whole ship, with her weapons and her watchful look-outs and her sixty-odd men sleeping below, was now his: he could use her intricate machinery, alter her course and speed, head out for the open Atlantic or run straight on the rocks. . . . He felt small and alone, in spite of the bridge look-outs and the signalman and the asdic rating who shared the watch with him: he was shivering, and he heard his heart thumping, and he wondered if he could bear it if they met a convoy, or if some accident—like the steering-gear breaking down— brought on a sudden crisis. He wasn't really fitted for this: he was a bank clerk, he was only twenty, he'd been commissioned for exactly eight weeks. . . . But the minutes of uncertainty passed, as *Compass Rose* held her steady course and nothing happened to disturb it: she was, it seemed, a going concern, and possibly he knew *just* enough to supervise her without some catastrophic blunder which nothing could retrieve.

Presently he began to enjoy himself.

Leaning over the bridge rail, he could see the whole fore-part of the ship clear in the moonlight: above him, the mast rolled through a slow, gentle arc against the dark sky: astern, their wake spreading and stretching out behind them was bounded by a thin line of phosphorescence that gave it a concise, formal beauty. He felt himself to be in the middle of a pattern, the focal point of their forceful advance: here was the bridge, the nerve-centre, with its faint glow from the binnacle and the dark motionless bulk of the two look-outs marking each wing, and here was himself, who controlled it all and to whom all the lines of this pattern led. Sub-Lieutenant Ferraby, Officer-of-the-Watch—he grinned suddenly to himself, and felt, for a moment, almost heroic. No one in the bank would believe this. But he must write and tell Mavis about it, as soon as he could. She *would* believe it.

The half-hourly relief of the bridge personnel interrupted this train of thought, setting the seal on his responsibility.

"Port look-out relieved, sir!"

"Very good."

"Starboard look-out relieved, sir!"

"Very good."

And up the voice-pipe from the wheelhouse, where the quartermasters were changing over: "Course north, ten west, sir—engine half ahead—Able Seaman Dykes on the wheel!"

"Very good."

At that moment he would not have been anywhere else in the world.

Presently the signalman of the watch, who had been standing by his side staring through his binoculars, straightened up and said: "Flashing light to starboard, sir."

When Ferraby found the light he counted the flashes carefully. "That's our next lighthouse," he said, when he had made sure of it. "It's still a long way ahead, though."

The signalman stamped his feet on the grating that ran the length of the fore-bridge, and said tentatively: "Bit cold up here, sir."

It was the first remark he had volunteered since they came on watch, and Ferraby looked at him out of the corner of his eye. He knew him by sight already: his name was Rose—a young, newly joined rating, younger even than Ferraby and only just qualified as an ordinary signalman. He was something like Ferraby in manner, too: shy, unsure of himself, ready to believe most of what he was told in totally new surroundings. Earlier, at the change of the watch, Ferraby had heard Leading Signalman Wells handing over to him, using an encouraging, almost fatherly tone that must have been reassuring to a boy standing his first night duty. "Now you don't need to get rattled," Wells had said. "You know the challenge, and the reply, and that's about all there's likely to

be, when we're routed independently. But if we meet anyone, and there's a signal, sing out for me straight away, and
I'll be up to give you a hand." The contrast between this
friendly backing, this verbal arm-round-the-shoulder, and the
sort of thing he himself had to endure from Bennett, had
been so marked that momentarily Ferraby had found himself
wishing he could be an ordinary signalman, with Wells to
help him, instead of a sub with a tough First Lieutenant
bullying him all the time. But he was not so sure of that feeling now, after half an hour in charge of the ship. If only it
could always be like this. . . .

He said: "Yes, it's damned cold," and feeling the need to
lead the conversation, he added: "What's it like below?"

"Warm enough, sir," answered Rose. "But it's very
crowded. And the walls—" he corrected himself hurriedly,
"the bulkheads sweat all the time. Makes everything wet
through. It takes a bit of getting used to."

"Is this your first ship?"

"Yes, sir."

"How long have you been in?"

"A month, sir. Just the training."

"What were you before you joined?"

Rose hesitated, and then answered: "I helped with a van,
sir."

A van-boy. . . . A van-boy, and now a signalman in a
ship that might go anywhere in the world and meet God-
knows-what hazards. . . . There was enough of a parallel
between Rose's change of status, and his own, for Ferraby
to be conscious of a strong fellow-feeling with him. But was
that a relationship encouraged by the Royal Navy? He shied
away from the thought and, hunching his shoulders which
were stiffening with cold, said: "I wonder if we could get
some tea?"

"There's some cocoa on in the galley, sir," Rose volunteered. "Shall I ask the bosun's mate?"

"Yes, do."

The cocoa, when it came up, was sweet and strong and
very comforting. They drank it together, side by side under

the cold sky, while beneath their feet the ship lifted gently to the swell, and the sea fell back from her cleaving bow and turned outward in a mile-long furrow, and their track was lost in the darkness astern.

Later in the watch, a cluster of lights low in the water told Ferraby that they were running into another bunch of the fishing boats that were all round the coast that night. This fleet of them lay directly on *Compass Rose's* course, and he wondered if he ought to call the Captain: but his spell on the bridge had given him plenty of confidence, and on an impulse he bent to the voice-pipe and spoke his first helm-order.

"Port ten."

The quartermaster's voice answered him. "Port ten, sir. . . . Ten of port wheel on, sir."

"Midships."

"Midships. . . . Wheel's amidships, sir."

"Steady."

"Steady, sir. . . . Course, north, twenty-five west, sir."

They held the new course for five minutes, till the fishing boats were abeam and well clear of them. Then he brought the ship back on her former course, and was just about to make a note of the manœuvre in the deck-log when from the Captain's voice-pipe there came a sudden call:

"Bridge!"

"Bridge, sir," answered Ferraby.

"What were you altering for, sub?"

"A fishing boat, sir," he said, compromising with the strict truth. "We're clear of it now." His surprise made him add: "How did you know, sir?"

He heard the Captain chuckle. "The steering engine makes a lot of noise down here. . . . Everything all right?"

"Yes, sir. The next light's coming abeam now."

He waited for a comment, but none came, and presently a slight snore told him that he need not wait any longer. Obscurely, he felt rather proud of that snore. It was the most definite compliment he had had so far in the ship.

. . .

It grew lighter: the sky imperceptibly paled: to the eastward, the land took on a harder outline, and beyond the nearest hills others began to come into view, their snow-summits waiting to catch the first shafts of the sun. Matching the sky, the sea round them paled also, turning from black to a livid grey; and a distant lighthouse, which had been beckoning them toward the horizon, struggled against the coming of daylight and faded till its beam was a faint, wan flicker against a mist of rising land. The whole length of the ship gradually emerged from a dark outline into a three-dimensional and solid structure with frost glistening all along the upper-works: on the bridge, figures and then faces came up sharp and clear—lined faces, grey with cold and fatigue, but relaxing now as the dawn cheered them.

Below, the ship stirred and came to life, welcoming or accepting the end of the watch. The smoke from the galley chimney thickened, and bore with it a coarse and cheerful smell of frying: feet rang on ladders and along the iron deck: from a hatchway aft the grey bristly face of Chief E.R.A. Watts peered at the daylight as if scarcely believing in it. The first night at sea was over.

Just before eight, Lockhart came up to the bridge to take over the watch. He had had nearly four hours' sleep and was feeling fresher than he had expected.

"All alone?" he asked, when he had had time to look round him.

"Yes," answered Ferraby. He could not resist elaborating. "I took the last two hours myself."

Lockhart smiled. "Is that so? And to think that I slept peacefully through it all. . . ." He looked at the nearest point of land. "How far have we got?"

Ferraby, showing him their position on the chart, asked: "Are you taking over? Where's Number One?"

"Eating breakfast," said Lockhart tonelessly. "Snorkers. Good-oh."

For a moment they stood side by side in the cold morning air. The sun was now just under the rim of the hills; it was a lovely morning. Still steady, still as tranquil as the day,

54

Compass Rose ploughed northward past magic islands. Lockhart sniffed the faint breeze. "Fun, isn't it?" he said.

"Yes," said Ferraby. "Yes, it is."

[*10*]

Vice-Admiral Sir Vincent Murray-Forbes, K.C.B.,
D.S.O., Royal Navy, sat at his desk in the operations building overlooking Ardnacraish harbour, playing despondently
with a silver paper-knife engraved: "Presented to Lieutenant-Commander V. Murray-Forbes, R.N., on relinquish-
ing command of H.M.S. *Dragonfly*. From the Ship's Company. October 1909. Good luck." He did not see the
engraved sentences: indeed, he had not read them for many
years; but they had a direct connection with his despond-
ency, and especially the date, which was incontrovertible.
It was something he carried with him always, like an unlucky charm; for it meant, by inference, that he was in his
sixtieth year, and too old to go to sea again.

The Admiral looked what he was: an old sailor, and surely
due for retirement after a lifetime of distinguished service in
the Navy. It was a lined face, strong, tremendously wrinkled
round the eyes: the broad stretch of gold braid on his sleeves
was impressive, and the rows of medal-ribbons seemed no
more than the face deserved. The D.S.O. was Jutland, the
K.C.B. represented a long and brilliant serial story, from
C.-in-C. China to C.-in-C. Home Fleet and then to a notable
shore appointment: the rest of the ribbons signified that he
had managed to stay alive a long time in various odd parts of
the globe. Too long, indeed, for his present peace of mind:
the year 1918, when he was captain in command of a
destroyer flotilla, had been the peak of his fighting days, and
now this new war had come too late for him to start them
all over again. For though he had managed to defer his over-
due retirement, it had not been for the reason that he had
hoped.

They would not send him back to sea. NOT REPEAT NOT'
TOO OLD, he wrote in firm capitals on the signal-pad in front
of him, and then, as firmly, scored it out again. But the
defiant scrawl represented something that could *not* be scored
out. Three months earlier, after intensive wangling, he had
very nearly brought off the sea-appointment that he craved
for; but fifty-nine years could not be gainsaid, and the Sea
Lord who was his personal friend had had to pass him by.
Instead—"A most responsible job," they reassured him:
"a very important one, where your experience will be vital."
So the only sphere where he really wanted to use that experience—afloat—was finally closed to him: the best answer
they could give him was Ardnacraish, destined to be the
training base for every new escort in the Western Approaches Command. It *was* important—damned important—
but it wasn't what he wanted; and now he looked at Ardnacraish and, with his eyes still turned back to that sea-going
appointment, he cursed it roundly.

Ardnacraish might have returned the compliment, though
with less justice: what the Admiral had done to it had had the
overriding sanction of war. But certainly there had been
changes. . . . If you took a small Scottish fishing village of
two hundred inhabitants in the remote Highlands, with one
inn, three shops, a slipway, and a small landlocked harbour:
if you decided that it had to be turned into a naval training
base, and transported there everything necessary for its
establishment—huts, store-rooms, sleeping-quarters, gear
and equipment of every sort: if you set up a signal tower and
a radio station, laid a defence boom, deepened the harbour,
and put down a line of mooring-buoys: if you drafted in a
maintenance and training staff of seventy officers and men,
and organized an additional floating population of two or
three hundred sailors at a time from visiting ships—if you
did all this, you got a certain result. It would probably be the
result you wanted: but you could hardly expect a sweet un-
spoiled Highland village to be a residual part of it.

Ardnacraish had been lovely: it would be lovely again,

when the alien visitation was over; but now it was a place for a job, a utilitarian necessity, and as such it was patchwork, ugly, and unrecognizable.

But it was his responsibility. . . . The Admiral looked out of the window at the harbour, across an intervening line of corrugated-iron roofs that housed the asdic and signal departments. There was, as usual, a brisk wind blowing: he could hear it rattling the ill-fitting doors of the other offices in the building, and he could see it ruffling its way across the harbour and sending small vicious waves slapping against the mooring-buoys. There were no ships in, at the moment, except the oiler and the tug attached to the base: the last one had left two days previously, and they were waiting for the next arrival, due that afternoon. She was to be a brand-new type, and the first of her class: a corvette—theatrical name, but an honoured one in naval history. He had her training program ready for her, and she would start it straight away.

It was a stiff program, though an experimental one still, since convoys themselves were as yet in the embryo stage, and one hardly knew what the escorts would have to contend with. But there were certain things that all ships had to do and to be, whatever job they were intended for: as a fundamental basis, they had to be clean, efficient, and alert. In this, almost everything depended on their officers, and, judging by the last war, there were going to be some pretty odd officers before the thing was over. This ship, he noted, had an R.N.R. captain, which meant, at any rate, a seaman in command. . . . The others, amateurs, might be worth anything or nothing.

The Admiral frowned. He would soon find out what they *were* worth, and what the ship was worth too: that was his job. He might be too old to take one to sea, but he was still a firm judge of what a ship should look like and how she should behave; and however long the war lasted, and whatever the urgency, no ship would leave his command that did not meet this lifelong standard.

There was a knock on the door, and a signalman entered.

57

The Admiral looked up. "Well?"

"*Compass Rose* entering harbour now, sir. Lieutenant Haines said to tell you."

"Has he signalled her a berth?"

"Yes, sir."

The Admiral got up, and walked across to the window again. A ship was just entering the narrows, moving very slowly, edging sideways to offset the crosswind: as he watched her, she lowered a boat that began to make for one of the central mooring-buoys. His eyes went back to the ship, and he appraised her carefully. She was small, smaller than he had expected: rather chunky, but not ungraceful if you discounted the clumsy-looking stern and the mast plumb in front of the bridge. She looked clean—and so she damned well ought to be, fresh from the builders—and the hands were properly fallen in fore and aft, in the rig-of-the-day. She was flying her pendant numbers, and a brand-new ensign. One gun on the fo'c's'le—a pom-pom aft—depth charges—nothing much else. . . . Something like an overgrown trawler. But she'd have to do more than trawler's work.

He watched her securing to the buoy, neatly enough, and then he turned to the signalman.

"Send a signal. '*Compass Rose* from Flag-Officer-in-Charge. Manœuvre well executed.' Then tell Lieutenant Haines to call away my barge. I'm going aboard now."

[*11*]

For three weeks they worked very hard indeed. From the moment that the Admiral's barge approached in a wide, treacherous sweep right under their stern and almost caught the Captain unawares, the ship's company was in a continual state of tension. If they were not out exercising with the submarine, they were doing gun drill or running through Action Stations in harbour: if they were not fighting mock fires or raising the anchor by hand, an urgent signal would order them to lower a boat and put an armed landing-party ashore on the nearest beach. In between times, relays of men attended drills and lectures ashore: sometimes, with half the crew thus absent and their normal organization unworkable, a fearsome directive from the Admiral would set them to some manœuvre that necessitated every available man tackling the nearest job, irrespective of his rating.

Stokers would find themselves firing guns: seamen had to try their hand at hoisting flag-signals: telegraphists and coders, gentlemanly types, would take on the crude job of connecting up filthy oil-pipes from the oiler. "Blast the old bastard!" said Bennett sourly, when some crisis or other found him hauling on a rope instead of watching other people do it: "I'll be cleaning out the lavatories next." Lockhart wished it might be true. . . . The three weeks' ordeal was exhilarating, and profoundly good for the ship, as far as training was concerned: but there were occasions when they all felt due for a holiday, and none too sure that it would arrive in time.

There were no holidays now: this was the time for winding up, for tuning to top pitch: they would have no other chance. Little by little the process advanced: the rough edges were smoothed off, the awkwardness of apprenticeship overcome and then forgotten. It was a progress they all acknowledged, and welcomed: their ship was coming alive, and for that reason she was a better place to live in, a surer weapon to use. There would come a time, they began to realize, when alertness and a disciplined reaction to crisis might save all their lives; if the price, now, were over-work and sometimes over-harshness, it was worth paying the score, and forgetting it as soon as it was paid. No weariness, no boredom, no grudge against authority, was worth setting against this ultimate survival.

The measure of their progress was nowhere more apparent than during the trips they made to sea, on exercises with the submarine attached to the base. The main purpose of these trips was to try out the asdic gear—the anti-submarine detector that was their main weapon—and to perfect the team-work between the asdic operators, the depth-charge crews, and the Captain, which would be a vital element in their future effectiveness. In those early days, the asdic set was an elementary affair, not much more than a glorified echo-sounder, working horizontally all round the ship, instead of vertically down to the sea-bed; but it was still a weapon of precision, it could still produce results if it were properly used. And certainly the hunts themselves, with a real, moving, elusive quarry to outwit, instead of the synthetic target that they practised on ashore, were the most exciting part of all their training.

At first they had very little success. Bennett, Lockhart, and Ferraby all took turns at manœuvring the ship during a hunt, and they all found the same inherent handicap—there were too many things to think about at the same time. The ship had to be handled, sometimes in bad weather that set her rolling like a metronome: the submarine had to be found, and held during the run-in: the asdic operators had to be controlled, and chivvied back onto the target if they showed signs of wandering: the engine revolutions had to be altered, the correct signals hoisted, the depth-charge crews warned, the right button pressed at the right moment. And if they forgot one of these things, the whole attack collapsed and had to be written off as a failure, a foolish waste of time attended by a deplorable publicity. . . . It was no wonder that, during the preliminary exercises, each of them in turn developed stage fright, and did their best to cover it by a mixture of bluff and pretended indifference. Bennett, naturally, was by far the best at this: to listen to him, nothing moving below the surface had a chance of survival when he was Officer-of-the-Watch, and precious little on top.

But gradually they improved: they learned various tricks and idiosyncrasies of the ship and the asdic set, they learned to anticipate what a hunted submarine would do next, they learned when it was safe to guess and when it was essential to make sure before moving in any direction. Their wits sharpened, and their applied skill too. And finally there came a day when in the course of six successive "runs" *Compass Rose* picked up the submarine each time and held it right down to the mock "kill": when, indeed, the submarine, surfacing at the end of its last encounter after trying every device and every evasion, signalled to them: "You're too good. Go away and try it on the Germans." At that moment of small triumph, it seemed a very good idea—and anything else a waste of energy. The time was very near when they would outgrow the schoolroom altogether, and insist on trying their armour on the adult world. They were confident that that armour would take a lot of denting. Even Chief E.R.A. Watts, when tackled straight, would admit that *Compass Rose* was running sweetly enough, and that his engines, at least, were proving themselves robust, tireless, and dependable. From Petty Officer Tallow there was now less talk of the glories of the *Repulse:* on a smaller scale, *Compass Rose* had won his affection.

There was one thing that did not improve, though they were busy enough to be able to ignore it most of the time: the situation in the wardroom. Ericson, watching his officers at work, was satisfied enough with their progress, from the professional angle: it was off duty, when they were isolated on board (there was nothing for them to do ashore, even when they braved the winter cold in search of distraction), that the bickering and the ill-humour started up again, taking the place of their working co-operation. It came to a head on one occasion, and he was forced to recognize it and to take action: he did so unwillingly, since discipline necessitated his admonishing the wrong man, but with the best will in the world he could not ignore a direct clash between Bennett and the other two.

It started with Ferraby: most things did: he was now established as the vulnerable element, the weak link that betrayed the rest of the chain. He tried hard enough, he was still eager to make a success of it: but that eagerness was blunted and poisoned all the time by the knowledge that, whatever he did, Bennett would find fault with it. Given

61

any sort of encouragement, and an occasional word of approval, he might have measured up to the new standard of effectiveness that *Compass Rose* as a whole had reached—he was not by any means stupid, he was adaptable and enthusiastic, he wanted above all to give of his best. But since this giving always met with the same reception, since whatever he did was wrong, and the fact was pointed out to him in the crudest terms, it was no wonder that he slipped deeper and deeper into a miserable hesitation. He grew to loathe and to fear that rough voice, which might at any moment call out "Ferrabee!" and then pick to pieces whatever he was trying to do; and hesitation, loathing, and fear were not a compound of any use either to himself or to the ship.

Lockhart saw what was happening, and did his best to stand in the way of Bennett's rougher attacks: it was this effort to shield Ferraby that led to an open rupture. It took place in the wardroom, one night when Ferraby, as Officer-of-the-Day, had come below again after evening Rounds. Though he had been up to the bridge, he had forgotten to check their anchor-bearings—a pure formality in this case, since there was no wind and in their sheltered harbour it would take a tidal wave to make *Compass Rose* drag her anchor; but Bennett, seizing the occasion as usual, had made it the subject of a prolonged and brutal tirade that Ferraby accepted without protest. When he was finally and contemptuously dismissed, and had left the wardroom, Lockhart, who had been a spectator, muttered something not quite under his breath. Bennett, who was standing by the sideboard pouring himself a drink, swung round.

"What did you say?" he snapped.

Lockhart came to a decision. "I said," he repeated more distinctly, "why don't you leave him alone? He's only a kid, and he's doing his best."

"It's not good enough."

"It would be if you gave him a chance."

Bennett slammed down his glass. "That's enough," he said roughly. "You keep out of it. I don't have to argue with you."

62

"You don't have to argue with anyone," said Lockhart moderately. "But can't you see that it's no good going on at Ferraby like that? It only makes him worse instead of better. He's that sort of person."

"Then he'd better change, pretty quickly," sneered Bennett.

"He's doing his best," Lockhart repeated.

"He's not. He's been no bloody use ever since I stopped him dipping his wick at Glasgow, and that's been the trouble all along."

Lockhart looked at him for a moment, and then said, with all the dispassion he could muster: "What a horrible man you are."

Bennett suddenly stiffened, his whole body rigid with fury. "Who the hell do you think you're talking to?" he shouted. "By God, you'd better watch out, or I'll land you in hell's own trouble! I'll see you stay a sub-lieutenant for the rest of the war, for a start."

Lockhart, who had had the one extra drink that took him over the borderline of discretion, looked pointedly at the two rings on Bennett's sleeve, and said:

"I'm not sure I want to be a lieutenant after all."

Bennett, now nearly beside himself, walked across the wardroom and stood over his chair. "One more crack like that, and I'll report you to the Captain."

"Try it," said Lockhart. He was beginning to feel fatalistic about the outcome of the scene: it might be suicidal to keep on, but if he knuckled under now it would cancel out the whole stand he had made. "Try it," he repeated. "The Captain's not *such* a bloody fool. I bet he knows how you treat Ferraby, at all events."

"He knows I treat Ferraby like that because Ferraby's a lazy bastard who's no bloody use to anyone." Bennett focused a venomous look on Lockhart's face, daring him to counter-attack. "And that's about true of you, too."

"It's not," said Lockhart, stung out of his control at last. He abandoned caution. "We both do a damned sight more work than you, anyway."

63

After which, there was really nothing to do but put on his cap and follow Bennett up to the Captain's cabin. The respectful gaze of Leading Steward Carslake, who had been an enthralled audience and who now came out of the pantry to watch the tense procession go by, was sufficient commentary on the seriousness of the clash. It seemed that only some vital exercise of authority could resolve it.

But the subsequent encounter in the Captain's cabin was an odd one, and less conclusive than either Bennett or Lockhart had expected. Ericson listened while Bennett put his case— fairly enough, since he was on impregnable ground; but even on the admitted facts he could not really decide how to deal with it. He had been expecting something of the sort for quite a long time, and now here it was: Lockhart had been a fool not to keep his temper, Bennett had been his natural unpleasant self—and he, as Captain, had to find the right answer, with a strong bias towards the maintenance of discipline. But what sort of discipline did he want to maintain?

The ideal solution was to tell Lockhart to behave himself, and Bennett not to be so tough; but that did not quite square with King's Regulations, and it was the letter of the law that had to be appeased. The next best thing was to find some negative ground on which to settle the matter, and he had an opening when Lockhart, in answer to a question about the origin of the row, said:

"I think Ferraby gets a rough deal, sir."

"It's not your concern whether someone else gets a rough deal or not," Ericson cut in briskly. "You've got your own job to do, without worrying how the First Lieutenant treats his officers."

"I realize that, sir." Lockhart, standing formally to attention, was still sensitive to atmosphere, and he guessed the Captain's dilemma; but having come so far he did not want the whole situation to melt away in vague generalizations about minding one's own business. "But if you think a friend of yours is being unfairly treated, the natural thing to do is to try and help him."

64

"Is it?" said Ericson ironically. "I should say that much the best plan was to keep clear of it, and let him work out his own salvation. Then we don't get this sort of argument, and"—he looked grimly at Lockhart—"argument between you and the First Lieutenant is something I'm not going to stand for."

"I know that, sir. I got a bit worked up, and—" he was about to say he was sorry, but somehow he could not bring himself to form the words. Instead he finished: "I'm not trying to get out of the consequences. But I do think that this sort of treatment"— he gestured towards Bennett— "is having an appalling effect on Ferraby. He just hasn't an ounce of self-confidence left."

Bennett, without looking at him, said: "I don't want any lectures on how to treat Ferraby."

Ericson glanced from one to the other—from Lockhart's serious, determined face, pale under the electric light, to Bennett's flushed self-confidence. Privately he thought: There's no solution really—they're just two unmixable people. Then he caught sight of his own face between them in the mirror: it was tough, square, a competent barrier between two opposing forces. He looked, in fact, a lot more convincing than he felt; he knew he was not handling this thing well, and it had to be handled perfectly, to dispose of it without a hang-over. The trouble was that he was dog-tired. The cabin, with its portholes closed since Darken Ship was piped five hours ago, was now stuffy and airless: they had had a long day at sea, and there was another one tomorrow. The Admiral's habit of slipping aboard "to see how things were getting along," without any more notice than the sight of his barge leaving the quay, was proving a constant source of irritation. Tonight, Ericson had not a great deal of energy left, and none at all for this sort of domestic upheaval.

But he made another effort, seeking to deal with the thing in black-and-white terms, without subtlety, disregarding the gross cleavage that lay in the background.

"Now look here," he began. "This has gone far enough, and it's not going to go any further. It's bad for you, and it's

65

bad for the ship." He looked at Lockhart. "I'm not going to have you interfering like this in things that don't concern you. Do you understand?"

"Yes, sir," said Lockhart. On this basis, he was now ready to let it go: he had not won, but neither had Bennett—unless there was something more to come.

Apparently there was nothing more. "Remember that, then," said the Captain. "I don't want to hear any more complaints about you, or I shall have to take some action—action you won't like. Now just forget. about the whole thing. There's plenty to do, without this sort of scrapping."

He stopped, and turned away: it seemed to be their dismissal. Bennett opened his mouth to speak, unable to believe that the matter was thus disposed of: what about the insolence, what about Lockhart's cracks, what about the denial of authority? He could not leave it like this. But he did not want to start things up again with Lockhart listening: it needed a less formal approach. He said:

"May I have a word with you, sir?"

Ericson, who had been expecting it, said: "All right, Number One." He nodded to Lockhart, who turned and left the cabin. "Well," said Ericson, a shade less cordially, "what's the trouble?"

"Sir," said Bennett, "I think Lockhart got away with it."

Ericson, disregarding the temptation to answer: "I quite agree with you," which would have been nearer the truth, said: "You've got to make allowances, Number One. He's a very new officer, and I think we've all been working pretty hard. It *was* a bit rough, I know, but I don't think it will happen again."

"I've had a lot of trouble with Lockhart," said Bennett aggrievedly. "I hoped you'd pull him up, sir. He needs stamping on, good and hard."

Ericson looked at him, tense and sweating in the close cabin, and thought: One of these days someone is going to hit you, and that means a court-martial, all because you're a tough character and have to show it all the time. He remembered a first mate rather like Bennett, back in the old days in the Far East Line: foul-mouthed, ready with his fists, never giving an inch of ground or a word of praise. He'd ended by killing his man—a Chinese seaman foolish enough to argue about some bad food. He'd got off with manslaughter, but that had been the end of him. On a less dramatic plane, Bennett might go the same way—or push someone else to it. There *were* people like that, doomed by their own intransigence, damned by their crudity: it was bad luck that one of them had landed up in *Compass Rose*.

He said, shortly: "I want to avoid having to stamp on people, as far as possible, Number One. There are other ways of getting them to work properly." He felt like adding something about Ferraby, and the need to treat him less roughly, but perhaps Bennett had had enough hints for one evening. Instead he said: "Give Lockhart a fresh start, and see what he makes of it," and then he turned away with a finality that even Bennett's thick skin could not resist. This was a scene that might go on for ever: he had had enough of it.

When Bennett had gone, his face registering the protest that had scarcely been allowed to come to life, much less to develop properly, Ericson walked out of his cabin, parted the thick blackout screens at the entrance to the companionway, and stepped onto the upper deck. The fresh air, though bitterly cold, came as a welcome relief: the night was clear, the little harbour easily seen, the small waves slapping against the ship's side an endless accompaniment to their vigil. He looked up at the sky: wispy clouds round the moon promised some wind later, but tomorrow's weather seemed as secure as their anchorage. Round him the familiar shipboard sounds were reassuring: the hum of the dynamos, the noise of a gramophone from the fo'c's'le, the clumping of the quartermaster's sea boots as he made his rounds further aft—all these were part of a life and a moment he savoured to the full. Night in harbour, after a hard day's work: there should be nothing to beat that.

But he was not *quite* satisfied: the recent scene with Bennett and Lockhart had left a bad taste. There had been too many loose ends, though if he had tried to deal with them in detail it would have been far more serious for Lockhart. And then there was Ferraby, adrift in circumstances he scarcely comprehended, as vulnerable as a baby that never grew any bigger or any cleverer. . . . He shrugged, and turned back to his cabin, glad to leave it all till tomorrow. There was only one real cure, anyway: they had to stop fighting each other, and fight the enemy instead.

Soon it was their last week at Ardnacraish, the end of their apprenticeship: the tuning-up process came to its full flower, and with it an access of confidence that reached all but the most unimpressionable elements.

Professionally, they were sure of themselves: they knew their ship, they knew their jobs in her. Now, no matter what they were asked to do, no matter how the Admiral or his staff stalked them, no matter what odd signals made Leading Signalman Wells suck his teeth and Bennett start sweating and shouting, they felt they could cope with it. There were occasional mistakes, lacerating to the dignity—as when one of the fo'c's'le party broke the wrong shackle on the cable and dropped the anchor and six feet of chain neatly over the bows and into thirty feet of water; but these were odd setbacks in a continuous process, small pebbles in the stream. All in all, they had made a success of Ardnacraish; even Ferraby, now that Bennett seemed to be holding his hand and moderating his voice, was beginning to improve: unexpectedly buoyant, he took a fresh lease and tried once more to fit himself in. . . . *Compass Rose*, eight weeks from the day she was commissioned, was now a working proposition.

During the final week they had been joined by another corvette, the next off the assembly line. Her name was *Sorrel*, and her captain, Ramsay, was an old friend of Ericson's; her arrival was a cheerful occasion, adding to the amenities of what was, in essentials, a bleak corner of the world. When they went out on trials with the submarine, *Sorrel* and *Compass Rose* hunted as a team, and this was another advantage, adding interest to exercises that were beginning to pall: they took it in turns to attack the submarine, while the spare ship stood off and passed cross-bearings, advice, and, occasionally, the ribald comments of the more successful performer. It was a useful foretaste of what could happen in convoy, when any number of escorts might join in a hunt, and would have to learn to do this, and make an effective contribution, without getting in each other's way.

Compass Rose's final exercise before she left was, appropriately, a practice-shoot at night.

At dusk they said good-bye to *Sorrel*, who was returning to harbour, and then for an hour they cruised about off the south end of the island, waiting first for the tug that was to tow their target for them, and then for the coming of night. It was one of those evenings which show the Scottish Highlands at their superb best: by good luck, their *envoi* from the peaceful world had a loveliness that they carried with them for many months afterwards. Sunset gave them a gold-and-red-streaked sky: dusk gave them a subtle-coloured back-cloth for the islands surrounding them—Mull and Iona and Colonsay: darkness itself came down from the hills in deep purple shadows that, reflected on the water round the ship, turned it to a sombre, royal hue. Then, in the deepening night, the hills were shut out altogether: the single light that marked the harbour entrance still stood guard for them, ten miles and more away, but that was the only element that bound them to the land. Alone on a dark noiseless sea, under a sky already pricked by the first stars, *Compass Rose* circled and lifted to the swell and waited for her rendezvous.

Up on the bridge, the waiting was focused down to a few alert men: the Captain at the front of the bridge; Lockhart, who was Officer-of-the-Watch, beside him; Leading Signalman Wells leaning against his lamp and staring through his binoculars; the two look-outs on the two wings completing the pattern. It was very cold: they felt it on their faces, they felt it on their stiff hands, they felt it in their legs and thighs as they stamped their feet. The canvas screens round the bridge were no protection: on their high platform, the waiting figures were simply part of the ship, bare to the weather, open to the sky.

Suddenly Leading Signalman Wells, intent on something that had caught his eye on their beam, straightened up.

"There she is, sir. Red eight-oh."

The vague blur to port resolved itself: under the growing moon, the tug emerged as a hard shape on the horizon, and the towed target as a black blob astern of her.

Wells spoke again. "Calling us up, sir!" He turned swiftly to the signalman of the watch, Rose, at the back of the bridge. "Take it down. . . . '*Compass Rose* from *Basher*.' "

"What a singular name for a tug," said Lockhart.

"Gives you fair warning," said the Captain. Lockhart smiled to himself. Now and again the Captain came out with a remark like that, disproving his professional inhumanity. It was the more refreshing for being so unexpected.

The dimmed signal-lights winked to each other across a mile of still water.

"Signal, sir!" said Wells presently. "From the tug: 'My course and speed, two-seven-oh, four knots. Length of tow, three hundred feet. Ready for you.' "

"Right," said the Captain. "Make to them: 'On our first run we will close from four thousand yards and fire three rounds. Please signal hits.' "

The lamps winked again, flickering across the darkness as if glad to find each other.

"Reply, sir: 'If any,' " said Wells, without expression.

"Humourist," said the Captain briefly. He bent to the voice-pipe. "Starboard twenty. Steer north." And then, to Lockhart: "Sound off Action Stations. We'll start this from the beginning."

The alarm bells, faintly and shrilly heard from below, set in motion a stirring, the length and breadth of the ship, which quickly filtered up to the bridge. Figures appeared on the gun platform, crowding round the gun: Petty Officer Tallow confirmed his presence at the wheel: the voice-pipe from the quarterdeck reported that Sub-Lieutenant Ferraby had the depth-charge partly closed up. As on so many occasions during the past three weeks, *Compass Rose* quickly came to life, filling in the gaps in her readiness, crowding the upper deck with men who no longer blundered about or impeded one another as they moved, but who made swiftly for their stations as if they had been walking about in full daylight. The hours of drilling and practice were paying a dividend already; if the future were to call upon it at a crucial moment, it was there, ready and available.

Lockhart's position at Action Stations was on the fo'c's'le, in charge of the gun: he had no sooner got there, clattering up the ladder in the darkness, and Leading Seaman Phillips had reported that the gun's crew was closed up, than he felt *Compass Rose* tremble as she increased speed: the wind of their advance struck cold on his face, prompting him to action. They loaded and stood ready, while the ship ran on over the dark water and the range shortened: then from the bridge came the shouted order: "Target bearing red four-five—range three thousand—open fire!" and from that moment the responsibility was his. *Compass Rose* had no refinements in the way of gunnery: in action, as now, it was to be a matter of shouting, and then local control from the gun platform itself. Lockhart set the range, and waited until the gun-layer, straining his eyes against the darkness, reported that he had found the target: then he gave the order: "Shoot!"

He had never seen the gun fired at night: close to, the effect was almost stupefying—a violent crash, and then a great burst of flame and smoke that momentarily blinded him and made him gasp. Through his binoculars he watched for the fall of shot, and presently it came: a tall spout of water, a plume of spray phosphorescent in the moonlight, in line with the target but well short of it.

"Up four hundred—shoot!"

Again the crash of the explosion, again the burst of flame, and the waiting for the shot to fall. This second time, accustomed to the noise, Lockhart could hear the shell whistling

7 1

and whining away into the darkness after the first report. Now they were over the target: the range must be closing quicker than he had thought, or else the first shot had been a bad one, fired as they rolled.

"Down two hundred—shoot!"

That was a good bracket—the spout of water was just short of the target. But that was the last round allowed to them. . . . The cease-fire gong sounded, and he called out: "Check, check, check!" to confirm it. Then he stood back, as the gun was cleared, and smelt the reek of cordite, and heard Phillips mutter: "The next one would have sunk 'em," and felt suddenly excited and pleased with himself. The noise and the flames and the sense of crisis were wildly novel to him: he had never done anything like it before, but it did seem—it *really* seemed—as if he had done quite well. . . . As if to confirm this, the Captain leaned over the edge of the bridge above him and said: "Not bad, Lockhart. Get ready for the next run." The sound of Bennett disagreeably clearing his throat in the background need not, he felt, be given any weight as a comment.

The second run was, by contrast, a resounding failure: it would not have frightened a rowing-boat. Their first shot fell short—so short, indeed, that Lockhart knew that the gun-layer had lost his head and fired on the forward roll, with the gun pointing downwards. The second was for some reason right out of line: he could, at a stretch, blame that on the quartermaster, who swung the ship off her steady course at the critical moment. The third fall, which was to make amends, Lockhart did not even see: they might never have fired it at all, for all the evidence they had, though probably it had gone far over and been obscured by the target. And that was the end of that run. . . . The noise and activity now seemed a great deal less dramatic, and the reflective silence from the bridge a positive insult. He said under his breath to Phillips: "We'll have to do better than this," and Phillips answered determinedly: "We'll do that, sir," and started a blasphemous harangue of the gun's crew, man by man. Lockhart, applying the principle of limited liability, walked casually out of earshot. He had delegated his authority, and it seemed to be in effective hands.

The harangue must have been a good one, for their last run was by far the best. One sighting shot, a little short, and then "Up two hundred—shoot!" and two hits plumb at the base of the target. The tug, impressed, flickered a message to them, and this time the Captain said: "Good shooting, Lockhart," and there was no repressive cough from Bennett. " 'Sink me the ship, Master Gunner,' " Lockhart quoted aloud, slightly over-elated: " 'Sink her, split her in twain: Fall into the hands of God, not into the hands of Spain.' " "Sir?" said Phillips interestedly. "Poetry," said Lockhart. "Sponge out, secure the gun, and then ask the leading steward to give you seven bottles of beer." He had never felt better in his life: at that moment, standing on the gun platform while the crew worked and chattered in the darkness, he would have shaken hands with Bennett or joined the Navy for a twelve-year stretch.

It was past midnight when they entered harbour: since it was the last exercise in their program, and the morrow was a genuine holiday, the late hour did not matter. *Compass Rose*, moving very slowly through the harbour entrance, was like a grey ghost slipping back to its lair, at some dead hour before the cock crew and ghosts must walk no more. The defence boom had been kept open for them, but nothing stirred as they slid by it and went gently up toward their buoy. The moon was still high, and every outline was clear: the bay had a silvery rim to it, marking the limits of their refuge, giving it a containing margin. They moved past the oiler, past the sleeping *Sorrel* with her shaded stern-light, and then, foot by foot, up to their mooring.

Standing in the eyes of the ship, torch in hand, Lockhart called out directions to the bridge, while the beam of the torch sent odd wavering reflections of the water along their hull. *Compass Rose* inched her way forward and came to a stop, her bows overhanging the buoy: Lockhart bent his shaft of light downward, picking out the white face of the rating perched on the buoy, and the wire, with the spring-clip at the end, snaking its way down to him. Then he turned and called out: "Hooked on, sir!" to the bridge: and they were at rest, and his part in the day was over.

A few minutes later the moorings were properly secured: the telegraph bell, faintly heard, which meant "Main engine finished with," set the seal on their arrival. The slack of the cable ran out noisily, starting up a hollow echo from the cliffs, and Leading Seaman Phillips, speaking out of the darkness to no one in particular, said: "I bet that wakes the Admiral." There was a small ripple of laughter from the fo'c's'le men: Lockhart wondered if Phillips had already drunk his beer. Then he took a last look at the moorings, and said: "All right—that'll do," and followed his party across the dark fo'c's'le and down the ladder. He was stiff and tired; but the last day had been the best, and *Compass Rose*, swinging to her buoy and peaceful under the moon, was something he unaccountably loved.

[*12*]

Once more, Vice-Admiral Sir Vincent Murray-Forbes sat at his desk in the operations building overlooking the harbour. Now he was writing a report: it was one of hundreds of reports, on ships and men, that he was to write, month in and month out, until the end of the war: on ships destined to be sunk or to survive, on men marked for killing, or for honour at the King's own hands. He did not know what lay in store for these ships or these men: it would not have made an atom of difference if he had been writing an epitaph on men due to be drowned tomorrow. He was concerned only with facts; and of these he had mustered a great many, during the past three weeks.

"H.M.S. *Compass Rose*," he wrote, in an old-fashioned, somewhat laborious longhand, "completed her program of training on February 2, 1940, and may be regarded as having passed out satisfactorily. The ship has been well worked up, and is clean and generally efficient. Further attention should be given (a) to fire fighting, which was below the requisite standard of speed, and (b) to the drill for Abandon Ship, which did not go smoothly on the only occasion on which it was tested. But with these reservations, the organization of H.M.S. *Compass Rose* now meets the high standard necessary to a ship engaged in the exacting task of convoy escort."

He consulted a batch of reports from his staff. "Gunnery," he wrote, as a sub-heading, and underlined it. "The single four-inch gun which is the sole major armament of this class of ship will only be adequate if constant attention is given to gun drill and to ammunition supply. H.M.S. *Compass Rose* did well in her various gun-trials, and the night-shoot was successful, both as regards the handling of the ship and the actual firing. Anti-aircraft shooting, conducted with a towed streamer-target, was less successful: it is recommended that more provision be made for anti-aircraft gun-control, possibly by loudspeaker operated from the bridge.

"Asdics," he went on, and underlined again. "On her arrival, H.M.S. *Compass Rose* was inadequately trained in this branch, and the Anti-Submarine Control Officer and the asdic ratings were clearly in need of intensive practice. When this had been provided, her efficiency improved rapidly, and she developed an effective anti-submarine team. Communication between the bridge and the depth-charge parties aft is still inadequate in this class of vessel: attention is drawn to my No. 242/17/1/40, addressed to Admiral Superintending Contract-Built Ships (repeated to C.-in-C. W.A.) in which various improvements are suggested.

"Depth-Charge Organization," he wrote. "Only constant practice will bring the depth-charge crews up to the high standard of efficiency necessary in this branch. Time-tests of reloading and firing were generally disappointing, and it is emphasized that speed and accuracy may be vital here when the ship is in action."

He added three short sub-headings: "Engine-Room Branch: satisfactory." "Telegraphy and Coding: adequate."

75

"Signal Branch: excellent." Then he took a fresh sheet of paper.

"H.M.S. *Compass Rose:* Reports on Officers," wrote the Admiral, and referred again to his notes. "Lieutenant-Commander George Eastwood Ericson, R.N.R.: Commanding Officer. This officer exhibited a high standard of seamanship, and showed himself expert at ship-handling. I judged him to be a conscientious and determined officer who, when he has gained more experience in this new class of ship, will extract everything possible out of his command. His relations with his subordinate officers appeared satisfactory, and it was clear that he inspired their confidence and would be followed by them without hesitation.

"Lieutenant James Bennett, R.A.N.V.R.: First Lieutenant and Anti-Submarine Control Officer," wrote the Admiral. "This officer has a remarkable self-confidence, and with more experience and application his executive capacity may come to match it. He tends to rely too much on his junior officers implementing his orders (and in some cases issuing them themselves). In the initial stages there were serious flaws in the internal organization of H.M.S. *Compass Rose*, doubtless due to this officer's inexperience. A downright, forceful personality who should make a good First Lieutenant when he learns to set an example of self-discipline.

"Sub-Lieutenant Keith Laing Lockhart, R.N.V.R.: Gunnery and Navigation Officer," wrote the Admiral. "I was impressed by this officer's competence, in novel surroundings and in a position of responsibility, when backed by very little practical experience. His gun's crews were well worked up, and he seemed to inspire confidence in the ratings in his division. He should develop into a good type of officer, very useful in a ship of this class. He should pay more attention to the regulations governing dress for officers when on duty.

"Sub-Lieutenant Gordon Perceval D'Ewes Ferraby, R.N.V.R.: Depth-Charge Control and Correspondence Officer," wrote the Admiral. "This officer lacks both experience and self-confidence, and appeared hesitant in giving orders. There is no reason why he should not develop into a useful officer, but he must learn to trust his own judgment, and to give the ratings under his charge the impression that he knows what he wants from them. His department improved during the latter stages of H.M.S. *Compass Rose's* course of training."

The Admiral drew a thick line under his report, and blotted it neatly. Then he added, at the bottom: "Addressed, Commander-in-Chief, Western Approaches: copies to Flag-Officer-in-Charge, Glasgow: Admiralty (C.W. Branch): H.M.S. *Compass Rose.*" Then he sat back, and rang for his secretary.

[*13*]

Ericson, at ease in his cabin, read his copy of this report with some satisfaction and a good deal of amusement. The Admiral had come well up to standard, by way of farewell: it was a perfect picture of Number One, despite the limits of official phraseology, and he liked especially the crack about Lockhart and "dress regulations"—Lockhart having mislaid his cap on one crucial occasion and greeted the Admiral with something between a wave and a bow. Then, as he folded the sheets of paper again, there was a knock on the door, and Leading Signalman Wells came in, a sealed envelope in his hand.

"Secret signal, sir," said Wells, in not quite his normal inexpressive voice. "The signal boat just brought it aboard."

Ericson ripped open the envelope, and read slowly and carefully. It was what he had been waiting for.

"Being in all respects ready for sea," said the pink slip, "H.M.S. *Compass Rose* will sail to join convoy AK14, leaving Liverpool (Bar Light Vessel) at 1200A 6th February, 1940. Senior officer of escort is in H.M.S. *Viperous*. Acknowledge."

77

Ericson read it through again. Then:

"Take this down," he said. " 'To Commander-in-Chief, Western Approaches, from *Compass Rose*. Your 0939 stroke four stroke two acknowledged.' And send it off straight away."

So they went to war.

PART TWO

1940: *Skirmishing*

[1]

The war to which they went had hardly settled down, even in broad outline, to any recognizable pattern.

The liner *Athenia* had been torpedoed and sunk, with the loss of 128 lives, on September 3, the first day of the war: the first U-boat sinking, to offset this ruthless stroke, was on September 14. Thus, at the beginning, the pace was hot—forty ships were sunk during that first September, and two fine warships, *Courageous* and *Royal Oak*, both went to the bottom before the turn of the year; but the pace did not last. The casualties had been mostly independent ships that happened to be at sea when war was declared; like the *Athenia*, they were in the wrong place at the wrong time; but with the growth of the convoy system this chance ill-fortune could be avoided, and ships and shipping companies were quick to see that any effort to remain in convoy, instead of straggling behind or charging proudly ahead of the pedestrian field, was worth while.

The U-boats were on the offensive—that was their role—but it was not a co-ordinated attack, nor even a very efficient one. Probably there were not more than a dozen of them at sea at any one time during this stage of the war, and so they hunted alone. They hung about off the coasts of Scotland and Ireland, and in the Bay of Biscay, on the look-out for stray ships that they could pick off at leisure; it was a series of individual forays—sometimes successful, sometimes a waste of time: the co-ordination and the control were to come later, and in the meantime the whole thing was unpredictable and rather amateurish. Britain was short of escorts, Germany was short of U-boats: the Atlantic was a very big ocean and, in winter weather, the finest hiding-place in the world. It was indeed like a game of hide-and-seek, played by a few children in an enormous rambling garden, with the light sometimes fading and the grown-ups calling out directions intermittently. And if some of the children were vicious and cruel, and pinched you when you were discovered, that was nothing unexpected in a nursery world.

Such was the battlefield of the Atlantic, when 1940 dawned. The danger was there, but the two sides were hardly engaged: the U-boats lurking always, but playing their luck instead of their skill. To join this untidy battle, *Compass Rose* sailed early in the year.

[2]

Their first convoy was a bloodless skirmish, as were many others in that momentary lull; but it was a useful foretaste of what was to come, as well as a proving of the ship in weather worse than they had yet met.

The sun was out as they sailed down into Liverpool Bay, on that fine February morning, to meet their convoy: it had pierced the early mist, melted the frost of their cold night passage, dried out their clothes with a cheerful warmth. Ericson knew the port well—he had lived there for ten years, and had sailed in and out of it scores of times: he looked for the familiar landmarks with an affectionate eagerness. As usual the first sight of land was the tall Blackpool Tower, away to the north: then the Bar Light Vessel, riding uneasily in the jumble of tide-ripped water that marked the entrance to the River Mersey; and then, faintly glimpsed in the mist and smoke up-river, the twin spires of the Liver Buildings, in the heart of the city. Somewhere there, in a little house on the Birkenhead side, Grace was undoubtedly knitting. . . . He had a moment's pang that they should be so near to each other and yet be unable to meet; and then he forgot it altogether. Five miles ahead of them their ships were coming out; they were led by a destroyer—an old V. and W. Class, which must be *Viperous*—already giving them the "interrogative" on her signal-lamp.

While Leading Signalman Wells was replying, first making *Compass Rose's* number and then taking down a long signal about the organization of the convoy, Ericson studied the line of ships coming toward them. They were of all shapes and sizes: tankers, big freighters, small ships that would surely have been better off in the coasting trade than trying the hazards of an Atlantic passage. Some were deep-laden, some were in ballast and uncomfortably high out of the water: they steamed in single file from the narrow Mersey channel: their pendants flew bravely in the sunshine, they seemed almost glad to be putting to sea again. . . . That could hardly be true, thought Ericson with a smile, remembering the tearful good-byes, the hangovers, the feeling of "Oh-God-here-we-go-again" that attended every sailing; but there was something about the file of ships—forty-six of them—that suggested a willingness to make the voyage, a tough confidence in the future.

There were U-boats in the way of that voyage, of course—or so it was said, because most ships and most men in that convoy had yet to meet one: there was, at any rate, a threat to use U-boats. Thus, as well as being important for these ships to sail to Boston and New York and Halifax and Rio, it was essential, as a simple matter of principle as well, that they should get through. The Atlantic had never been specifically a British ocean; but it was even less a German one, and now was not the time for it to change its nationality.

Ferraby, hanging about at the back of the bridge (it was not his watch) was more stirred by the sight of those ships than he had ever been before. He liked everything about this convoy: he liked its air of purpose as it cracked on speed

81

after the cautious passage down-channel: he liked individual ships—particularly the tough and shapely tankers: he liked the men on board who waved cheerfully to *Compass Rose* as she passed down the line towards the tail of the convoy. This sort of thing—this moment of significance and determination, this comradeship, this sea-brotherhood—was what he had had in mind when, at the training establishment, he volunteered for corvettes: there had been times when it had seemed impossible of attainment, when he was convinced that he was going to be fobbed off with a third-rate drama of pretence and frustration: now he knew that all his wishes were coming true.

Here were the ships, assembling for their long uncertain voyage: here was *Compass Rose*, appointed to guard them: here was Ferraby himself, a watchkeeping officer—or practically so—charged specifically with a share of that guardianship. His pale face flushed, his expression set in a new mould of determination, Ferraby surveyed the convoy with pride and a feeling of absolute proprietorship. *Our* ships, he thought: *our* cargoes, *our* men. . . . None would be surrendered, of this convoy or of any other, if it depended on any effort of his.

Ferraby's eyes were new, and took a good deal on trust: other eyes—Ericson's among them—were not new, and to them, it must be admitted, the convoy was somewhat more impressive than the escort, which reflected perfectly the pinched circumstances of the Royal Navy at this stage. To shepherd these forty-six ships through waters that were potentially the most treacherous in the world, there had been provided one fifteen-year-old destroyer, of a class that, though valiantly manned and valiantly driven, was really far too slight and slender for the Atlantic weather: two corvettes —one a prewar edition of crude design, the other *Compass Rose*; a trawler; and a rescue tug that already, in the sheltered waters of Liverpool Bay, was bouncing about like a pea on a drum. Five warships—four and a half would be nearer the truth—to guard forty-six slow merchantmen was not a reassuring prospect for the experts on either side. . . . But there it was: the best that could be done. And since there were no more ships to be had, something else would have to fill the gap: skill and luck must somehow bring about what a rational probability could not hope to effect.

Compass Rose was kept busy all that afternoon. It meant a long day for the Captain, who had been on the bridge since first light; but certainly he could not leave it now, when there was really no one else who could be trusted to handle *Compass Rose* in close company with other ships. So he stayed on, wedged in a corner of the bridge, drinking successive cups of tea and giving endless helm-orders, while they worked through the various tasks that *Viperous* had set them. First they had to see that all the ships had sailed, checking their names and numbers against the long list that had been signalled to them: then they had to round up the stragglers and coax them into a closer formation: then— most trying of all—they had to pass a verbal message over the loud-hailer to each of the forty-six ships, and, since it concerned an important alteration of their course during the night, make absolutely sure in each case that the instructions had been understood.

Over and over again they repeated that message: first the Captain, then Lockhart (who had the afternoon watch), then Leading Signalmen Wells, then the Captain again. Some ships were deaf, and needed endless repetitions: some were foreign, and had to summon a man from the depths of the stokehold to take the message: some were having their afternoon sleep, and doubtless thought the booming voice was all part of the same bad dream.

"God Almighty!" said Ericson at one point, when five minutes' hailing of a big tanker had produced nothing more than a vague salute from a man in a bowler hat on the bridge: "You'd think they *wanted* to get lost tonight. Try them again, sub."

"Hallo, Number Thirty-Two," Lockhart called wearily through the loud-hailer. "Hallo, Number Thirty-Two. I have a message for you. Take it down, please."

The tanker ploughed on, while *Compass Rose* kept jaunty pace with her, like a Pekinese harbouring designs on a greyhound.

"Can we use the siren, sir?" asked Lockhart. "They don't seem to hear the human voice."

"We'll use the gun in a minute." Ericson grasped the wire and blew a prodigious blast on the siren. The man in the bowler hat walked to the wing of the bridge and stared at them.

"Number Thirty-Two—I have a message for you!" Lockhart called out swiftly. "Take it down, please."

The man on the tanker cupped his hand to his ear.

"Oh God, the bastard's deaf," said Lockhart despairingly, forgetting that the hailer was still switched on. The crisp comment boomed across the intervening thirty yards of water, and evidently found its mark: the man took his hand down and shook his fist at them instead.

"You've hurt his feelings, sub," said the Captain.

"Mistake, sir—sorry." Lockhart was indeed considerably taken aback by what he had done, and when next he spoke he tried to make amends by assuming a winning tone: through the loud-hailer, it sounded revolting, like a dance-band crooner wooing the customers. "Message for you, Number Thirty-Two. Important alteration of course. Please take it down."

In answer the man on the tanker raised a megaphone and shouted to them. Faintly over the water came the words:

"Don't be so bloody rude. I'll report you to the Board of Trade."

Then he went inside and shut the door of the bridge-shelter firmly behind him. They had to wait until the change of the watch brought a new man to the bridge, before they could attract any further attention at all.

That first night with the convoy was a restless affair that gave them very little sleep. They were still organized on a two-watch basis—that is, the Captain and Ferraby alternated with Bennett and Lockhart, four hours on and four hours off.

It was a trying arrangement at the best of times, hard on the endurance and the temper: even if they could fall asleep as soon as they came off watch, they had to wake and dress and climb up to the bridge again, almost before they had turned over. But this was not the best of times, and *Compass Rose* far from a restful place when they were off duty. The wind was rising, and the Irish Sea with it: the ship responded to the movement with a deplorable readiness, rolling and thumping as if she were being paid by the hour for her travail. In the noisy turmoil between-decks, sleep was barely possible, even to men already dog-tired.

There were other things. An aircraft, flying low over the convoy, brought them needlessly to action stations at two o'clock in the morning: one of their ships, straggling in the rear (where *Compass Rose* was stern escort), needed constant chivvying to keep it in touch with the main body. Their progress was dishearteningly slow: Chicken Rock Light, at the south end of the Isle of Man, was their mark for so long that at times it was difficult to believe that they would ever leave it behind and reach the open sea. Altogether, the first night at their appointed job was not reassuring: if it could be as trying as this, with no enemy to fight and only a few odd incidents to contend with, what would it be like when they met the real ordeal?

There was no answer to this question; not that night, nor at any time during the next seventeen days, which was the duration of the trip. But soon, in any case, they forgot to wonder about it: they had enough to deal with, in the simple course of nature. The second day saw them make more tangible progress, northwest between Scotland and Northern Ireland; and nightfall gave them, as their last sight of land, the lovely rain-washed hills of the Mull of Kyntyre, and Islay away to the north. Then they turned due westward, to the open sea and the teeth of the wind, and the deep-sea voyage had begun. As a final introduction to it, U-boats were reported in the area immediately ahead.

They never met those U-boats, which were doubtless thankful enough to stay submerged and escape the fury of the weather; for it was the weather that was the most violent enemy of all. For eight days they steamed straight into a westerly gale: five hundred miles at a grindingly slow pace, buffeting through a weight of wind that seemed to have a personal spite in every blow it dealt. The convoy was dispersed over more than fifty square miles: the escorts were out of touch most of the time: it was impossible to establish any sort of "convoy speed" because they were no longer a composite body, just a lot of ships making the best they could of the vile Atlantic weather. The big ships in the van slowed down till they had almost lost steerageway, and tried to preserve some sort of order; but the smaller ones still straggled away behind, virtually heaving-to at the height of the gale and often having to steer many degrees off their true course, simply in order not to batter themselves to pieces. On the eighth day, *Viperous*, which had had a very bad time and had lost two men overboard, signalled: "Convoy disperse—proceed independently": in the circumstances, the signal had an irony that they were scarcely in the mood to enjoy.

The escorts collected: *Viperous* with damage to her bridge superstructure, the old corvette minus one of her boats, *Compass Rose* intact but rolling villainously, the trawler riding well, the tug tossing about with a ludicrous, almost hysterical violence as she tried to keep pace with the rest. They had a rendezvous with the incoming convoy, and they found it—somehow: in that wilderness of wind and rain, with visibility hardly more than five hundred yards at any time, they found the single pinpoint in mid-Atlantic that brought them up with the ships they were waiting for. It was navigation of a very high order; it had been *Viperous's* responsibility, and Ericson, with years of experience behind him, found himself watching *Viperous's* bridge rolling through a sixty-degree arc, and wondering, somewhere between amazement and deep admiration, how on earth her captain had managed it. Taking sights and fixing their position, under these conditions, was very nearly impossible: somehow it

86

had been done, and done with the absolute accuracy of fleet manœuvres in calm weather.

They turned for home, with the new convoy of thirty-odd ships that, in the better weather to the westward, had managed to preserve a reasonable formation. But now, with the fierce wind behind them, it was more uncomfortable still; and another U-boat alarm involved "evasive routing" that took them many miles off their proper course and kept them nearly two days extra at sea. Aboard *Compass Rose*, conditions were indescribable. She rolled furiously, with a tireless malice allowing of no rest for anyone. Cooking was impossible, even had they not exhausted their fresh meat and vegetables many days previously: the staple diet was tea and corned beef, at breakfast, lunch, and dinner, for nearly a fortnight on end. Everything was wet through: some water had come down a ventilator and flooded the wardroom: forward, the mess-decks were a crowded hell of saturated clothes, spare gear washing about round their feet, food overturned—and all the time the noise, the groaning slamming violence of a small ship fighting a monstrous sea. There seemed no end to it. *Compass Rose*, caught in a storm that could take hold of her bodily and shake her till the very rivets loosened: a storm that raged and screamed at her and never blew itself out until they were in the shelter of the land again: *Compass Rose*, adrift on this malignant ocean, seemed doomed to ride it for ever.

Bennett, disliking the experience they were all sharing, said so with honest persistence. He was now the most vocal of the wardroom, complaining with an ill-temper coloured by a real uneasiness: the rotten ship, the lousy convoy, the bloody awful weather—these were the sinews of an unending dirge that was really grounded in fear. Like the others, he had never seen weather like this, or imagined it possible: he knew enough about ships to see that *Compass Rose* was going through a desperate ordeal, but not enough to realize that she was built to survive it, and would do so. He doubted their safety, and doubt was translated by a natural process into anger. He had made a fool of himself over working out their position, too—so much so that the Captain, taking the sextant from him, had said: "Leave it, Number One—I'd rather do it myself": it had not helped matters.

He should have done something about getting the mess cleared up in the fo'c's'le, but he couldn't be bothered. He should somehow have organized at least one hot meal a day, even if it were only warmed-up tinned beans: the galley fire was unusable, but with a little ingenuity it could have been done in the engine room. This, again, was more trouble than he was prepared to take. Instead, he sulked, and shirked, and secretly longed to be out of it.

Not much more of this for him, he decided: there were other ways of winning the war. . . . It was all so tiring, too: if he hadn't been able to hand the watch over to Lockhart, and get forty winks now and again, he'd have been out on his feet.

Lockhart was desperately tired, and rather numbed, for nearly all that voyage. His thin wiry body was not built to withstand the cold: he was not yet accustomed to staying awake and alert when every nerve under his skin was crying out for sleep, and bitter cold and wakefulness were all that the present offered. Bennett might shirk his watch, spending most of it inside the asdic shelter: he himself could not do so. Four hours on, and four off, for seventeen days at a stretch—that was his share: and the hours "on" were an unending strain, trying his eyes and his tired body to the limit. And when he stumbled down the ladder at the end of his watch, there was little relief to be had: tea and corned beef in the shambles of the wardroom, with water washing about all over the place and the furniture lashed together in one corner, and then the effort to sleep, wedged in his bunk against the endless rolling of the ship, with the light left burning in case of an alarm, and the thought, nagging all the time, that he must get up and face the wind and the sea again within a few hours. When he *did* face it again, and felt the gale whipping and tearing at his face and clothes, and *Compass Rose* lurching under his feet as if the world itself were drunk, it was with a body from which every instinct save a dumb endurance had been drained.

There was one night he remembered especially, toward the end of the trip, when the wind had veered to the north and the gale was at its height. A gigantic sea was running at them from the beam: *Compass Rose* would rise to it as if she were going up in a lift, balance herself uneasily at its peak, and then fall away into the trough of the wave with a wicked sideways roll. Sometimes the next wave, towering up in its turn, would catch them as they lay there sluggishly, and beat down on them before they could rise. That was the moment when the heart quailed: when solid tons of water fell with a thunderous drumming on the bridge and the upper deck, and the spray flew over in clouds, wind-driven and cutting. The storm was indeed incredibly noisy: the water crashed and thudded against their side, the wind howled at them out of the blackness as if it had a conscious intention of terror. Round them was nothing but a waste of sea, a livid grey whipped up here and there to white foam; and then beyond it, like a threatening wall, the surrounding dark, the chaos and flurry of the night.

With Bennett dozing inside, Lockhart was clinging to the rail in one corner of the bridge, staring through misted binoculars at the single merchant ship on which he was keeping station. He was wet through, and cold to the bone: his feet inside the sodden sea boots squelched icily whenever he moved: from the pinched skin of his face the water ran down, riming his eyes and lips with salt. He felt little resentment against Bennett, who should really be doing this job: he had a general disgust that someone nominally his senior should be content to evade responsibility at a moment like this, but he was really feeling too remote from personalities to care. For him, the world had resolved itself into a storm, and a small blur to leeward of *Compass Rose*: the blur was a ship that he must not lose, and so, for hour after hour, he nursed *Compass Rose* in her station, altering the engine revolutions, edging over when the blur faded, and away again when it loomed too large.

He was roused at one point from this tremendous concentration by someone nudging him, and he turned round to see a figure in the darkness beside him.

"Who is it?" he asked. It could hardly be Bennett.

"Coxswain, sir," said a voice.

"Hallo, coxswain! Come to see the fun?"

"Just for a bit of air, sir."

They both had to shout: the wind caught the words on their very lips and whipped them away into the night.

"I brought a mug of tea up, sir," Tallow went on. And as Lockhart took it gratefully, he added: "It's got a tot in it."

Tea and rum. . . . When Lockhart bent down to shelter behind the rail, and took a sip, it ran through him like fire: it was the finest drink he had ever tasted. He was oddly moved that Tallow should have taken the trouble to make tea at two o'clock in the morning, add a tot of his own rum, and negotiate the difficult climb up to the bridge with it. He could not see Tallow's face, but he divined a sympathy in his manner that was nearly as warming as the drink.

"Thanks, coxswain," he said when he had finished it. "I needed that." He raised his binoculars again, confirmed that *Compass Rose* was still in station, and relaxed slightly. "What's it like below?"

"Terrible, sir. Couldn't be worse. It'll take us a week to get straight, after this lot."

"Not much longer," said Lockhart, though he did not feel that very acutely. "Two or three days, and we'll be in shelter."

"Can't be soon enough for me, sir. Proper uproar, this is. A lot of the lads wish they'd joined the Army instead."

They talked till the end of the watch, shouting at each other against the storm. Lockhart was glad of the company: it was a tiny spark of warmth and feeling in a furious and inhuman onslaught. They would need a lot of that, if the Atlantic were going to serve them like this in the future.

. . .

Physically, Ferraby was in a worse way than any of them. He had been acutely seasick during most of the voyage, but he never gave in to it: always, when it was time for him to go on watch, he would drag himself up the ladder, his face the colour of a dirty handkerchief, and somehow last out the four hours on the bridge. Then he would stumble below again, and force himself to eat, and be sick once more, and lie down on his bunk, waiting for sleep to blot out the clamour of the storm, and his misery with it. Often sleep would not come, and he lay awake throughout his time off watch. Those were the worst moments of all, when doubt as to whether he could go on with this job pressed on his consciousness like a living weight of guilt.

Toward the end, the strain nearly proved too much for him. This was particularly so when he had to go on watch at night, after an hour or so of sleep snatched in the stuffy heaving cabin. He would get into his sea boots and duffle coat, listening to the sounds of the storm outside, and the thud of water hitting the side of the ship and the deck overhead. Then he climbed slowly up the ladder, tired beyond belief, fearing the wind and the misery waiting for him up on the bridge: watching the square of dark sky at the entrance above him, to see if the gale was passing. He was very weak, and without any will except to last out this watch, and the next one, and a few more until they made harbour. Once, he stopped halfway up the ladder, and found himself crying. "Mavis," he said—and went on, as if his wife had answered him from somewhere up above.

He bore his ordeal alone, bravely: his set white face invited nothing save the kindness of ignoring it. He did not give in, because to fail to go on watch, to confess his defeat, would have been worse than any seasickness, any fatigue, any wind or rain or fury. There was no way out that was not shameful; and that was no way out.

The Captain carried them all.

For him, there was no fixed watch, no time set aside when he was free to relax and, if he could, to sleep. He had to control everything, to drive the whole ship himself: he had to act on signals, to fix their position, to keep his section of the convoy together, to use his seamanship to ease *Compass Rose's* ordeal as much as possible. He was a tower of strength, holding everything together by sheer unrelenting guts. The sight of the tall tough figure hunched in one corner of the bridge now seemed essential to them all: they needed the tremendous reassurance of his presence, and so he gave it unstintingly, even though the hours without sleep mounted to a fantastic total.

He was tired—he could not remember ever having been so tired—but he knew that he was not too tired: there were always reserves. . . . It was part of the job of being captain, the reverse side of the prestige and the respect and the saluting: the tiny ship, the inexperienced officers, the unbelievable weather—he had taken these on as well, and they would not defeat him. So he dealt with everything that came, assuming all cares out of an overflowing strength: he was a professional—the only one among amateurs who might in the future become considerable assets to him but at the moment were not very much help—and the professional job, at sea, was not without its rewarding pride. It had to be done, anyway: he was the man to do it, and there was no choice and no two answers.

They grew, almost, to love him, toward the end of the voyage: he was strong, calm, uncomplaining, and wonderfully dependable. This was the sort of captain to have: *Compass Rose* could have done with nothing less, and *Compass Rose*, butting her patient way homeward under the blows of the cruel sea, was lucky to have him.

No voyage can last for ever, save for ships that are sunk: this voyage ran its course, and presently released them. There came an afternoon—the afternoon of the sixteenth day—when the horizon ahead was not level, but uneven: not the pale grey of the sky, but the darker shadow that was the land. The foothills of Scotland came up suddenly, beckoning them onward: their rolling lessened as they came under the lee of the northern coastline: presently, toward dusk, they were in shelter, and running down toward the home port that promised them rest and peace at last. It was difficult to realize that the worst was over, and that *Compass Rose*, on a steady keel, could become warm and dry again: it was difficult to believe in the relaxation that had been so relentlessly denied them. It must be an illusion, or a swindle: probably the Irish Sea would open up at the other end, and they would find themselves in deep water once more, fighting another round of the same exhausting battle. They had been on trial for so long that the acquittal did not seem to ring true.

So the first convoy ended. It had been a shock—the more so because of the doubt, in the background, as to how they would fare in action with U-boats, if action were added to so startling an ordeal. But they did not think of this straight away: that night, tied up alongside the oiler after seventeen days of strain, they were all so utterly exhausted that a dead and dreamless sleep was all they were fit for.

[*3*]

It seemed that they were to be stationed permanently at Liverpool, and there they settled down, as part of the Liverpool Escort Force that was gradually being built up. The centre of naval activity was Gladstone Dock, down-river and away from the town: it was already crowded with destroyers and sloops, and the corvettes that were now beginning to leave the shipyards in substantial numbers. The forest of masts, the naval parties moving on the dockside, and the huts and store-rooms put up for their use, were all heartening symptoms of a growing escort strength; but they were matched by a steady increase in the number and size of convoys, which made demands on the naval potential almost impossible to meet. It was clear that many chances would have to be taken with the safety of merchant ships, for a long time to come.

Among the corvettes to arrive at Liverpool was *Sorrel*, who, delayed at Ardnacraish by some clash with the Admiral that she was not particularly ready to discuss, joined her sister ship soon after their second convoy.

Ericson was not notably pleased that *Compass Rose* was based on Liverpool; in fact, he was inclined to resent the fact, without being too sure why. The theory was admirable: they came in from a convoy, and there was Grace, knitting away in her little house across the river and waiting for him. But it was an undeniable distraction, at a time when he wanted to concentrate exclusively on the ship: and, in some indistinct way, it seemed to be cheating—he had embraced a hard life and an exacting job, and here now was another embrace, to make things pleasant after all. . . . He could not have said why he found that wrong, and certainly he never hinted anything of the sort to her; but it was a fact that he preferred to live on board when they were in harbour, and was faintly irritated at having to find excuses for doing so.

The man it suited most was Tallow: his home also was in Birkenhead, just over the river from Gladstone Dock, and he had no false notions as to the relative comforts of *Compass Rose* and No. 29, Dock Road. . . . It was a home he shared with his widowed sister Gladys, who had kept house for him ever since her husband died, four or five years previously: whenever he came back on leave, his room was waiting for him, and a cheerful welcome as well. Gladys Bell (Bell had been a postman) worked in a Liverpool office, supplementing a tiny pension: she was fortyish, plain, good-natured, and she and Tallow got on very well together, in an undemanding sort of way. He had hoped that she would marry again, even though he would lose thereby; but there had never been any sign of it, and by and by the idea ceased to worry him. If a decent widowhood suited her, it certainly suited him.

When he went round to the house on their second night in

harbour, and walked into the tiny gaslit kitchen with a "Well, Glad!" which had been his greeting ever since she could remember, her plain sallow face lighted up at the surprise. She had not seen him for six months.

"Bob! Where've you sprung from, lad?"

"We're in for a bit," he said. "It's our home port—couldn't be better."

"Well, that's nice." Her mind darted immediately to the larder, wondering what she could give him on his first night ashore. "Have you had your tea?"

"Tea?" he smiled mockingly. "Have you ever known me have my tea on board, when I can get your cooking just by crossing the river?"

There was a hesitant cough behind him in the doorway.

"Oh," said Tallow awkwardly. "Brought a friend, Glad. Chief E.R.A. Watts. Same ship."

"Come into the front," she said, when they had shaken hands and mumbled to each other. "This kitchen's not fit to be seen."

In the front parlour, she lit the gas: the overcrowded room sprang to life, as if the hissing noise had been a stage direction. It was the best part of the shabby old house, carefully cleaned and cherished: the creaking wing-chairs were comfortable, the mahogany table sat four-square and solid in the middle, the ornaments were mostly souvenirs brought home by Tallow himself, from Gibraltar and Hong Kong and Alexandria. Lace curtains gave them a genteel privacy, at the cost of three quarters of the available light: from the mantelpiece, Tom Bell the postman regarded them importantly, as if he carried registered letters for each one of them.

Gladys turned from the flaring gaslight, and looked at the two men with pleasure. They were both very smart—spotless jackets, gold badges, knife-edge creases to their trousers: she found herself wondering, not for the first time, how they managed to keep their clothes so nice, in the cramped quarters on board.

"How's the new ship?" she asked her brother.

The two men exchanged glances, before Tallow answered:

"She'll never live to be old, I'd say."

Watts laughed, scratching his bald head. "That's about the size of it, Mrs. Bell. We've had a rare trip, I can tell you."

"Was it very rough?"

"Rough as I've ever known it," said Tallow. "We were chucked about like—like—" he sought for a suitable simile, and failed. "Remember I wrote you how small she was? I didn't tell you the half of it. We were standing on our heads, most of the time."

"What about those submarines?"

"*We* were the submarine, I should say." Watts, warming to the friendly atmosphere, chipped in with a readiness rare to him. "Never got our heads above water for days on end. Must be the new secret weapon—the corvette that swims under water."

Gladys clicked her lips. "Well, I never. . . . You must be ready for a bit of a rest."

"I'm ready for a pint," said Tallow with alacrity. "How about it, Glad? Anything in the larder?"

She shook her head. "I wasn't expecting you, Bob. Why not walk round to the Three Tuns while I'm getting the tea?"

Tallow cocked his eye at Watts. "What d'you say?"

Watts nodded. "Suits me."

"Half an hour," said Gladys firmly. "Not a minute more, otherwise it'll spoil."

"What are you going to give us?"

"Never you mind."

They collected their caps, and made for the door gradually, like boys preparing to play truant and pretending to do something else. She watched them amusedly as they sidled out. Men. . . . But it sounded as if they'd earned it. She went through to the kitchen and made ready, happily, to welcome them back as they deserved. Later, in the cosy parlour with a big fire going, they all enjoyed themselves: the two men talked of the trip, and of other trips, while she sat back and listened to them, and threw in an occasional comment. She did not like the sound of *Compass Rose;* but when she said so, bluntly, they were curiously quick to put in a good word for the ship, to make excuses for this and explain away that. Men, again. . . . But it was good to have them there, and to know that they were relaxed and happy, after the hard times.

As soon as they got in at the end of their first trip, Ericson applied for another officer to be appointed to the ship; it was clear that there was far too much work for a First Lieutenant and two subs to handle, leaving out of account the chance that accident or illness might make them more short-handed still. He presented a good case, arguing the matter first with a faintly supercilious staff officer who seemed to think that corvettes were some kind of local defence vessel, and then incorporating his arguments in a formal submission to the Admiralty: it must have been an effective document, since their Lordships acted on it within three weeks. Sub-Lieutenant Morell, they said, was appointed to *Compass Rose*, "additional for watchkeeping duties"; Sub-Lieutenant Morell would join them forthwith.

Morell arrived, fresh from the training establishment, accompanied by an astonishing amount of luggage: he was a very proper young man, so correct and so assured that it appeared fantastic for him to grace anything as crude as a corvette. In peacetime he was a junior barrister, a product of the other London that was so great a contrast to the Bohemian world Lockhart knew and worked in: Lockhart, indeed, could only imagine him in black coat and pin-stripe trousers, moving from his chambers in Lincoln's Inn to a sedate lunch-party at the Savoy, or later, impeccably tail-coated, squiring the least impulsive of the season's debutantes to Ciro's or the Embassy. He was grave, slow-moving, and exceedingly courteous: in his brand-new and beautifully cut uniform he seemed far better suited to a diplomatic salon than to *Compass Rose's* rough and ready wardroom. He was a living reproof to the solecism of displaying emotion. He was, inevitably, an Old Wykehamist.

He and Bennett could hardly be expected to mix. On the first evening, at dinner, Morell watched, with an expression of disbelief that Lockhart found ludicrous, as Bennett greeted the tinned sausages with his usual salute, tucked his napkin under his chin, and fell to on this deplorable dish. Morell offered no comment, but it was clear that the scene had made an impression: later, when he and Lockhart were alone in the wardroom, he remarked: "I understand the First Lieutenant comes from one of the Dominions," with an absence of expression that was itself the best substitute for it.

"Australia," answered Lockhart, himself non-committal.

"Ah. . . . I have met one or two Australians—usually the victims of confidence tricksters. We can never persuade them that in London they are likely to encounter people with sharper wits than their own."

"It's amazing how people still fall for that sort of thing."

"It is not amazing," said Morell, after reflection. "But it is, at least, continually strange. . . . Do we often have tinned sausages for dinner, by the way?"

"Very often."

"Whether this war is long or short," said Morell, after reflecting again, "it is going to *seem* long."

That was the only comment he made that could have been construed as any kind of criticism. But in spite of this discretion, he must have come into early collision with Bennett: next afternoon, when work was over, he sought out Lockhart and asked him, with some formality, for guidance.

"The First Lieutenant used an expression which is novel to me," he began. "I wish you'd explain what it means."

"What was it?" asked Lockhart, with an equal gravity.

"He said—ah—'Don't come the acid with me.'" Morell screwed up his eyes. "'Come the acid' . . . I must confess I have not heard that before."

"What were you talking about?"

"We were discussing the best way of dismantling the firing-bar on the asdic set." he paused. "That's not too technical for you?"

"No," said Lockhart. "But it may have been too technical for Bennett. He's been trained in a rougher school."

"That may well be the case. . . . So 'coming the acid' . . ."

"It means that you probably corrected him without wrapping it up enough."

Morell smiled: it was the first time Lockhart had seen him do so. "I could hardly have been more diplomatic."

"You must have overdone it, then."

The other man sighed. "How strange to meet Scylla and Charybdis in Atlantic waters. . . . Perhaps I should explain the allusion. There were—"

"Do not," said Lockhart, with a fair approximation of Bennett's accent, "come the acid with me."

"Ah!" exclaimed Morell. "Now I understand."

They both laughed. Lockhart was glad that Morell had joined them: he promised to enliven the wardroom, though with little intention of so doing, and the wardroom could do with all the enlivenment possible.

[4]

The first few convoys followed the pattern of their initiation. They still worked with *Viperous* as leader of the group, which had been strengthened by *Sorrel* joining it: they were still, as a fighting escort, untried by the enemy. There were submarines about—other convoys kept running into them—but so far their luck had held: the log recorded no shot in anger, only a succession of comments on the weather. This, at least, continued to put *Compass Rose* to the test: whatever the season, it seemed that the Atlantic could never wholly abandon its mood of violence.

But the longer days of spring and early summer did, in fact, afford them some relief: watchkeeping by day was certainly less of a strain, whatever antics the ship was going through. They were now divided into three watches, four hours on duty and eight off: Bennett and Lockhart were both on their own, and Morell and Ferraby shared the third watch together. The eight hours off duty were so great an advantage, bringing them fresh to their watch, that it was almost impossible to believe that they had once done without them. Certainly the new arrangements suited Ericson, who could now sleep most of the long day and be available, comparatively rested, at any time during the night. Of his watch-keeping officers, he found that Bennett was all right as long as nothing unexpected happened: that Lockhart was completely trustworthy, and not afraid to call him in good time to deal with any crisis: and that Morell and Ferraby, between them, added up to something like a dependable pair of hands and eyes. He could hardly expect more, from this cheerfully amateur collection.

But the nights were still a strain and a challenge to them all, whether the enemy were near or far. Darken Ship was piped at sunset each day: from that moment, no glimmer of light must show either in the convoy or among the escort—the faintest gleam might beckon a submarine that otherwise would have no suspicion ships were in its area. That moment when they drew the covers on was always significant: usually there had been some sort of U-boat warning during the day, and if other convoys were running into trouble it must, sooner or later, be their own turn. Thus there would be a feeling throughout the ship, each time dusk fell, that they were approaching uncertainty again, extending the chances of action: from then on, at any moment, there *might* be a U-boat sniffing the air a few miles off, there *might* be a torpedo track, there *might* be a bang close by them—or even in their own guts. The canvas screens were drawn across the entrances, the lights were dimmed inside, the galley fire damped down: *Compass Rose*, steaming through the cold evening air toward a horizon barely distinguishable from the sky, became a grey shadow clinging to other shadows that she must not lose. In thick weather, when the moon was down, to keep their correct station on the convoy as it hurried through the essential darkness was a strain on the attention and the eyesight that left them, at the end of their four hours, exhausted and blinking with fatigue. But if they lost the convoy, or got grossly out of station, the price was not simply a red face in the morning: it might be a U-boat piercing the gap they had left, and lives and ships on their conscience.

There were other cares at night, complicating a plain effort of seamanship. The current orders were that escorts were to zigzag, so that they could move faster and lessen the chance of being hit themselves; it was a sensible precaution, and one they all approved of, but a zigzag on a pitch-black night, with thirty ships in close contact adding the risk of collision to the difficulty of hanging on to the convoy, was something more than a few lines in a Fleet Order. Lockhart, who now kept a permanent middle watch—midnight to four a.m.—and on whom the brunt of the dark hours fell, evolved his own method. He took *Compass Rose* out obliquely from the convoy, for a set number of minutes: very soon, of course, he could not see the other ships, and might have had the whole Atlantic to himself, but that was part of the manœuvre. Then he turned, and ran back the same number of minutes on the corresponding course inwards: at the end, he should be in touch with the convoy again, and in the same relative position.

It was an act of faith that continued to justify itself, but it was sometimes a little hard on the nerves. He once had a nightmare, and later evolved a fairy story, in which *Compass Rose*, steaming towards the convoy again on the inward course, never met it: she went on and on, over a blank dark sea that presently paled with daylight, and there was never a ship in sight. . . . And once the Captain had come up, when they were at the very limit of the outward leg and out of touch with the convoy, and had looked about him as if he could scarcely believe his eyes.

"Where are they, Lockhart?" he asked with a certain grimness.

Lockhart pointed. "There, sir. . . . We're on the outer zigzag," he added, to justify a blank horizon. "We'll meet them again in seven minutes."

Ericson grunted. It was not a reassuring sound, and Lockhart, counting the minutes, wondered what on earth he was going to say if this time his nightmare came true. When at last the ships came up again, black and solid, he had a surge of relief that he felt the Captain was aware of.

"Zigzagging on time?" said Ericson curtly.

"Yes, sir."

"Check your course each time you alter. Don't leave it to the quartermaster—he might make a mistake." Then he walked off the bridge without further comment. That was what Lockhart liked about the Captain: if he trusted you, he showed it—he didn't fiddle about in the background, pretending to do something else, and all the time watching you like a nursemaid. And he was quite entitled to be worried, and to ask questions when he felt like it: if they did lose the convoy, whichever one of them was responsible, it was, as far as the official record went, the Captain's fault.

What Lockhart found especially annoying was handing over his watch to Bennett. By tradition, the First Lieutenant had the morning watch—four a.m. to eight: Bennett followed the custom as far as the actual time went, but in other respects he scarcely justified his position. It was mortifying to cling on to the convoy all through the middle watch, keeping exact station and a fast, accurate zigzag, and hand over *Compass Rose* in a pinpoint position at the end of it; and then to hear, as he left the bridge, Bennett saying: "Signalman! See that ship there? Tell me if we start to lose her," and then settling down inside the asdic hut. One of these days, thought Lockhart, they might all forfeit their lives simply because Bennett had a dislike of fresh air. But it was hardly a matter he could complain of, officially. It would have to wait till the Captain took notice of it.

At this stage—still unwarlike, still a tame apprenticeship —they found hardest to bear the monotony of rolling, with,

as an occasional variant, the shuddering crunch with which
Compass Rose greeted a head sea. The rolling affected every
single thing they did, on watch or off. Often they had to
cling to the bridge rail for four hours at a stretch, drenched
and cold, while the ship disgraced herself with a tireless
forty-degree roll; and then, off watch and supposedly resting, they had to eat their meals with the food continually
slopping into their laps, and the wardroom furniture creaking and sliding and occasionally breaking adrift altogether
and hurtling across the room. They were always being hurt,
in spite of a continual watchfulness: doorways hit them as
they were leaving their cabins: they were thrown out of
their bunks as soon as sleep relaxed their tense care, and all
round them on the floor would be books and papers and boots
and clothes, which some especially violent roll had released
from control.

It was tremendously exhausting, this never being able to
rest without something going wrong, something hitting
them, something coming adrift and breaking, or making a
noisy clatter for hour after hour. There was a damnable
rhythm about the movement: they got tired of it, they got
tired of always hanging on to something, they got tired of
paying for a moment's forgetfulness with bruised legs and
shoulders, cut lips, wrenched ankles. But they could not
escape it: it was an inherent element in going to sea in corvettes. Sometimes, up on the bridge, they would watch
Sorrel being chucked about like a cork, and the spray going
over as she punched her way through a rough sea, and they
would think how tough she looked, and what a pretty picture, handsome and determined, she made. It was a pity that
the reality, in *Sorrel* as in *Compass Rose*, was so infinitely
unpleasant.

One of their convoys, about this time, was a classic in this
respect. After nine days on the outward trip, they had turned
for home, with some hope of making a quick passage and
getting back in less than a week. It did not work that way.
. . . The gale that sprang up did more than scatter the convoy: it kept every single ship in it hove-to for two days on

end, waiting for the weather to moderate. In those two days, *Compass Rose* covered eighteen miles—sideways, and due south: she spent them in company with a small merchant ship that had engine trouble and asked for someone to stay with her. For all the forty-eight hours, *Compass Rose* circled very slowly round the derelict, taking three hours to complete each circuit, moving with agonizing slowness against the mountainous seas and rolling, rolling, rolling all the time, as if she wanted to tear her mast out.

They lost one of their boats, which went clean under a huge wave and never came up again: they lost some oil drums that were stowed aft: they lost their patience many times, but patience had to return, and sweat it out to the end. . . . When the storm finally blew itself away, they spent another twenty-four hours hunting for the convoy and reassembling it. They were at sea for twenty-two days on that trip: at the end, *Compass Rose*, and her crew with her, looked as if they had all been through the same tidal wave, emerging in tatters at the end of it.

They found, on all their convoys, that the food soon became intolerably coarse and dull. *Compass Rose* carried enough fresh meat, bread, and vegetables for five days: after that, their diet was the same dreary procession of tinned sausages, tinned stew, hard biscuit, and tea. (The tinned stew came in an ornate container labelled "Old Mother Jameson's Farm House Dinner." Said Morell, surveying the dubious mixture on his plate: "I must remember *never* to go to dinner at Mrs. Jameson's.") It was enough to support life, and that was all one could say about it: since they ate these horrible meals in a wardroom that was sooner or later flooded out, or, at the best, ran with sweat throughout the voyage, the pleasures of the table in *Compass Rose* never threatened to seduce them from their duty.

They found, all the same, that there were times when they could still relax—that some moments at sea were enchanting. Now and again, an afternoon watch on the bridge would prove so perfect a way of passing the time that it seemed almost ludicrous for them to be paid for it. The convoy was in formation, and not menaced by U-boats: the hot spring sunshine poured down from a flawless sky: the brave ships advanced in line, leaving behind them, like *Compass Rose*, a broad white sparkling wake that meant a smooth passage and a day nearer home. On the bridge, there was nothing to do but check the change of course as they zigzagged, and keep an eye on *Viperous* in case she woke early from her afternoon siesta: for the rest, it was warmth, cool clean air, a steady ship under one's feet, and an occasional sound—a gramophone, the swish of a hose, the clang of an emptied bucket—to prove that *Compass Rose* carried nearly ninety men on this prosperous voyage.

They found that some nights, especially, had a peaceful loveliness that repaid a hundred hours of strain. Sometimes, in sheltered water, when the moon was full, they moved with the convoy past hills outlined against the pricking stars: slipping under the very shadow of these cliffs, their keel divided the phosphorescent water into a gleaming wake that curled away till it was caught and held in the track of the moon. It was then that the watches went pleasantly, with the night air playing round the ship like the music of Prospero's isle: Morell and Ferraby would talk idly of their homes, or Lockhart and Wells, sharing a later watch, would make it go swiftly in reminiscence and conjecture. These magic nights, unmarred by fatigue or any alarm, were very few: when they were granted, their sweetness remained for long afterwards. Once or twice Ericson, coming up to the bridge in the early hours of the morning, would find it, and the whole ship, so peaceful and so softly lapped by darkness that it was hard to recall the purpose of their voyage. *Compass Rose*, afloat on a calm sea, seemed to shed every attribute save a gentle assurance of refuge.

They found, to meet those other nights which were so brutal and so prolonged, that they were toughening up. They became cunning at anticipating what the next big sea would do to the ship, and expert at avoiding its consequences: to hang on as they moved from place to place, to wedge themselves so that even the relaxation of sleep would not dislodge them, to keep themselves warm, and their clothes water-proof—these were lessons that the harsh school drove home until they were ingrained. Even the lack of sleep was less damaging now: they developed the facility of snatching odd moments of it whenever possible, and for the rest they could, if need be, stay awake for an astonishing number of hours without losing the edge of alertness. The process of accepting the hard necessities of their life meant that much of their normal feeling was blunted: Lockhart, finding himself one evening discarding the volume of essays he had bought before sailing in favour of the crudest and most trivial of the current magazines, thought, with faint alarm: Hell, I'm getting as bad as Bennett. . . . But it was in a sense true, and necessary as well: the time for sensibility was past, gentleness was outdated, and feeling need not come again till the unfeeling job was over.

They found, above all, that one part of every trip could be actively enjoyed: the last day of it, when they were in sheltered water and getting ready for their return to harbour. Now was the time when, running down the Irish Sea and making the last turn for home, they set to work to tidy up the ship after the chaos of the voyage: portholes were opened to the cleansing breeze, wet clothes stripped off and hung out to dry, the furniture and the tables and stools in the mess-decks released from their lashings and set out properly. The sun gleamed on the saturated decks, and dried them off swiftly, leaving a rime of salt: round the bows, the porpoises and the seagulls played, crossing and recrossing their pathway as if clearing a way of welcome for them.

The convoy, the line of ships they had been guarding for so long, began the last mile of its journey, up-river to the docks: deep-laden, crammed to the decks with cargo, immensely worth while, it struck a note of thankful pride as it was safely delivered. The escort parted, steaming in single file past their charges and further up-river. For them, at last, here was the haven where they would be: peace alongside the oiler, the mail coming aboard, hot baths, clean clothes, rest and sleep after many days and nights had denied them all these things.

[5]

Suddenly it was time for their first spell of leave: six days, for half the ship's company and all the officers save one, so that *Compass Rose* could have her boilers cleaned and a few small repairs carried out. It was their first break since the ship was commissioned, five months previously; they felt that they had earned it, and Ericson, while not encouraging them in this view, privately admitted that they were right.

He himself, sitting opposite Grace in a comfortable armchair for six successive evenings, could not get used to the stillness of the house. Aboard *Compass Rose* there was always something stirring; even when she was in harbour, there were engine-room fans and dynamos going all the time, there was the quartermaster clumping round the upper deck, there were signals coming down, and the noise of Morse from the W/T office, and the wardroom radio doing its best to cheer the lonely-hearted sailors, cradled in the deep of Gladstone Dock. Here there was nothing, save the click of Grace's knitting needles and the rustle of coal in the grate. Her mother had postponed her visit, though she might descend on them in the near future: John, their son, was away at sea— Ericson still had not managed to meet him since *Compass Rose* was commissioned, even though they went in and out of the same port. So, in the silent house, they sat opposite each other. To Grace, it was nothing out of the ordinary: to Ericson himself, it was an unsettling contrast with what must be his true habit of life.

There were other things he could not get used to. It was a woman's house, soft and rather frilly: the cushions multiplied on the sofa, the ornaments were brittle and inescapably gay, the tablecloth was a lace affair that caught against his hands whenever he moved them. He felt out of place: he felt

107

as if he were somehow breaking training, at a time when a hard austerity was the essential choice. Sleeping with Grace in the big double bed upstairs had an indulgence, an added warmth, that he did not really want to enjoy. She was his wife, but to lie with her, even in passive sleep, had a sensual element that betrayed his instinct for celibacy.

If she was aware of this subtle withdrawal, she gave no sign: for very many years she had taken things at their face value, her husband included, and a war was not the time to question what lay below the surface of any reasonable relationship.

"You're restless, George," she said, one night when he had tossed and turned till past midnight, and finally woken her from a comfortable dream. "Can't you get to sleep?"

"It's the bed," he answered irritably. "I can't get used to it."

"I thought sailors could sleep anywhere." Between waking and sleeping, her common sense had a fugitive quality that occasionally betrayed her into flippancy. Ordinarily, she would never have made so derivative a comment.

"This one can't."

"Shall I make some tea?"

"No, thank you."

Now that he had woken her, he wanted nothing except that she should go to sleep again and leave him to his isolation. The longer they talked in this intimate setting, the deeper he was involved in a softer world that might destroy his resolute spirit. Even in peacetime, he had sometimes resented this recurrent surrender: sea-going was really a job for a single, tough man. Now, in war, relaxation seemed a form of treason. . . . The odd, overdramatic thoughts continued to pursue him, as Grace turned over and went to sleep again. He had never felt quite like this before: perhaps he was worrying too much, perhaps he *did* need a spell of leave after all. But that didn't mean letting everything slip. Tomorrow he would go down to the ship again. Just to look around, just to see how she was getting on.

. . .

1940: *Skirmishing*

Bennett was talking to a woman in a hotel bedroom. She was the usual woman—infinitely tainted, infinitely practised, hard as nails; it was the usual room. The hotel stood, or rather lay in wait, at the back of the dock area; it was dedicated to a fornication so incessant and so transitory that there were often more people passing up and down the stairs than using the bedrooms. It was like a dirty hive, serving a machine-made sexuality, emitting a drone of love. . . . If Bennett had known that the building housed, at that particular moment, four members of *Compass Rose's* crew besides himself, it would probably have struck him as a form of insubordination. He would not have considered that he himself was in the wrong place.

Now he untied his tie before the tarnished mirror, while behind him the bedsprings creaked as the woman composed herself for the encounter. While thus occupied, they made the conversation appropriate to the moment.

"Did you have a nice voyage, dear?"

"Lousy," said Bennett briefly. "Gets worse every time. I reckon I'm going to quit."

"You can't do that, can you?"

"I'll find a way. They can't keep me cooped up in a little crap-boat like that for ever."

"It must be funny on a boat—a lot of men all jammed up together. What d'you talk about?"

Bennett, who was taking off his trousers, paused. "What do you think?"

"Love, eh? Love all the time, I suppose."

"Something like that."

"They say sailors are all the same." The woman, whom no violence and no crudity incidental to her trade could now surprise, sketched a sentimental sigh. It was a minor triumph of artifice over conviction. "There was a bit in the *Mirror* about it the other day—how they were always on the look-out for pen pals."

"First I've heard of it," said Bennett. He leered. "They're always on the look-out for something, but they don't want to use a pen in it."

The woman smiled mechanically. For her, no indecent jokes were new, or funny, but they seemed to entrance the customers. One man had nearly fallen out of bed, telling her about a friend of his who got cramp on the job and had to be carted off to hospital, with the girl beside him on the stretcher. For the life of her, she couldn't crack a smile about that one. . . .

"Well," said Bennett, turning to the bed, "this is what I've been waiting for."

"My!" said the woman, almost immediately. "You *are* passionate, aren't you. Sure you're not French?"

"There's only one thing French about me," said Bennett, and roared with sudden laughter.

The woman smiled again. Very comical. . . . "I'm sure you must be French," she insisted. "They say they're too bloody passionate to live."

"You can't hold on to it for ever," said Bennett explanatorily. "I've been carrying this lot around for four months."

"It all adds up, doesn't it?" said the woman vaguely. "Careful now. . . ."

Morell, who had very much wanted a quiet evening at home, said:

"Of course, darling. Where would you like to go?"

Elaine Morell did not answer immediately. There were so many lovely places, and they only had five days to cover them. . . . Of course, she could go anywhere she liked, whether he were here or not, but it was nice to make the most of him while he *was* here—he looked so sweet in his uniform, even though the single thin stripe was a bit depressing. She pulled a face at herself in the dressing-table mirror, adjusted a curl at the nape of her neck, and said:

"You decide, darling. It's your leave, after all."

Morell, lounging behind her on the quilted bed, wondered if that were quite true. He wondered, indeed, whether anything really belonged to him, where his wife was concerned: he found her so incredibly lovely and persuasive that all his will, all his competent judgement, could be swamped on the instant, and he would surrender the most cherished project at a flick of her fingers. The world saw him as a grave young man, with a capable brain, developing judgment, and a future in the law; it did not see, it could not guess, how his marriage had proved a sensual solvent for this whole fabric.

She was a minor actress, on the fringe of the West End stage: she was not appearing at the moment—the war seemed to have made her so very busy in other ways. . . . When Morell had married her, it was almost as if he were playing a part himself, so incongruous did the combination of himself and this glamorous creature seem: the incongruity had been solved by his ceasing, for all intents and purposes, to be himself at all, when he was with her. He spoke to her as he spoke to no one else, with a tender diffidence that none of his friends would have recognized or credited: he listened to her talking, and answered her, as if the brittle chatter of her lovely mouth had been his Lordship's address to the jury. He also did exactly as he was told.

At this moment, for instance, he was desperately tired: it would be the third night running they had gone out to dine or to dance, and he wanted peace, he wanted Elaine to himself. But from the beginning she had proclaimed that she wished to show him off everywhere, and so it had been a procession of cocktail parties, restaurants, and night clubs: even on his first evening, they had not returned home to their flat until four in the morning. Of course, she had made it up then, made it up with a cunning intensity that had, after three months without her, swamped and overthrown his senses. It seemed that she had felt that too. "Darling," she had said, with that murmur in her throat which could stir something inside him, even in a moment of satiety, "darling, you must go away more often, or something—that was terrific!"

In the face of so fierce a welcome, how difficult to refuse her anything; and if he did refuse her (though this was a thought for secrecy), how quickly that fervour might dry up. . . . She was beautiful—not in a remote fashion, but with a face that beckoned, a mouth formed only for kissing, and a body so soft, so shapely, and so glowing that its only conceivable purpose was to fuse with the sinewed imprint of a man's. She had, for Morell, a sensual pull that two years of marriage had never assuaged: her moving limbs induced in him an almost insane urgency, her body seemed to flicker for his delight. Even, as now, to watch her dressing, perfuming her neck and shoulders, adjusting a brassière to encase her flawless breasts, was intolerably exciting. . . . Whenever she wanted, she could promote this frenzy: whenever she did not want, the frenzy was there in a yet more desperate degree.

Of course she demanded too much, of course she betrayed the cool man he had imagined himself to be. But a single glance of hers, a single movement, squared the account, making it natural and essential to please her, and boorish to do otherwise. And, once again, if he *didn't* please her, if he failed to follow her lead in anything, it became dangerous, it was more than he dared. There were so many other people. . . .

One of these other people, indeed, had telephoned, on Morell's first evening at home. From her bath Elaine had called: "Answer that, darling—I'm wet," and when he lifted the receiver a man's voice, against a background of music and other voices, had broken in immediately:

"Elaine? There's a swell party here, but we need that beautiful body—how about coming over?"

Morell said, rather foolishly: "Hallo?"

"Oh, sorry," said the voice. "Who's that?"

"Morell."

"*Who?*"

"Morell."

"Oh—yes." An odd laugh. "Sorry, old boy, I didn't know you were back."

"I'll tell my wife you called," said Morell. "Who is it speaking?"

"Doesn't matter—forget it. G'bye." He sounded rather drunk, but not as drunk as all that.

That evening, once again, they danced till very late, in a

night club so hot, so noisy, and so uninhibited that it might have been part of a zoo. It was very crowded: Elaine seemed to know a great many people, among them half a dozen Air Force pilots who came up in a solid procession to ask her to dance. At one point, clinging to Morell in the twilight of the dance floor, she had stroked his sleeve and murmured: "Darling, how long before you get promoted?" and he had ceased to be proud of her head on his shoulder, and felt rather foolish instead. But, as usual, she drove all that away as soon as they were home: in bed at last, erotic with alcohol, she swamped and sucked him of fervour till the fatigue of love became an aching reality, and sleep the only drug to ease it.

It was his leave, after all.

With Mavis, Ferraby spent a wonderful and tender period. She was now living with her mother, and the circumstances— a cramped, suburban house at Purley, a lack of privacy at meals and in the evenings—were not ideal; but it was so lovely to see her again, so lovely to *be* somebody, to be con- sidered and deferred to, after the brusque contempt of *Compass Rose*, that the drawbacks were forgotten. The free- dom from constraint, and the fading out of the hatred at close quarters, were tangible blessings; and in their private times together, the return to tenderness proffered so startling a contrast that, to begin with, he could scarcely believe it.

"He must be absolutely beastly!" said Mavis indignantly, when Ferraby had told her something of Bennett's manners and methods. "Why do they allow it?"

"It's discipline," said Ferraby vaguely. He did not really believe this, nor had he, for very shame, told her the full story; but he did not want the shadow to stay where it had fallen. "The First Lieutenant's meant to run the ship, really, and that means the officers as well."

"But he needn't be so horrid about it."

"He's like that."

"They oughtn't to allow it," she said again. "I'd like to give him a piece of my mind."

Dear Mavis, so sweet and attractive in slacks and the blue

Angora jersey, with her little face screwed up in anger and sadness. . . . He kissed her, and said: "Let's forget about it. How about going for a walk?"

"If you're not too tired."

He looked at her, and smiled. "Why should I be too tired?"

She blushed, not meeting his eye. "Gordon Ferraby, you're a disgrace. . . . You know quite well what I meant."

He felt very masculine as he took her arm.

But the mention of Bennett's name must have started a train of thought that remained with him. That night he dreamed of *Compass Rose* in a storm, and of Bennett shouting at him and refusing to let him issue the right helm-orders, so that they were in danger of running ashore: he woke up, yelling at the top of his voice and sweating with panic, just as the ship drove through smoking breakers towards a line of rocks. . . . Mavis, putting her arms round him, was appalled at the feel of his wet trembling body and at the idea, which each shudder communicated, of an emotional turmoil greater than he could bear: when he apologized for the noise he had made, it was as if he were excusing some hopeless deformity for which he deserved all the pity in her heart.

"I must have been dreaming," he muttered hoarsely. "I'm sorry, darling."

"What was the dream about, Gordon?"

"The ship."

"Tell me."

"I've forgotten." But after a moment he did start to tell her, while she held him close and listened with misgiving and with a new understanding compassion flooding through her: for in the end he told her everything—his fears and failures, the guilty doubt of his fitness for the job, the true story of the last few months. It was easier in the dark, with her head on his shoulder, and, as usual with her, there was no shame in confession; indeed, it was she who was the more moved when he had finished, who suffered his own fear of returning after the leave was finished, and felt it as her own miserable dilemma. Above all, she was shaken by the revelation, which nothing in his cheerful letters to her had even hinted at. This was not the man she knew and had married: what had they done to him?

They talked far into the night. There was little she could give him save the assurance of her own confidence: it sounded pathetically inadequate against the wretched background he had sketched for her. She remembered for long afterward a single stubborn sentence of his, which he repeated whenever she suggested that he might ask for a different job: "I can't give up something I volunteered for." She could not persuade him either that the job was proving infinitely harder than he had imagined, and might thus be honourably abandoned, or that Bennett was so horrible a complication that the whole basis of his engagement was changed. Somewhere deep inside him, an obstinate self-destroying will was at work, forbidding him to surrender.

For some reason, after that night, she hoped that she would have a child as soon as possible.

Lockhart, having lost the toss, stayed aboard as duty officer. It would be his turn for leave next time, and in any case he found that he did not mind being left behind: he had recently been promoted to Lieutenant, and the extra gold ring on his sleeve burned bright with new responsibility. . . . It was, also, the sort of rest he needed, and in his spare time he occupied himself much as he would have done on leave—reading, listening to the radio, unwinding the tight coil of the past few months. *Compass Rose*, with her boilers blown down and no fans working, was cool and silent: it was odd to feel the ship, hitherto so active and alive, sinking back into a suspended laziness that matched his own. There was very little to do, and nothing that demanded any sort of concentration on his part: he saw the hands fall in after breakfast, and told Leading Seaman Phillips what had to be done in the way of sweeping and painting: he opened the mail, in case there were anything urgent: he dispatched the libertymen ashore, clean and tidy, at four o'clock; and he went round the ship at nine in the evening, to see that all was secure for the night. Meals were something of a picnic: both the leading cook and Carslake, the leading steward, were on leave, and his welfare was in the hands of the second steward, Tomlinson, who had once had a coffee-stall in the Edgware Road and whose methods were better suited to a quick turn-over in saveloys and hot pies, cash only, and no back answers, than to the gentler world of the wardroom. But since, being alone, Lockhart had revived his peacetime habit of reading all the time he was eating, the slapdash service and the in-different food did not greatly worry him.

They were tied up alongside *Viperous*, which was also boiler-cleaning: it was the first time he had been able to ex-amine a destroyer in close detail, and he took advantage of their neighbouring position to go aboard several times. His opposite number, also left on board for the leave period, was a young R.N. sub-lieutenant who, though aware of his in-feriority of rank, could hardly take an R.N.V.R. lieutenant seriously: Lockhart was amused to watch the struggle be-tween his natural respect for a two-ringer and his natural contempt for an amateur. There was nothing amateur about *Viperous*, certainly: the rigid R.N. atmosphere, allied to the almost professional glamour of a destroyer, was a potent combination. *Viperous* and *Compass Rose* might be doing the same job, and they might share the same hardships; but there was no doubt which of them was the elder brother, with an elder brother's unchallenged status. Their relative positions in the hierarchy, however, now seemed to matter less than they had done at the beginning. Lockhart was coming to be-lieve in corvettes, as were many other people: they were the smallest ships regularly employed on Atlantic convoys—the trawlers and tugs had been withdrawn as unsuitable—and sea-going in corvettes was already appropriating a toughness and a glamour of its own.

He had one or two visitors during the leave period. Among them was Lieutenant-Commander Ramsay, the captain of *Sorrel*, who came aboard one morning and put his head round the wardroom door.

"Anyone in?" he asked loudly. He was a cheerful individual, red-faced and stocky, with a rolling West Country accent: reputed to be a disciplinary terror in his own ship, he appeared to shed it as soon as he crossed the gangway.

"Hallo, sir!" Lockhart put aside his newspaper. "Come in."

"Is your captain on board?"

"No, he's on leave still. Will you have a drink?"

"Aye. Gin, please . . . I see you got that second stripe. How's that First Lieutenant of yours?"

Lockhart grinned. "Bearing up."

"Makes you hop about a bit, doesn't he?"

"He—er—maintains a stiff discipline, yes."

Ramsay smiled in his turn. "One way of putting it. . . . Here's luck."

They gossiped for some little time, mostly about their own escort group and the job that corvettes were doing: they both betrayed the half-humourous resignation that seemed inevitable when those who sailed in corvettes were talking shop together. Ramsay related in detail a mishap to *Sorrel* that had occurred on the last convoy—a huge wave had broken right *over* her bridge, smashed two windows in the charthouse, and bent the rail nearly a foot out of the true. *Compass Rose* could not quite match that experience, Lockhart decided after rummaging in his memory, though there was a morbid interest in trying to do so on her behalf. . . . Ramsay, when he rose to leave, said, out of the blue:

"Maybe you'll get a First Lieutenant's job yourself, one of these days."

The remark made Lockhart both pleased and thoughtful for some time afterwards. It was an idea that had never even occurred to him; now that he examined it, it did not seem so fantastic as it might have at the beginning of the year.

His principal other visitor was Ericson himself, who slipped aboard one day toward the end of their leave, and walked round the ship with an air so suspicious and so proprietary that Lockhart found himself imagining half a dozen things he had either done wrong or failed to do at all. But the Captain seemed to be satisfied that *Compass Rose* was

117

coming to no harm: he stayed to have lunch on board and, as if to mark the difference between this occasion and the normal times when the ship was working, he dropped all formality and proved himself very good company on a new and level plane. He was especially interesting when he talked about his own apprenticeship in the Navy, and the quick learning that the war had now made necessary, compared with the wearisome year-to-year grind of peacetime seagoing and the desperately slow promotion that rewarded it. Lockhart had the impression that Ericson was now becoming convinced of something—perhaps the capability of amateurs like himself—which before he had rejected out of hand. . . . Altogether, it was one of the most pleasant meals he had ever had in *Compass Rose:* it left him with a feeling of respect, almost of hero-worship, for Ericson, which a little earlier he would have dismissed as a surrender of individuality. Some of his peacetime convictions, it seemed, were being rubbed off: if the ones that took their place were as natural and as unforced as this new regard, it did not matter at all.

[6]

On the evening of their return from leave, Lockhart, Morell, and Ferraby were all in the wardroom when Bennett stumbled down the ladder and entered the room. He was undeniably drunk, and most of his trouser buttons were undone: the general effect was so unpleasant that it was difficult to include him in their company without exhibiting a strong reaction. For some moments he busied himself at the sideboard, while they watched him in silence; then he turned round, glass in hand, and focused his eyes on each of them in turn.

"Well, well, well," he said with foolish emphasis. "Good little boys, all back from leave at the proper time. . . . How did you tear yourself away?"

No one answered him.

The full glass slopped over his coat as he gestured drunkenly. "Matey lot of bastards, aren't you?" He eyed Lockhart with confused belligerence. "What's been happening while I've been away?"

"Nothing at all."

"I suppose you were slipping ashore the whole time." He took an enormous gulp of whisky, coughed, and only just held on to it. His eyes moved unsteadily round to Morell and Ferraby. "And as for you married men—married—" he lost the thread of what he was going to say, but unfortunately started again. "You had a wonderful time. Don't tell me."

"It was very pleasant," said Morell after a pause.

"I bet you left a bun in the oven, both of you," said Bennett thickly. Then suddenly he turned a grey-green colour, and lurched out of the room. They heard him stumbling up the ladder, and the clang of the lavatory door behind him.

"Now what on earth does that peculiar phrase mean?" asked Morell, when he had gone.

Lockhart, considerably embarrassed, said: "I shouldn't worry about it if I were you."

"But what?" Morell insisted.

Lockhart explained, as delicately as he could, the reference to pregnancy. It could not be made to sound in the least delicate, and the reaction was what he had expected. Ferraby flushed vividly and looked at the floor: Morell lost his normal air of indifference and for a moment his face had a startling expression of disgust and anger.

"What a monstrous man he is!" he said in the uncomfortable pause that followed. "How can we get rid of him?"

"I've an idea he might get rid of himself," answered Lockhart, glad of the change of subject. "He didn't like that last convoy at all. I wouldn't be surprised if he gave this job up."

"How could he do that?" asked Ferraby, in a voice so subdued and spiritless that it was almost a whisper.

Lockhart gestured vaguely. "Oh, there are ways. . . . If I were he, I think I should get a duodenal ulcer. For some reason the Navy takes them very seriously—if they suspect anything like that they put you ashore straight away, in case something blows up while you're at sea."

"One of us had better tell him," said Morell after re-flection. "I wouldn't like him to be in any doubt as to how to go about it, just for want of a word of advice."

"I should say he knows," remarked Lockhart.

"How wonderful if he did go," said Ferraby, in the same small voice. "It would make such a terrific difference."

"Funnier things have happened."

"But not nicer," said Morell. "Not in my experience, at least."

By one of those coincidences that occasionally sweeten the crudest circumstances, Lockhart's forecast came exactly true. The very next day, at lunch, Bennett, who had been eating with his accustomed fervour, suddenly clapped his hands to his stomach and gave a realistic groan.

"Jesus Christ!" he said, in a voice suppressed by tension and mashed potato. "That hurt!"

"What's the matter?" said Ericson, looking at him with non-committal interest.

"Hell of a pain. . . ." Bennett gave another groan, yet more heart-rending, and doubled up across the table. His hands were still clasped to his stomach, and his breath came heavily through clenched teeth. It was difficult, for a variety of reasons, not to applaud the occasion.

"Better lie down," said Ericson. "Take it easy for a bit."

"Jesus, it's agony!"

"Perhaps you have a bun in the oven," said Morell suavely. He raised his eyebrows as he saw Lockhart struggling with laughter.

Bennett levered himself upright, and tottered towards the door. "Reckon I'll lie down," he mumbled. "It may pass off." He went through the doorway toward his cabin, moaning with great clarity.

"Bad luck," observed the Captain.

"Most moving," said Morell. "I imagine there's nothing

we can do to help him." The remark was so clearly a statement of non-intention that Lockhart could hardly stop
laughing out loud.

Ericson looked round the table suddenly. "What are you
all grinning at?" he demanded.

"Sorry, sir," said Lockhart, who was the most uncon-
trolled offender. "I was thinking of something."

Morell frowned, with a wonderful air of disapproval. "It
hardly does you credit, at a time like this," he said stiffly.
"If the First Lieutenant is in pain, I should not have thought
you would be able to laugh at anything else."

Ericson looked from one to the other, started to speak, and
then let it go. They were behaving rather badly: but he himself was conscious of a certain lightening of the atmosphere,
now that Bennett had taken himself off, and it was hardly
honest to check the same feeling in other people. . . . The
only drawback to the slightly farcical occasion was the possibility of Bennett's really being ill: for *Compass Rose* was at
twelve hours' notice for steam, and likely to sail the next
day.

His foreboding was accurate enough. Bennett complained
of pain all that afternoon: he went off to the naval hospital
the same evening, and he did not return. When Ericson summoned Lockhart to his cabin next morning, he had on his
desk two signals that did not go well together. One was their
sailing orders, for four o'clock: the other was about Bennett.

"The First Lieutenant won't be back for some time, Lockhart," Ericson began. "He's got a suspected duodenal ulcer."

"Oh," said Lockhart. He felt inclined to laugh, at the way
it had all fallen into place so neatly, and then he had a sudden
thought which brought him up sharply. Something else was
falling into place, something that concerned him intimately,
something for the bright future. He waited for the Captain
to speak, knowing what he was going to say, almost fearing
to hear it in case it should be less than he hoped.

Ericson was frowning at the two signals. "We sail this
afternoon, and we'll have to go without him. There's no

121

chance of getting a relief by then, either." He looked up. "You'll have to take over as Number One, and organize the watches on that basis."

"Yes, sir," said Lockhart. His heart, to his secret surprise, had raced for a moment, as if to mark a violent pleasure. First Lieutenant. . . . It could be done, and it would have to be—he wouldn't have another chance like this one, for a very long time.

"I'll help you with it," Ericson went on. "You should be able to carry on until a relief arrives."

"I can carry on anyway."

"Can you?" Ericson looked at him again. Lockhart had spoken with a kind of informal resolution that was a new thing in their relationship.

"Yes, sir."

"All right," said Ericson after a pause. "I'll see. . . . Do your best this time, anyway."

Lockhart walked out of the cabin with that precise determination.

The first convoy, with the new job to do, was a challenge, and Lockhart took it on happily. As far as watchkeeping was concerned, it gave him an easier run: he now had the morning watch, from four a.m. until eight, and in this early part of the summer that meant almost four hours of daylight watchkeeping, instead of the strain and difficulty of a totally dark middle watch. But there were many other things that went with his promotion, added responsibilities that must always be borne in mind: from the first afternoon, when after a final check-up with Tallow he reported *Compass Rose* "ready to proceed," he was never clear of the routine interruptions that the proper execution of his job entailed, and never free of worry lest he had forgotten something. He did not mind, because he was professionally and personally interested, as well as immensely eager to make a success of it; but on that convoy, as on many others still to come, he worked harder than he ever had before.

In essence, he had to present the Captain with a going concern, a smoothly run ship that would not fail him in any trial. In harbour it involved one range of responsibility, concerned mostly with discipline, topping up stores and ammunition, and the organization of working-parties so as to keep the ship clean and efficient: at sea it took on a more vital quality, closer to the war and with less margin for error. Weapons had to be tested daily; parties detailed to deal with the odd things that went wrong: watches had to be changed or strengthened; the mess-decks visited twice a day to see that they were tidied up and as dry as possible—otherwise life on board became even more grossly uncomfortable than it need be: at nightfall, *Compass Rose* must fade into the twilight with no light showing, no weapon out of order, and no man on board in any doubt of what he must do, whatever the circumstances. It was a full program; but he was strengthened by Ericson's backing, which was strong and continuous, and pleased also by the reaction of Morell and Ferraby. They gave him a cheerful co-operation: freed from Bennett's heavy-handed regime, and wanting above all to make a success of the substitution, they went out of their way to help him through the first uncertain period.

For they *were* free of Bennett: he faded away into a dilatory background of hospital boards and recurrent examinations, and they never saw him again. Lockhart's promotion was confirmed, not without some misgivings, by Western Approaches Command; and the new officer who arrived to fill the gap, one Sub-Lieutenant Baker, was junior to Ferraby and, if his hesitant air was anything to go by, likely to remain so. The new team assembled and settled down, making of *Compass Rose* a different ship altogether. The wardroom was now a pleasant place where they could relax and feel at ease, without a morose and critical eye singling them out for comment: after six months of suspicion and the most oafish kind of tyranny, it made for a happy freedom that they did not want to abuse. The same feeling spread throughout the ship, filtering down to the lower deck, where Bennett's crude methods had aroused the most resentment and the strongest reaction in terms of idling and shirking: the idea that Lockhart, though no fool, was a better man to work for, produced, as it often does, more work and not less. There were of course, to start with, one or two efforts at taking advantage of the more reasonable rule, notably by libertymen who returned on board late and produced elaborate excuses for doing so; but after one conspicuous offender, claiming to have been involved in a boarding-house fire, had been informed by Lockhart (who had taken the trouble to find out) that the night in question had been the first one for four months on which the Liverpool Fire Brigade had not been called out, and had then been sent to detention by the Captain, the number of men ready to "try it on" showed a steep decline.

Ericson, observing the general improvement, was pleased with his experiment. He had gone to a good deal of trouble to get Lockhart's appointment confirmed, in the face of a stubborn sort of disbelief ashore, and the trouble was worth while. Both he and *Compass Rose* had gained something that might be even more valuable in the near future.

There was one job of Lockhart's that had been his ever since he had joined *Compass Rose* and had admitted, in a moment of inattention, that one of his great-uncles had once been a surgeon at Guy's Hospital; and that was the job of ship's doctor. So far it had involved him in nothing more than treating toothache, removing a splinter from a man's eye, and advising, with no sort of experience to guide him, on a stubborn case of lice-infestation: all the serious cases went to the naval hospital ashore, and as yet nothing in this class had ever occurred at sea. Vaguely he realized that this would not always be so: other corvettes had had casualties to deal with, after ships in convoy had been torpedoed, and sooner or later he himself would be faced with an experience he was little fitted for. It was a thought he shied away from, because he had a real doubt as to how he would meet the ordeal: nothing in his life, not even a casual motor accident, had brought him into contact with blood and violence, and he feared a reaction that might be ineffective or foolish. "Fainting at the sight of blood"—the stock phrase sometimes occurred to him, with a discomforting twinge of anxiety. Suppose that was what happened, suppose he could not help it. . . . The job of doctor was the only one on board that, in moments of introspection, he wanted to relinquish.

But so far it had been a sinecure: so far, their most challenging medical problem had been sufficiently beyond his scope for him to be justified in rejecting it.

The occasion had been the start of a convoy, when the line of ships was forming up after the slow progress down-river. A near-by tanker had started signalling to *Compass Rose*, and Wells, receiving the message, passed it on to the Captain.

"From the tanker, sir," he said. " 'Have you a doctor on board or can you give medical advice?' "

Ericson looked at Lockhart, who was also up on the bridge. "How about it, Number One?"

"I'll have a crack at it, sir," said Lockhart. "I can't do much harm at this distance."

"All right." He turned to Wells. "Make to them: 'Medical advice available. What are symptoms?' "

There was a pause, while the lamps flickered again. Then Wells, reading the reply, suddenly said: "Oh!" in a startled voice. It was the first time Lockhart had ever seen him surprised, and he wondered what could be coming. With no sort of expression, Wells gave the "message received" signal, and then said:

"Reply, sir: 'Tight foreskin.' "

There was a reflective silence on the bridge.

"Sir," said Lockhart, "I honestly don't know."

"Does you credit," answered Ericson. It was one of those remarks he occasionally made, which endeared him to Lockhart as something more than a good captain. "I don't think we have any experts on board, have we?"

"No, sir," said Lockhart.

" 'Afraid we cannot help your patient,' " Ericson dictated to Wells, " 'Will ask destroyer, which has a doctor.' Send that off. . . . Fine start for a twenty-one day convoy," he said thoughtfully. "That'll teach him not to go to *that* address again."

The subsequent exchange of signals with *Viperous* was of a kind that does not figure in the official log: at the end of it, Lockhart had less inclination to continue his medical career than ever before. Later, in mid-Atlantic, they inquired after the casualty, and received the answer: "Patient enjoyed a good night." "We know that," was Morell's dry comment. "It was the original trouble."

And then, suddenly, being the doctor wasn't funny any more.

Dunkirk, that fabulous flight and triumph, was their signal for joining battle: from then onward, almost every convoy they escorted suffered some sort of attack, either from U-boats or aircraft, and the loss of ships began to be an inevitable part of their sea-going. Dunkirk, as it was bound to, made a great difference to the balance of things in the Atlantic: the operation itself drew off many ships, destroyers and corvettes alike, from regular convoy-escort, and some of them were lost, others damaged, and still others had to remain in home waters when it was over, to be on hand in case of invasion. The shortage of escorts at this stage was ludicrous: even with the arrival of fifty obsolescent destroyers that America had now made available to the Allies, convoys sailed out into the Atlantic with only a thin token screen between them and the growing force of U-boats. When, after Dunkirk, the Royal Navy turned its attention to the major battle again, it was to find control of the battlefield threatened by a ruthless assault, which quickened and grew with every month that passed.

There was another factor in the altered account. The map now showed them a melancholy and menacing picture: with Norway gone, France gone, Ireland a dubious quantity on their doorstep, and Spain an equivocal neutral, nearly the whole European coastline, from Narvik to Bordeaux, was available to U-boats and, more important still, as air bases for long-range aircraft. Aircraft could now trail a convoy far out into the Atlantic, calling up U-boats to the attack as they circled out of range: the liaison quickly showed a profit disastrous to the Allies. In the three months that followed Dunkirk, over two hundred ships were sent to the bottom by these two weapons in combinations, and the losses continued at something like fifty ships a month till the end of the year. Help was on the way—new weapons, more escorts, more aircraft: but help did not come in time, for many ships and men, and for many convoys that made port with great gaps in their ranks.

It was on one of these bad convoys, homeward bound near Iceland, that *Compass Rose* was blooded.

When the alarm bell went, just before midnight, Ferraby left the bridge where he had been keeping the first watch with Baker, and made his way aft towards his depth charges. It was he who had rung the bell, as soon as the noise of air-craft and a burst of tracer bullets from the far side of the convoy indicated an attack; but though he had been prepared for the violent clanging and the drumming of feet that followed it, he could not control a feeling of sick surprise at the urgency that now possessed the ship, in its first alarm for ac-tion. The night was calm, with a bright three-quarter moon that bathed the upper deck in a cold glow, and showed them the nearest ships of the convoy in hard revealing outline; it was a perfect night for what he *knew* was coming, and to hurry down the length of *Compass Rose* was like going swiftly to the scaffold. He knew that if he spoke now there would be a tremble in his voice, he knew that full daylight would have shown his face pale and his lips shaking; he knew that he was not really ready for this moment, in spite of the months of training and the gradually sharpening tension. But the mo-ment was here, and somehow it had to be faced.

Wainwright, the young torpedoman, was already on the quarterdeck, clearing away the release-gear on the depth charges, and as soon as Wainwright spoke—even though it was only the three words "Closed up, sir"—Ferraby knew that he also was consumed by nervousness. . . . He found the fact heartening, in a way he had not expected: if his own fear of action were the common lot, and not just a personal and shameful weakness, it might be easier to cure in company. He took a grip of his voice, said: "Get the first pattern ready to drop," and then, as he turned to check up on the depth-charge crews, his eye was caught by a brilliant firework display on their beam.

The attacking aircraft was now flying low over the centre of the convoy, pursued and harried by gunfire from scores of ships at once. The plane could not be seen, but her swift progress could be followed by the glowing arcs of tracer bullets, which swept like a huge fan across the top of the convoy. The uproar was prodigious—the plane screaming through the darkness, hundreds of guns going at once, one or two ships sounding the alarm on their sirens: the centre of the convoy, with everyone blazing away at the low-flying plane and not worrying about what else was in the line of fire, must have been an inferno. Standing in their groups aft, close to the hurrying water, they watched and waited, wondering which way the plane would turn at the end of her run: on the platform above them the two-pounder gun's crew, motionless and helmeted against the night sky, were keyed ready for their chance to fire. But the chance never came, the waiting belts of ammunition remained idle: something else forestalled them.

It was as if the monstrous noise from the convoy must have a climax, and the climax could only be violent. At the top of the centre column, near the end of her run, the aircraft dropped two bombs: one of them fell wide, raising a huge pluming spout of water that glittered in the moonlight, and the other found its mark. It dropped with an iron clang on some ship they could not see—and they knew that now they would never see her: for after the first explosion there was a second one, a huge orange flash that lit the whole convoy and the whole sky at one ghastly stroke. The ship—whatever size she was—must have disintegrated on the instant; they were left with the evidence—the sickening succession of splashes as the torn pieces of the ship fell back into the sea, covering and fouling a mile-wide circle, and the noise of the aircraft disappearing into the darkness, a receding tail of sound to underline this fearful destruction.

"Must have been ammunition," said someone in the darkness, breaking the awed and compassionate silence. "Poor bastards."

"Didn't know much about it. Best way to die."

"You fool," thought Ferraby, trembling uncontrollably, "you fool, you fool, no one wants to die. . . ."

From the higher vantage-point of the bridge, Ericson had watched everything; he had seen the ship hit, the shower of sparks where the bomb fell, and then, a moment afterward, the huge explosion that blew her to pieces. In the shocked silence that followed, his voice giving a routine helm-order was cool and normal: no one could have guessed the sadness and the anger that filled him, to see a whole crew of men like himself wiped out at one stroke. There was nothing to be done: the aircraft was gone, with this frightful credit, and if there were any men left alive—which was hardly conceivable—*Sorrel*, the stern escort, would do her best for them. It was so quick, it was so brutal. . . . He might have thought more about it, he might have mourned a little longer, if a second stroke had not followed swiftly; but even as he raised his binoculars to look at the convoy again, the ship they were stationed on, a hundred yards away, rocked to a sudden explosion and then, on the instant, heeled over at a desperate angle.

This time, a torpedo. . . . Ericson heard it: and even as he jumped to the voice-pipe to increase their speed and start zigzagging, he thought: "If that one came from this side of the convoy, it must have missed us by a few feet." Inside the asdic hut, Lockhart heard it, and started hunting on the danger-side, without further orders: that was a routine, and even at this moment of surprise and crisis, the routine still ruled them all. Morell, on the fo'c's'le, heard it, and closed up his gun's crew again and loaded with star-shell: down in the wheelhouse, Tallow heard it, and gripped the wheel tighter, and called out to his quartermasters: "Watch that telegraph, now!" and waited for the swift orders that might follow. Right aft, by the depth charges, Ferraby heard it, and shivered: he glanced downward at the black water rushing past them, and then at the stricken ship, which he could see quite clearly, and he longed for some action in which he could lose himself and his fear. Deep down in the engine room, Chief E.R.A. Watts heard it best of all: it came like a hammer-blow, hitting the ship's side a great splitting crack, and when, a few seconds afterwards, the telegraph rang for an increase of speed, his hand was on the steam valve already. He knew what had happened, he knew what might happen next. But it was better not to think of what was going on outside: down here, encased below the waterline, they must wait, and hope, and keep their nerve.

Ericson took *Compass Rose* in a wide half-circle to starboard, away from the convoy, hunting for the U-boat down what he presumed had been the track of the torpedo; but they found nothing that looked like a contact, and presently he circled back again, toward the ship that had been hit. She had fallen out of line, like one winged bird in a flight of duck, letting the rest of the convoy go by: she was sinking fast, and already her screws were out of water and she was poised for the long plunge. The cries of men in fear came from her, and a thick smell of oil: at one moment, when they had her outlined against the moon, they could see a mass of men packed high in the towering stern, waving and shouting as they felt the ship under them begin to slide down to her grave. Ericson, trying for a cool decision in this moment of pity, was faced with a dilemma: if he stopped to pick up survivors, he would become a sitting target himself, and he would also lose all chance of hunting for the U-boat: if he went on with the hunt, he would, with *Sorrel* busy elsewhere, be leaving these men to their death. He decided on a compromise, a not too dangerous compromise: they would drop a boat, and leave it to collect what survivors it could while *Compass Rose* took another cast away to starboard. But it must be done quickly.

Ferraby, summoned to the quarterdeck voice-pipe, put every effort he knew into controlling his voice.

"Ferraby, sir."

"We're going to drop a boat, sub. Who's your leading hand?"

"Leading Seaman Tonbridge, sir."

"Tell him to pick a small crew—not more than four—and row over toward the ship. Tell him to keep well clear until she goes down. They may be able to get some boats away themselves, but if not, he'll have to do the best he can. We'll come back for him when we've had another look for the submarine."

"Right, sir."

"Quick as you can, sub. I don't want to stop too long."

Ferraby threw himself into the job with an energy that was a drug for all other feeling: the boat was lowered so swiftly that when *Compass Rose* drew away from it and left it to its critical errand the torpedoed ship was still afloat. But she was only just afloat, balanced between sea and sky before her last dive; and as Tonbridge took the tiller and glanced in her direction to get his bearings, there was a rending sound that carried clearly over the water, and she started to go down. Tonbridge watched, in awe and fear: he had never seen anything like this, and never had a job of this sort before, and it was an effort to meet it properly. It had been bad enough to be lowered into the darkness from *Compass Rose*, and to watch her fade away and be left alone in a small boat under the stars, with the convoy also fading and a vast un-friendly sea all round them; but now, with the torpedoed ship disappearing before their eyes, and the men shouting and crying as they splashed about in the water, and the smell of oil coming across to them thick and choking, it was more like a nightmare than anything else. Tonbridge was twenty-three years of age, a product of the London slums condi-tioned by seven years' naval training; faced by this ordeal, the fact that he did not run away from it, the fact that he re-mained effective, was beyond all normal credit.

They did what they could: rowing about in the darkness, guided by the shouting, appalled by the choking cries of men who drowned before they could be reached, they tried their utmost to rescue and to succour. They collected fourteen men: one was dead, one was dying, eight were wounded, and the rest were shocked and prostrated to a pitiful degree. It was very nearly fifteen men: Tonbridge actually had hold of the fifteenth, who was gasping in the last stages of terror and exhaustion, but the film of oil on his naked body made him impossible to grasp, and he slipped away and sank before a rope could be got round him. When there were no more shadows on the water, and no more cries to follow, they rested on their oars, and waited; alone on the enormous black waste of the Atlantic, alone with the settling wreckage and the reek of oil; and so, presently, *Compass Rose* found them.

Ferraby, standing in the waist of the ship as the boat was hooked on, wondered what he would see when the survivors came over the side: he was not prepared for the pity and horror of their appearance. First came the ones who could climb aboard themselves—half a dozen shivering, black-faced men, dressed in the filthy oilsoaked clothes they had snatched up when the ship was struck: one of them with his scalp streaming with blood, another nursing an arm flayed from wrist to shoulder by scalding steam. They looked about them in wonder, dazed by the swiftness of disaster, by their rescue, by the solid deck beneath their feet. Then, while they were led to the warmth of the mess-deck, a sling was rigged for the seriously wounded, and they were lifted over the side on stretchers: some silent, some moaning, some coughing up the fuel oil that was burning and poisoning their intestines: laid side by side in the waist, they made a carpet of pain and distress so naked in suffering that it seemed cruel to watch them. And then, with the boat still bumping alongside in the eerie darkness, came Tonbridge's voice: "Go easy—there's a dead man down here." Ferraby had never seen a dead man before, and he had to force himself to look at this pitiful relic of the sea—stone cold, stiffening already, its grey head jerking as it was bundled over the side: an old sailor, unseamanlike and disgusting in death. He wanted to run away, he wanted to be sick: he watched with shocked amazement the two ratings who were carrying the corpse: "How can you bear what you are doing?" he thought, "how can you touch—it? . . ." Behind him he heard Lockhart's voice saying: "Bring the whole lot into the fo'c's'le—I can't see anything here," and then he turned away and busied himself with the hoisting of the boat, not looking behind him as the procession of wrecked and brutalized men was borne off. When the boat was inboard, and secure, he turned back again, glad to have escaped some part of the horror. There was nothing left now but the acrid smell of oil, and the patches of blood and water on the deck: nothing, he saw with a gasp of fear and revulsion, but the dead man lying lashed against the rail, a yard from him, rolling as the ship rolled, waiting for daylight and burial. He turned and ran towards the stern, pursued by terror.

In the big seamen's-mess-deck, under the shaded lamps, Lockhart was doing things he had never imagined possible. Now and again he recalled, with a spark of pleasure, his previous doubts: there was plenty of blood here to faint at, but that wasn't the way things were working out. . . . He had stitched up a gash in a man's head, from the nose to the line of the hair—as he took the catgut from its envelope he had thought: "I wish they'd include some directions with this stuff." He had set a broken leg, using part of a bench as a splint. He bound up other cuts and gashes, he did what he could for the man with the burnt arm, who was now in-sensible with pain: he watched, doing nothing with a curious hurt detachment, as a man who had drenched his intestines and perhaps his lungs with fuel oil slowly died. Some of *Compass Rose's* crew made a ring round him, looking at him, helping him when he asked for help: the two stewards brought tea for the cold and shocked survivors, other men offered dry clothing, and Tallow, after an hour or two, came down and gave him the largest tot of rum he had ever seen. It was not too large. . . . Once, from outside, there was the sound of an explosion, and he looked up: by chance, across the smoky fo'c's'le, the bandaged rows of wounded, the other men still shivering, the twisted corpse, the whole squalid confusion of the night, he met the eye of Leading Seaman Phillips. Involuntarily, both of them smiled, to mark a thought that could only be smiled at: if a torpedo hit them now, there would be little chance for any of them, and all this bandaging would be wasted.

Then he bent down again, and went on probing a wound for the splinter of steel that must still be there, if the scream of pain the movement produced was anything to go by. This was a moment to think only of the essentials, and they were all here with him, and in his care.

It was nearly daylight before he finished; and he went up to the bridge to report what he had done at a slow dragging walk, completely played out. He met Ericson at the top of the ladder: they had both been working throughout the night, and the two exhausted men looked at each other in silence, unable to put any expression into their stiff drawn faces, yet somehow acknowledging each other's competence. There was blood on Lockhart's hands, and on the sleeves of his duffle coat: in the cold light it had a curious metallic sheen, and Ericson looked at it for some time before he realized what it was.

"You must have been busy, Number One," he said quietly. "What's the score down there?"

"Two dead, sir," answered Lockhart. His voice was very hoarse, and he cleared his throat. "One more to go, I think— he's been swimming and walking about with a badly burned arm, and the shock is too much. Eleven others. They ought to be all right."

"Fourteen. . . . The crew was thirty-six altogether."

Lockhart shrugged. There was no answer to that one, and if there had been he could not have found it, in his present mood: the past few hours, spent watching and touching pain, seemed to have deadened all normal feeling. He looked round at the ships on their beam, just emerging as the light grew.

"How about things up here?" he asked.

"We lost another ship, over the other side of the convoy. That made three."

"More than one submarine?"

"I shouldn't think so. She probably crossed over."

"Good night's work." Lockhart still could not express more than a formal regret. "Do you want to turn in, sir? I can finish this watch."

"No—you get some sleep. I'll wait for Ferraby and Baker."

"Tonbridge did well."

"Yes. . . . So did you, Number One."

Lockhart shook his head. "It was pretty rough, most of it. I must get a little book on wounds. It's going to come in handy, if this sort of thing goes on."

"There's no reason why it shouldn't," said Ericson. "No reason at all, that I can see. Three ships in three hours: probably a hundred men all told. Easy."

"Yes," said Lockhart, nodding. "A very promising start. After the war, we must ask them how they do it."

"After the war," said Ericson levelly, "I hope they'll be asking us."

[8]

They sailed on eleven convoys that year: sometimes to Iceland, sometimes to Gibraltar, sometimes to the pinpoint in mid-Atlantic that was their rendezvous with the incoming ships. As winter drew on, the weather took a natural turn for the worse: but once the appalling discomfort and the tiredness were accepted, they grew to welcome the rising wind and the falling glass, for the respite of another kind that these brought. For at least they provided cover for the convoy: a black night, with a stiff sea running, was a form of insurance against attack, which they were ready to pay for as long as was necessary. At that time, U-boats had not reached the stage of development when they could fire torpedoes at almost any level: and the bad weather, in any case, made the ships hard to find and harder to hit. At the beginning, they never thought that they would welcome an Atlantic gale: as time went on, no other sort of weather suited them so well.

But the wind did not always blow, the moon was not always obscured by cloud. There were many repetitions of that first losing convoy: the tally of survivors gradually mounted, the total of ships lost pursued a steady upward curve. Something, it was clear, would have to be done about this question of survivors, if it was to be worth while fishing them out of the water; for corvettes, which were detailed for the bulk of this rescue work, were really ludicrously inadequate for the job. They needed a doctor, or at least a qualified sick-berth attendant, to see to the wounded and exhausted men: it was futile, it was senseless, to risk the ship in picking them up, only to have them die on board, from shock or burns or oil-poisoning that could not be properly treated.

Corvettes needed other things for this work, too: spare clothes, spare blankets, a proper sick-bay, drugs to ease pain. They even needed more canvas, for sewing up the dead. A lot of such things, which had not been foreseen, were now emerging into grisly reality.

It was on this note of inadequacy, this scrambling waste of effort and courage, that 1940 drew to its close. Another, more memorable, note was struck, too, just before the end. On Christmas morning they saw a ship, loaded with iron ore, break in half and sink in less than one minute: she went down like a stone in a pond, leaving nothing save an oily scum and four men on the surface of the water. This was the record so far, out of many quick kills: it still had power to shock. But then all the losses, the deaths, the scale of slaughter, still startled and moved them.

They should have known that things were just warming up.

PART THREE

1941: *Grappling*

[*1*]

They started the new year with a piece of domestic drama that in its untidiness and its inherent futility somehow reflected the wider battle.

The centre of the storm was a small able seaman by the name of Gregg. Gregg was one of the fo'c's'le party, in Morell's division: the latter knew little about him save that he was quiet and dependable, and had never been in any sort of trouble during the whole of the fifteen months he had been in *Compass Rose*. It was therefore something of a surprise when Gregg failed to return on board at the end of their stay in harbour, and was not to be found by the time the ship left on her first convoy of the year. They sailed without him, after leaving with the shore authorities sufficient particulars to ensure that he would not be stranded on the dockside when he returned. The post mortem and the clearing up would have to wait: all that was involved now was the nuisance of being short-handed—the trouble in store, like the other details and duties of life in harbour, was shelved, while the sea claimed all their attention.

But certainly the trouble was there, when they got back home. Absence without leave was sufficiently serious: to miss one's ship completely was in a higher scale of crime altogether, since if one did so, and the ship was involved in any kind of action, one was liable as well to a charge of desertion in the face of the enemy. Ericson, surveying Able Seaman

Gregg when he was brought up at Captain's Defaulters, on the morning after their return to harbour, waited with some interest to hear what he had to say. He might conceivably have some legitimate excuse that would disentangle him altogether—though it was hard to see what this could be. Alternatively, there might be something that would lessen the seriousness of the charge. Ericson hoped for this extenuation, since Gregg was a decent kid who had not been in trouble before: otherwise the thing might involve sending him to detention, and he would probably be permanently spoilt.

The crisis broke when Gregg refused to say anything at all.

The evidence on one side was simple: he had left the ship one afternoon, he had missed her when she sailed, he had reported back on board the morning she returned to harbour: the absence without leave for seventeen days was not disputable. But when Ericson asked for an explanation, he was met by a shake of the head, and a muttered "Nothing to say, sir" that brought him up short.

"You must have something to say," said Ericson sharply. He looked at the small sandy-haired figure in front of him, and tried to analyse the man's expression. It was not quite apologetic, it was not quite shy, it was certainly not rebellious; it had a sort of submissive determination that was, in the circumstances, rather brave. . . . "I want to know why you left the ship," Ericson went on, "and what you've been doing while we've been at sea. You've got to account for yourself—otherwise you'll be in serious trouble."

They all stared at Gregg: the Captain, Lockhart, Morell, and Tallow, who had marched him up to the table. The expressions on the ring of faces varied: the Captain, as judge, was non-committal, Morell looked puzzled, Lockhart wore his First Lieutenant's disciplinary frown, and Tallow exhibited the professional disgust of a man who had no patience with defaulters and not the smallest belief in their excuses. In the middle of it all, braving the storm, Able Seaman Gregg preserved his unblinking air of reserve. "When did you last

138

see your father?" thought Lockhart inconsequently, and frowned yet more determinedly still. This sort of thing was no longer allowed to be funny.

"Well," said Ericson after a pause. "I'm waiting."

"Nothing to say, sir," repeated Gregg in the same flat tone. Tallow drew in his breath with a sharp hiss, and Ericson, hearing it, was somehow reminded of the whole weight of tradition, the machinery of naval justice, that lay behind this moment. Soon he would have to apply that tradition, balancing the seesaw of crime and punishment, and the idea seemed wasteful and futile, when all it boiled down to was himself and a forlorn able seaman who would not try to save his own skin.

He wanted to find the real reason that lay behind it, and he wanted to rescue Gregg from a situation that, with the best will in the world, must always be weighted against him. He tried again.

"That's just silly," he said reasonably. "I don't know what you're trying to cover up, but I shouldn't think it's worth it. You know that I can send you to detention for this?"

"Yes, sir," mumbled Gregg.

"I don't want to do that, because you haven't been in trouble before and your divisional officer tells me you're a good worker. But unless you give me an explanation I haven't any alternative." He paused. "How did you come to miss the ship, and what have you been doing the last seventeen days?"

There was still no answer. Gregg looked stolidly out in front of him, his eyes just below the level of Ericson's chin, maintaining the foolish contest of wills, which could only have one end. The noises of the ship and the dockside seemed suspended, waiting for the scene to resolve itself. To Lockhart it seemed, fancifully, that this might never happen, that Gregg need never answer, that they might wait there for ever, till they all grew old and the war was over and no one cared any more. . . . Perhaps Ericson had something of the same feeling, for he straightened up suddenly and said:

"Stand over."

"Stand over," repeated Tallow, with the tiniest edge of doubt in his voice. And then, with more force: "On caps!" he continued automatically. "About turn! Quick march!"

When Gregg was out of earshot, Ericson turned to Morell.

"I'll see him again tomorrow," he said. "In the meantime, you'd better have a talk with him and try and find out what it's all about. I don't want to send him up without knowing what's behind it."

"Yes, sir," said Morell.

"Is he married?"

"Yes, sir."

"Ask him if there's anything wrong there. . . . Coxswain!"

"Sir?"

"Stand Gregg over till tomorrow morning."

"Aye, aye, sir."

"Next case."

But when Morell saw Gregg later that day, down in his cabin, he took a different line. There was less need for formality here, and less occasion for care in what one said: he could treat Gregg as he would have treated a witness in court, a witness who knew something but might have to be wheedled or bullied or tricked into revealing it. With no one listening, and no record to keep, the relationship of officer to rating could be stretched a long way outside the normal pattern.

"The Captain's doing his best for you," Morell said shortly, when Gregg once more repeated his stubborn "nothing-to-say" formula. "Probably a damned sight more than you deserve, but that's nothing to do with me. What he's trying to get at is, what made you suddenly walk ashore and miss the ship. Why don't you tell him?"

"I don't want to say, sir," said Gregg, with the same finality as before.

"You'd rather have a month's detention?"

Gregg's expression changed to a sulky frown, but he said nothing.

"That's what it would mean, you know," Morell went on.

"It'll be a black mark against you for the rest of your time in the Navy, it'll always be there, on your conduct sheet."

"I'm only in for the war, sir."

"Well, how long do you think that's going to last? You want to get on, don't you? You don't want to stay an able seaman for two or three years more? How can you be recommended for leading seaman if you do this sort of thing, and then refuse to say anything about it?"

"I don't know, sir."

"You'd better talk, Gregg." Morell changed his tone. "What's it all about? Where did you go to? Did you go home?"

After a pause: "Yes, sir," said Gregg, swallowing. "I went to London."

"Well, that's something. . . . Is there anything wrong there?"

"Not now, sir."

"Was there?"

"Yes."

"What?"

The obstinate, blank look returned. "I don't want to say."

"You know I won't repeat it to anyone."

"You'll repeat it to the Captain," said Gregg shrewdly.

"I don't have to. . . . And that's only two people, anyway: it won't go any further."

Gregg shook his head. He was wavering, but he still could not face whatever it was that filled his mind. "It will, if I say it up at the table. It'll be all over the ship then."

Morell frowned. "What you say at Defaulters *doesn't* go all over the ship. You know that perfectly well. . . . Now let's get this straight. There was some trouble at home?"

"Yes, sir."

"With your wife?"

"Yes."

"What sort of trouble?"

Gregg gestured, rather pathetically. "The usual."

"How did you hear about it?"

"Someone wrote—a pal at home."

"And you went off home to try to fix it up?"

"Yes."

"Why didn't you tell me?"

No answer.

"You see what it's got you into," said Morell hardly. "What the hell do you think your officers are for, if not to help you when this sort of thing happens?"

"I didn't know, sir. . . . I wanted it kept a secret."

"How can it be a secret, when you're absent without leave for seventeen days?"

"But no one knows about it still, sir—only you."

"But you're going to tell the Captain," said Morell.

"I don't want to do that. I'd rather go to cells, and have done with it."

"Don't be a bloody fool," said Morell. "I don't say you'll get off, but it might make a lot of difference. He's a human being, you know."

"But I can't tell it all up at the table," said Gregg desperately. "Not with all of you listening."

"We don't have to be listening. You know you can see the Captain privately, if it's a family matter, don't you?"

"Yes, sir."

"Well?"

Gregg came to a sudden decision. "I'd like to do that, sir."

"Why didn't you say so this morning?"

"I didn't think of it."

"You'd have saved yourself a lot of trouble. And been a lot more popular." Morell stood up. "All right—I'll arrange for you to see him this afternoon."

Gregg looked scared. "What do I say, sir?"

"You tell him exactly why you went home, and what happened when you got there."

"And it won't go any further?"

"No."

"And I'll maybe get off?"

142

"I don't know. Probably not altogether. But it'll give you a better chance than simply refusing to speak. That can only have one end, can't it?"

"Yes." Gregg smiled suddenly. "Thanks a lot, sir."

"There's nothing to thank me for." It was time to return to normal, time to drop the curtain again. "You're not clear yet, not by a long chalk. Now get back to work. I'll send for you when the Captain wants to see you. And this time, tell him the truth—everything—and don't waste any more time."

It was doubtful if Gregg could have brought himself to tell his story, even then, if he had not been coaxed and persuaded up to the very last moment. But Ericson, forewarned by Morell of what was at the heart of the trouble, was at special pains to make it easy for him. With Gregg in his cabin he gave ostentatious orders that he was not to be disturbed: he made him sit down, he gave him a cigarette, and he led off his questions as if taking it for granted that Gregg would have no embarrassment about telling him everything. And when the man still hesitated, sitting on the edge of his chair, stiff and sweating in his number-one suit with the gold badges, Ericson suddenly leant forward and said:

"You're married, Gregg, aren't you?"

"Yes, sir."

"Did you go home to see your wife?"

Gregg's eyes flickered upwards once, and then down again. His voice was not much above a whisper. "Yes, sir."

"You'd better tell me about it," said Ericson. "You want to tell somebody, don't you?—apart from the trouble you're in over it?"

He looked away as the other man struggled to answer. But the lead was enough, the balance was tipped: now at last, up in the quiet cabin, with the sun filtering through the porthole and the muted sound of water running against the hull, Gregg told his appalling story.

It had begun with a letter, waiting for him when *Compass Rose* got back from her last trip: a letter from a pal.

143

Dear Tom, [it said] *of course it's none of my business, but I've been up and down the old street once or twice, thinking of calling on Edith and asking how you're getting along, and then I haven't liked to go in because she's got company already. Dear Tom, there's a lot of talk about it, a car outside the house at all hours, they say he's a traveller for one of the big firms. I seen him once saying goodbye, they were laughing. I didn't like it, Tom, I thought I'd write and tell you. If I done wrong I'm sorry, you know me, always putting my foot in it. Keep cheerful, you better ask for a bit of leave and straighten it up, it all comes of these chaps being in a reserved bloody occupation, shooting's too good for some, yours till the cows come home.*

"I had to go, sir," said Gregg, twisting his hands together. At that moment there was more than certainty in his voice: something like defiance. "I had to go, straight away. When you get a letter like that . . . I wasn't due for leave even next time it came round, and that was three weeks ahead. I had to see what was going on. We've only been married six months."

And so he had gone, without a word to anyone, that same afternoon: slipping ashore with the libertymen, catching the last London train from Lime Street station, arriving about eleven at night, getting the bus out to Highgate.

"What happened then?" asked Ericson, when the pause had stretched to unbearable limits.

"It's a little house, sir," said Gregg, "a nice little house. It used to be my mother's—she left it to me. When I walked up from the bus stop, it was just like the letter said." The defiance was gone now, swallowed up in misery: he was re-living the horrible moment. "When I got to the house, the car was outside the door, and—and there was a light on up-stairs."

Gregg paused, and frowned: the imprint of emotion on the smooth round face was very moving. "See what I mean, sir? Downstairs, it was dark."

"Yes," said Ericson, "yes, I see."

For a moment Gregg hadn't known what to do, he'd been so taken aback, so horrified, so sick with it. He had stood in the dark street, looking from the car up to the light, the terrible bedroom light. "I didn't need telling any more, sir: there was enough to bet on, there. . . . I waited a long time, thinking what to do, and then I thought: 'Well, give her a chance, she's only a kid really, and lonely by herself,' so I walked up the path whistling a bit, and I made a lot of noise opening the door and going inside. . . . You see, I love her, sir," he said, with simple determination, as if only he knew about love. "We've been married just the six months."

But now there was a long silence that Ericson could not break, so clearly pitiful was the feeling behind it: the word "love" must have struck a hopeless note of memory. When Gregg started again, it was as if the key had now changed to something darker, more horrible still: as if this part of the story, which he had not yet shared with anyone, had a special forbidden quality that made them both guilty, teller and hearer alike.

Gregg's wife had called out when she heard the door go: scared, she sounded, and there was a lot of moving about. . . . She said: "Who is it?" and he answered: "Tom," and there was whispering that made him feel angry and sick at the same time. He had switched on the light in the hall and waited, knowing quite well what they were doing and what the whispering meant: they were wondering if it could be bluffed out, what the evidence was, how much he had seen and guessed. But evidently they soon decided that it was hopeless, for now a man's voice spoke quite loud, and when Edith called out: "I'm coming down," it had a sulky note of defiance.

"I still didn't know what to do, sir—I couldn't make sense of it at all. She'd always been so different, there'd never been anything like this. We were only married a couple of leaves back—you read the banns for us, here on board." Ericson suddenly remembered that this was so: he could even recall, with a queer distaste, having read "Edith Tappett, spinster, of the Parish of Highgate, London," and wondering what a

145

girl with so unromantic a name could be like. Now he knew: now they both knew. . . . "Pretty soon she came down," Gregg went on, speaking rather fast and looking at the floor. "She hadn't got dressed, even then: she was all anyhow, in her dressing-gown."

Ericson thought: that's something he'll never forget: what a horrible thing to have in one's mind, for ever and ever. . . . But Gregg was hurrying on, leaving one scene for another yet more terrible, as if his choice were so rich and so wide that he need not stay long over one aspect of it.

"She'd had a bit to drink, sir—I could tell that. But that wasn't enough for her to talk the way she did. You'd have thought it was all *my* fault. 'I've got a friend,' she said, 'I wasn't expecting you'—just like that. And when I said: 'Friend?—what do you mean, friend?' she said: 'There's no need to shout, Tom, you don't want any trouble, surely?' And then she called out: 'Walter,' and after a minute the man came down the stairs. *He* didn't care," said Gregg, with fury and misery in his voice, "he walked down the stairs doing up his coat. . . . A big flashy chap, well dressed, full of himself—you could tell he did this sort of thing every day of the week." Gregg looked up and then down again, flushing, remembering a deep humiliation. "He was twice the size of me, sir. I couldn't even—I couldn't—" His voice tailed off into an empty realm of cowardice and despair, where only his defeat, his still-raw shame, was real.

"Never mind that," said Ericson quickly, as if there were no significance in the pause, the moment of abasement. "Tell me what happened next. What did your wife say?"

"You should have let me know, Tom," was what his wife had said. "How was I to tell you'd be back?" And then she had actually introduced them, and the man had said: "Ah, the sailor home from the sea," and Gregg had told him to get out, and the man had answered: "We don't want any unpleasantness, thank you." It was all part of a topsy-turvy nightmare in which Gregg could not get his bearings at all. "After he'd gone, we had it out properly, but I couldn't get her to see it straight at all." Gregg's voice still held some of the astonishment of that moment. "She said she'd got used to—to love, sir, with me, and she couldn't do without it. She said it had been going on for two months. She said that this chap had talked her into it, but she wasn't really sorry, only on my account. She said it was the war, and lots of people did it. . . . She acted like a different person. In the end we just went off to bed. She was with me that night, sir, though—though I could hardly touch her at first."

There was now a much longer pause, almost as if Gregg had finished putting his side of the affair and were waiting for the verdict. But that could not be the end of the story, thought Ericson, looking down at his desk: it was horrible enough, and it excused a good deal as far as Gregg's behaviour went, but it only accounted for two days—three at the outside—and he had been away for seventeen. . . . He waited, wanting to prompt the other man but unable to find a way that would not sound brutal or indifferent: he had been moved by the recital—horrified, even—and he did not want it to seem as if he considered it of no account, or was brushing it aside in favour of a strict, immovable justice. But presently Gregg took up the story again, without any reminder: perhaps he had merely been collecting his thoughts, perhaps there was worse to come.

"That was the first day, sir," he said, "and I stayed two more, just to make sure—I'd still be back in time to catch the ship, and that way it didn't seem it would be so bad." He looked swiftly at the Captain, aware that he was taking a lot for granted, but the latter made no sign: the verdict, the judgement, was to come at the very end. . . . "She was just like she used to be in the old days," Gregg went on: "she stopped talking about the other chap, she didn't say anything more about these funny ideas, she seemed to have forgotten all about it, except when I spoke about it at the end. But before I left I asked her what was going to happen, and she promised faithfully to give it another try. So I went off to catch the early train—" Ericson could tell there was yet another climax coming, another stroke of pain, from Gregg's swifter, shorter breathing, and the way his words came faster and faster, "and I missed it because of the traffic, and I came back, thinking I'd spend the day with her and catch the train in the evening, and she wasn't there—the house was empty, and she'd taken her case as well."

This time Ericson was afraid that Gregg was going to break down altogether: his voice came to a sudden stop, and his mouth, working and trembling uncontrollably, seemed on the point of puckering into tears. It was a moment of surrender: he looked young and capable and smart in his uniform, and then, above the neatly rolled collar and the clean white flannel, his defeated face destroyed the picture utterly. Without a word Ericson went to his cupboard, poured out some whisky, and handed the glass to Gregg: because it was so unusual a thing to do, so far outside the normal, it was capable of being a failure and a mistake. For a moment Ericson wondered if at a later date, when Gregg had forgotten the worst of this matter, he might translate the occasion into different terms: perhaps boasting cheekily in the mess-decks: "Trouble? Not *me!* The skipper gave me a tot of whisky and told me to come back any time. . . ." But no, it would not be like that. The giving of the whisky seemed to surprise Gregg into an effort of control: as he sipped it, looking round the cabin and out through the sunlit porthole, his mouth and face firmed again, and he prepared to go on. What he had said, and what he had still to say, was desolate, but not too desolate for ordered speech.

It was possible, he had thought, that his wife might be at her mother's, over at Edgware; even though she had said nothing about going, she was in the mood for impulsive action. So to Edgware he went, by bus, only to draw another blank. "She wasn't there, and she hadn't been there for weeks. I could see her mother thought it was funny, but I wasn't answering any questions. Then I went to see my pal, the one that wrote the letter, but he'd gone back after his leave and they didn't know anything. So I left it, and went home again."

He had been alone in the empty, silent house for a week.

148

As he dismissed it thus, in a single sentence, Ericson tried to visualize what it must have been like: the waiting, the loneliness, the suspicion, the knowledge of betrayal. "I had to stay, sir, in case she came back," he said, and Ericson could not, for pity, deny the claim. "I'd have gone looking for her, but I didn't know where to look—there was the whole of London. And then I got an idea, I should have thought of it before. There was a married friend of hers, woman I never cared for, over the other side of London, down White City way. I thought she might be staying there, so I went over, and asked at the house. She said the wife *had* been there, a few days back, but had gone away again, she didn't know where." The story was pouring out now, unchecked by any reserve: in the silent cabin the words and sentences, clumsy and ill-formed, yet flowed with an eloquent readiness towards their cruel end. "I thought she was telling lies, there was something in the way she looked, so I hung about a bit, watching for the car, and then I turned into the first pub I came to, for a pint and something to eat, and there they were, the two of them, sitting down and drinking port." He swallowed. "She was laughing, and then she looked up and said: 'Look who's here.' "

Ericson thought he was going to stop, as he had stopped many times before, but the whisky had done its work—or perhaps it was the story itself, which could not be delayed at so crucial a point.

"I asked what she was doing there, instead of being at home," Gregg went on immediately, "and she said there was no harm in having a drink. Then I said: 'Where've you been the last week?' and she said: 'Staying with Else'—that's this woman. I said I wasn't going to stand for it, and the man said: 'What you need is a drink.' I said: 'I don't want a drink from you—if this goes on I'm going to see about a divorce.'

"I didn't really mean it, I just wanted to give him a scare. He said: 'You've got no evidence.' So I said: 'How about you coming down the stairs that night?' and he said: 'I was just saying good night to Mrs. Gregg—it was quite innocent.' And then he winked at her and she laughed like a— like a rotten tart."

"What an accurate description," thought Ericson, "how can he want her now, how can he feel anything but hatred and disgust?" But in Gregg's voice there was neither of these: when he said "rotten tart" he was not condemning, he was mourning what he and she had lost. There was no trace of rationality in it, no balancing of right and wrong: there was simply the incalculable instinct of love, of what people feel—or feel that they should feel—when they undertake to bind themselves to other people. Even now, it seemed, Gregg did not question the validity of that binding: the bargain might be bad, but it was a bargain still—and all this sprang from "love," a word in a book, a scene in a film, a foolish core of determination in a man's brain.

Gregg was continuing, with quiet assurance. "I was going to say something to him about that, sir, but then he said: 'You needn't worry, anyway, I'm off to the States next week, big buying job.' And the wife said: 'First I've heard of it, Walter, when are you going?' and he said: 'Thursday— I'll come round to say good-bye,' and I said: 'Like hell you will—you don't come near the house again.' It was funny, sir, he didn't try to argue the toss about that, he just said: 'Have it your own way, then'; I think what I said about the divorce must have rattled him a bit, but perhaps he'd had enough of it anyway. Then he stood up and said to the wife: 'Thanks a lot, see you again one of these days,' and she said, very surprised: 'Do you mean good-bye, Walter?' and he walked off, and by and by she started crying and I took her home."

At that, Gregg paused and looked at Ericson, as if judging how he would receive what he was going to say next: he was near the end now, and he must, in spite of his earlier indifference, have felt it necessary to justify himself while he had the chance. Ericson was careful to keep his expression as non-committal as possible: even now, there was no verdict to be given, no comforting words to forestall the threat of discipline. This was still a private hearing, out of the main stream, with the normal course of events held in suspense.

Gregg seemed to gather himself together. "That was the Friday, sir," he said. "I'd been adrift ten days already, and this chap didn't leave till the next Thursday, six more days." He swallowed again. "I still couldn't go, sir, I still couldn't leave her, even now it wasn't safe: he might change his mind and come round to the house, and if he didn't, I knew she'd be off to meet him if she got half a chance. . . . So I thought I'd stay on, and keep her there with me: I was in the rattle anyway, whatever happened, and there was only one way to make sure she didn't see him. Even then it was touch and go. We went to the pictures once, and she got up to go to the Ladies', and after a bit I went out myself, and I just caught her as she was going out through the front entrance. After that, we stayed at home all the time. . . . She used to cry a lot: she was always on at me, wanting to go out—I was afraid to go to sleep, towards the end, and then I locked up all her clothes and hid the key where she couldn't find it." He passed his hand over his forehead. "But one night—it was the Wednesday, the night before this chap left—she waited till I was asleep and broke the cupboard open and got dressed, and then something woke me up, and she tried to run for it, and I got to the door first and she was screaming and pulling at me, I thought she'd go mad. . . . I stayed awake all that night, to make sure, and then in the morning she saw it was too late, and she kind of gave up and I knew it was all right to leave. . . . I wasn't going to talk to her at all about it, I wanted to forget it and start afresh; but when I was saying good-bye she said: 'Will you be in trouble?' and I said yes, I would, and she said: 'I'm in trouble too, Tom,' and then she said she was going to have a baby."

Ericson looked at the floor. There was only one question to be asked, and not for a million pounds could he have asked it. But then suddenly Gregg asked and answered it for him, in one swift brave stroke.

"The kid'll be mine, sir, and that's all there is to it."

"Love again," thought Ericson, with wonder in his heart: love the unfailing cure, no matter how hideous the deception, how vile the betrayal. . . . Now that the story was done, he wanted to dispose of it as quickly as possible: it was clear that Gregg could not be punished for something that had tried him too high, that he was simply not equipped to deal with, and there was a wise provision for mercy available in such cases. But in spite of his willingness to spare Gregg any further ordeal, there was one point to be made; and it must be driven home at once, if only in fairness to other men who, caught in the same circumstances, did not take the law into their own hands but stayed within the framework of discipline. He turned in his chair.

"Thank you for telling me this, Gregg—I shall think it over before your case comes up again tomorrow. At the moment there's only one thing I want to say, but it's something you ought to remember." He summoned an incisiveness he did not wholly feel. "Your officers aren't there just to run the ship and give orders—they're there to help you as well. In a case like this, if you'd come to me as soon as you got that letter I could have given you special leave, and then you wouldn't have had to break ship. And we could have arranged for someone to visit your wife, while you were away." He smiled—very briefly, for it was not a smiling moment: the miserable face opposite him was the only proper measure of its quality. "Just remember that the Royal Navy has a routine for *everything*, whether it's for going into battle, or for taking a shell out of a gun when it's jammed and may explode, or for helping in domestic trouble like yours. It's usually the only workable routine there is, the best available, because the Navy looks after its own." He saw that for some reason Gregg was near to tears again, and he broke off: the point had been made, and he could not bring himself to hammer it further home. "That's all for now. Ask the First Lieutenant to see me."

When Gregg had gone, Ericson sat for a long time in thought. On one point, thought was straightforward. Gregg's story would have to be checked—that could be done on the spot, in London, as a matter of routine—and if it were true, he could legitimately let him off altogether: even though Gregg had done wrong, even though women and marriage and emotion should not play a part in war. . . . But he knew that the story *was* true—and it was here that thought strayed uncontrollably: there had been no acting in that anguish, no lies behind the pitiful story. Some women were worthless, and some were getting bored with the war: when the two things coincided, no result, however mean or sordid, should ever come as a surprise.

[2]

Presently the turn of the year was left behind, and the lengthening days that marked the spring brought them onc respite at least—easier nights at sea. Morell's middle watch, indeed, was now the only one that passed in complete darkness; and soon, as spring gave way to early summer, even he was allowed a partial relief from the strain of hanging on to the convoy and guessing at black shadows for four hours on end. During the last half-hour of his watch, toward four o'clock in the morning, there would be a faint lifting of the darkness in the east: through his binoculars the horizon would lose its vagueness and take on a harder outline, and the ships that lay in his line of sight began to abandon their gloomy neutrality and grow into three-dimensional figures again. By the time Lockhart came up to relieve him, at the change of the watch, it was possible to distinguish in detail the upper-works of *Compass Rose* and the faces of the men up on the bridge: when they said good morning to each other, it was a matter of recognition and not guesswork. And then, within half an hour, it was the dawn, and the start of another day— a day further out into the Atlantic, or a day nearer home. Lockhart would survey the calm collection of ships, and per-haps drop back a mile or so to encourage the stragglers: the Captain would come up, grey and bristly from an uncomfortable night in his berth in the wheelhouse, and look about him and sniff the air, and then wander from side to side of the bridge, sextant in hand, ready to catch the last stars before they died with the sun; and finally, to mark the end of the night, Tomlinson the young steward sidled up and collected the sandwich plates and the derelict cocoa cups, the debris of the night's picnic.

That was the simple outline of dawn, as it came to *Compass Rose* on dozens and scores of mornings; but many dawns had more to them than this. Often, tragically, daybreak was the time for counting heads, for closing gaps in the ranks, for signalling to *Viperous* the total of survivors and the total of the dead. For now, with 1941 advancing, they were a year older, and so was the war; and the further it progressed the deeper they seemed to be involved in failure and setback.

The tide was now set and running strongly against all Allied shipping: over a full two thirds of the Atlantic the attackers had the initiative, and they held on to it and gave it ruthless force and effectiveness. It was like a dark stain spreading all over this huge sea: the area of safety diminished, the poisoned water, in which no ship could count on safety from hour to hour, seemed swiftly to infect a wider and wider circle. In the background, the big ships skirmished and occasionally came to blows: the *Hipper*, the *Scharnhorst*, and the *Gneisenau* emerged on raiding forays, the *Hood* was sunk by one prodigious shot at eleven miles' range, and then, in a swift counterstroke, the destruction of the *Bismarck* squared the account. But these were dramatic surprises, highlights of a ponderous and intermittent warfare: plying to and fro ceaselessly, the convoys fought their longer and bloodier battle against a multiplying enemy.

The enemy was planning as well as multiplying. At last, the U-boats were co-ordinating their attack: they now hunted in packs, six or seven in a group, quartering a huge area of the convoy route and summoning their full strength as soon as a contact was obtained. They had the use of French, Norwegian, and Baltic ports, fully equipped for shelter and maintenance: they had long-range aircraft to spot and iden-

tify for them, they had numbers, they had training, they had
better weapons, they had the spur of success. . . . The first
concerted pack-attack sank ten out of twenty-two ships in
one convoy: the monthly record of sinkings mounted—fifty-
three in one month, fifty-seven in another. The U-boats
gradually extended their operations further westward, until
there was no longer, in mid-Atlantic, a safe dispersal-area
for the convoys; neither from Britain, Canada, nor Iceland
(which had now been drawn fully into the strategic pattern)
could complete air cover be provided, and the escorts themselves were limited in their endurance. So the stain spread,
and the ships went down. There were countermeasures:
patrolling aircraft extended their range, a number of merchant ships were provided with fighters launched by catapult,
and the quality of the weapons in the escorts improved
slowly: to mark this improvement, one month in the middle
of 1941 saw seven U-boats sent to the bottom—the highest
total of the war. But seven U-boats was not enough: there
were still too many of them hunting and striking, and not
enough escorts to screen the convoys: there was still a vast
margin that could only be covered by luck and human endeavour, and neither of these could match the standard and
the pace of the enemy, or stop the slaughter.

Of this slaughter, *Compass Rose* saw her full share. It was
no longer a surprise when the alarm bell sounded, no longer
a shock to see the derelict humanity that was hoisted over the
side after a ship went down: it was no longer moving to
watch the dying and bury the dead. They developed—they
had to develop—a professional inhumanity toward their job,
a lack of feeling which was the best guarantee of efficiency:
time spent in contemplating this evil warfare was time
wasted, and rage or pity was something that could only come
between them and their work. Hardened to pain and destruction, taking it all for granted, they concentrated as best they
could on fighting back and on saving men for one purpose
only—so that they could be returned to the battle as soon as
possible.

. . .

Ferraby and Baker, the two juvenile leads, shared the first watch, from eight until midnight. Following the contemporary corvette fashion, they had both grown beards: in some curious way it made them look younger instead of older, and also rather unconvincing, like the naval personnel in a provincial revival of *H.M.S. Pinafore*. ("Nice drop of horticulture you've got there," a visitor to the wardroom had said, surveying the effect: the remark had earned, from Morell, the highest raised eyebrows of the war so far.) Baker, who had arrived on board a year previously as a shy young man with a vague background in accountancy, had shed none of his diffidence in the intervening period: he and Ferraby were alike in many ways—in their automatic acceptance of authority, no matter how flimsy its basis, in their lack of confidence, in their fear that sooner or later the test of war would reveal their shortcomings. . . . . When they talked together, it was on a level plane of protective humility, as men talk when, in an outer office, they are waiting to be interviewed for a job they do not think they will get: it is no good showing off to each other, because neither is worth impressing, and raised voices or a cocksure attitude may be overheard, and lead to their disqualification before they have even faced the boss. . . . But latterly, Ferraby had secured an appreciable lead: he was now a father, and when the two of them were together he exhibited the first stirrings of paternal consequence.

"Did you mind it being a girl?" asked Baker one night, when, as usually happened at sea, the conversation turned to the gentler background of home. "Or did you really want a boy?"

"It didn't seem to matter what it was, as long as *she* was all right," said Ferraby frankly. "You get so worried towards the end. . . . Of course she had her mother there, to look after her, but all the same I was glad when it was over." Even now, he could not think of that night, just before the end of his last leave, without acute discomfort: Mavis's cry as she woke suddenly, about midnight, the frantic telephoning, the ambulance that would not come, the agonized waiting past

dawn, past midday, past half another night. . . . To see
Mavis and the baby together, next morning, two heads on
the pillow instead of one, had made up for most of it; but it
could not wholly kill the force of memory. "It was a bit of
luck I was on leave when it started," Ferraby went on.
"Otherwise I don't know what I'd have done, thinking about
it happening while we were at sea."

"My turn for leave next," said Baker, reacting to the
cherished word. "Two more convoys, I should say—about
six weeks."

Six weeks. . . . That started, in Ferraby, a fresh train of
thought that he was not ready to share with Baker, or with
anyone else. Six weeks was a long time in the Atlantic, at
this stage, when the next six hours—or six minutes, for that
matter—might bring them disaster. There were so many
U-boats on the hunt: sooner or later, he was sure, one of
them was going to get *Compass Rose* in its sights. Ferraby was
never free of that fear, nowadays: it was as if, when Bennett
left, he had to exchange one tyranny for another, as if the
fear of Bennett would only give way to the fear of being
torpedoed. Of all of them on board, Ferraby was the least
hardened to what was going on: he could not forget the
nodding head of the dead man, that first time they had picked
up survivors, he could not forget the recurrent alarm, the
inevitable attack, the slim chance of survival. Even now, as
he talked to Baker or looked at the ship they were stationed
on, he was uncomfortable and nervous, preoccupied with
what the next few moments might bring: it was getting toward midnight, the end of their watch, and this was the time
when things so often happened—the bang, the flare from a
torpedoed ship, the explosion in the heart of the convoy. And
if they did not happen in this first watch, they could happen
in the next one, the middle—and that was worst of all.

At midnight, every night at sea, Ferraby was free to go
below, and turn in, and sleep undisturbed till breakfast
time: he had never found this possible save at the very beginning and the very end of a voyage, when they were in
safety and shelter. There was something in the very act of

157

lying down below the waterline that tortured his imagination: it seemed quite impossible that *Compass Rose* would not be torpedoed during these dark hours, and that the torpedo, when it struck, would not rip its way into the very cabin where he lay. . . . Night after night, when they were out in the deep of the Atlantic, these thoughts returned to him: he would lie there, while the ship rolled and groaned and the water sluiced past a few inches from his bunk, sweating and staring at the bulkhead and the rivets that bound the thin plating together. That plating was all that stood between him and the black water: he waited in terror for the iron clang, the explosion, the inrush of water, the certainty of being trapped and choked before he could make a move. One terrible night he *had* managed to get to sleep, even though there had been warnings of a submarine pack in their vicinity: after an hour of sweating nervousness he had dozed off, and then, between waking and sleeping, he had heard a monstrous explosion that seemed to come from within the ship itself, and as he leapt from his bunk the alarm bell clanged, followed by a rush of feet, and he had felt a surge of blinding panic as he raced for the ladder and the open sky.

Out on the upper deck, where at last he gasped the free air, the scene was like a scene from hell. One of the escorts had fired a snowflake rocket—a big flare that could illuminate a two-mile circle and was meant to lime-light any submarine that might be on the surface: its yellow brilliance now hung over the wild water, showing him the convoy straining against the storm, and *Sorrel* racing off to starboard, hunting and guessing, and then, quite close to them, a ship, badly listed, already on her way down. Even as he watched her, there was a sudden gush of flame from her funnel, and she seemed to fall apart: a filthy waft of burnt oil and paint and steam came toward them, the very smell of death, and she was gone, quenched by the sea. Ferraby leaned against a stanchion, physically sick: that ship might have been *Compass Rose*, and the men now trapped and drowned might have been their own crew, and the place where the torpedo had struck, his own cabin. For many nights after that, he could not bear to go below after he came off watch: he would wander about the upper deck, or curl up in a corner at the back of the bridge, or in the alleyway by the wheelhouse: wakeful till dawn, fingering his safety light and his blown-up life-jacket, waiting in taut apprehension for their turn to come. He had seen other men like this, rescued survivors who would not go below again even to snatch a meal, and he had wondered at their fear and their obsession. Now he wondered no more.

But this was something he could share with no one—and especially not with Mavis, who now must never know the extent of his terror and his danger. They had taken a small house outside Liverpool, and he saw her every time *Compass Rose* was in harbour: the recurrent meeting and separation and good-bye was sweet and harassing at the same time, not helping him at all. . . . More and more, the war was making demands on him beyond his capacity, presenting a bill that his bankrupt spirit could not meet.

[3]

Lockhart had come to rely on Ericson, and to admire him unstintingly in the process. He was everything a captain should be: the centre of calm on the bridge, whatever was happening, a fine seaman who could handle *Compass Rose* with absolute assurance, a tireless personality who took infinite pains over every part of his job, whether it was rounding up stragglers, or fixing their position at sea, or cherishing their paintwork when they came alongside the oiler. He seemed irreplaceable: it was therefore something of a shock when he was suddenly put out of action, and Lockhart had to take the ship himself for the last five days of a convoy. Ericson was thrown out of his bunk one night when *Compass Rose*, at her most captious, achieved a forty-five-degree roll, and he broke a rib: the slightest movement gave him intense pain, and it was out of the question for him to appear up on the bridge. Lockhart signalled the casualty to *Viperous*, and with a good deal of misgiving took over command for the rest of the trip.

He had of course no choice in the matter, though that did not make it any easier. But once the initial challenge was met, the preliminary awe overcome, he found that he was enjoying himself: he was playing a new role, and it seemed to be within his range. . . . Of course it was ludicrous, really: the idea of a free-lance journalist called Lockhart roaming the Atlantic in entire charge of a thousand-ton ship and a crew of eighty-eight men would have raised a laugh in any prewar Fleet Street bar. But this was no longer prewar, and the mould was different: he had had eighteen months of training for this moment, eighteen months of watching Ericson and imbibing, unconsciously, the function of command, and when the moment came it seemed not much more than an easy step upward, with an extra tension to mark the occasion and a certain humorous surprise to spice it. That was one of the best things about the Navy—in wartime at least: it taught you quickly, it taught you well, it taught you all the time: suddenly you woke up with a direct responsibility for a valuable ship and a section of a convoy and a lot of men, some of them your friends, and it seemed as if you were simply turning another page of a book you knew by heart already.

When Ericson, grumbling between the bouts of pain, took to his bunk, *Compass Rose* was nine hundred miles west of the Irish Channel, butting along as stern escort to a slow convoy that had already had its fill of headwinds and U-boat scares. But then the luck changed: the wind dropped, and they made their five-day approach to land without any further warnings and not a single genuine alarm. Lockhart reorganized the watches so as to leave himself free of any set hours: being new to the job, and not having Ericson's developed confidence, he stayed awake far longer than he need have done and spent an average of two thirds of every day up on the bridge. He had to be ready for surprises, and the safest way to do that was to be on the spot at all the likely times. . . . Now and again he went down to report to the Captain, who would repeat, on each occasion, the same insistent questions: was the convoy closed up, was *Compass Rose* in her proper station, were there any U-boat warnings, had Lockhart taken his sights carefully and worked out their position, what did the weather look like? The only question he never asked directly was: "Are you worried about what you're doing?" and Lockhart was grateful for the implied confidence. The nearest Ericson got to such a query was when he remarked, going off at a tangent:

"I don't suppose you thought this could ever happen, a couple of years ago."

Lockhart smiled. He was standing in the middle of the Captain's cabin, still muffled against the cold outside, his sea boots and duffle coat making an odd contrast with Ericson's elegant dressing-gown.

"A couple of years ago, sir," he answered, "my only command was a five-ton yawl, rather pretty, mucking about in the Solent."

"How big a crew?"

"*She* was rather pretty, too."

"Get back on the bridge," said Ericson, "before my temperature goes up."

Thank God for a good captain, thought Lockhart as he made his way up the ladder again: for a good *man*, too, a man to respect and to like, whatever the circumstances. During the last few months, their relationship had developed a great deal, on welcome lines of friendship: close to each other all the time, and liking the success of the arrangement, they had come to ration their formality, confining it to the necessary public occasions and leaving the rest on an easier plane. Lockhart still called the Captain "sir," in public or private, because that was the way he felt about it; but the two of them, trusting each other's competence and viewing the whole thing as an effective partnership, had come a long way since Lockhart first stepped into the Clydeside dock-office, a year and a half previously.

The easy voyage drew to its close, with no more disturbing incident than when an Iceland trawler, southbound, tried to cut at right angles through the convoy in semi-darkness, and had to be headed off from so daring a project. In the narrows between Scotland and the north of Ireland, the convoy split, some ships making for the Clyde, others southward to Cardiff and Barry Roads, and the main portion to Liverpool Bay. Going down the Irish Sea and closing the Liverpool coastline meant, for Lockhart, a sharpening of the tension, like the last part of a training course that concludes with a formidable test-paper. In these confined waters, much could happen if anything went wrong with their navigation or if they failed to stay alert: there was a treacherous coastline to be watched, and a great deal of shipping moving up and down it, as well as the usual sprinkling of offshore fishing boats, some with lights, some without, and all of them trailing nets of unknown length and complexity. Fishing boats, indeed, were a hazard of a special character. The Admiralty had for centuries been receiving claims from imaginative fishermen who, as soon as they saw a ship-of-war within five miles of them, immediately shook their fists at heaven and swore blind that their nets had been overrun and torn to ribbons. Their Lordships had even introduced a "Fishing Boat Log" as a countermeasure: whenever fishing boats were sighted at sea, their exact position was to be noted down and an estimate given of their distance away. It did not always do the trick, but at least it sorted the brazen claims from the merely frivolous.

Lockhart was on the bridge for the whole of the last night, checking their course, making sure of the various buoys and lights as they were sighted, leaving nothing to chance: he understood now how immensely tiring Ericson must have found it at the beginning of their commission, with untried, inexperienced officers as his sole help, and a ship whose performance and handling were, even for a professional seaman, largely a matter of guesswork. When dawn came round again, and found the convoy safely past the Isle of Man and heading east for Liverpool and home, Lockhart was conscious of an immense relief, and wearily thankful that, except for the business of docking *Compass Rose* (which he was still nervous about), the hardest part of the trip was over. The sun drying out the decks and the seagulls playing triumphantly round the bows seemed a reflection of this holiday mood. He had had nothing spectacular to cope with; but it had all been new, and if anything had gone wrong there could have been no more public demonstration of his shortcoming.

The holiday, however, had been declared too soon. He was just thinking of going below to shave and change, leaving the easy final watch to Baker, when he saw *Viperous* heading for the stern of the convoy, moving with the high speed, enormous wash, and unnecessary air of drama that were the things he most envied in destroyers. . . . She cut between the last two ships of the wing column, turned in a flurry of foam, and edged up alongside *Compass Rose*.

"Switch on the loud-hailer," said Lockhart quickly. He had no idea what was coming, but there was likely to be a conversation involved. From the destroyer's bridge he saw binoculars raised and turned his way: at a lower level, the two crews leaned over their respective rails, and, recognizing their friends here and there, exchanged the repartee appropriate to a homecoming.

From *Viperous* the loud-hailer boomed out suddenly, carrying a pleasant, deep voice with the crisp inflection of authority.

"How's your captain?" it asked.

Lockhart raised his microphone. "About the same," he answered. "It hurts a good deal—he's still turned in."

"Give him my best wishes. . . ." There was a short pause. "We're due for leave today, and I want to get in early to see about our pay. Do you think you can lead the convoy in? The Bar Light Vessel's about nine miles ahead."

"Yes," said Lockhart. It wasn't a moment for hesitation, though he had very little idea of what was required of him. "Yes, I can do that."

"The commodore's just signalled them to form single file," the voice went on. "Take station ahead of him as soon as they've done that. When you get up to Gladstone Dock, make the usual arrival signal—thirty-eight ships, convoy BK108. I'll explain about us."

"Yes, sir," said Lockhart, recalling the need for formality. *Viperous's* captain, the senior officer of the escort group, was a young commander with a forceful reputation.

For a moment longer the two ships kept level pace. "All right," came the voice from *Viperous*. "I'll leave you to it. But don't let them go too fast—the harbourmaster doesn't like it." Somewhere deep within the destroyer the engine-room telegraph clanged, and she suddenly jumped forward, throwing out a bow wave like the slicing of a huge cream cake. "We will now," said the disappearing voice, authoritative to the last, "give you our impersonation of a greyhound of the ocean." And *Viperous* drew swiftly away, leaving *Compass Rose* as if standing still, and Lockhart pondering the superiority of destroyers over all other ships. If only one could press a button like that aboard *Compass Rose*, and leave the fleet behind. . . .

But he had more to do than yearn for better things. The convoy was forming into single line, ready for the narrow passage up-river, and he had at least six miles to make up before he was in station at the head of the column. *Compass Rose* could not rival *Viperous's* swift get-away, but she did her best: the hull throbbed as the revolutions crept upwards, and presently they were passing ship after ship on their way to the front of the convoy. Lockhart noticed, without paying much attention to it, that the sun had gone in and that it had turned suddenly colder; but he was not prepared for what followed after. They were just drawing level with the fourth ship of the convoy, and he had sighted the Bar Light Vessel, marking the entrance to the river itself, about two miles ahead of them, when the Bar Light Vessel disappeared; and as he stared round him, unwilling to believe that visibility could have deteriorated so swiftly, the convoy disappeared also, sponged out like chalk from a slate. It was fog, fog coming down from the north, fog blowing across their path as thick as a blanket and blotting out everything on the instant.

Lockhart leaned over the front of the bridge, momentarily appalled. The fog enveloped them in great thick wafts of vapour, cold and acrid; he could see the tip of their gun-barrel, twenty feet in front of him, and nothing more at all— no sea, no ships, not even *Compass Rose's* own stem. It was like moving inside a colourless sack, isolated and sightless— and then suddenly he heard the other occupants of the sack, a wild chorus of sirens as the convoy plunged into the fog bank. It had taken them by surprise, when they had just crowded into a single compact line: many ships were less than their own length from the next one ahead of them, and the convoy was telescoping like a goods train when the brakes are applied. Now, unsighted, moving blindly in the raw and luminous air, they were doing the only thing left to them—making as much noise as possible, and praying for the fog to lift.

Lockhart's moment of panic did not last. *Compass Rose* had been in fog before, and he had admired Ericson's calmness and sure control of the situation: now he simply had to follow that example. There was a temptation to sheer away from the convoy, and take an independent line altogether, but that had to be resisted: in a fog, one had to trust other ships to hold their course, and do the same oneself, otherwise it was impossible to retain a clear picture of what was going on. One single ship, losing its nerve and trying to get out of trouble in a hurry, could destroy that picture, and with it the whole tenuous fabric of their safety, and bring about disaster.

At the moment all the ships were comfortably to starboard, and he set to work to plot, inside his head, the varying notes of their sirens. The nearest one, with the deep note, was a big tanker they had been passing when the fog came down: the ship ahead of her made a curious wheezing sound, as if some water had got into her siren. The commodore's ship, at the head of the column, had another distinguishable note; and above them all the authoritative voice of the foghorn on the Bar Light Vessel, two miles ahead, supplied as it were the forward edge of the pattern. Beyond that foghorn they could hardly go in safety, for there the channel narrowed to a bare fifty yards: if the fog did not lift, and the convoy had to anchor, it must be done within a time limit of not more than twenty minutes.

Lockhart had the picture in his head, for what it was worth: and beside him in the raw air of the bridge the others —Morell, Baker, Leading Signalman Wells, the two look-outs—tried to contribute their own quota of watchfulness and interpretation. For the sounds were deceptive—they all knew that well: it was possible that a siren which seemed to be coming clearly from one side was being reflected off the fog bank, and came in fact from some unknown area of danger. *Compass Rose* ran on, over the oily water, with the ghostly company beside her keeping a distance and a formation that could only be guessed at: the rest of the convoy seemed to recede, while the four sounds Lockhart was especially on the alert for—the big tanker, the ship ahead of her, the commodore, and the Bar Light Vessel—succeeded in even rotation, with *Compass Rose* as the fifth element in the pattern. As long as that pattern held, and the fog blew over or dispersed, they were safe.

Suddenly he raised his head, and was conscious of Wells jerking to attention at the same time. A new siren had sounded, an intruder in the pattern, and it seemed to be coming from their port bow—the side away from the convoy, the side that had been clear. "Ship to port, sir?" said Wells tentatively, and they waited in silence for the sound to come again. One—that was the tanker: two—the ship ahead of her: three—the commodore: four—a prolonged wail from the Bar Light Vessel. Then *five*—a wavering blast, nearer now, coming from that safe space to port that had suddenly assumed an imminent danger. Lockhart felt his scalp lifting and prickling as he heard it. It might be anything—a ship coming out, a stray from the convoy, an independent ship creeping along their own path: but it was *there*, somewhere in the fog, somewhere ahead of them and to port, steaming along on God-knows-what course and getting nearer with every second that passed.

He gripped the front of the bridge rail and stared ahead of him. He knew without turning round that the others were watching him: he was the focus now, *Compass Rose* was in his grip, and her safety and perhaps all their lives depended on what he did next. Their own siren sounded, tremendously near and loud, and then the safe four in succession, and then the damned fifth—nearer still, dead ahead or a little to port. He said: "Slow ahead!" surprised at the calmness of his voice: the telegraph clanged, the revolutions purred downward to a dull throbbing, the slop and thresh of their bow wave died to a gentle forward rustling. But the tension did not die: he felt himself taut and sweating as *Compass Rose* ran on, nearing the edge of the known pattern and nearing also that fifth ship, the doubtful element that could wreck them all. If the commodore did not give the signal for anchoring he *must* do something—either stop dead, or take a wide sheer to port, away from the crowd and the danger: they could not simply run on, swallowing up the safety margin, surrendering foot by foot their only security. He heard Morell by his side cough: the damp air mingled with the sticky sweat under his hair, so that drops ran down his forehead: their own siren boomed out suddenly, just above their heads: he had a quick vision of what might lie a few seconds ahead—the crash, the grinding of wood and metal, the wrecked bows, the cries of men trapped or hurt in the messdecks: he felt all the others watching him, trusting and yet not trusting, hoping that he could meet this inexorable crisis —and then suddenly the port look-out called out: "Ship to port, sir!" and forty yards away, in the fog that suddenly cleared and the sunshine that suddenly broke through, a small coaster slid past them and down the side of the convoy. He felt a great surge of relief as the last wisps of fog blew away, showing him the lines of ships still intact and the Bar Light Vessel riding clear on the smooth water. As suddenly as the danger had come, it had been taken away again. It was a full reprieve: he had done his best, and the best had been good enough, and now *Compass Rose* steamed on with the rest of them, toward the familiar landmarks of home.

An hour later they were in the thick of the Mersey traffic, leading the slow and stately progress up-river to the convoy anchorage. The long line of ships stretched behind them, deep-laden, travel-stained, proud and yet matter-of-fact: ships they had guarded for many days, ships they knew well by sight from this and earlier convoys, ships they had cursed for straggling or admired for skilful handling. It was another convoy—Lockhart had lost count by now, but perhaps it was their sixteenth, perhaps their twentieth: another great company of ships, safe home with hundreds of men and thousands of tons of supplies, after running the gauntlet of the weather and the worst that the enemy could do. Perhaps pride *was* the keynote, pride and a sober thankfulness: the supplies were needed, the men were precious, and their own *Compass Rose* was a well-loved hostage to fortune. . . . Wells said suddenly: "Commodore calling up, sir!" and there was silence on the bridge as he took and acknowledged the message from the big freighter that led the convoy. Then Wells turned from his signal-lamp.

"From the commodore, sir. 'Nice to see those Liver birds again. Thanks and good-bye.' "

Lockhart looked up river, toward the great gilded birds that topped the Liver Building in the heart of Liverpool. He shared the commodore's sentiment, down to the last tip of their wings. . . .

"Make: 'They look bigger and better every time. Good-bye to you,' " he dictated to Wells. He waited while the message was dispatched and then, with a curious sense of disappointment, he gave the helm-order that took *Compass Rose* in a wide sheer away from the convoy and toward their own berth at the oiler. The job was done, the release was official, but to part company now was like surrendering a foster child one had learned to love. . . . Earlier, he had been worried about manœuvring *Compass Rose* up to the oiler, but now he took her alongside with a careless skill, as if he had done it every day for the past year. After the weight of the last few days, after the ordeal of the fog, there seemed nothing that he could not do. When finally he gave the order: "Finished with main engines," and went down to report to Ericson, he felt at least ten years older, and triumphant in his maturity.

[4]

There was the life at sea, crude, self-contained, sometimes startling: there was the tender life of home, when leave came round; and there was the medium world of life in harbour, when they rested from one convoy and prepared for the next one. Of the three, harbour routine gave them perhaps the most vivid sense of being one unit of a complex weapon engaged in a huge and mortal battle.

Gladstone Dock, where nearly all the Western Approaches escorts roosted, had in two years developed into a vast, concentrated hive of naval activity. Strategically, the Battle of the Atlantic was controlled from the underground headquarters in Liver Buildings: down in Gladstone Dock, and in other smaller docks grouped along the waterfront, the ships that fought the battle, the crude pawns that did the work, lay in tiers, three and four abreast along the quayside, salty, shabby, overworked, overdriven; fresh and wet from the encounter, resting thankfully, or waiting for the next tide to take them out again. . . . They looked workmanlike, without much elegance, but tough and dependable: they were close packed, stem to stern, their masts reaching for the sky, their level fo'c's'les towering over the jetty—the jetty that was itself crowded with sheds and training huts and an untidy jumble of gear and spare parts and oil drums and newly delivered stores. But it was the ships that drew and focused the eye: the lean grey destroyers, the stocky sloops and corvettes, the trawlers that swept the fairway—this was the whole interlocking team that had the battle in its hands. Here in Gladstone Dock was the hard shell for the convoys, the armour of the Atlantic: it did not shine, it was dented here and there, it was unquestionably spread thin and strained to the limit of endurance; but it had stood the test of two brutal years, and it would hold as long as the war held, and for five minutes longer.

The men who manned these ships were cast in the same mould. For sailors, the Battle of the Atlantic was becoming a private war: if you were in it, you knew all about it—you knew how to watchkeep on filthy nights, how to surmount an aching tiredness, how to pick up survivors, how to sink submarines, how to bury the dead, and how to die without wasting anyone's time. You knew, though not in such detail as your own particular part of the job, the over-all plan of the battle, and the way it was shaping. You knew, for example, that at this moment the score was running steadily against the convoys; you knew by heart the monthly totals of sinkings, the record and the quality of other ships in other escort groups, the names of U-boat commanders who had especially distinguished themselves by their skill or ruthlessness. The whole battle was now a very personal matter, and for sailors involved in it there was a pride and a comradeship that nothing could supplant. For they were the experts, they were fighting it together, they had learnt what it took from a man, and the mortal fury that, increasing from month to month, tested whomever was sucked in, from the highest to the lowest, down to the fine limits of his endurance.

This was especially true of the men who sailed in corvettes, the smallest ships loose in the wild Atlantic at this desperate stage: when they foregathered in harbour after the tough convoy, the triumphant attack, the miserable loss and slaughter, they were very conscious of their calling. . . . They read about themselves in the newspapers, they quoted the ludicrous headlines that lagged so far behind the truth; but deep within himself each man knew that the public reputation, the corvette label, was a reflection of something that, when isolated at sea, always confronted him with a mixture of triumph and horror, that was a stark and continuous chal-

lenge, that really did take a man to survive. . . . When a
sailor said: "I'm in corvettes," he might be alert for the
answering: "That must be tough—I believe they roll their
guts out": but whatever the answer, whatever the scale of
sympathy or incomprehension, the truth kept him company,
and in his private mind he could be proud of it.

Alongside each other, in harbour, one wardroom visited
another: a taste of someone else's gin and a new angle to
flotilla gossip enlivened the set routine and the waiting for
action. But there was little to distinguish between the men
themselves: whatever the ship, they were the same kind of
people—amateurs who had graduated to a professional skill
and toughness. When Ericson looked round his own wardroom, he saw in theory a journalist, a barrister, a bank clerk,
and a junior accountant; but these labels now were meaningless—they were simply his officers, the young men who ran
his ship and who had adapted themselves to this new life so
completely that they had shed everything of their past save
the accent it had given them. It was the same in other ships:
all the corvettes were officered on these lines: the new experimental craft had taken their men to school with them,
and had developed swiftly and evenly into units remarkable
for their dependability, and essential to the struggle. It was
no wonder that, when they met and relaxed between convoys,
these young men all exhibited, like a brand-name, the dis-
dainful confidence of the elect. To sail in corvettes was a
special kind of test and a special distinction, and none could
know it better than themselves.

It coloured—it was bound to colour—their feelings for
other men who were not in the battle. During her time in
harbour, *Compass Rose* had many contacts with the shore
staff, who supervised the continuous program of gunnery
and asdic training that filled most of the working days between convoys; and there were many visitors on board—
experts of all kinds to check their equipment, signalling and
engineering staff, liaison characters, religious performers:
men with excellent reasons for coming aboard, and men with
none at all save a militant thirst and the chance of slaking it

at any one of a dozen floating bars. . . . There was indeed a very wide range of callers, and it was fair to say that most of them were welcome, since most of them were hard-working, helpful, genuine, and wistfully honest when they proclaimed their longing to go to sea instead of sitting out the war in an office job ashore. But there were others, nibbling and sipping at the outside of the real core; professional callers, who could be counted on to come aboard at eleven in the morning with some transparent excuse, anchor themselves in the wardroom with a glass in one hand and the bottle convenient to the other, and stay there with so established an air that the final choice lay between closing the bar or asking them to lunch. . . . Some of them acted a part, and the talk would run on their eagerness to go to sea, if only they could shake off this infernal catarrh; others did not even bother to do this, and exhibited only the complacency that went naturally with a soft job, plenty of spare time, and a prescriptive right to scrounge free drinks for several hours a day. When one was recovering from two or three weeks of vile weather at sea, with perhaps a rough convoy thrown in, and the memory of men gasping out their lives in the very wardroom where one sat, it was particularly hard to be civil to a man who seemed to regard the whole thing as an agreeable joke, and his own soft role in it as the reward of a natural talent.

For the most part their reaction, even among themselves, was silence, a tacit contempt that could hardly find expression without acknowledging what they thought of their own job. But sometimes this contempt overflowed. There was one occasion aboard *Compass Rose* when, lunch having been delayed for a full hour by a determined stayer who would not take even the broadest hint that the morning gin-session was over, they sat down at the lunch table in a state of frustrated impatience. Ericson was ashore, and Lockhart, sitting at the head of the table and helping himself to nearly congealed steak-and-kidney pie, voiced the general feeling when he said:

"That man really is the limit. He comes aboard every single day we're in harbour, and I don't suppose he does a stroke of work while he's here." He looked at Morell. "What did he do for us this morning?"

"He had eight gins," answered Morell evenly. "Apart from that, he said our gun was very nice and clean."

"Flotilla Gunnery Officer!" exclaimed Lockhart savagely. "I'd like to take that gun and—"

"Quite so," said Morell. "But I claim the right to pull the trigger."

Ferraby, picking at his food at the bottom of the table, broke in. "Don't you remember him at *King Alfred*?" he asked Lockhart. "He was there the same time as us. He said he was going into Coastal Forces."

Lockhart nodded. "I remember his face vaguely."

"You've had plenty of time to refresh your memory," said Morell.

"What makes me specially angry," went on Lockhart, "is his general attitude—the way he looks at the war. He comes aboard here, drinks our gin, doesn't pretend to be the slightest use to us, and then talks about the war and the Navy as if they were both some kind of racket, specially invented to give him a soft job."

"That's probably exactly what the war has meant for him," said Morell. "There are hundreds of people like that, you know: they don't see the point of it, they don't *want* to see the point of it—they get themselves a nice easy job, with a bit of extra pay attached, and the longer the war goes on the happier they are. They're not fighting, or helping to fight, because they don't see the thing as a fight at all. It's simply a little cosmic accident which has given them a smart uniform and the chance to scrounge cigarettes at duty-free prices."

"But how many people do see it as a fight?" Baker did not often join in wardroom discussions, but this time he seemed to have nerved himself to take part. He looked round the table, rather hesitantly. "We all feel pretty close to it here, I suppose, but even so—" he floundered for a moment, "even when we're at sea, it's difficult to feel that we're there because we've got to win the war and beat the Germans. Most of the time it's not like being in a war at all—it's just doing a job because everyone else is doing it, and if it was the French instead of the Germans we'd do it just the same, without asking any questions."

"I know what you mean," said Lockhart after a pause. "Sometimes it *is* like being caught in a machine, a machine which someone else is working and controlling." He hesitated. The true answer was of course that one should have taken sufficient interest in politics before the war to understand what the war was about, and to feel a personal and overwhelming desire to win it; but for someone like Baker, barely out of his teens and with the narrowest of interests, the criticism would have been harsh. His trouble was not lack of interest, but immaturity. "But all the same," he went on, "we *are* in it, and we *are* fighting; and even if we don't consciously give it a melodramatic label like 'fighting for democracy' or 'putting an end to fascist tyranny,' that's precisely what we're doing and that's the whole meaning of it."

Morell looked at him curiously. "You really feel that, don't you?"

"Yes." Then, conscious that the others were looking at him with an equal curiosity, Lockhart relaxed, and smiled. "Yes, I'm a very patriotic character. It's the only thing that keeps me going."

There was a knock at the wardroom door, and the quartermaster came in.

"Gunnery Officer, sir," he said formally.

"Yes?" said Morell.

"The officer who went ashore a while ago just came back, sir."

"Oh God!" said Lockhart involuntarily.

"He asked me to give you this, sir." The quartermaster held out an envelope. "Said he forgot about it."

"Thank you," said Morell. He took the envelope, and slit it open with a knife. An imposing-looking sheet of foolscap fell out. Morell glanced at it, and his face assumed a ludicrously startled air. "Good heavens!" he muttered. "It's not possible."

"What is it?" asked Lockhart.

"An amendment to the new Flotilla Gunnery Orders that came out yesterday," answered Morell. "Our friend has justified his existence at last."

"Anything important?"

"Oh yes. In fact it's fundamental. . . ." Some element of control in his voice made them all look up. "I will read it to you. 'Flotilla Gunnery Orders,' " he read out, his inflection infinitely smooth. " 'Amendment Number One. Page two, line six. For 'shit' read 'shot.' "

Among the many ships they encountered regularly at Liverpool were some manned by men of the Allied navies, men who had either escaped in the ships themselves and made their way to Britain, or had been recruited on their arrival and drafted to a British ship that had been turned over to them. There were, among others, several Dutch minesweepers, a Norwegian corvette, and a French submarine-chaser of so dramatic a design that it was difficult to tell, at a first glance, whether she was sinking or not. Such ships, and such men, set a curious problem: the problem of whether to take them seriously, and count on them as honest and effective allies, or to discount them altogether and treat them as an unexpected piece of decoration, acceptable as long as they did not get in the way of more serious preoccupations but hardly to be rated as ships of war and men of action.

The trouble was that they varied: sometimes they were convincing, sometimes not. The "foreign" ships were of course essentially self-contained: isolated in a strange country and cut off from their own defeated peoples, their officers and men had a wary reserve in dealing with strangers that was difficult to break down. One wanted to understand them, to make allowances, to sympathize with their position; but there were so many other things to think about that the curious, the almost tender complication of appreciating an exile's feelings was too much trouble altogether, unless one were in an exceptionally sympathetic mood. . . . Sometimes it did seem worth while, when they could be persuaded to talk freely; for many of them had exciting stories to tell of how they came to be fighting for the Allies, stories so very much more significant than simply signing on the dotted line and stepping into an R.N.V.R. uniform: stories of drama and intrigue when their countries were on the verge of defeat, of escape seen as the only salve for honour, of taking desperate decisions under cover of a passive acceptance, of fighting and eluding, of breathing suddenly the free air of England. . . . They all shared this basic excitement, in many and varied forms, and they shared also a sadness, a looking backward toward what they had left behind; but even in sadness they varied, even here there were degrees of plausibility.

The Dutch and the Norwegians seemed essentially serious and dependable: they too had this backward glance—many of them had heard nothing of their friends and families since their countries had been cruelly overrun in 1940—but they matched it by a forward look as well, a positive effort to regain and re-establish what they had lost, a fighting back toward home and peace with honour. Their ships always made a remarkable impression, because the men themselves seemed to have remarkable qualities; by cutting themselves off from their homes they had cleared the ground for a single-minded effort, and this effort, involving the seamanlike virtues of cleanliness, patience, and courage, was reflected in all they did and most of what they said. By chance, it was Ericson who summed up this feeling, after spending an evening in one of the Dutch minesweepers in Gladstone Dock.

"I like those Dutchmen," he said to Lockhart next morning, when they were walking round the upper deck during Stand-Easy. "They take the whole thing seriously—everything's related to the war, or if it isn't they don't want to hear about it. Even when I said it was a pity Princess Juliana had had three daughters in a row, instead of a son, their captain got terribly red in the face and said: 'If you think we don't fight for daughters, I smash you. Come outside.' Of course," added Ericson reasonably, "we'd had a few glasses of schnapps—but he was quite determined about it. . . . That's the kind of man I like to have minesweeping in front of a convoy: not these bloody Frogs, all yearning for home and missing the corners."

For the Frenchmen were different: that was something which could not be denied. It happened that Lockhart went aboard the French ship on a good many occasions, to take advantage of the food (which was exquisite) and the chance of talking French; and he could not help being aware of a dubious quality, a fugitive relaxation that seemed to infect the whole ship. It was not that their basic allegiance was in question, but that they had been defeated by events and were not wholly convinced that France could now be rescued from her degrading situation. They talked of General de Gaulle with respect, but they seemed always to leave a margin for events to deteriorate: if de Gaulle failed, they were going to shrug it off—*faut pas penser, faut accepter*—and put their money on a different horse, even the one labelled Laval and running in the colours of collaboration. . . . They were no longer proud, as the Dutch and the Norwegians were proud: they talked much more of their homes and their families, much less of the job they were doing: they longed openly for home, home on any terms, home by surrender if it could not be regained by victory: at times it seemed that their mainspring was not *la patrie* but *l'amour*—a four-letter urge that, by an odd coincidence, seemed to render them impotent. . . . It was a pity; Lockhart, who had lived in Paris and admired all things French, found it profoundly sad; but it was a manifestation of the Gallic spirit in adversity which could not be disguised.

In the course of an argument the captain of the French ship, somewhat less than sober, said to Lockhart one night: "You don't really trust us, do you?" He used the tone of voice, the bitter inflection, that seemed to add: "We do not mind, because you are a barbarous nation anyway." But the stain was there, and was thus acknowledged; and the charge of Anglo-Saxon insensibility could not wipe it out, nor pretend that it was the product of a simple misunderstanding.

There were, as yet, no Americans officially upon the scene: their two years' neutrality had not yet been ended by the galvanic shot-in-the-arm of Pearl Harbor. But here and there they were to be met: flyers relaxing at Liverpool between trans-ocean trips, and sailors in the anonymous middle reaches of the Atlantic. For they were now escorting some of the convoys, from American ports to a point where they could be taken over by the British escort: strange-looking destroyers, with long names often beginning with "Jacob" or "Ephraim," would appear from the mist, and spell out Morse messages very slowly and gently, for the dull British to assimilate as best they could. "They must think we're a lot of kids," said Leading Signalman Wells disgustedly one day, when an exceptionally prudent American operator had tried his patience to the limit. "It's like Lesson Number One back in barracks. And what a bloody ignorant way to spell 'harbour'. . . ." But the main reaction was a pleasant sense of comradeship: it was good to have some more ships lending a hand, at this time of strain, and the fact that the trans-Atlantic link was being completed in this natural way, Americans handing over to British, gave the latter a grateful and brotherly satisfaction. The Americans were still out of the war; but between lend-lease, and this unobtrusive naval effort, they were certainly doing their best round the edges.

Others were not. There are degrees of neutrality, just as there are degrees of unfaithfulness: one may forgive a woman an occasional cold spell, but not her continued and smiling repose in other men's arms. Even in the grossest betrayal, however, whether of the marriage vow or the contract of humanity, there could be variations of guilt: for example, one could understand, though one could not condone, the point of view of such countries as Spain or the Argentine, which had political affinities with Germany and did not disguise their hatred of England and their hopes of her defeat. They had never been married to democracy in the first place. . . . But it was difficult to withhold one's contempt from a country such as Ireland, whose battle this was and whose chances of freedom and independence in the event of a German victory were nil. The fact that Ireland was standing aside from the conflict at this moment posed, from the naval angle, special problems that affected, sometimes mortally, all sailors engaged in the Atlantic, and earned their particular loathing.

Irish neutrality, on which she placed a generous interpretation, permitted the Germans to maintain in Dublin an espionage-centre, a window into Britain, which operated throughout the war and did incalculable harm to the Allied cause. But from the naval point of view there was an even more deadly factor: this was the loss of the naval bases in southern and western Ireland, which had been available to the Royal Navy during the First World War but were now forbidden them. To compute how many men and how many ships this denial was costing, month after month, was hardly possible; but the total was substantial and tragic. From these bases escorts could have sailed farther out into the Atlantic, and provided additional cover for the hard-pressed convoys: from these bases, destroyers and corvettes could have been refuelled quickly, and tugs sent out to ships in distress: from these bases, the Battle of the Atlantic might have been fought on something like equal terms. As it was, the bases were denied: escorts had to go "the long way round" to get to the battlefield, and return to harbour at least two days earlier than would have been necessary: the cost, in men and ships, added months to the struggle, and ran up a score that Irish eyes a-smiling on the day of Allied Victory was not going to cancel.

From a narrow legal angle, Ireland was within her rights: she had opted for neutrality, and the rest of the story flowed from this decision. She was in fact at liberty to stand aside from the struggle, whatever harm this did to the Allied cause. But sailors, watching the ships go down and counting the number of their friends who might have been alive in-

stead of dead, saw the thing in simpler terms. They saw
Ireland safe under the British umbrella, fed by her convoys
and protected by her air force, her very neutrality guaranteed
by the British armed forces: they saw no return for this protection save a condoned sabotage of the Allied war effort;
and they were angry—permanently angry. As they sailed
past this smug coastline, past people who did not give a
damn how the war went as long as they could live on in their
fairy-tale world, they had time to ponder a new aspect of
indecency. In the list of people you were prepared to like
when the war was over, the man who stood by and watched
while you were getting your throat cut could not figure very
high.

Liverpool was a sailors' town, and she went out of her
way to make this generously plain. From the merchant ships
lining the quays and docks, from the escorts cramming Gladstone Dock, hundreds of men poured ashore every night, intent on enjoying their short hours of liberty: they got drunk,
made disturbances, thronged the streets and the public-
houses, monopolized the prostitutes, seduced the young girls,
and accommodated the married women—and Liverpool forgave them all, and still offered her hospitality unstintingly.
It was difficult to estimate the contribution to morale that
Liverpool made, during this wartime invasion; but the happy
background, the sure welcome, which continued for year
after year, was a memorable help to sailors, giving them
something to look forward to after weeks at sea, something
that could take the sting out of loneliness as well as exhaustion.

Compass Rose, of course, came in for her share of this
generosity; after being based there for eighteen months, most
people on board had contacts ashore, and could be sure of the
home cooking and the blessed normality of family life, which
was itself the best tonic of all. Some of *Compass Rose's* crew
had married Liverpool girls, or had brought their wives up
to live there: the ship now seemed to belong to Liverpool,

and as long as their luck held and she was not transferred to the Clyde or Londonderry, the two other big Western Approaches bases, they were very happy in the situation—the best compromise between war and peace which was possible.

Ericson also was glad of this permanent tie with the shore, which made for a contented crew and less likelihood of serious leave-breaking; he was even reconciled, on his own account, to the consolidation of his domestic life, with Grace as the placid background and the little house in Birkenhead as his resting place between convoys. He did not concentrate any the less on *Compass Rose;* and the fact that Grace's mother was now living with them, and was installed in a permanent position on the left side of the fireplace, meant that he need not feel guilty about sleeping on board if the need arose. The other Birkenhead resident, Tallow (now a Chief Petty Officer), was growing positively sleek on his sister Gladys's cooking; and he was deriving a certain amount of amusement from the situation between Gladys and Chief E.R.A. Watts, who had been a persistent and welcome visitor ever since *Compass Rose* was first stationed at Liverpool. Watts was a widower with grown-up children, Gladys was a widow comfortably past the age of romantic ardour; it was a quiet affair, a placid understanding that, come the end of the war, they would settle down together and, between his pension and her modest savings, make a go of it. . . . When Watts had first broached the subject to Tallow, it was in such a roundabout way that the latter could hardly grasp what he was driving at: but when Watts finally muttered something about "getting fixed up after the war," light broke through.

"Why, that's fine, Jim!" exclaimed Tallow. The two men were alone in the petty-officers' mess, and on an impulse, Tallow leaned forward and held out his hand. They shook hands awkwardly, not looking at each other, but there was warmth in Tallow's voice as he went on: "Best thing that could happen for her. And for you, too. You've asked her, eh?"

"Sort of. . . ." Watts was still embarrassed by the display of feeling. "We've got a—an understanding, like. The only thing is—" he paused.

"What's the trouble?"

"She was a bit worried about you. I mean, she's been housekeeping for you for a long time, hasn't she? She didn't want you to be disappointed."

"Oh, forget about it!" Tallow smiled. "Might get married myself one of these days—you never know. You go ahead, Jim, and I'll give the bride away, any time you like."

"Can't see it happening soon," answered Watts. "Not with the war going the way it is. Longest bloody job I ever saw."

"You're right about that. . . . Don't worry over me, anyway: just name the day, and I'll dance at your wedding."

But that was not to be. For Liverpool, the sailors' town, was soon to pay for that label in the most brutal way imaginable; and a tiny part of that payment bore away with it Watts's modest hopes of happiness.

[5]

Even far down-river, at the Crosby Light Vessel, they knew that something was wrong; and as they made their way upstream at the tail of the convoy many of the crew clustered on the upper deck, shading their eyes against the strong May sunlight and looking toward the city they had come to know as home. Morell, who was standing on the fo'c's'le with the men getting out the mooring wires, trained his glasses up the river towards the Liver buildings: there seemed to be a lot of smoke about, and here and there a jagged edge to the skyline which he had never noticed before. . . . At his side he suddenly heard Leading Seaman Phillips exclaim: "Christ! It's copped a packet!" and then he smelt—they all smelt— the acrid tang of the smoke blowing down-river, and his eyes, focusing suddenly on a big warehouse just above Gladstone Dock, discovered that it was split from top to bottom, that one half of it was a gigantic heap of rubble, that the rest was blackened and smouldering. His binoculars, traversing steadily across the city and over to the Birkenhead side, showed him many such buildings, and scores of small houses lying ruined in the centre of a great scorched circle: there were fires still burning, there was a heavy pall of smoke lying over the northern part of the city, there were gaps, whole streets missing, rows of houses misshapen and torn. He dropped his glasses, shocked by the scale of the destruction, the naked ruin of a city that they had left prosperous and unharmed; and then he caught the eye of one of his fo'c's'le party, a young seaman whose wife, he knew, had recently come to live in Liverpool.

"What—what's it like, sir?" asked the man hesitantly.

"Not too good, I'm afraid," answered Morell. "It looks as if they've been raided several times."

"Bastards!" said Phillips, to no one in particular. "Look at those houses. . . ."

The smoke and the dirty air, the smell of destruction, blew thick and strong across the river toward them; and such was their homecoming.

From the signal station they were ordered to go straight into Gladstone Dock. "I hope they didn't get the oiler," said Ericson, as Wells read out the message to him. "She'd go up like a Roman candle. . . ." He had been looking through his glasses at the Birkenhead side of the river, where his own house was: the damage there was on a special scale of fury, as if the bombers, trying for the docks, had mistaken the neat rows of houses for the near-by quayside, and had triumphantly unloaded. Or perhaps they had not minded what they hit. . . . *Compass Rose* veered suddenly across the river, and Ericson called out, in sharp tones: "Watch her head, coxswain!" and up the voice-pipe came Tallow's answering voice: "Sorry, sir!" and Ericson remembered that he was not the only one who had a personal interest in what had happened at Birkenhead. Thankfully he decreased speed, and set a course for the squat stone entrance to Gladstone Dock. At least they would know soon, at least they had not to wait for the uncertain mail or the chance flight of rumour, to learn the worst.

As they came alongside the southern quay of the dock-basin, a berthing party of half a dozen men from the nearest destroyer ran along to meet them and to take their mooring wires. The first heaving-line whipped across from ship to shore, establishing contact once more after a fortnight at sea, and Leading Seaman Phillips, standing high on the fo'c's'le head, called out:

"What's been going on?"

One of the berthing party, a tough three-badge able seaman, looked up and grimaced. "You've missed something, mate!" he shouted back. "Eight nights on end—that's all we've had: bombers coming over every night as thick as bloody sparrows. They've made a right mess of this town, I can tell you."

"Go on," said Phillips. "What's got it worst?"

The A.B. gestured vaguely. "All over, I reckon—Bootle, Birkenhead, Wallasey. And down in the town too: there isn't any Lord Street left—they got the lot, both sides. Worst bombing of the war, the papers said. I don't want any worse myself. . . . There was an ammunition ship just alongside here, blazing all over, but they towed her out into the middle of the river before she went up." He gestured again, more vividly. "Best dose of salts I've ever had. . . . Give us your head-rope."

From the bridge above them a remarkably cold voice said: "Stop talking and get on with those wires." Phillips winked at the man standing on the quay below him, and got an answering jerk of the head. They both knew, to within very fine limits, just how long such a conversation could go on.

Presently, when they were secure and Ericson, up on the bridge, had rung off the engines, he turned to Lockhart.

"Number One."

"Sir?"

"There'll be a lot of requests for special leave, probably.

You'd better cancel ordinary leave, and give it to ratings who have homes or relatives ashore."

"Aye, aye, sir."

"See that these wires are squared off. I'm going ashore to telephone."

There were a lot of other candidates for the telephone: a small procession of men, anxious to establish contact, queueing up outside the single dockside call-box, waiting patiently, not talking to each other. Ericson got through, and spoke for a moment to his wife: she sounded subdued, but at least she was there. . . . Ferraby, whose small house was on the outskirts of the city, had the same comforting luck: but Tallow, when it came to his turn, could not get his number at all, simply the high continuous note that meant "line out of order." When he was back on board, and making a hurried toilet in the petty officers' mess before going ashore again, Watts said tentatively:

"I'd like to come with you, Bob."

Tallow, who was shaving, nodded his head. "Yes, Jim. You come along."

"They might just have damaged the telephone wires," said Watts after a pause.

Tallow nodded again. "It might be that."

But the nearer they got to the house, after crossing the river by ferryboat, the more they knew that it was *not* that. From the landing stage they walked up hill toward Dock Road, slowly because of the blocked roads and the rubble and glass and smashed woodwork that was strewn over the streets; the trail of wrecked houses and the smell of newly extinguished fires was a terrible accompaniment to their journey. They did not talk to each other, because the cruel destruction was saying it all for them: there was no need to speculate on what they were going to find, when the odds mounted with every pace they took, with every shop and little house that had been blasted to ruins. Presently, walking in step side by side, smart and seamanlike in their square-cut uniforms, they turned the last corner, or the place where the last corner should have been, and looked down Dock Road.

185

There wasn't a great deal left of Dock Road: the two corner houses just beside them had gone, and three more further down, and then there was a great hole in the centre of the roadway, and then, further down still, a ragged heap of rubble where another house had sprawled into the street. It must have been a stick of bombs, as neatly placed as the buttonholes in a dress. . . . Tallow looked at the furthest point of destruction, sick and hurt: he said, somewhere between surprise and fatalist calm: "That's the one, Jim, I know it is," and he started foolishly to run. Watts, possessed by the same urgency, kept pace with him, and they went at a steady jog-trot down the street: past the first lot of wrecked houses, past the second, past the crater in the roadway, and up to the last shattered corner. Number 27 was half ruined by blast: so was Number 31. Number 29 had taken the full force of a direct hit.

Number 29, Dock Road. . . . Under the bright afternoon sunshine the wreck of the little house seemed mean and tawdry: there was flayed wallpaper flapping in the wind, and half a staircase set at a drunken angle, and a kitchen sink rising like some crude domestic altar from a heap of brickwork. The house had collapsed upon itself, and then overflowed into the garden and the roadway: the broken glass and the rubble slurred under their feet as they came to a halt before it. It was not a house any more, this place where, between voyages, Tallow had been so comfortable and content, and Watts had stumbled out a halting proposal of marriage, and Gladys had made a warm cheerful haven for them all; it was simply a shapeless mass slopping over from its own foundation, a heap of dirt and rubbish over which drifted, like a final curse, the smell of burnt-out fire. Some men—a rescue squad in dusty blue overalls—were picking over the ruins like scavengers who did not know what they were seeking.

After a moment of hesitation Tallow accosted the nearest of them, a big man in a white steel helmet.

"How did it happen?" he asked.

Scarcely looking at him, the rescue man said: "Don't ask bloody silly questions. I'm busy."

"It's my house," said Tallow, without expression.

"Oh. . . . " The rescue man straightened up. "Sorry, mate. . . . We get more bloody fools hanging round these jobs than I ever saw in my life." He looked at Tallow with rough compassion. "Direct hit, this one. Middle of the raids —about five days ago. You been away?"

"Yes. Just got back."

By his side, Watts said: "We didn't know about this."

There was a silence, while the dust stirred and settled. With an effort, Tallow put his question.

"How about the people inside, then?"

The rescue man looked away from him, and across the street. "You'd better ask at the warden's post, down there." He pointed. "They see to all that."

"But what about them?" said Tallow roughly. "Do you know or don't you?"

This time the rescue man looked directly at him, searching for words as he stared. "You can't expect much, mate, not after this. We got them out. Two women. Don't know their names. Ask over there, at the warden's post. They'll tell you all about it."

"Were they dead?" asked Tallow.

A moment of hesitation; then: "Yes, they were dead."

On their way across the street towards the warden's post, Tallow said: "It was probably Mrs. Crossley. She used to sit with Gladys in the evening."

Inside the warden's post, a brick shelter on the street corner, three men were sitting at a table playing cards. Two were young, and one was an oldish man with grey hair. As Tallow and Watts entered, stooping under the low doorway, one of the young men glanced up and called out in mock alarm:

"Look out, lads—the Navy's here!"

The oldish man put down his cards and said: "Just in time for a cup of tea. Always glad to see the Navy."

"Name of Tallow," said Tallow briefly. "Number 29, Dock Road." He jerked his head back. "You know—the one across the street. What happened?"

There was a long shocked silence, while the three men stared at Tallow, the smiles fading from their faces, the cheerful welcome evaporating into shame. Then the old man stuttered and spoke:

"Mr. Tallow—yes. That was your house, wasn't it? I'm very sorry, very sorry indeed." He fumbled with some papers on the rough deal table, concealing his raw embarrassment. "Mr. Tallow. . . . I reported it to the Town Hall, of course. Two casualties—yes, I've got it down here. Mrs. Bell, Mrs. Crossley. . . . Didn't they notify you?"

"We've only just got in. Been at sea for a fortnight. When did it happen?"

"May the fifth. That's five days ago, isn't it?" He read the names again. "Mrs. Bell, Mrs. Crossley. Would they be relatives of yours?"

Tallow swallowed. "Mrs. Bell was my sister. Mrs. Crossley was a friend."

The old man shook his head. "I'm very sorry to hear it. If there's any help we can give—"

"What did they do with—"

One of the young men, the one who had greeted them so cheerfully, stood up suddenly. "Take it easy, chum," he said quietly. "Here—sit down for a minute."

"When was the funeral?" asked Tallow. He did not sit down.

"Two days ago." The young man coughed. "There were some others, you know. Twenty-one altogether."

"Twenty-one? All from Dock Road?"

"Yes. It was a bad night."

Standing in the entrance behind Tallow, Watts stirred suddenly. "Where was it? The funeral, I mean."

"Croft Road Cemetery." The old man answered this time. "It was very tasteful, I can assure you of that. The Mayor and Corporation attended. They were all together in one big grave, and the floral tributes—" he paused, and his tone altered suddenly. "They can't have known anything, Mr. Tallow. It was all over in a minute—in a second. They can't have suffered at all."

"No," said Tallow. "I see that."

"It's a sort of comfort," said the old man gently.

"Yes," said Tallow. "Thank you. I'll come back in a day or two."

Outside, the sunshine was very bright after the gloom of the warden's post. The two men stood side by side, not looking at each other, staring at the house and the men climbing over the rubble. Some children were playing in the front garden, setting up a wall of bricks and then knocking it down. A dusty and desolate peace lay over everything.

"I'm sorry, Bob," said Watts after a pause. "Real sorry."

"I'm sorry too, Jim. On your account, I mean. I know how you felt. We've both lost—" Tallow straightened his shoulders suddenly. "Well, that's that, anyway. Let's make a move." He began to walk back slowly up Dock Road, and Watts fell into step beside him. "It's funny," said Tallow as they were passing the jagged crater, "but I still can't hardly believe it." He looked up at the sky, the innocent treacherous sky. "It doesn't make sense, really," he went on, astonishment and pain in his voice. "You come in from sea, feeling real glad to be back, and then you go home and find that people you thought were alive and happy, were really dead and buried while you were still two days out. . . . It doesn't make sense," he repeated vaguely. "Jim, I think I want a drink."

[6]

They did four more convoys, of the rough nervous character that marked most convoys nowadays; and then, at high summer, they were given what they had been looking forward to for many months—a refit, with the long leave that went with it; the first long leave since *Compass Rose* was commissioned. They had all wanted that leave: many of them needed it badly: life on Atlantic convoys was a matter of slowly increasing strain, strain still mounting toward a crucial point that could not yet be foreseen, and it took its toll of men's nerves and patience, as surely as of ships. It showed itself in small ways—leave-breaking that had no hope of escaping punishment, quarrelling in the wardroom, an outbreak of petty thieving in the mess-decks—and its only cure was a proper rest, free of routine, free of danger, free of discipline. As long as that rest was granted, they could take on the burden again, and sweat it out to the end; but without such a pause, irritation and inefficiency could gain ground at a startling pace.

Not less than her crew, *Compass Rose* herself needed the respite. It was the first substantial break in service since she had left the Clyde, nearly two years before: apart from necessary minor repairs, designs had altered, weapons improved, and personnel increased, and there was a lot to be done to bring her up-to-date with the newest corvettes. She was due for an entirely new bridge, roomier and better protected, with the mast tucked away behind it in authentic Naval fashion: she could now have a properly equipped sick-bay, new depth-charge rails and throwers, and a superior asdic set that would do everything except tell them the name of the opposing U-boat. The total list of alterations and additions was a substantial one; and *Compass Rose*, sinking back gratefully in the hands of the shipyard, turned her face from the sea and settled down to a six weeks' course of rejuvenation.

With two thirds of the ship's company on leave, and only Baker to keep him company in the wardroom, Lockhart was very conscious of this slacking-off process. He had postponed his own leave in order to see *Compass Rose's* refit properly launched—that was specifically his job—and as he wandered round the ship, checking over what had to be done from the long complicated defect list, he felt a curious sense of disappointment to see how swiftly *Compass Rose* had

ground down to a full stop. She should have held on longer
than this. . . . A few days before, she had come in from sea
as a going concern, and a good one—smart, efficient, controlled by a routine that, after two years, had no loose ends
of any sort; now, at a stroke, the routine was broken, and
she had relapsed into a hulk, a dead ship tied to the jetty—
dirty and untidy, her boilers cold, her men gone, her mainspring run down. He could hardly believe that she could
deteriorate so quickly and completely.

He watched the workmen removing great chunks of the
bridge with acetylene-cutters, he watched the sparks falling
on the useless gun-mounting from which the gun had been removed; he wandered aft, disconsolate, to where the welders,
busy on the new depth-charge rails, had bent the old ones into
fantastic and unusable shapes. He knew that *Compass Rose*
would come back again, stronger and better than ever; but
at this moment of dissolution it was sad to see a ship, which
had been so taut and trim, lose the name of action over a
single week-end.

There were other things during those first days of the refit
which he liked even less. He could not help contrasting the
disciplined and cheerful crew of *Compass Rose*, and the infinitely hard work that, day after day, they took as a matter
of course, with what passed for the war effort among the
dockyard workers. Perhaps this was a bad shipyard; but
good or bad, the contrast was obvious, with unpleasant implications as well. Some of them worked hard and honestly,
most did not: most of them jogged along at a take-it-or-leave-
it pace, talked and shirked in corners half a dozen times a day,
and knocked off with so great a punctuality that when the
whistle went they were already streaming across the gangway, homeward bound. Many times Lockhart interrupted
card games down in the engine room, out of sight of the foreman: there was one hardy poker school that assembled every
afternoon in the asdic compartment, locked the door on the
inside, and played out time till five o'clock, deaf to everyone
but the dealer. . . . Considering that these men led a protected life, free of discipline or compulsion, that they had

their homes to go to at the end of every day, that the calls on their labour were restricted to set hours, and that they were paid a great deal more than any rating on board, it was difficult not to feel impatience and contempt at their grumbling grudging contribution. They were among the people whom sailors fought and died for; at close quarters, they hardly seemed to deserve it.

On one occasion, Tallow came to Lockhart in a high state of indignation. "Just come and look at this, sir," he said, hardly able to get the words out, and led the way up to the boat-deck. Alongside the boats were the Carley floats—safety rafts each equipped with paddles, a keg of water, and a watertight tin of provisions sufficient to last for a week or so. There were two Carleys, and there should have been two tins of food: now, after a week in dockyard hands, there were none.

"Those bloody dockies!" said Tallow, allowing himself an unusual freedom. "Stealing food that might keep a man alive after he's been torpedoed. . . . By God, I'd like to put some of them on a raft in the middle of the Atlantic, and let them work it out for themselves! Isn't there anything we can do, sir?"

"I'm afraid not." Lockhart surveyed the rifled Carley floats with melancholy calm. He had learnt a lot of things during the past few days. "We can complain, of course— I'll see the dockyard superintendent about it—but it won't bring the stuff back and it won't teach people what an appalling thing this is to do." He looked at Tallow. "They just haven't got the same idea, coxswain, and that's all there is to it."

"It's time they were taught it," muttered Tallow angrily. "And these are the chaps who go on strike whenever they feel like it—more pay, less work, and no cross words from the foreman. I wish they could swap jobs with us, just for one trip. They'd know when they were well off, then."

Newspaper accounts of strikes, which they would read when they returned to harbour, made sailors, indeed, sometimes wonder what on earth they were fighting for. . . . It really seemed a reversal of common sense, to put it no higher, that once he was in uniform a man had to do exactly what he was told, without arguing, for an infinitesimal wage and in extreme discomfort, while the man from the house next door, in civilian clothes but with the same stake in the war, could hold the country up to ransom until he got exactly what he wanted. Sailors did not talk much about it, because they were busy and preoccupied with what they had to do, and were not very vocal anyway; but it was there in the background, tied up with the black market, with people who wangled extra food and wasted petrol that had cost men's lives on its journey to England: it was part of the whole rotten minority racket that, in moments of frustration, could induce a rage so wild that it poisoned all pleasure in the job, and all pride in its fulfilment.

Normally, Ericson would have spent a good deal of time on board during the refit: the temptation to prowl round continuously, while so many strange things were being done to *Compass Rose*, would have been irresistible. But for the first time since the war started, his leave had coincided with his son's, and he found himself eager to spend as much time as he could at home, making the most of a meeting that chance might not bring round again for a long time, and another sort of chance might destroy altogether. Young John Ericson, out of his apprenticeship, was now a Fourth Officer: the blue uniform with its single gold stripe sat oddly on his awkward, boyish figure, and Ericson, watching him covertly as he sat on the sofa that, a few years before, he had scrambled over or used as a rocking-horse, could hardly believe that the boy was now entitled to wear the man's rig. He had grown up so fast, almost while Ericson's back was turned, and, most fantastic of all, he was doing the same job as his father. . . .

In the evening, the family circle round the fireside had a touch of unreality about it. Ericson sat in his usual armchair, reading or talking: Grace knitted busily at one end of the sofa, and young John, miraculously adult, sat puffing a shiny new pipe at the other. Opposite Ericson, in the other armchair, the old lady did the cross-words and impressed her will on them all. Grace's mother had mellowed a little, Ericson decided, but not much: she still tried to rule the roost, she still behaved as if she were the only grown-up in a houseful of children. It was lucky that he himself was home so seldom, and that he had *Compass Rose* to retreat to, when things got on his nerves. For the old lady, spiderlike, was not going to move now—that was obvious: she was installed for the duration, and the household had to be regrouped round her, in a way that the Captain of one of His Majesty's ships-of-war could hardly accept as natural.

Part of the unreality lay in their conversation: they talked of everything but what was uppermost in their minds, the force that had brought them all together and might separate them again at any moment—the war. Both Ericson and his son, indeed, were ready enough to talk of it, but before the women they were curiously shy: sitting round the fireside, they remembered enough of the job they were sharing to know that it could not be put into fireside words. When they did come anywhere near the subject, it was simply to chaff each other in the traditional Royal and Merchant Navy rivalry: the only things that could be mentioned about their partnership were the frivolous variations on the surface— the different helm-orders, the different rates of pay, the things that mattered least of all. And then, breaking in on their talk, Grace would say: "I'm sure it doesn't make any difference how fast a corvette can go. You all have to go along together, don't you?" And the old lady, scratching away at the evening paper, would mumble: "What's a word of eleven letters meaning 'futility?' " and the whole family would unite to solve this major problem. . . . So they sat on, night after night: two men, two women, closely bound, yet far apart: feeling the weight of war, and disregarding it in favour of the lightest alternative they could think of.

Once during that meeting, Ericson and his son did talk. It was towards the end of John's leave, when Ericson, moved by a hunger for close companionship which he could scarcely define, proposed a bus ride into the country and a long walk over the Cheshire moors. The bus took them inland, through the unlovely Birkenhead suburbs and the ribbon-development that lay beyond; and then, leaving the bus, they struck northwestward on foot, and walked toward the sea. They walked steadily for four hours, under the warm sunshine, meeting the breeze that blew in from the Irish Sea and the Atlantic itself: their isolation, in these wild surroundings, part of an England they knew and loved, brought them close together, and they talked as they might have talked at sea, sharing a watch on a calm night. They talked of the job they were doing, the matter that lay in the forefront of their minds: the things that were happening to the convoys, the ships and friends they had lost, the truth behind the statistics and the bald or misleading newspaper announcements. But it was not until the late afternoon, when they reached the northwest coast and lay on a hillside sloping to the sea, and watched, on the horizon, a line of ships heading out into the Atlantic, that they spoke at last without reservation and without shyness, acknowledging their secret feelings.

"It's just plain murder, Dad," said John Ericson at one point, when they touched again on the happenings of the last few months, and the fearful total of sinkings. "You can't call it anything else. . . . The same thing happens to convoy after convoy, only a little worse each time. How long can they go on sending us to sea, when it's an absolute certainty that half the ships won't come back?"

"Some convoys get through, John," said Ericson defensively.

"Damn few. . . . Oh, we're not blaming the escorts—they do the best they can, and it's pretty good all the time. It's just that the convoy system doesn't seem to be *working*. You ought to hear our old man on the subject! We can go fifteen knots, any time we like, and yet we have to jog along at seven and eight knots, stuck in a convoy for three weeks on end, a sitting target for the U-boats."

"You're still better off in a convoy, instead of steaming independently. The figures prove it."

"It doesn't feel like it, when those torpedoes are flying

round, and the only signal you can get from the Commodore is 'Maintain convoy speed'. . . . And watching ships and people that you know, being blown up or sunk or bombed, every time you put to sea. Sometimes I feel as if—" he paused.

"What, John?"

"Are you ever afraid, Dad?" The young face, an unformed version of his own, turned towards Ericson anxiously. "Really afraid—trembling, I mean—when you know there's going to be an attack?"

"I think we all are. . . . " Ericson lay on his back, staring at the blue and gold sky, speaking as casually as he could. "I know that I am, anyway. The only thing is to show it as little as you can—because it's catching—and to try and do your job as well as you would if you *weren't* afraid." He examined a sprig of heather with great attention. "There's nothing much in being afraid, John: if a man tells you that he isn't, on our job, he's either a liar or such a cast-iron bloody fool that he's not worth talking to."

"I get the needle pretty badly sometimes."

"Well, you're not a liar, at least."

They both laughed. There was between them now a closeness, a trusting confessional honesty, which they had never reached before.

"I think of you a lot, Dad, when I'm at sea," John went on after a pause. He too was staring at the sky, which with the approach of evening was losing colour swiftly. On the far horizon, the line of sea and sky began to blur as the sun dipped towards the water. "Particularly when I see those corvettes chasing round the convoy. They're so incredibly small. . . ."

"There's something to be said for being a small target."

"There's something to be said for ten thousand tons of solid ship underneath you, in an Atlantic gale."

"I think of you too, John." Ericson, cherishing the moment of intimacy, the first since childhood, hardly knew how to phrase what was in his mind. "We're both doing the same job, and we know the sort of job it is, and I can't help being anxious about you. Anxious and—proud of what you're doing. When I was your age, I hadn't got anything like as far. So just take care of yourself, won't you?—I want to be able to celebrate the next armistice properly. . . . We must think about catching our train, John, or your grandmother will be on the warpath again."

John grinned as he got to his feet. "She's a terror, isn't she?"

"She certainly keeps us all in order, yes."

"Oh, it's all right for me," said John, grinning again. "I'm not the captain of *my* ship."

In the garden of the small house just outside Liverpool, Ferraby played with the baby. The baby, a girl, was now six months old: pretty, gurgling, crawling unsteadily, and answering her name—Ursula—with an ecstatic bubbling noise. Ferraby loved everything to do with being a father, from wheeling the pram out in the afternoons to preparing a bath at the exact temperature: even to be woken up in the middle of the night was an acceptable part of fatherhood, establishing his connection firmly. But most of all he liked simply to be with the child, watching her, talking to her, feeling her minute fingers curling round his own. He felt no need for any more exciting kind of activity, these days: his whole leave was passing in this simple and tender fashion, and he would have chosen nothing else. But now, as he played in the sunshine, holding the warm body, touching the soft petal skin, his thoughts were far away: his thoughts were of steel and storm, the ugliest thoughts in the world.

Such moods and such thoughts came in waves, and he could not now control them. At any time of the day or night, his mind would go back to *Compass Rose*, and the way his leave was running out, and what would take the place of this respite, which must soon come to an end: sometimes, as now, the contrast between terror and tenderness, the extremes of his two lives, overwhelmed him with its futility. At one and the same time, he felt the sweetness of the present, here in the garden, and the threat of the future that lay out in the

Atlantic: he felt that he could only face one of them, and it was not the future—the future was too hard and too evil, and he hated it with all his soul.

He no longer told Mavis anything of this, though sometimes he told the baby.

Now, as he sweated with his thoughts and his prophetic fear, the baby, gurgling again, crawled to the edge of the rug and fell gently onto her face in the grass. The swift wailing changed magically as Ferraby picked her up and held her close to him. Mavis, brought out of the house by the noise, checked her step and stood watching them, a smile on her face. Bless his heart. . . . It was lovely to see Gordon so relaxed and so happy.

Young Baker said: "Yes, Mother—I'd love to," and went upstairs to put on his collar and tie. It was the fourth time he'd been out to tea with his mother that week; but she enjoyed it so much, she got so much fun out of showing him off, that it was impossible to say no to her. There was nothing else to do, anyway.

As usual, he was spending his leave at home, in his mother's small house in a Birmingham suburb. For the first few days it had been fun to be fussed over, to enjoy the good cooking and the undoubted comfort of his mother's housekeeping, to be the male centre of a soft feminine flutter. But soon this had begun to pall: he could not help realizing that this was not the sort of flutter he wanted, nor quite the sort of softness either. . . . Baker was nineteen years old, a shy, anxious-to-please young man whose normal instincts, as yet ungratified, were somewhat heated by his predilection for the more furtive brands of erotica: he collected the pin-up girls from *Esquire* and similar publications, he subscribed to "art" magazines, he even possessed, hidden under a pile of shirts in his wardrobe, a series of postcards that recorded the athletic aspects of love in unusual variety. But so far, no one had appeared in support of these day-dreams: the only girls he met at home were the approved daughters of his mother's friends, selected, it seemed to him, for their inherent wholesomeness, and his only feminine contact at Liverpool was a Wren in the Pay Office, who was much too interested in her career to spare any attention for a sub-lieutenant, and met his tentative advances with a smile as thin as his single stripe. . . . So he spent his time ashore, and his leave periods, balanced between hope and despair: hope that somewhere, just around the next corner, was the girl he so much wanted, and despair when the next corner proved inevitably bare. It was so unfair: other people had girls, and did all sorts of things with them: even in the cinemas there was a maddening activity in the back row: only he, it seemed, was still waiting for the right one to come along, to ease this futile longing.

From the foot of the stairs his mother called out: "Tom! It's time we started," and he put on his coat and prepared to go down. Another tea party. . . . But you never knew: perhaps, this time, the girl would be there, and she would smile and they would recognize each other instantly, and somehow they would get away from the crowd, and she'd start to do the most marvellous things to him, and it would happen at last.

There *was* a girl there, as it turned out, but she was terrible: awkward, sallow, flat-chested—no sort of help at all. He could not even imagine himself kissing her. . . . They sat round in a formal circle, drinking tea and eating cucumber sandwiches: Mrs. Keyes, Mrs. Ockshott, Mrs. Henson, his mother, an old chap who was somebody's husband, the girl who was somebody's daughter, and himself in the place of honour—the young Naval officer snatching a brief hour of peace between fearful voyages. The conversation, indeed, ran on something like these lines: on such occasions, his mother made obvious efforts to draw him out, and the simplest course was to play up to her and lay it on as thick as possible. It was easy to expand in this uncritical atmosphere.

"Sometimes," he said, munching, "it's so rough that we can't put anything on the table at all. We eat things straight out of the tin, or just go without."

The ladies clicked their tongues sympathetically, and his mother said: "Fancy that!" in fond horror. He caught the girl's eye fixed on him admiringly. But she was so ugly. . . . She was sitting with her knees apart, he observed, exposing the kind of safety knickers that you sometimes saw in advertisements, with elastic round the thighs. No good at all. . . . He took another sandwich.

"Yes," he went on recklessly, "I remember the steward bringing some corned beef up to the bridge for me. It was the first food I'd had for—for two days. The funny thing was, when it arrived I just couldn't eat it. Exhaustion, I suppose."

"Fancy that!" said his mother again. And then: "Tell us about that man who was drowning, Tom. You know—when you went overboard in the storm."

"Oh—that. . . ." The girl, though still looking at him, had now closed her legs. "You're welcome," he thought, and passed his cup for some more tea. "It's nothing much," he began, marshalling his thoughts rapidly. "But one night, when the Captain called for volunteers—"

He made the story into a good one—almost too good, if the face of the only other man in the room was anything to go by. But the women lapped it up: and the ugly girl was positively hypnotized by everything he did and said. He enjoyed the admiration while it lasted, but on the way home he relapsed into boredom and frustration again. What did those old cows and that awful girl matter? He was just throwing the stuff away. . . . He really wanted to tell these stories sitting by the fireside, with a different kind of girl—*the* girl—resting her head on his knees, and looking up at him, and not minding when his hand moved gradually down under the top of her dress.

How wonderful it would be, he thought, to be married, really married.

Morell, nursing a glass of brandy, sat in the warm, subtly feminine sitting-room of the flat in Westminster, watching the clock and waiting till it was time to fetch his wife from the theatre. His uniform jacket lay on the chair opposite him, waiting also for the moment to move. But the moment, much as he wanted it, was not yet here.

The clock showed five past ten, which meant another half hour before he could reasonably start: Elaine did not like him hanging round the theatre or her dressing-room when she was on the stage, and she was rarely ready to leave— make-up off, clothes changed—before eleven o'clock each night. (At sea, he had pictured himself waiting in her dressing-room, playing with the make-up box, talking to her dresser, until she came off stage; but it had not worked out like that.) Many times he had found himself wishing that the run of the play would come to an end, but it showed no sign of doing that: besides, the wish was purely selfish—she would have been so disappointed. . . . But certainly the engagement meant that he had not seen much of her during his leave: six evening shows a week, and two matinees as well, left her with very little spare time, even leaving out of account the extra appointments—lunches, dinners, cocktail parties—that seemed to go naturally with being in a current West End play.

Morell sipped his brandy, while the clock crawled towards the half hour. His mood was morose and uncertain, in spite of the fact that they would be meeting again very soon: the trouble was that he could not count on the meeting being a happy one.

At the beginning, Elaine had seemed genuinely regretful of the time they must spend apart. "Oh darling, what a shame!" she had exclaimed, on the night of his arrival. "Just when you've got long leave, I've got a part in a play that's actually going to run. . . . But never mind," she had continued, rubbing her face against his shoulder, "fetch me at the theatre, and I'll make it up to you afterwards." And later that night, when he had claimed her at the stage door and taken her home, she did make it up to him, with all the sensual tenderness he remembered from the past. Indeed, it had been like that for three or four nights, without a shadow of hesitation on her part, so that he was immensely, violently happy. And then, and then. . . .

What did it amount to, exactly, the obvious deterioration? What had made her attention fade, and his happiness and confidence with it? To begin with, it had been the fault of living in a crowd: people ringing up all the time, engagements she would not cut, late parties after the play was over, parties from which he was excluded. "But darling," she would say "it's no good you coming along. It's just theatre people, probably talking shop the whole time. You'd be bored to bits." And when he had remonstrated further: "Darling, I've *got* to go," she would insist, with an edge of irritation. "It's important—it might mean more work when this play is finished." There was no getting past that argument: or none that she would recognize as valid.

It was no good asking questions, either. "Oh, just a party," she would say, when he wanted to know where she was going. "You don't know the people—you probably wouldn't like them, anyway." Question and answer, question and silence, question and angry protest. (But he could not help the questions: he was wretchedly jealous of every moment of their separation.) "Oh darling, don't *heckle!*" she would answer finally, when his probing reached a foolish level of persistence. "It's driving me mad. . . ." And that would be that. He wanted to explain to her where it was driving *him*, but he had begun to be afraid of any sort of emotion, any groping beyond the normality of their life together, any experiment. He had so much to lose, and it seemed clear, for some reason, that he could afford it far less than she. Each time he tried to re-establish himself, the effort was feebler, the ground more surely lost, the abject surrender more obvious.

He really had no weapons, and he had already betrayed the fact, with fatal effect upon them both.

There was something else, too, worse than all this, something he noticed quite early on in his leave: a subtle lessening of her fervour, a certain automatic response, so that he could not decide, in cold blood, whether she were genuinely moved in love, or merely a competent performer. . . . There had been one moment, a moment of ludicrous detachment when, close as they were, he had seemed to be observing her from an immense distance, and had suddenly found himself making up a speech in his head. "This woman, as your Lordship will observe," the strange words formed just behind his tongue, "makes love with a degree of technical competence which—" but he had not been able to complete the sentence. Indeed, suddenly cold and sick, it was all he could do to complete the act of love, so as not to betray himself, and her.

There was nothing definite to go on, and nothing definite to comfort him either. Worst of all, he was no longer able to talk to her about it, to ask for reassurance and to receive it. They shared a house and a bed, they shared an easy conversation and a range of jokes; but they shared nothing below the surface—the candour and the closeness were gone, and he was afraid to challenge their passing, for fear of what he might uncover.

The clock struck the half-hour, and with a thankful readiness he rose to put on his coat. As he moved, the telephone rang.

For a full minute he let it ring unanswered. Almost certainly it was one of her friends, her intolerable friends—the women with their quick malicious tongues, the fat men with wandering hands and contracts in their pockets, the juvenile leads who were very nearly homosexuals but were willing to try anything, the stage riff-raff swelled by home-based officers on the make. . . . But the ringing persisted, and finally he crossed to the side table and lifted the receiver.

It was Elaine.

"Darling," she began, speaking quickly as if knowing that he was going to object, "I've been asked to a party, after the show tonight."

"Oh," he said, non-committally.

"I *must* go, darling. Readman will be there. You know—the producer."

"All right," he said, after a pause. He had other words ready, but he knew they would not be effective. "Can I fetch you from anywhere?"

"No. I'll be so late, darling."

203

"You know it doesn't matter. Where will you be?"

"I don't know, really." The edge of irritation was creeping into her voice again. "We'll probably go on somewhere. Don't you worry."

But foolishly he persisted. "Ring me up, then. I can come along anywhere, any time." "Oh darling," he thought, "you're my wife, and this is the last week of my leave, and I want you here, not at parties with other people." But these also were words that were not effective.

"That's so silly—" she began—and then, treacherously, she disposed of the matter in a swift series of sentences, leaving him no time to answer. "Really it'll be too late, darling. And don't wait up for me. Get some sleep, and I'll see you in the morning. Good-bye."

He had already opened his mouth to start another pleading sentence when he heard the telephone click. Presently the dialling-tone began.

He sat down again, and took up the glass of brandy, conscious only of a shattering disappointment. Then, before he had time to control the direction of his mind, he thought suddenly of two things, in swift and horrible succession. He did not know what wretched instinct presented them so vividly, but once they were there he could not drive them out again. He remembered, first, the huge bruise he had found on Elaine's thigh, the first night of his leave. She bruised very easily; it had been rather a joke on their honeymoon, and on their first night it was still a joke. "I knocked it getting out of a taxi," she had answered when he asked her. "Fine story!" he had grumbled, and then, in a different mood: "May I bring you another taxi—pretty soon?" and she, in answer: "The meter's ticking up already. . . ." A charming scene, melting into frenzy—but now he remembered only the readiness of her first answer.

The second thing he thought of made him get up and, with a clear sense of shame, go into the bathroom. Hanging behind the bathroom door was a sponge-bag, a special sponge-bag in which Elaine kept her "things." He leaned against the wall, unwilling to put, even secretly to himself, so disgusting a question. Then he reached out his hand, and took the sponge-bag from its hook, and opened it, loathing himself, and looked inside.

What he was looking for was not there.

Of course, it was not conclusive. Once—rather a long time ago—she had said: "Oh, I always want to be ready for you." It could have, even now, a simple and tender explanation.

But as soon as he was back in the sitting-room, and had sat down, he began to imagine, in very terrible detail, Elaine making love with someone else.

Lockhart also spent his leave in London, though on a less emotional plane. Indeed, there were times when, if he had been offered some kind of overflow from Morell's situation, he might have taken it on just to keep his hand in. At sea, he was aware in himself of a celibate dedication to the work he was doing: a long leave ashore was inclined to probe the chinks in that armour, reminding him of a different sort of past and exposing a human weakness for sensual indulgence which he had imagined was stowed away with his civilian clothes. But, in the event, the occasion never offered, and his leave passed as a tranquil extension of the male world that the past two years had made normal for him.

He stayed in a borrowed flat in Kensington, the owner of which was absent on some mysterious mission to America; after living for so long in a crowd, he might well have been lonely. But on his doorstep was London, his own fine town, shabby and bomb-damaged but with all her offerings unimpaired: the people, the bars, the theatres, the concerts, the simple slow walks down streets that ended at the river or the green open parks—these were all here under his hand, and he made the most of them, with a thankful appetite for variety.

He met a great many people—by chance, by coincidence, by arrangement, by misfortune: of them all, he best remembered two. They were not good examples of wartime London, and they were not the pleasantest people he met;

but they stuck in his memory, just as, at a children's birthday party, it is the child who is sick or who loses its temper who makes the most lasting impression—particularly on the adults.

He met, in the Café Royal, a man who had been, for a brief and inglorious period, his employer in an advertising agency in London. Lockhart had taken on the job, some time in the middle thirties, when he was broke—indeed, he would scarcely have considered it in any other circumstances, so foolish and irksome was it from the very beginning. His work consisted of writing advertising copy in praise of food: in outlining the style to be aimed at, his employer, a large fat man by the name of Hamshaw, tried to communicate his own sense of mission, and was clearly taken aback by Lockhart's somewhat frivolous approach. Matters proceeded uneasily for some months: more and more of Lockhart's stuff was returned to him, marked "too harsh," "too stiff," "a softer approach, please," once even "the reference to saliva is indelicate." There came a day when Lockhart's projected phrase to round off a dog-biscuit advertisement: "Dogs like 'em," was rejected in favour of: "No more toothsome morsel has ever been offered to the canine world," and he knew that, broke or not, his patience was exhausted.

He waited for the chance of a parting gesture, and the chance came. On his desk one morning was a note from Hamshaw: "Please let me have a suitable slogan for Bolger's Treacle Butterscotch." Lockhart considered for a moment, scribbled a line at the bottom of the page, picked up his hat, and walked out. Not till some hours later did Hamshaw, nosing round the copy room, light upon the farewell effort: "Bolger's Butterscotch—Rich and Dark like the Aga Khan."

Even in those days, Hamshaw had been sufficiently pompous; now, appointed to control the thought of entire subcontinents on behalf of the Ministry of Information, he was positively Olympian. He greeted Lockhart with a detached bow, and said: "Ah, Lockhart—come and share my table" as if he were offering Holy Communion to a dubious backslider. When they had chatted warily for some time:

1941: *Grappling*

"A fine service, yours," said Hamshaw with deliberation, gently massaging a ponderous chin. "But I must confess that at the Ministry we find you—shall we say?—a little backward."

"Backward," repeated Lockhart non-committally.

Hamshaw nodded, popped a sandwich into his mouth, and nodded again. "Yes. We'd like to see a little more readiness to release material—about the Atlantic, and so forth. It's very difficult to get the Admiralty to co-operate, very difficult indeed."

"I think they take security fairly seriously."

"My dear Lockhart, you can't teach me anything about *security!*" said Hamshaw, as if it were his own personal conception. "I can assure you we have that *very* much at heart. What we want is more willingness to publicize what's going on, once the demands of security are met. These successes—if successes they are—are no good unless people hear about them, no good at all."

Lockhart frowned, not seeing why he should accept this nonsense, even as a matter of social convenience. "A sunk U-boat is sunk," he said shortly, "whether it's on the front page in two colours or not. The advertising afterwards doesn't affect it at all."

"The *advertising*, as you call it," Hamshaw looked at him portentously, alert for any disrespect, "is valuable from the morale point of view. The national morale, which is one of our prime concerns, needs a continual supply of favourable news items to sustain it. Indeed, I think it is safe to say that the war could not be fought for one single day without the constant public inspiration which we supply. However," he went on, perhaps aware of Lockhart's wandering attention, "I mustn't ride off on my hobby-horse, absorbing though it is. Tell me about your own work. You find it personally satisfying?"

"Something like that," said Lockhart.

"In many ways," said Hamshaw, staring into the middle distance, "it is a great pity you did not stay with us. I was able to take some of my staff with me to the Ministry—

those I particularly trusted—and they have all done well.
You might have had a junior controllership by now—possibly
even a sectional directorship."

"God bless my soul!" said Lockhart.

"Oh yes, there is great scope for advancement—very great
scope indeed. But perhaps you are happy enough where you
are."

"Yes," said Lockhart, "I think I am."

"Well, that is all that matters. It is all one war," went on
Hamshaw with frightful condescension, "all one great cause.
We realize that very fully, I assure you. We cannot all be
charged with supplying the driving force for the battle—the
services play an honourable part in the field itself."

"How vulgar you make it sound," said Lockhart evenly,
as for the second time in their joint lives he picked up his hat,
preparatory to flight. "But bear with us a little longer. We
are trying to get integrated in your war machine."

"Now I've angered you, somehow," said Hamshaw re-
proachfully.

"Yes," said Lockhart, "somehow you have," and left him
to work it out. It would doubtless be dismissed as some re-
grettable form of war psychosis.

Later that evening, in the bar of a Fleet Street pub, he met
a fellow journalist by the name of Keys, whom he had not
seen since the beginning of the war. Keys was considerably
older than himself, a tough and seasoned senior reporter on
the staff of one of the popular dailies; like Hamshaw, his
natural inclinations seemed to have been stimulated and in-
tensified by war, and where he had once been something of a
sceptic about human nature in general, he was now crudely
cynical about every aspect of the war, and the motives of
anyone who had the remotest connection with it. With no
prompting at all save the whisky at his elbow, he treated
Lockhart to a diatribe of extraordinary violence, embracing
the whole of Britain: indeed, not one of his fellow country-
men escaped the lash. The politicians were feathering their
nests without regard to the common good, the industrialists
were selling shoddy war-material at fantastic profits, all the

newspapers without exception were lying their way through the struggle, ignoring Allied setbacks and inventing successes to put in their place. The working class were loafers to a man; and servicemen, of course, were the dupes of a huge national confidence trick, if no worse. . . .

"There's nothing to choose between us and the Germans, anyway," concluded Keys savagely, staring at Lockhart's uniform as if it were some kind of prison garb, shameful to anyone who wore it. "We're both after the same thing—the domination of Europe, and the markets that go with it. The Germans are just a bit more honest about it, that's all."

"Um," said Lockhart non-committally. The bar was crowded, and he did not want to attract attention by an argument that was bound to be futile, and might become unpleasant. Just above their heads was a large sign, in Gothic characters, which read: THERE IS NO DEPRESSION IN THIS HOUSE. It might be better to take his cue from that.

"By God!" exclaimed Keys, seeming to lash himself into a sudden fury, "I've had to write more claptrap about the great Allied war effort, the last few months, than I would have thought possible. It's enough to turn your stomach."

"Why do it, then?"

Keys shrugged. "For the same reason you're wearing that uniform," he answered, with a bitter inflection.

"I doubt it," said Lockhart shortly.

"Don't fool yourself. . . . There's a war, and you join up like a good little boy, because everyone else is doing it. There's a war, and my paper has to plug the patriotic angle because it would be unsalable otherwise, and I have to turn the stuff out because I'd lose my job if I didn't. It's the same reason—the fear of not toeing the line, and of being unpopular if you don't follow the crowd like a lot of bloody sheep."

"There are other reasons," said Lockhart.

Keys snorted derisively. "I suppose you're going to tell me the whole Navy's fighting for God, King, and country."

"It's an idea that lies behind a lot of what we feel," said Lockhart, without heat. "It *isn't* just a war for right and justice, with all the merit on one side, I know, and there's enough truth in that 'domination of Europe' thesis to make one think twice before accepting patriotic speeches at their face value. But if we lost, or if we hadn't declared war in the first place, we wouldn't have a chance of establishing *any* of the things we believe in. What do you suppose England would be like, if the Germans were running it?"

"More efficient," said Keys.

Lockhart smiled. "I see I'm not likely to make much headway," he said good-humouredly. He found it, for some reason, impossible to be annoyed with Keys, who had lived so long with the-news-behind-the-news that he could hardly distinguish a genuine emotion from a counterfeit one, and was quite unaffected by either. "I'll just have to carry on in my patriotic day-dream. . . . It's a *real* feeling, sometimes, you know," he went on quietly, "and a lot of people have died for it already."

"More fools they," said Keys contemptuously.

"Ah yes," said Lockhart, "but they couldn't know that, could they? They've only got the newspapers to go by, and you people do *such* a good job."

Lockhart got slightly drunk that night, possibly as an antidote, and it was in a mood of detached intoxication, weaving his way down the long slope of Piccadilly towards Knightsbridge and home, that he tried to sort out his impression of the day's encounters. Of the two men, Hamshaw and Keys, he infinitely preferred the latter's approach to the war: he might be bitter and cynical about it, but at least he was not deluding himself, at least he was free of the pompous haze of grandeur with which Hamshaw had surrounded himself and the war and his role in it. War was not like that: no sacred cause, served exclusively by pledged knights, was involved; on the other hand, war was not Keys's brand of shoddy commercial dogfight, either. There had been something in what he said, some slender basis for the idea that the fight was between equally guilty contestants, each determined on European ascendancy; but not enough to resolve it finally into a simple and selfish struggle, with nothing to choose between the eventual winners. Keys had rationalized his own bitterness, which might spring from a dozen different causes; it might even be grounded, deep down, in the fact that he was too old to be of any practical use in the war and, being excluded for what perhaps seemed an ignoble reason, was determined to shrug off the whole business.

"We can't all be born at the same time," said Lockhart aloud, addressing the façade of a big block of flats at Rutland Gate. But perhaps Keys wasn't as logical, as infinitely wise, as he himself was at this moment. Keys was too old for fighting: therefore, to him, fighting was a worthless preoccupation, and the war a cut-throat extension of commercial travelling.

Of course there must be something more. . . . Lockhart had never been a professed patriot: even now, closely involved in the fight, he could feel no dedication save to the necessity of winning—and *then* seeing about a fair and equitable settlement. But the winning was paramount: the alternative meant disaster, for everything he stood for and felt, and subjection to a cruel, impersonal, and loathsome tyranny that would bring the curtain down on human hope.

There must be Germans, too, who felt like that: good ones, deluded, but sincere and equally concerned with the humanities: good soldiers, good sailors, good airmen who felt they were destroying a perverted English attempt at conquest. It was a pity that they had to be killed as well. . . .

"I'm a German, really," he said out loud again, pausing to rest against a convenient lamp-post. "Nothing to choose between us. . . . But my part of Germany's got to win, and then we'll start parcelling the whole thing out again."

"Yes, sir," said the policeman who suddenly appeared at his side. "Have you got far to go home?"

Lockhart blinked, and focused his eyes with an effort. The figure that was now before him seemed enormous in the lamplight. "Why are policemen always taller than I am?" he asked complainingly. "Now, in Germany—"

"How about a taxi?" asked the policeman, with the usual

all-embracing patience. "You'll get one a little way back, in Knightsbridge."

"A fine night for walking," said Lockhart.

"A fine night for sleeping," said the policeman, reprovingly. "They're all asleep round here. We don't want to wake them up, do we?"

"Were you ever in the Navy?" asked Lockhart, with a vague idea of establishing a friendly contact.

"No, sir," said the policeman, "I've had no luck at all." A taxi, coasting slowly past on its way back to town, turned neatly at a wave of his hand, and ground to a standstill beside them. "What's the address, then?"

Lockhart gave it, and stood wavering as the policeman opened the taxi door. The annoying part about being drunk was that everyone was so much more efficient than oneself. . . . He paused, with one foot on the step of the cab.

"I was walking home quite quietly," he said.

"Yes, sir," said the policeman.

"I don't want any trouble," said the taxi driver, an oldish man in a thick green overcoat. "Navy or no Navy."

"This is all right," said the policeman, slamming the door as Lockhart subsided on the seat. Through the open window he added: "You sure of that address?"

"Yes," said Lockhart. "Engraved on my heart."

"All right," said the policeman. He nodded to the taxi driver. "Off you go."

"We've got to win," said Lockhart, by way of valediction.

"Don't I know it," said the policeman. "But not all in one night. Leave something for tomorrow."

"What's it like in them battleships?" asked the taxi driver over his shoulder, about a mile further on.

"I should think it's absolutely terrible," answered Lockhart, who was trying to light a cigarette and disentangle his gas mask at the same time.

"I only asked," said the taxi driver sourly. "They can sink, for all I care."

"Don't you want to win the war?" asked Lockhart, astounded.

"There's a lot of things I want," said the taxi driver. He gave a swift and meaning glance at his meter. "Double fare after twelve o'clock, you know."

"Nonsense," said Lockhart.

The taxi driver clapped on his brakes, and brought the cab to a standstill. "What did you say?" he asked grimly.

"I was born in this town," Lockhart began, with a clarity of thought that astounded even himself. "You know perfectly well—"

It was not a satisfactory evening.

But this was not the note on which his leave ended: neither this, nor Hamshaw, nor Keys. He carried away with him a very different sort of memory. For on his last night in London he went to the theatre, to a non-cerebral musical comedy that was the only thing he could get a seat for; and there, when the lights went up for the interval, he saw a sight that stayed with him afterwards for very many months.

It was a party of R.A.F. officers from some hospital—a hospital that supposedly dealt with plastic surgery cases. The six young men in air force uniform were all the same: Lockhart, looking sideways along the row, received so frightful an impression of disfigurement that for a moment he thought it must be a trick of lighting and shadow. But it was no trick: the faces *were* all shattered in the same formless way, mutilated alike by wounds and by slapdash surgical repair: puckered by scars or by burning, twisted into living caricature, lacking eyebrows, lacking ears, lacking lips and chins; greyish-yellow where fire had scorched them, livid red where they were scarred, a line of violence and pain that shocked Lockhart nearly to sickness. Beside each terrible face was a fresh young one—a girl's; and the girls were all smiling and talking animatedly and looking closely into the *other* faces, without flinching, and the other faces, which were not equipped to smile and hardly even to talk, looked back at them searchingly, with dreadful alertness. . . .

"They oughtn't to allow them in," whispered a woman sitting just behind him. "What about decent people's feelings?" "Shut up, you flaming bitch," thought Lockhart, nearly saying it aloud, and then, looking down the row again toward the wounded men, as many other people were looking, drawn by the magnet of this insane ugliness: "You poor bastards," he thought again, "I hope you're going to be all right—in time, in a year or two. . . ." This, and nothing else, was the war; this was the part you couldn't glamourize, or belittle, or pretend about in any way. He was glad when the lights went down again, but glad only for their sakes, for the cover of darkness which they must welcome: for himself, after the initial shock, he had felt more at home with this cruel evidence of the fight than with anything else in London. Indeed, the wounded men were a good token of the best of this city, scarred and fired in the same way: maimed for life, maybe, but talking and working and playing with what was left, and never to be daunted now or in the future.

It was the right kind of memory to take back from leave: the unsoftening kind, the dream-of-home that ran no risk of tenderizing the spirit. Lockhart took it with him thankfully.

They hardly knew *Compass Rose*, by the end of her refit: she seemed to have moved right out of the corvette class altogether, and to have been graduated with unexpected honours. The new bridge was a replica of a destroyer's, with a covered chart-table and plenty of room to walk about: the sick-bay, presided over by a sick-berth attendant who had actually been a country vet at one period, was properly fitted up and stocked for most of the emergencies they had met so far. There were more depth charges and anti-aircraft guns: there was the new asdic set: above all, there was now a brand-new weapon altogether—radar.

Radar—the most formidable invention in sea warfare—had been slow in coming to them. By now, all the escort destroyers had it, and a lucky corvette or two; but Ericson, who had applied many times during the past year for it to be fitted, had always come away discouraged. "You haven't a hope," the man in charge of such things at headquarters had told him, whenever he raised the question. "There are all sorts of ships ahead of you. In fact," said the man, who was not a smooth-spoken character, "as far as radar is concerned, corvettes are sucking on the hind tit. You'll just have to wait until everyone else has had a go."

"What a pity Bennett is not still with us," remarked Morell, who had overheard the conversation. "The phrase would have delighted him. . . ."

But now at last they had it, mounted on the bridge in all its glory and promise. Radar was the one thing they needed, the one weapon that the Atlantic war had long demanded: a means of making contact at night or in thick weather with whatever lay in waiting near by. It could detect a U-boat on the surface at a considerable distance, and show its course and speed: on its fluorescent screen radar gave a "picture" of the convoy or of near-by ships, a picture that simplified station-keeping at night to such a degree that it was difficult to see how they had ever done without it. There need be no more hanging-on and punishing the eyes at night, since radar did it all: no more searching for lost ships or for the incoming convoy—there they were, clearly picked out on the screen, scores of miles away. It was going to be a help and a comfort—that they all realized; and beyond this, perhaps it would, as a weapon, even start to equalize the Atlantic score, meeting the cunning and secret attack with a delicate revealing finger, the best that science could do for man.

They were fitted with it in time to return to sea when the battle was climbing to crucial heights; in time for the worst convoy of all so far.

[7]

The smiling weather of that late summer helped them to settle down to sea-going again, after the relaxation of their refit. It was a curious business, this tuning up of men and machinery, and in some cases it caught both of them unawares.

Compass Rose hit the knuckle of the jetty—fortunately not very hard—on her way out of dock, owing to a small defect in her reversing gear; and one seaman, to his lasting shame, was actually seasick on the five-minute trip across the river to top up at the oiler. . . . But these were odd items in a quick process of re-establishment: when they picked up their convoy off the Bar Light Vessel they were already halfway back to the old routine, and by the time they were two days out, clear of land and heading in a wide southwesterly circle for Gibraltar, the ship was fighting fit again. The weather gave them a wonderful succession of sunlit days and calm nights; and, conscious of their luck in sailing for hour after hour over a deep blue, mirror-calm sea, the sort of warm and lazy trip that cost a guinea a day in peacetime, they quickly made the transfer from land to seafaring. It was, from many angles, good to be back on the job again: clear of the dubious and emotional tie of land, they were once more part of an increased escort—two destroyers and five corvettes—charged with the care of twenty-one deep-laden ships bound for Gibraltar. This was their real task, and they turned to it again with the readiness of men who, knowing that the task was crucial, were never wholly convinced that the Navy could afford to let them take a holiday.

The treachery of that perfect weather, the lure of the easy transition, were not long in the declaring.

It started with a single aircraft, possibly an old friend, a four-engined Focke-Wulf reconnaissance plane that closed the convoy from the eastward and then began to go round them in slow circles, well out of range of any gunfire they could put up. It had happened to them before, and there was little doubt of what the plane was doing—pinpointing the convoy, shadowing it, noting exactly its course and speed, and then reporting back to some central authority, as well as tipping off any U-boats that might be near by. The change this time lay in the fact that it was occurring so early in their voyage, and that, as they watched the plane circling and realized its mission, the sun was pouring down from a matchless sky onto a sea as smooth and as lovely as old glass, hardly disturbed at all by the company of ships that crossed it on their way southward. Unfair to peace-loving convoys, they thought as they closed their ranks and trained their glasses on the slowly circling messenger of prey: leave us alone on this painted ocean, let us slip by, no one will know. . . .

At dusk the plane withdrew, droning away eastward at the same level pace: up on the bridge, preparing to darken ship and close down for the night, they watched it go with gloomy foreboding.

"It's too easy," said Ericson broodingly, voicing their thoughts. "All it's got to do is to fly round and round us, sending out some kind of homing signal, and every U-boat within a hundred miles just steers straight for us." He eyed the sky, innocent and cloudless. "I wish it would blow up a bit. This sort of weather doesn't give us a chance."

There was nothing out of the ordinary that night, except a signal at eleven o'clock addressed by the Admiralty to their convoy. "There are indications of five U-boats in your area, with others joining," it warned them, with generous scope, and left them to make the best they could of it. As soon as darkness fell the convoy changed its course from the one the aircraft had observed, going off at a sharp tangent in the hope of escaping the pursuit: perhaps it was successful, perhaps the U-boats were still out of range, for the five hours of darkness passed without incident, while on the radar screen the compact square of ships and the out-lying fringe of escorts moved steadily forward, undisturbed, escaping notice. *Viperous*, making her routine dash round the convoy at first light, signalled: "I think we fooled them" as she swept past *Compass Rose*. The steep wave of her wash had just started them rolling when they heard the drone of an aircraft, and the spy was with them again.

The first ship was torpedoed and set on fire at midday. She was a big tanker—all the twenty-one ships in the convoy were of substantial size, many of them bound for Malta and the eastern Mediterranean: it was a hand-picked lot, a valuable prize well worth the pursuit and the harrying. And pursued and harried they were, without quarter: the swift destruction of that first ship marked the beginning of an eight-day battle that took steady toll of the convoy, thinning out the ships each night with horrible regularity, making of each dawn a disgusting nursery-rhyme, a roll call of the diminishing band of nigger-boys.

They fought back, they did their best; but the odds against them were too high, the chinks in their armour impossible to safeguard against so many circling enemies.

"There are nine U-boats in your area," said the Admiralty at dusk that night, as generous as ever; and the nine U-boats between them sank three ships, one of them in circumstances of special horror. She was known to be carrying about twenty Wrens, the first draft to be sent to Gibraltar: aboard *Compass Rose* they had watched the girls strolling about the deck, had waved to them as they passed, had been glad of their company even at long range. The ship that carried them was the last to be struck that night: she went down so swiftly that the flames which engulfed the whole of her after-part hardly had time to take hold before they were quenched. The noise of that quenching was borne over the water toward *Compass Rose;* a savage hissing roar, indescribably cruel. "By God, it's those poor kids!" exclaimed Ericson, jolted out of a calm he could not preserve at so horrible a moment. But there was nothing that they could do: they were busy on a wide search ordered by *Viperous,* and they could not leave it. If there were anything left to rescue, someone else would have to do it.

Four of the girls *were* in fact picked up by another merchant ship, which had bravely stopped and lowered a boat for the job. They were to be seen next morning, sitting close together on the upper deck, staring out at the water: there was no gay waving now, from either side. . . . But the ship that rescued them was one of the two that were sunk that same night: she too went down swiftly, and *Compass Rose,* detailed this time to pick up survivors, could only add four to her own total of living passengers, and six to the dead. Among these dead was one of the Wrens, the only one that any ship found out of the draft of twenty: included in the neat row of corpses Tallow laid out on the quarterdeck, the girl's body struck a note of infinite pity. She was young: the drenched fair hair, the first that had ever touched the deck of *Compass Rose*, lay like a spread fan, outlining a pinched and frightened face that would, in living repose, have been lovely. Lockhart, who had come aft at dawn to see to the sewing up of those that were to be buried, felt a constriction in his throat as he looked down at her. Surely there could be no sadder, no filthier aspect of war. . . . But there were many other things to do besides mourn or pity. They buried her with the rest, and added her name to the list in the log, and continued the prodigal southward journey.

Six ships were gone already: six ships in two days, and they still had a week to go before they were near the shelter of land. But now they had a stroke of luck: a succession of two dark nights that, combined with a violently evasive alteration of course, threw the pursuit off the scent. Though they were still on the alert, and the tension, particularly at night, was still there, for forty-eight hours they enjoyed a wonderful sense of respite: the convoy, now reduced to fifteen ships, cracked on speed, romping along toward the southern horizon and the promise of safety. Aboard *Compass Rose*, a cheerful optimism succeeded the sense of ordained misfortune that had begun to take hold; and the many survivors they had picked up, wandering about the upper deck in their blankets and scraps of clothing or lining the rails to stare out at the convoy, lost gradually the strained refugee look that was so hard on the Naval conscience. Hope grew: they might see harbour after all. . . .

So it was for two days and two nights; and then the aircraft, casting wide circles in the clear dawn sky, found them again.

Rose, the young signalman, heard it first: a stirring in the upper air, a faint purring whisper that meant discovery. He looked round him swiftly, his head cocked on one side: he called out: "Aircraft, sir—somewhere. . . ." and Ferraby and Baker, who had the forenoon watch, came to the alert in the same swift nervous movement. The throbbing grew, and achieved a definite direction—somewhere on their port beam, away from the convoy and toward the distant Spanish coast. "Captain, sir!" called Baker down the voice-pipe, "sound of aircraft—" But Ericson was already mounting the bridge ladder, brought up from his sea-cabin by the hated noise. He looked round him, narrowing his eyes against the bright day, and then: "There it is!" he exclaimed suddenly, and pointed. On their beam, emerging from the pearly morning mist that lay low on the horizon all round them, was the plane, the spying eye of the enemy.

They all stared at it, every man on the bridge, bound together by the same feeling of anger and hatred. It was so unfair. . . . U-boats they could deal with—or at least the odds were more level: with a bit of luck in the weather, and the normal skill of sailors, the convoy could feint and twist and turn and hope to escape their pursuit. But this predatory messenger from another sphere, destroying the tactical pattern, eating into any distance they contrived to put between themselves and the enemy—this betrayer could never be baulked. They felt, as they watched the aircraft, a helpless sense of nakedness, an ineffectual rage: clearly, it was all going to happen again, in spite of their care and watchfulness, in spite of their best endeavours, and all because a handful of young men in an aircraft could span half an ocean in a few hours, and come plummeting down upon their slower prey.

Swiftly the aircraft must have done its work, and the U-boats could not have been far away; within twelve hours, back they came, and that night cost the convoy two more ships out of the dwindling fleet. The hunt was up once more, the pack exultant, the savage rhythm returning and quickening. . . . They did their best: the escorts counter-attacked, the convoy altered course and increased its speed: all to no purpose. The sixth day dawned, the sixth night came: punctually at midnight the alarm bells sounded and the first distress-rocket soared up into the night sky, telling of a ship mortally hit and calling for help. She burned for a long time, that ship, reddening the water, lifting sluggishly with the swell, becoming at last a flickering oily pyre that the convoy slowly left astern. Then there was a pause of more than two hours, while they remained alert at action stations and the convoy slid southward under a black moonless sky; and then, far out on the seaward horizon, five miles away from them, there was a sudden return of violence. A brilliant orange flash split the darkness, died down, flared up again, and then guttered away to nothing. Clearly it was another ship hit—but this time, for them, it was much more than a ship; for this time, this time it was *Sorrel*.

They all knew it must be *Sorrel*, because at that distance it could not be any other ship, and also because of an earlier signal they had relayed to her from *Viperous*. "In case of an attack tonight," said the signal, "*Sorrel* will proceed five miles astern and to seaward of the convoy, and create a diversion by dropping depth charges, firing rockets, etc. This may draw the main attack away from the convoy." They had seen the rockets earlier that night, and disregarded them: they only meant that *Sorrel*, busy in a corner, was doing her stuff according to plan. . . . Probably that plan had been effective, if the last two hours' lull was anything to go by: certainly it had, from one point of view, been an ideal exercise, diverting at least one attack from its proper mark. But, in the process, someone had to suffer: it had not cancelled the stalking approach, it did not stop the torpedo being fired: *Sorrel* became the mark, in default of a richer prize, meeting her lonely end in the outer ring of darkness beyond the convoy.

Poor *Sorrel*, poor sister-corvette. . . . Up on the bridge of *Compass Rose*, the men who had known her best of all were now the mourners, standing separated from each other by the blackness of night but bound by the same shock, the same incredulous sorrow. How could it have happened to *Sorrel*, to an escort like themselves. . . . Immediately he saw the explosion, Ericson had rung down to the wireless office. " '*Viperous* from *Compass Rose*,' " he dictated. " '*Sorrel* torpedoed in her diversion position. May I leave and search for survivors?' " Then: "Code that up," he snapped to the telegraphist who was taking down the message. "Quick as you can. Send it by R/T." Then, the message sent, they waited, silent in the darkness of the bridge, eying the dim bulk of the nearest ship, occasionally turning back to where *Sorrel* had been struck. No one said a word: there were no words for this. There were only thoughts, and not many of those.

The bell of the wireless office rang sharply, breaking the silence, and Leading Signalman Wells, who was standing by the voice-pipe, bent down to it.

"Bridge!" he said, and listened for a moment. Then he straightened up, and called to the Captain across the grey width of the bridge. "Answer from *Viperous*, sir. . . . 'Do not leave convoy until daylight.' "

There was silence again, a sickened, appalled silence. Ericson set his teeth. He might have guessed. . . . It was the right answer, of course, from the cold technical angle: *Viperous* simply could not afford to take another escort from the screen, and send her off on a non-essential job. It was the right answer, but by Christ it was a hard one! . . . Back there in the lonely darkness, ten miles and more away by now, men were dying, men of a special sort: people they knew well, sailors like themselves: and they were to be left to die, or, at best, their rescue was to be delayed for a period that must cost many lives. *Sorrel's* sinking had come as an extraordinary shock to them all: she was the first escort that had ever been lost out of their group, and she was, of all the ones that could have gone, their own chummy-ship, the ship they had tied up alongside after countless convoys, for two years on end: manned by their friends, men they played tombola with or met in pubs ashore: men they could always beat at football. . . . For *Sorrel* to be torpedoed was bad enough; but to leave her crew to sink or swim in the darkness was the most cruel stroke of all.

"Daylight," said Morell suddenly, breaking the oppressive silence on the bridge. "Two more hours to wait."

Ericson found himself answering: "Yes"—not to Morell's words, but to what he had meant. It was a cold night. With two hours to wait, and then the time it would take them to

run back to where *Sorrel* had gone down, there would be very
few men left to pick up.

There were in fact fifteen—fifteen out of a ship's company
of ninety.

They found them without much difficulty, toward the end
of the morning watch, sighting the two specks which were
Carley rafts across three miles or more of flat unruffled sea.
However familiar this crude seascape had become to them,
it was especially moving to come upon it again now: to approach the loaded rafts and the clusters of oily bodies washing about among *Sorrel's* wreckage: to see, here and there in
this filthy aftermath, their own uniforms, their own badges
and caps, almost their own mirrored faces. . . . The men
on the rafts were stiff and cold and soaked with oil, but as
Compass Rose approached, one of them waved with wild
energy, foolishly greeting a rescuer not more than twenty
yards away from him. Some of the men were clearly dead,
from cold or exhaustion, even though they had gained the
safety of the rafts: they lay with their heads on other men's
knees, cherished and warmed until death and perhaps for
hours beyond it. Ericson, looking through his binoculars at
the ragged handful that remained, caught sight of the grey
face of *Sorrel's* captain, Ramsay, his friend for many years.
Ramsay was holding a body in his arms, a young sailor ugly
and pitiful in death, the head thrown back, the mouth hanging open. But the living face above the dead one was hardly
less pitiful. The whole story—the lost ship, the lost crew,
the pain and exhaustion of the last six hours—all these were
in Ramsay's face as he sat, holding the dead body, waiting
for rescue.

It was a true captain's face, a captain in defeat who
mourned his ship, and bore alone the monstrous burden of its
loss.

Lockhart, waiting in the waist of the ship while the survivors were helped aboard, greeted him with impulsive
warmth as he climbed stiffly over the side.

"Very glad to see you, sir!" he exclaimed eagerly. Everything about Ramsay—his expression, his weary movements,

his reeking oilsoaked uniform,—was suddenly and deeply moving, so that to have saved his life, even in these tragic circumstances, seemed a triumph and a blessing. "We were all hoping—" he stopped awkwardly, watching Ramsay's face. He knew immediately that it would be wrong, terribly wrong, to say: "We were all hoping that we'd pick *you* up, anyway." That was not what Ramsay himself was feeling, at that moment. Rather the reverse.

"Thanks, Number One." Ramsay, straightening up, turned round and gestured vaguely towards the men still on the rafts. "Look after them, won't you? One or two of them are pretty far gone."

Lockhart nodded. "I'll see to all that, sir."

"I'll go up to the bridge, then." But he lingered by the rails, watching with hurt eyes as the remnants of his crew were helped or hauled or lifted tenderly inboard. In the middle of the crowd of men working, he was unassailably withdrawn and private in his grief. When the living were seen to, and they were starting on the dead, he turned away and walked slowly towards the bridge ladder, his oily bare feet slurring and slopping along the deck. Lockhart was glad to be kept busy and preoccupied at that moment. It was not one to be intruded on, upon any pretext.

To Ericson, up on the bridge, Ramsay presently held out his hand and said:

"Thanks, George. I'll not forget that." The west-country accent was very prominent.

"Sorry we couldn't be here earlier," said Ericson shortly. "But I couldn't leave the screen before daylight."

"It wouldn't have made much difference," answered Ramsay. He had turned away, and was once more watching the bodies coming inboard, and the other bodies that disfigured the even surface of the sea round *Compass Rose*. "Most of them were caught below, anyway. We broke in half. Went down in a couple of minutes."

Ericson said nothing. Presently Ramsay turned back to him and said, half to himself:

"You never think that *you'll* be the one to catch it. It's

something you can't be ready for, no matter how much you think about it. When it does happen—" he broke off, as if at some self-reproach he did not know how to voice, and then the moment itself was interrupted by Signalman Rose, alert at one of the voice-pipes.

"Signal from *Viperous*, sir," he called out. "Addressed to us. 'Rejoin the convoy forthwith.' "

"Something must be happening," said Ericson. He walked to the head of the bridge ladder, and looked down at the waist of the ship. The two rafts were cleared now, but there were still twenty or more bodies floating within a circle of half a mile round them. "I'd have liked to—" he began uncertainly.

Ramsay shook his head. "It doesn't matter, George," he said quietly. "What's the odds, anyway? Leave them where they are."

He did not look at anyone or anything as *Compass Rose* drew away.

What had happened, as they discovered when they caught up the convoy, toward midday, was that another ship had been torpedoed, in broad daylight, and *Viperous* was rightly anxious to close up all the escorts as soon as possible. There could be no pause, no respite in this long chasing battle: certainly the dead had no claim—not even when, as now, they were beginning to outnumber the living. By noon of that seventh day, the tally of ships remaining was eleven— eleven out of the original twenty-one; behind them were ten good merchant-ships sunk, and countless men drowned, and one of the escorts lost as well. It was horrible to think of the hundreds of miles of sea that lay in their wake, strewn with the oil and the wreckage and the corpses they were leaving behind them: it was like some revolting paper-chase, with the convoy laying a trail from an enormous suppurating satchel of blood and treasure. But some of it—the Wrens, and *Sorrel*, and the screams of the men caught in the first ship lost, the burning tanker—some of it did not bear thinking about at all.

It was not a one-sided battle, with repeated hammer-strokes on the one hand and a futile dodging on the other but it was not much better than that, in the way it was working out; there were too many U-boats in contact with them, not enough escorts, not enough speed or manœuvrability in the convoy to give it a level chance. They had fought back all that they could. *Compass Rose* had dropped more than forty depth charges on her various counter-attacks, some of which should have done some damage: the other escorts had put up a lively display of energy: *Viperous* herself, after one accurate attack, had sufficient evidence in the way of oil and wreckage to claim a U-boat destroyed. But as far as the overall picture was concerned, all this was simply a feeble beating of the air: with so many U-boats in their area, miracles were necessary to escape the appalling trap the convoy had run into, and no miracles came their way. There was no chance of winning, and no way of retreat; all they could do was to close their ranks, make the best speed they could, and sweat it out to the end.

Compass Rose had never been so crowded, so crammed with survivors. It was lucky, indeed, that they had the new sick-bay and the sick-berth attendant to deal with their wounded and exhausted passengers: Lockhart could never have coped with the continual flow single-handed. But apart from the number of people requiring attention, they had collected a huge additional complement of rescued men—far outnumbering, indeed, their own crew. There were fourteen Merchant Navy officers in the wardroom, including three ship's captains: there were a hundred and twenty-one others —seamen, firemen, cooks, Lascars, Chinese—thronging the upper deck by day, and at night crowding into the mess-decks to eat and sleep and wait for the next dawn. During the dark hours, indeed, the scene in the darkened fo'c's'le was barely describable. Under the shaded yellow lamp was a scene from the Inferno, a nightmare of tension and confusion and discomfort and pain.

The place was crammed to the deckhead: men stood or sat or knelt or lay in every available space: they crouched under the tables, they wedged themselves in corners, they stretched out on top of the broad ventilating shafts. There were men being seasick, men crying out in their sleep, men wolfing food, men hugging their bits of possessions and staring at nothing: wounded men groaning, apparently fit men laughing uneasily at nothing, brave men who could still summon a smile and a straight answer. It was impossible to pick one's way from one end of the fo'c's'le to the other, as Lockhart did each night when he made the Rounds, without being shocked and appalled and saddened by this slum corner of the war; and yet somehow one could be heartened also, and cheered by an impression of patience and endurance, and made to feel proud. . . . Individuals, here and there, might have been pushed close to defeat or panic; but the gross crowding, the rags, the oil, the bandages, the smell of men in adversity, were *still* not enough to defeat the whole company. They were all sailors there, not to be overwhelmed even by this sudden and sustained nightmare: they were being mucked about, it was true, but it would have to be a lot worse than this before they changed their minds about the sea.

There was another sort of nightmare that kept recurring to Lockhart as he looked at the throng of survivors, and at *Compass Rose's* seamen making their cheerful best of the invasion, and met a puzzled or a frightened face here and there in the crowd. Suppose, like *Sorrel*, they were hit; suppose they went down in a minute or so, in two broken halves, as *Sorrel* had done: what would happen in there, what sort of trapped and clawing shambles would develop as they slid to the bottom? The details could not really be faced, though it was possible that other people in the fo'c's'le were occupying their spare time in facing them. Once, when Lockhart was adjusting a survivor's bandaged arm, the man said:

"Be all right for swimming, eh?"

Lockhart smiled. "Sure thing. But you won't be doing any more swimming on this trip."

The man looked straight at him, and jerked his head. "You're dead right there. If anything happens to this lot, we're snug in our coffin already."

. . .

227

The afternoon that they rejoined the convoy, another signal came from the Admiralty. "There are now eleven U-boats in your area," it ran. "Destroyers *Lancelot* and *Liberal* will join escort at approximately 1800."

"Two 'L' Class destroyers—that's grand!" said Baker enthusiastically, down in the wardroom at tea time. "They're terrific ships. Brand-new, too."

"They'd better be very terrific indeed," said Morell, who was reading a copy of the signal. "Eleven U-boats works out at one to each ship left in the convoy. I very much doubt," he added suavely, "whether their Lordships really intended such a nice balance of forces."

Lockhart smiled at him. "Getting rattled, John?"

Morell considered for a moment. "I must admit," he said finally, "that this is *not* a reassuring occasion. Whatever we do, those damned U-boats get inside the screen every time. We've lost almost half our ships, and we're still two days away from Gibraltar." He paused, "It's odd to think that even if nothing else happens, this is probably the worst convoy in the history of sea warfare."

"Something to tell your grandchildren."

"Yes, indeed. In fact, if you guarantee me grandchildren I shall recover my spirits very quickly."

"How can he guarantee that you have grandchildren?" asked Baker who was, aboard *Compass Rose* at least, a dull conversationalist.

"If they're as stupid as you," said Morell, with a flash of impatience so rare that he must in truth have been nervous, "I hope I don't have any."

They were all feeling the same, thought Lockhart in the offended silence that followed: irritable, on edge, inclined to intolerance with each other. The tiredness and strain that had mounted during the past week was reaching an almost unbearable pitch. There could be no cure for it save gaining harbour with the remnants of their convoy, and that was still two days ahead. He suddenly wanted, more than anything else in the world, to be at peace and in safety. Like the rest of them, like all the escorts and all the merchant ships, he had very nearly had enough.

The two destroyers joined punctually at six o'clock, coming up from the southeast to meet the convoy, advancing swiftly toward it, each with an enormous creaming bow-wave. They both exhibited, to a special degree, that dramatic quality which was the pride of all destroyers: they were lean, fast, enormously powerful—nearer to light cruisers than destroyers—and clearly worth about three of any normal escort. They made a cheerful addition to the ships in company, thrashing about valiantly at the slightest scare or none at all, darting round and through the convoy at a full thirty-five knots, signalling in three directions at once, and refusing to stay still in any one position for more than five minutes at a time.

"Proper show-off," said Leading Signalman Wells, watching them through his glasses as they sped past on some purely inventive errand. But there was a touch of envy in his voice as he added: "All very well for them to dash about like a couple of brand new tarts—they haven't had the last week along o' this lot."

At dusk the two newcomers settled down, one ahead and one astern of the convoy, completing the atmosphere of last-minute rescue that had accompanied their arrival. They were doubtless well aware of the effect they had produced. But theatrical or not, their presence did seem to make a difference: though there was an attack that night, all that the circling pack of U-boats could account for was one ship, the smallest ship in the convoy. She was hit astern, and she went down slowly: out of her whole company the only casualty was a single Lascar seaman who jumped (as he thought) into the sea with a wild cry and landed head first in one of the lifeboats. In the midst of the wholesale slaughter, this comedy exit had just the right touch of fantasy about it to make it seem really funny. . . . But even so, this ship was the eleventh to be lost, out of the original twenty-one: it put them over the halfway mark, establishing a new and atrocious

229

record in U-boat successes. And the next night, the eighth and last of the battle, when they were within three hundred miles of Gibraltar, made up for any apparent slackening in the rate of destruction.

Three more ships, that last night cost, and one of them— yet another loaded tanker to be torpedoed and set on fire— was the special concern of *Compass Rose*. It was she who was nearest when the ship was struck, and she circled round as the oil, cascading and spouting from the tanker's open side, took fire and spread over the surface of the water like a flaming carpet in a pitch-black room. Silhouetted against this roaring backcloth, which soon rose to fifty feet in the air, *Compass Rose* must have been visible for miles around: even in swift movement she made a perfect target, and Ericson, trying to decide whether to stop and pick up sur- vivors, or whether the risk would not be justified, could visualize clearly what they would look like when stationary against this wall of flame. *Compass Rose*, with her crew and her painfully collected shipload of survivors, would be a sitting mark from ten miles away. . . . But they had been detailed as rescue ship: there were men in the water, there were boats from the tanker already lowered and pulling away from the tower of flame: there was a job to be done, a work of mercy, if the risk were acceptable—if it were worth hazarding two hundred lives in order to gain fifty more, if prudence could be stretched to include humanity.

It was Ericson's decision alone. It was a captain's moment, a pure test of nerve: it was, once again, the reality that lay behind the saluting and the graded discipline and the two- and-a-half stripes on the sleeve. While Ericson, silent on the bridge, considered the chances, there was not a man in the ship who would have changed places with him.

The order, when it came, was swift and decisive.

"Stop engines!"

"Stop engines, sir. . . . Engines stopped, wheel amid- ships, sir."

"Number One!"

"Sir?" said Lockhart.

"Stand by to get those survivors inboard. We won't lower a boat—they'll have to swim or row towards us. God knows they can see us easily enough. Use a megaphone to hurry them up."

"Aye, aye, sir."

As Lockhart turned to leave the bridge, the Captain added, almost conversationally:

"We don't want to waste any time, Number One."

All over the ship a prickling silence fell, as *Compass Rose* slowly came to a stop and waited, rolling gently, lit by the glare from the fire. From the bridge, every detail of the upper deck could be picked out: there was no flickering in this huge illumination, simply a steady glow that threw a black shadow on the sea behind them, that showed them naked to the enemy, that endowed the white faces turned toward it with a photographic brilliance. Waiting aft among his depth-charge crews, while the flames roared and three boats crept toward them, and faint shouting and bobbing lights here and there on the water indicated a valiant swimmer making for safety, Ferraby was conscious only of a terror-stricken impatience. "Oh God, oh God, oh God," he thought, almost aloud: "Let us give this up, let us get moving again. . . ." Twenty feet away from him in the port waist, Lockhart was coolly directing the preliminaries to the work of rescue —rigging a sling for the wounded men, securing the scrambling nets that hung over the side, by which men in the water could pull themselves up. Ferraby watched him, not with admiration or envy but with a futile hatred. "Damn you," he thought, once more almost saying the words out loud: "How can you be like that, why don't you feel like me —or if you do, why don't you show it?" He turned away from the brisk figures and the glowing heat of the flames, his eyes traversing the arch of black sky overhead, a sky blotched and streaked by smoke and whirling sparks; he looked behind him, at the outer darkness that the fire could not pierce, the place where the submarines must be lying and watching them. No submarine within fifty miles could miss this beacon, no submarine within five could resist chancing a torpedo, no submarine within two could fail to hit the silhouetted target, the stationary prey. It was wicked to stop like this, just for a lot of damned Merchant Navy roughs. . . .

A boat drew alongside, bumping and scraping: Lockhart called out: "Hook on forrard!" there were sounds of scrambling: an anonymous voice, foreign, slightly breathless, said: "God bless you for stopping!" The work of collection began.

It did not take long, save in their own minds; but coming toward the end of the long continued ordeal of the voyage, when there was no man in the ship who was not near to exhaustion, those minutes spent motionless in the limelight had a creeping and paralytic tension. It seemed impossible for them to take such a reckless chance, and not be punished for it; there was, in the war at sea, a certain limiting factor to bravery, and beyond that, fate stood waiting with a ferocious rebuke. "If we don't buy it this time," said Wainwright, the torpedoman, standing by his depth charges and staring at the flames, "Jerry doesn't *deserve* to win the war." It did seem, indeed, that if *Sorrel* could be hit when she was zigzagging at fourteen knots, there wouldn't be much trouble with *Compass Rose;* and as the minutes passed, while they collected three boatloads of survivors and a handful of swimmers, and the huge circle of fire gave its steady illumination, they seemed to be getting deeper and deeper into a situation from which they would never be able to retreat. The men who had work to do were lucky: the men who simply waited, like Ericson on the bridge or the stokers below the waterline, knew, in those few agonizing minutes, the meaning of fear.

It never happened: that was the miracle of that night. Perhaps some U-boat fired and missed, perhaps those within range, content with their success, had submerged for safety's sake and broken off the attack; at any rate, *Compass Rose* was allowed her extraordinary hazard, without having to settle the bill. When there were no more men to pick up, she got under way again: the returning pulse of her engine, heard and felt throughout the ship, came like some incredible last-minute respite, astonishing them all. But the pulse strengthened and quickened, in triumphant chorus, and she drew away from the flames and the smell of oil with her extra load of survivors snatched from the very mouth of danger, and her flaunting gesture unchallenged. They had taken the chance, and it had come off; mixed with the exhilaration of that triumph was a sober thankfulness for deliverance, a certain humility. Perhaps it would not do to think too much about it: perhaps it was better to bury the moment as quickly as possible, and forget it, and not take that chance again.

Another ship, on the opposite wing, went down at four o'clock, just before dawn; and then, as daylight strengthened and the rags of the convoy drew together again, they witnessed the last cruel item of the voyage.

Lagging behind with some engine defect, a third ship was hit, and began to settle down on her way to the bottom. She sank slowly, but owing to bad organization, or the villainous list the torpedoing gave her, no boats got away; for her crew, it was a time for swimming, for jumping into the water, and striking out away from the fatal downward suction, and trusting to luck. *Compass Rose*, dropping back to come to her aid, circled round as the ship began to disappear; and then, as she dipped below the level of the sea and the swirling ripples began to spread outward from a central point that was no longer there, Ericson turned his ship's bows towards the centre of disaster, and the bobbing heads that dotted the surface of the water. But it was not to be a straightforward rescue; for just as he was opening his mouth to give the order for lowering a boat, the asdic set picked up a contact, an undersea echo so crisp and well-defined that it could only be a U-boat.

Lockhart, at his action station in the asdic compartment, felt his heart miss a beat as he heard that echo. At last. . . . He called through the open window: "Echo bearing two-two-five—moving left!" and bent over the asdic set in acute concentration. Ericson increased the revolutions again, and turned away from the indicated bearing, meaning to increase the range: if they were to drop depth charges, they would need a longer run-in to get up speed. In his turn, he called out: "What's it look like, Number One?" and Lockhart, hearing the harsh pinging noise and watching the mark on the recording set, said: "Submarine, sir—can't be anything else." He continued to call out the bearing and the range of the contact: Ericson prepared to take the ship in, at attacking speed, and to drop a pattern of depth charges on the way; and then, as *Compass Rose* turned inward towards the target, gathering speed for the onslaught, they all noticed something that had escaped their attention before. The place where the U-boat lay, the point where they must drop their charges, was alive with swimming survivors.

The Captain drew in his breath sharply at the sight. There were about forty men in the water, concentrated in a small space: if he went ahead with the attack he must, for certain, kill them all. He knew well enough, as did everyone on board, the effect of depth charges exploding under water— the splitting crash that made the sea jump and boil and spout skyward, the aftermath of torn seaweed and dead fish that always littered the surface after the explosion. Now there were men instead of fish and seaweed, men swimming toward him in confidence and hope. . . . And yet the U-boat was there, one of the pack that had been harassing and bleeding them for days on end, the destroying menace that *must* have priority, because of what it might do to other ships and other convoys in the future: he could hear the echo on the relay-loudspeaker, he acknowledged Lockhart's developed judgement where the asdic set was concerned. As the seconds sped by, and the range closed, he fought against his doubts, and against the softening instinct of mercy; the book said: "Attack at all costs," and this was a page out of the book, and the men swimming in the water did not matter at all, when it was a question of bringing one of the killers to account.

But for a few moments longer he tried to gain support and confidence for what he had to do.

"What's it look like now, Number One?"

"The same, sir—solid echo—exactly the right size—*must* be a U-boat."

"Is it moving?"

"Very slowly."

"There are some men in the water, just about there."

There was no answer. The range decreased as *Compass Rose* ran in: they were now within six hundred yards of the swimmers and the U-boat, the fatal coincidence that had to be ignored.

"What's it look like now?" Ericson repeated.

"Just the same—seems to be stationary—it's the strongest contact we've ever had."

"There are some chaps in the water."

"Well, there's a U-boat just underneath them."

"All right, then," thought Ericson, with a new unlooked-for access of brutality to help him: "All right, we'll go for the U-boat. . . ." With no more hesitation he gave the order: "Attacking—stand by!" to the depth-charge positions aft; and having made this sickening choice he swept in to the attack with a deadened mind, intent only on one kind of kill, pretending there was no other.

Many of the men in the water waved wildly as they saw what was happening: some of them screamed, some threw themselves out of the ship's path and thrashed furiously in the hope of reaching safety: others, slower witted or nearer to exhaustion, still thought that *Compass Rose* was speeding to their rescue, and continued to wave and smile almost to their last moment. . . . The ship came in like an avenging angel, cleaving the very centre of the knot of swimmers: the amazement and horror on their faces was reflected aboard *Compass Rose*, where many of the crew, particularly among the depth-charge parties aft, could not believe what they were being called upon to do. Only two men did not share this horror: Ericson, who had shut and battened down his mind except to a single thought—the U-boat they must kill: and Ferraby, whose privilege it was to drop the depth charges. "Serve you bloody well right!" thought Ferraby as *Compass Rose* swept in among the swimmers, catching some of them in her screw, while the firing-bell sounded and the charges rolled over the stern or were rocketed outward from the throwers: "Serve you right—you nearly killed us last night, making us stop next door to that fire—now it's our turn."

There was a deadly pause, while for a few moments the men aboard *Compass Rose* and the men left behind in her wake stared at each other, in pity and fear and a kind of basic disbelief; and then with a huge hammer-crack the depth charges exploded.

Mercifully the details were hidden in the flurry and roar of the explosion; and the men must all have died instantly, shocked out of life by the tremendous pressure of the sea thrown up upon their bodies. But one freak item of the horror impressed itself on the memory. As the tormented water leaped upward in a solid grey cloud, the single figure of a man was tossed high on the very plume of the fountain, a puppet figure of whirling arms and legs seeming to make, in death, wild gestures of anger and reproach. It appeared to hang on a long time in the air, cursing them all, before falling back into the boiling sea.

When they ran back to the explosion area, with the asdic silent and the contact not regained, it was as if to some aquarium where poisoned water had killed every living thing. Men floated high on the surface like dead goldfish in a film of blood. Most of them were disintegrated, or pulped out of human shape. But half a dozen of them, who must have been on the edge of the explosion, had come to a tidier end; split open from chin to crotch, they had been as neatly gutted as any herring. Some seagulls were already busy on the scene, screaming with excitement and delight. Nothing else stirred.

No one looked at Ericson as they left that place: if they had done so, they might have been shocked by his expression and his extraordinary pallor. Now deep in self-torture, and appalled by what he had done, he had already decided that there had been no U-boat there in the first place: the contact was probably the torpedoed ship, sliding slowly to the bottom, or the disturbed water of her sinking. Either way, the slaughter he had inflicted was something extra, a large, entirely British-made contribution to the success of the voyage.

By the time they were past the Straits, and had smelt the burnt smell of Africa blowing across from Ceuta, and had shaped a course for Gibraltar harbour, they were all far off balance.

It had gone on too long, it had failed too horribly, it had cost too much. They had been at action stations for virtually eight days on end, missing hours of sleep, making do with scratch meals of cocoa and corned-beef sandwiches, living all the time under recurrent anxieties that often reached a desperate tension. There had hardly been a moment of the voyage when they could forget the danger that lay in wait for them and the days of strain that stretched ahead, and relax and find peace. They had been hungry and dirty and tired, from one sunrise to the next: they had lived in a ship crammed and disorganized by nearly three times her normal complement. Through it all, they had had to preserve an alertness and a keyed-up efficiency, hard enough to maintain even in normal circumstances.

The deadly part was that it had all been in vain, it had all been wasted: there could have been no more futile expense of endurance and nervous energy. Besides *Sorrel*, which was in a special category of disaster, they had lost fourteen ships out of the original twenty-one—two thirds of the entire convoy, wiped out by a series of pack-attacks so adroit and so ferocious that countermeasures had been quite futile. That was the most wretched element of the voyage—the inescapable sense of futility, the conviction that there were always more U-boats than escorts and that the U-boats could strike, and strike home, practically as they willed.

The escorts, and *Compass Rose* among them, seemed to have been beating the air all the time: they could do nothing save count the convoy's losses at each dawn, and make, sometimes, a vain display of force which vanished like a trickle of water swallowed by an enormous sea. In the end, they had all sickened of the slaughter, and of the battle too.

To offset the mortal bleeding of the convoy, by far the worst of this or any other war, *Viperous* had sunk one U-boat: a second had probably been destroyed; and *Compass Rose* herself had collected 175 survivors—nearly twice the number of her own crew. But this seemed nothing much, when set alongside the total loss of lives: it seemed nothing much, when measured against the men they had depth-charged and killed, instead of saving; it seemed nothing much, when shadowed by the stricken figure of *Sorrel's* captain, wordless and brooding at the back of their bridge as *Compass Rose* slid into the shelter of Gibraltar Harbour, under the huge Rock that dwarfed and mocked the tiny defeated ships below.

At half past eight on the evening of their arrival, there was a knock on the door of the Captain's cabin. Ericson, sitting in his armchair with a glass in his hand and a half-empty bottle of gin on the side-table, called out: "Come in!" in a voice from which all expression save an apathetic listlessness had vanished. He had been drinking steadily since four o'clock, in an attempt to forget or to blur the edges of certain scenes from their recent voyage. It had not been successful, as a glance at his face showed all too plainly.

In answer to his invitation three extraordinary figures entered the cabin: three tall, very fair men, all dressed alike in sky-blue suits of an excruciating cut, vivid shirts with thick brown stripes, and yellow pointed shoes. They stood before him, like a trio from some monstrous vaudeville act, looking down at the figure slumped in the chair with expressions half doubtful, half smiling: they had the air of men who expect to be recognized and welcomed, and yet are uncertain of their exact status in novel circumstances. They were like three public-school boys who had strayed, by accident, into the headmaster's side of the house.

The Captain stood up, rocking slightly on his feet, and

focused his eyes with an effort. "Who—" he began, and then he suddenly recognized them. They were three of his late passengers, the captains of Norwegian ships, who had been living in the wardroom for the past three or four days after being picked up as survivors. The last time Ericson had seen them, they had been wearing what was left of their uniforms; now, it was clear, they had been ashore, and some Gibraltar outfitter had done his worst for them in the way of civilian clothes. It was a highly efficient disguise for men who, when properly dressed as ship's captains, could exhibit a formidable air of competence and toughness.

The tallest and fairest of them, possibly the elected spokesman, took a pace forward, and said, in a voice just over the borderline of sobriety:

"Good evening, Captain. We came back to thank you for our lives."

Ericson blinked. "Didn't recognize you," he said, his voice equally blurred. "Come in. Sit down. Have a drink."

"Thank you, no," said the first speaker.

"Thank you, yes," said the man just behind him, with perverse readiness. "I wish to drink with this brave man who stopped his ship in the middle of a fire, and gave me my life."

"And me," said the third man, who had the worst suit and the vilest shirt of all, "me, I have the same wish, much stronger. And for my wife too, and my three children."

"That's fine," said Ericson, a trifle embarrassed. "Let's sit down. What'll you have?"

But when they were all three provided with glasses, and had settled down on the hard cabin chairs, the conversation lagged. There had been a formal toast to their rescuer, and much repetition of the word "Skoal!" each time they drank; apart from that, there did not seem much to say. Ericson was too near to his brooding thoughts to switch over to conviviality at such short notice; and the three visitors, who had clearly included any number of bars in their shopping tour ashore, were further handicapped by their halting English. Ericson, with an effort, complimented them on their new and appalling clothes: there were more drinks, and more cries of

The Cruel Sea

"Skoal!": and then a stone-wall silence fell, one of those silences which demonstrate instantly that all the conversation that has gone before, no matter how lively, has been an arid social artifice. Finally it was broken by the first of the three captains, who leaned forward in his chair and said solemnly:

"We know that you have much to think about."

"Yes," said Ericson, "I've been thinking."

"You are sad?"

"Yes," said Ericson again. "I'm pretty sad."

The second captain leaned forward in his turn. "The men in the water?"

Ericson nodded.

"The men you had to kill?" asked the third captain, completing the chorus.

"The men I had to kill," repeated Ericson after a pause. He remembered having once seen a Russian play with dialogue like this. Perhaps Norwegian plays were the same.

"It was necessary to do it," said the first captain decisively, and the other two nodded. "Yes," said the second. The third one said: "Skoal!" and drank deeply.

"May be," answered Ericson. "But that didn't make them look any prettier, did it?"

"It is war," said the second captain.

"Skoal!" said the first.

"I wash my hands, please," said the third.

When he came back, Ericson roused himself momentarily. "I really thought there was a submarine there," he said. "Otherwise I wouldn't have done it." He realized how foolish that must sound, and he added: "I had to make up my mind. I've put it all in the report."

"There is no blame," said one of the captains.

"But there may be thoughts," said another.

"Naturally there will be thoughts."

"For thoughts there is gin," said the first captain, with an air of logic.

"Skoal!" said Ericson.

It went on like that for a very long time. It was neither better, nor worse, than being alone. But when his three visitors had gone, Ericson did not relax: he simply reached out his hand for the bottle again. It was quite true that for thoughts there was gin.

It was Lockhart who finally found him, some time after midnight, leaning over the rail just outside his cabin, staring down at the water, muttering vaguely. Lockhart himself, though he had had less to drink, was in no better case as far as his private thoughts were concerned. Earlier that evening he had gone ashore with Lieutenant-Commander Ramsay, *Sorrel's* captain, to see the latter to his billet in the nearby Naval Barracks: it had been a sad, silent walk through streets and crowds whose cheerfulness was not infectious, and they had parted almost as strangers. Now Lockhart was back on board, but he felt quite unable to turn in: he had the jitters, like nearly everyone else in the ship, he was exhausted beyond the point of relaxation, his brain had too much company for sleep.

But when he came to the end of his pacing of the iron deck, there was the Captain, leaning over the rail in helpless defeat. Someone on board was even worse off than himself. . . . The big tough figure stirred as Lockhart approached, and turned toward him.

"Are you all right, sir?" asked Lockhart.

"No," answered Ericson readily. "I don't mind telling *you* that I'm not." His tone was thick and slurring: it was the first time Lockhart had ever heard it so, and after their two years of close association it was hard to identify the surrendered voice with the competent one he knew so well.

Lockhart came close to him, and leaned against the rail also. They were on the side away from the quay: before them was the harbour, ghostly under the moonlight, and ahead was the black shadow of the aircraft carrier *Ark Royal*, their nearest neighbour, and behind towered the huge Rock of Gibraltar, the haven for which they had been steering for many days and nights. All round them the ship, at rest after her disastrous voyage, was oppressively silent.

"You've got to forget all about it," said Lockhart, suddenly breaking through the normal barrier of reserve that separated them. "It's no good worrying about it now. You can't change anything."

"There *was* a submarine," shouted Ericson in a furious voice. He was now helplessly drunk. "I'm bloody well sure of it. . . . It's all in the report."

"It was my fault, anyway," said Lockhart. "I identified it as a submarine. If anyone killed those men, I killed them."

Ericson looked up at him. Incredibly, there were tears in his eyes which glittered like bright jewels starting from a mask, proclaiming his weakness and his manhood in the same revealing moment. Lockhart looked at them in amazement and compassion: how moving was that pale working face, how comforting, after their ordeal, the glistening tears of this strong man. . . . He made as if to speak, wanting to forestall Ericson and save him from further revelation; but the other man suddenly put his hand on his shoulder and said, in an almost normal voice:

"No one killed them. . . . It's the war, the whole bloody war. . . . We've just got to do these things, and say our prayers at the end. . . . Have you been drinking, Number One?"

"Yes, sir," said Lockhart. "Quite a lot."

"So have I . . . First time since we commissioned . . . Good night."

Without waiting for an answer he turned and lurched towards his cabin entrance. After a moment there was a thud, and Lockhart, following him into the cabin, found that he had collapsed and was lying face downwards in his armchair, dead to the world.

"Sir," said Lockhart formally, "you'd better get to bed."

There was no sound save Ericson's heavy breathing.

"You poor old bastard," said Lockhart, half to himself, half to the prone figure spread-eagled below him, "you poor old bastard, you've just about had enough, haven't you?" He considered getting the other man's clothes off and somehow bundling him into his bunk, but he knew he would never be able to do it—the helpless fourteen-stone weight would be far too much for him. Instead he began to heave the Captain's body round so as to settle him comfortably in the armchair, talking out loud as he did so. "I can't get you to bed, my dear and revered Captain, but I can at least snug you down for the night. . . . You'll have quite a head when you wake up, God bless you—I don't think I'd like to be one of your defaulters tomorrow morning. . . . Get your legs out straight. . . ." He eased Ericson's collar and tie, looked down at him for a moment more as he lay relaxed in the arm-chair, and then moved toward the doorway. "That's the best I can do for you," he murmured, his hand on the light-switch. "Wish it could be more, wish I could *really* cure you. . . ." He clicked off the light. "Drunk or sober, Ericson, you're all right. . . ."

He was already halfway through the doorway when he heard the other man's voice behind him, vague and sleepy.

"Number One," said Ericson, "I heard that."

"That's all right, sir," said Lockhart, without embarrassment. "I meant it. . . . Good night."

There was silence as he went out, silence as he climbed down the ladder to the deserted wardroom. All round him, as on the upper deck, the exhausted ship lay in the embrace of sleep, hoping to forget the horrible past. Lockhart dwelt for a moment on that past, and his own guilty part in it; then he unlocked the sideboard, set out a bottle and a glass, and, following what now seemed an excellent example, drank himself into insensibility.

[8]

Morell sat at ease on a balcony overlooking the main street of Gibraltar, gravely sipping a tall glass of Tio Pepe sherry so exquisitely pale and dry that it was an honour to welcome it upon the tongue.

Below him the crowds were thickening as the libertymen thronged ashore from the many ships in harbour. There was so much here that was new, to do and to see: the shops carried their full cargos of silk stockings and scents, the gharries threaded their way down the narrow streets with their canopies ruffled by the breeze, and from the cafés and beer halls the music and the laughter beckoned continuously; it was all part of the fun, part of the novel landfall. They always enjoyed their visits to Gibraltar; and now, as far as *Compass Rose* was concerned, it came as a special balm for their defeat, underlining the wonder of having survived so fearful a voyage. Morell, like the rest of them, was welcoming it all with open hands: after a week in harbour, the hot sunshine, the chance of relaxing in their white tropical rig, the swimming parties to the eastern side of the Rock, the strange faces in the street, the glamour of visiting a foreign port, still showed no signs of palling. There was nothing much on the credit side of that voyage; but if one were lucky enough to be alive at the end of it, instead of dead like most of *Sorrel's* crew, Gibraltar seemed a particularly good place to be alive in.

They felt, too, that they themselves had a special status here. Rumours of the disaster to the convoy had spread swiftly among the personnel of the base: it was enough to remark, in the Naval Mess ashore: "We were with AG93," for an alert silence to intervene, and for curious speculative glances to focus on the speaker. AG93 was a convoy with a reputation: anyone who had sailed with it ought by rights to be either round the bend, or dead. . . . It was something to have earned even this dubious *cachet*, in a port that was playing so dramatic a part in the war and where the big ships, whose base it was, were earning worldwide reputations for courage and daring.

Ark Royal, for example, lay next ahead of them in the harbour below, the sheer of her bows climbing like an overhanging cliff up to the enormous flight-deck that crowned her superstructure. She was now the most hunted ship on the seven seas, the target for the bombs, the torpedoes, and the boastful lies of the enemy: with her were the battle cruiser *Renown* and the rest of "Force H," that famous company of ships which had fought the convoys through to Malta in the face of a ferocious opposition, and could still find time to trail the *Bismarck* to her death, a thousand miles to the northward. Grouped round them in the teeming harbour were the lesser vessels—the destroyer flotillas, the fleet minesweepers, the clutch of submarines that harassed the coastwise shipping of the western Mediterranean: across the bay in Algeciras, smugly privileged, were the spying eyes of the enemy, sheltering under the wing of Spain whose contribution to victory this was: far to the eastward were Crete and Greece, now in the throes of a bloody rout; and over all the fabulous Rock stood guard, that impregnable honeycomb of tunnels and lifts and ammunition and stores and guns, holding the Straits by the throat, and a thousand square miles of ocean in the same mortal grip.

Morell called for another glass of sherry, and sat on in his soft delectable corner of the fortress, watching the declining sun and the lengthening shadows of the evening, sipping the delicate drink in complete contentment. Presently there was vague shouting and the sound of some disturbance in a café further down the street; but he did not bestir himself to look over the balcony rail, nor was he in the least curious about the noise. If it were anyone from *Compass Rose* in trouble, he would hear all about it in the morning; if not, they could murder each other with jagged bottle-tops, for all he cared. . . . He wanted nothing more from this moment: no excitement, no complication, no angel in the path. They had had their ordeal, they had survived it, and it was good, very good, to be at ease at last.

[9]

On the sixth day of their journey home, late in the forenoon watch, Chief E.R.A. Watts came up to the bridge with a worried frown on his face. So far, things had been going well with their return convoy: there had been no shadowing aircraft, no scares about U-boats waiting for them, no drama of any sort. It made a nice change. . . . But now there was a chance of things not going well at all, and it was he who had to break the news.

"Captain, sir!" Watts stood at the back of the bridge, awkwardly shifting his feet on the smooth white planking. He never came up there if he could help it, because it made him feel entirely out of place: his proper station was on the engine-room "plate" three decks below, among the pipes and the gauges that he understood so well; this open-air stuff, with look-outs and flag-signals and water dashing past all round, was not his cup of tea at all. Even his overalls and oily canvas shoes looked funny, with everyone else dolled up in sea boots and duffle coats. . . . Ericson, who had been preparing to check their noon position, and enjoying the sunshine at the same time, turned round at the sound of his voice.

"Well, Chief? Anything wrong?"

"Afraid so, sir." Watts came forward, rubbing his hands on his overalls. His grey creased face was full of concern. "I've got a bearing I don't like the feel of at all. Running hot, it is—nearly red-hot. I'd like to stop and have a look at it, sir."

"Do you mean the main shaft, Chief?" Ericson knew that his knowledge of the engine room, sufficient for normal purposes, did not include all the technical refinements, and he wanted to get his facts straight.

"Yes, sir. Must be a blocked oil-pipe, by the look of it."

"Any good if we slow down? I don't want to stop if we can help it."

Watts shook his head vigorously. "If we keep the shaft turning it's liable to seize up, sir. And I can't trace the oil line back from the main feed unless we stop engines. It's one of those awkward corners—the after bearing, right up against the gland space."

Ericson, struggling to give form to the sketchy picture in his mind, frowned in concentration. But the answer seemed fairly clear. If a main bearing were running hot, it wasn't getting its proper ration of oil: if the oil were continuously denied, and the melting point of the metal were reached, the bearing and the surrounding sleeve would be welded into one, and the main shaft would be locked. That was, comparatively speaking, a straightforward piece of mechanical mystery . . . For a moment he cast about in his mind for possible alternatives, but he knew there were none. They would have to do the least healthy thing in the war at sea— stop in mid-ocean, with their engine put out of commission.

"All right, Chief," said Ericson, making up his mind to it. "I'll send a signal, and then ring down for you to stop. Be as quick as you can."

"I'll be that, sir."

They were just in visual touch with *Viperous*, who was zigzagging in broad sweeps across the van of the convoy. When *Compass Rose* signalled her news, the answer was laconic:

"Act independently. Keep me informed."

"Acknowledge," said Ericson briefly to Rose, who was signalman of the watch. Then: "Starboard ten. Stop engines," he called down to the wheelhouse; and *Compass Rose*, turning in a wide sweep away from the convoy, lost way and came gradually to a standstill.

Up on the bridge they waited in silence, while the convoy steamed past them, and the corvette that had the stern position altered course to pass close by, like an inquisitive terrier that does not know whether to wag its tail or to bark. Down below in the engine room, Watts and a leading stoker called Gracey set to work on their examination of the oil feed. It was indeed an awkward corner, jammed up against a bulkhead and barely approachable: to trace the trouble they had to pick out the suspect oil-pipe from an array of a dozen, and then take it to pieces in sections to find out which part of it was blocked. The engine room was very hot: they were forced to bend nearly double as they worked, groping for the joints from opposite sides of the piping because there was not room for them to stand side by side: sections of the pipe could not be brought out and examined before other sections of other pipes had been loosened and removed. It was a full two hours before they had located the trouble—an L-shaped, curved section that appeared to be totally blocked.

Watts stepped backward and straightened up, holding the pipe in one hand and wiping his sweaty forehead with the other. "Now what?" he said rhetorically. "How do we find out what's inside this?"

"Suck it and see, I suppose," answered Gracey, who was a lower-deck comedian of some note.

"Get a piece of wire," said Watts coldly. Some people were allowed to be funny to Chief E.R.A.'s, but leading stokers were not included in this licensed category. "Not too thick. . . . I'm going up to report to the Captain."

After two more hours of steady work, they were still no further on. Whatever had got inside the pipe seemed to be stuck there immovably: it couldn't be blown out, it couldn't be pushed through, it couldn't be melted or picked to pieces. Waiting on the bridge of his useless ship, Ericson found it hard to restrain himself from storming down to the engine room and telling them to stop loafing and get on with it; but he knew that this would have been futile, as well as unfair. Watts was doing his best: no one else on board could do better. At four o'clock, with the last ships of the convoy now out of sight below the horizon, Ericson had sent a signal by R/T to *Viperous*, explaining what was happening; there had been no answer beyond a bare acknowledgment, and it was clear that *Viperous* was setting him a good example in trusting him to make the best of the repair and to rejoin as soon as possible.

He stood wedged in a corner of the bridge, staring down at the dark oily water that reflected the overcast sky; behind him, Ferraby and Baker, who had the watch, were idly examining the pieces of a Hotchkiss anti-aircraft gun that one of the gunnery ratings was stripping. The asdic set clicked and pinged, monotonously wakeful, the radar aerial circled an invisible horizon: the two look-outs occasionally raised their binoculars and swept through their respective arcs—forward, aft, and forward again. *Compass Rose* was entirely motionless: her ensign hung down without stirring, her vague shadow on the water never moved or altered its outline. She was waiting for two things—for her engine to start again, and for the other thing that might happen to her, without warning and without a chance of defending herself either. Who knew what was below the surface of the dark sea, who knew what malevolent eye might be regarding them, even at this moment? In the nervous and oppressive silence, such thoughts multiplied, with nothing to set against them save the hope of getting going again.

On the quarterdeck aft, some of the hands were fishing. If Ericson had told them that they were fishing in at least a thousand fathoms of water, as was in fact the case, it would probably have made no difference. Fishing—even with bread-crumb bait dangling six thousand feet above the ocean bed— was better than doing nothing, at a moment like this.

Down below in the engine room, Chief E.R.A. Watts had come to a certain decision. It involved considerable delay, and some danger of wrecking everything beyond repair; but there was no choice left to him.

"We'll have to saw the pipe up," he said to Gracey, at the end of another futile bout of poking and picking at the obstruction. "Bit by bit, till we find the stoppage."

"What then?"

"Clear it out, and then braze the whole thing together again."

"Take all night if we do that," said Gracey sulkily.

"Take all the war if we don't," retorted Watts. "Get a hacksaw, while I tell the Captain."

Watts was actually up on the bridge when *Viperous* appeared in sight again. She came storming down from the northwestward at about five o'clock in the afternoon, her big signal-lamp flickering as soon as she was over the horizon; she wanted to know everything—the state of their repairs, the chances of their getting going again, and whether they had had any suspicious contacts or seen any aircraft during their stoppage. In consultation with Watts, Ericson answered as best he could: they had located the trouble, and would almost certainly be able to clear it, but it would probably take them most of the night to do it.

Viperous, who had stopped her swift approach as soon as she was in effective touch, circled lazily about ten miles off them while the signals were exchanged. Then there was a pause, and then she signalled:

"Afraid I cannot spare you an escort for the night."

"That is quite all right," Ericson signalled back. "We will sleep by ourselves." He put that in in case *Viperous* were feeling sad about the arrangement. It was perfectly true that two escorts could not be spared from the convoy during the night; there could be no argument about the rightness of that decision.

There was another pause. *Viperous* began to shape up towards the northward horizon again. When she was stern-on to them:

"I must leave you to it," she signalled finally. "Best of luck." She began to draw away. Just before she got out of touch she signalled again: "Good night, Cinderella."

" 'Good night, dear elder sister,' " Ericson dictated to Rose. But then he cancelled the message, before Rose started sending. The captain of *Viperous* was just a little bit too elder—in rank—for him to run the risk.

The repairs did not take all the night, but they took many trying hours of it. Watts had to cut the oil-pipe eight times before he found the exact point of obstruction; this was at the joint of the elbow, and consisted of a lump of cotton waste hardened and compressed into a solid plug. The question of how it got there gave Watts half an hour of abusive and infuriated speculation, and left Leading Stoker Gracey, along with the rest of the engine-room complement, in sullen contemplation of the whole system of Naval discipline. But time was not there to be wasted: even as he raged and questioned, Watts was working swiftly on the pieces of piping, brazing them together again into something like the same length and curve as they had had before. The result did not

look very reassuring, and once they were delayed and very
nearly defeated by a section that succumbed to the heat of
the blow-lamp and collapsed into solid metal: but finally the
whole pipe was cleared and smoothed off, and they set to
work to coax it back into position again.

Outside, dusk had come down, and then the night. With
its coming, they took extraordinary precautions against discovery: Lockhart went round the upper deck three or four
times to ensure that the ship was properly darkened and that
no chink of light would betray them: the radios in the wardroom and the mess-decks were closed down, and stringent
orders given against unnecessary noise: the boats were swung
out, ready for lowering, and the lashings of the rafts cast off
—in case, as Tallow put it morbidly, they had to make a rush
job of swimming. "And if any of you," he added to the hands
working on the upper deck, "makes a noise tonight, I'll
have his guts for a necktie." Their situation now involved a
worse risk than any stopping or loitering had done before,
because this time they were quite helpless: if a torpedo
passed right underneath them, they could only wave good-
bye to it, and wait for the next one. As the hours passed, the
tension became unbearable: this was the sea, the very stretch
of water, that on their outward voyage had seen so many men
go to their death, and here they were, sitting on it like a
paralysed duck and waiting for the bang.

But there was nothing to do except wait. Watch succeeded
watch: the hands tiptoed delicately to their stations, instead
of clumping along the deck or stamping their sea boots on
the iron ladders, as they usually did: *Compass Rose* floated
motionless, with the black water occasionally slapping
against her side: a brilliant quarter-moon hung in the mid-
Atlantic sky, showing them all the outlines of their hazard.
Throughout the ship there was the same tension, the same
disbelief in the future, the same rage against the bloody stokers down below who had let the engine get gummed up, and
were now loafing and fiddling about. . . . Lockhart had it
in mind to give the watch on deck, and the other spare hands,
something definite to do, to take their attention away from

the present danger; but everything he thought of—such as fire drill or lowering a boat to the waterline—involved noise and probably the flashing of torches on the upper deck, and in the end he abandoned the idea and left them alone. Waiting in idleness was bad for the nerves; but the risk attending anything else might be worse still.

Ericson spent all these hours up on the bridge: there was no other station for him at such a moment, and no other choice in his mind. The look-outs changed half-hourly: cocoa came up in relays from the wardroom: the asdic and the radar kept up their incessant watch: curbing his immense impatience, Ericson sat on, enthroned like some wretched ragamuffin chief on the bridge of his useless ship. Mostly he stared at the water and the horizon, sometimes at the bright moon that no cloud would obscure: occasionally he watched the shadowy figures on the upper deck, the men who waited there in silent groups, collected round the guns or the boats, instead of going below and turning in. This was a new thing aboard *Compass Rose*. But he could not find fault with their prudence, he could not blame them for their fear.

There was an example of this nervous strain much closer at hand. Ferraby had not been below decks since the ship came to a stop, and now he was curled up in a blanket at the side of the bridge: he lay on his back, his hands clasped behind his head, his inflated life-jacket ballooning out like some opulent bosom; he had been there since he came off watch, at midnight, and he had never stirred or changed his position. Ericson had thought that he was dozing; but once, taking a turn round the bridge, he had noticed that the other man's eyes were wide open, and that he was darkly staring at the sky overhead. There was a sheen of perspiration at his temples. He was very far from sleep. . . . Ericson paused in his pacing, and looked down at the pale face.

"All right, sub?" he asked conversationally.

There was no answer, and no sign that he had been heard. But Ericson did not persist with his question: this was a time to disregard people's reactions, to look past them without comment. The ship had been stopped, a still and defenceless target, for over twelve hours: *Sorrel* was fresh in all their minds: this was where it had all happened before. It was no wonder that, here and there, nerves stretched to breaking point were jumping and quivering in the effort to hold on.

He walked to the front of the bridge again, and sat down without another word. Ferraby could not help what was happening to him: no blame attached to him for his raw nerves, any more than a newborn child could be blamed for weighing six pounds instead of eight. The womb of war had produced him thus. But somewhere at the back of his mind Ericson was conscious of a strange sort of envy, an irritated consciousness of what a huge relief it would be to relax his grip, to surrender the unmoving mask of competence, to show to the world, if need be, his fatigue or fear. . . . "Gibraltar," he thought suddenly: "I gave up there, Lockhart saw it"—but that had been alcohol, alcohol and guilt, nothing else. And it was not to happen again, it was not to happen now. . . . Waiting in the darkness, watching the silver ripples crossing the track of the moon, he slowly tightened up again.

Only once during that night was there an interruption of their vigil, but it was an interruption that startled them all. In the stillness that followed the change of the watch, just after midnight, breaking harshly in upon the sound of lapping water, there was a sudden burst of hammering from below, a solid succession of thuds that resounded throughout the ship. Everyone came to attention, and looked at his neighbour in quest of reassurance: secretly they cursed the men working in the engine room, for re-awakening their fear and their hatred. The noise could be heard for miles around. . . . On the bridge, Ericson turned to Morell, who had just taken over the watch.

"Go down and see Watts," he said crisply. "Tell him to stop the hammering or to muffle it somehow. Tell him we can't afford to make this amount of noise." As Morell turned to go, Ericson added, less formally: "Tell him the torpedo will hit him first."

That was perfectly true, thought Morell, as he climbed

down successive ladders deep into the heart of the ship: to go below the waterline at a moment such as this was like stepping knowingly into the tomb. He could not help feeling a comradely admiration for the men who had been working patiently, ten feet below the surface of the water, for so many hours on end: it was part of their job, of course, just as it had sometimes been part of his own to be up on the exposed bridge when an aircraft was spraying them with machine-gun fire: but the cold-blooded hazard involved in working below decks in the present circumstances seemed to demand a special category of nervous endurance. If a torpedo came, the engine-room crew must be an instant casualty: they would have perhaps ten seconds to get out, as the water flooded in, and those ten seconds, for a dozen men fighting to use one ladder in the pitch darkness, would mean the worst end to life that a man could devise. . . . But hazard or not, they oughtn't to make so much noise about what they were doing: that was stretching their necks out too far altogether.

The hammering stopped as he slid down the last oily ladder to the engine room itself, and Watts, hearing his step on the iron plating, turned to greet him.

"Come to see the fun, sir? It won't be long now."

"That's my idea of good news, Chief," answered Morell. No settled Naval hierarchy could ever make him address Watts, who was nearly old enough to be his grandfather, with anything save an informal friendliness. "But the Captain's a bit worried about the noise. Can you do anything to tone it down?"

"Pretty well finished now, sir," said Watts. "We were just putting one of those brackets back. . . . Could you hear the hammering up top?"

"Hear it? There were submarines popping up for miles around, complaining about the racket."

There was a short laugh from the handful of men working round the oil pipe: down there, even the funniest jokes about submarines were only just funny. . . . Morell looked round the circle of faces, harshly lit by the naked hand-lamp clipped to a nearby stanchion: they all shared the same look, the same factors of expression—tiredness, concentration, fear in the background. He knew them all by sight—Watts, Leading Stoker Gracey, a couple of young second-class stokers named Binns and Spurway who were always getting drunk ashore, an apprentice E.R.A. called Broughton who was a Roman Catholic—but he had never known them quite like this: the labels and the characters he usually attached to them seemed to have been stripped and melted away, leaving only the basic men whose brains and fingers either could or could not patch up the oil pipe before a submarine caught them, and whose faces reflected this uncertain future. There was no pettiness about them now, no individual foible, no trace of indiscipline: as they worked, Care sat on their shoulders, Time's winged chariot was at their backs (Morell smiled as the odd phrases, incongruous in the glare and smell of the engine room, returned to him), and they knew this all the time and it had purged them of everything save a driving anxiety to finish what they had to do.

"Any signs of submarines, sir?" asked Gracey after a pause. He was a Lancashireman: he pronounced the hated word as "soobmarines," giving it a humorous air that robbed it of its sting. Said like that, it was hardly a submarine at all, just something out of a music-hall, no more lethal than a mother-in-law or a dish of tripe. How nice, thought Morell, if that were true.

"Nothing so far," he answered. "The convoy seems to be quite happy, too. But I don't think we want to hang about here too long."

Watts nodded. "Seems like we're sitting up and asking for it," he said grimly. "If they don't get us now, they never will."

"How much longer, Chief?"

"Couple of hours, maybe."

"Longest job we've ever had," said Gracey. "You'd think it was a bloody battlewagon."

"Me for barracks, when we get in," said Broughton. "I'd rather run the boiler-house at Chatham than this lot."

"Who wouldn't?" said Spurway, the smallest and usually the drunkest stoker. "*I'd* rather clean out the dockside heads, any day of the week."

Morell suddenly realized how intensely nervous they had all become, how far they had been driven beyond the normal margins of behaviour. He said: "Good luck with it," and started up the ladder again. At the top the stars greeted him, and then the black water. A small chill wind was stirring, sending quick ripples slapping against their side. Alone in the dark night, *Compass Rose* lay still, waiting.

[*10*]

In the cold hour that stretched between two and three a.m., with the moon clouded, and the water black and fathomless as sable, a step on the bridge ladder. But now it was a different sort of step: cheerful, quick-mounting, no longer stealthy. It was Chief E.R.A. Watts.

"Captain, sir!" he called to the vague figure hunched over the front of the bridge.

Ericson, stiff and cold with his long vigil, turned awkwardly towards him. "Yes, Chief?"

"Ready to move, sir."

So that was that, thought Ericson, standing up and stretching gratefully: they could get going, they could leave at last this hated corner, they could make their escape. The relief was enormous, flooding in till it seemed to reach every part of his body: he felt like shouting his congratulations, seizing Watts's hand and shaking it, giving way to his light-headed happiness. But all he said was: "Thank you, Chief. Very well done." And then, to the voice-pipe: "Wheelhouse!"

"Wheelhouse, bridge, sir!" came the quartermaster's voice, startled from some dream of home.

"Ring: 'Stand by, main engines.'"

Very soon they were off: steaming swiftly northward, chasing the convoy: the revolutions mounted, the whole ship grew warm and alive and full of hope again. There was no need to look back: they had, by all the luck in the world, left nothing of themselves behind and given nothing to the enemy.

At about six o'clock, with the first dawn lightening the sky to the eastward, they "got" the convoy on the very edge of the radar screen. Lockhart, who was Officer-of-the-Watch, looked at the blurred echo appreciatively: it was still many miles ahead, and they would not be in direct touch till mid-morning, but it put them on the map again—they were no longer alone on the waste of water that might have been their grave. He woke the Captain to tell him the news, as he had been ordered to: it seemed a shame to break into his sleep with so straightforward an item, which might well have been kept till later in the morning, but the orders had been ex-plicit—and probably Ericson would sleep the easier for hear-ing that they were in touch again. Indeed, the sleepy grunt that came up the voice-pipe in answer to Lockhart's informa-tion seemed to indicate that Ericson had only just risen to the surface, like a trout to a fly, to take in the news, before diving down fathoms deep to the luxury of sleep once more. Lock-hart smiled as he snapped the voice-pipe cover shut again. After such a night, the Captain deserved his zizz.

The morning watch progressed toward its ending at eight o'clock: the light grew to the eastward, blanching the dark water: Tomlinson, the junior steward, foraging for the cups and sandwich-plates of the night's session, went soft-footed on the wet and dewy deck, like a new character in a suddenly cheerful third act. The engine revolutions were now set near their maximum: *Compass Rose's* course was steady, aiming for the centre of the convoy ahead: Lockhart had nothing to do but stamp warmth into his feet and keep an appraising eye on the radar screen as the range closed and the pattern of ships hardened and took shape. It was good to see that compact blur of light, as welcome and as familiar as the deck under his sea boots, gaining strength and edging nearer to them: they had been away from it too long, they wanted, above all, an end to their loneliness, and here it was at last, tangible and expectant, like a family waiting to greet them at the finish of a journey. . . . His thoughts wandered: he responded automatically as the quartermaster and the look-outs changed for the final half hour of the watch: *Compass Rose*, breasting the long Atlantic swell and shifting gently under his feet, might have been a train rocking over the last set of points as it ran into Euston station. At the end of the platform there would be—he jerked to attention suddenly as the bell rang from the radar compartment.

"Radar—bridge!"

Lockhart bent to the voice-pipe. "Bridge."

The voice of the radar operator, level, rather tired, not excited, came up to him. "I'm getting a small echo astern of the convoy, sir. Can you see it on the repeater?"

Lockhart looked at the radar screen beside the voice-pipe, a replica of the one in the operator's compartment, and nodded to himself. It was true. Between the convoy and themselves there was now a single small echo, flickering and fading on the screen like a candle guttering in a gentle draught. He watched it for half a minute before speaking. It was never more than a luminous pinpoint of light, but it always came up, it was persistently *there* all the time: it was a contact, and it had to be accounted for. He bent to the voice-pipe again.

"Yes, I've got it. . . . What do you make of it?" Then, before the man could answer, he asked: "Who's that on the set?"

"Sellars, sir."

Sellars, thought Lockhart: their Leading Radar Mechanic, a reliable operator, a man worth asking questions. . . . He said again: "What do you make of it?"

"Hard to tell, sir," answered Sellars. "It's small, but it's there all the time, keeping pace with the convoy."

"Could it be a back-echo off the ships?"

"I don't think so, sir." Sellars's voice was dubious. "The angle's wrong, for a start."

"Well, a straggler, then?"

"It's a bit small for a ship, sir. . . . Do you see the ship right out to starboard—probably one of the escorts? That one's a lot bigger."

Lockhart stared at the radar screen. That, again, was quite true. On the edge of the convoy pattern, away to starboard, was a single detached echo that was probably a corvette; and it was appreciably bigger than the speck of light they were querying. He found himself hesitating, on the verge of reporting the strange echo to the Captain, and yet not wanting to wake him up from his deserved sleep without good reason. It could be one of many things, all of them harmless: it could be a fault in the set, which was not yet clear of its teething troubles: it could be a straggler from the convoy (though its size was against it): it could conceivably be a rainstorm. Or it could—it *could*—be something that they really wanted to see. . . . After watching for a full two minutes, while the echo strengthened slightly, maintaining level pace with the convoy as before, he said to Sellars: "Keep your eye on it," and then, unwillingly, he crossed to the Captain's voice-pipe and pressed the bell.

When he came up to the bridge, knuckling his eyes and rubbing his stiff face, Ericson was not in the best of tempers. He had had a bare four hours' sleep, interrupted by the first convoy-report; and to have it broken into again, just because (as he phrased it to himself) there was a bloody seagull perched on the radar aerial and the First Lieutenant hadn't got the sense to shoo it away, did not seem to him the best way of greeting the happy dawn. He grunted as Lockhart pointed out the echo and explained how it had developed: then he looked up from the radar screen, and said briefly:

"Probably a straggler."

"It's a lot smaller than the other ships, sir," said Lockhart tentatively. He recognized the Captain's right to be short-tempered at this God-forsaken hour of the morning, but he had taken that into account when he woke him up, and he wanted to justify the alarm. He pointed to the screen. "That's the stern escort, I should say. This thing is at least ten miles behind that."

"M'm," grunted Ericson again. Then: "Who's the radar operator?" he asked, following Lockhart's own train of thought.

"Sellars, sir."

Ericson bent to the voice-pipe, and cleared his throat with a growl. "Radar!"

"Radar—bridge!" answered Sellars.

"What about this echo?"

"Still there, sir." He gave the range and the bearing. "That makes it about ten miles astern of the last ship of the convoy."

"Nothing wrong with the set, is there?"

"No, sir," said Sellars, with the brisk air of a man who, at ten minutes to eight on a cold morning, was disinclined for this sort of slur, even coming from a bad-tempered captain. "The set's on the top line."

"Have you had an echo like this before?"

There was a pause below. Then: "Not exactly, sir. It's about the size we'd get from a buoy or a small boat."

"A trawler? A drifter?"

"Smaller than that, sir. Ship's boat, more like."

"H'm. . . ." Ericson looked at the radar screen again, while Lockhart, watching him, smiled to himself. It was clear that his bad temper was fighting a losing battle with his acknowledgment of Sellars's competence. Behind them, the rest of the bridge personnel, and Baker, who had just come up to take over the watch, were also eying the Captain speculatively, alert for any decision. But when it came, it was still a surprise.

"Sound Action Stations," said Ericson, straightening up suddenly. And to the wheelhouse, in the same sharp voice: "Full ahead! Steer ten degrees to starboard."

Lockhart opened his mouth to speak, and then snapped it up shut again. Taken by surprise, he had been about to say something phenomenally silly, like: "Do you really think it's a submarine, sir?" The loud, endless shrilling of the alarm bells all over the ship, and the thud of heavy boots along the decks and up the ladder, gave the best answer of all

to this foolish speculation. . . . He stood by the battery
of voice-pipes, conscious of more than the usual excitement
as the various positions were reported to him, and he acknowledged the reports. The pattern and the sequence of
this were yawningly familiar, it was all old stuff, they had
been doing it, in fun or in earnest, for two whole years; but
this time, this time it really might have some point to it. . . .

One by one the voices pricked his eagerness.

Ferraby from aft: "Depth-charge crews closed up!"

Morell from the fo'c's'le: "Gun's crew closed up!"

Baker from amidships: "Two-pounder gun closed up!"

Chief E.R.A. Watts from far below: "Action steaming-
stations!"

Tallow from the wheelhouse: "Coxswain on the wheel,
sir!"

Lockhart gave a swift glance round him, and fore and aft,
a final check for his own satisfaction. The bridge look-outs
were at their places on the Hotchkiss guns: Leading Signalman Wells was ready by the big signal-lamp. Grouped round
the four-inch gun just below the bridge, the steel-helmeted
crew stood alert, with Morell staring ahead through his
binoculars and then turning back to direct the loading: far
aft, Ferraby was the centre of another group of men, clearing away the safety lashings from the depth charges and preparing them for firing. Satisfied, Lockhart turned to the
Captain, presenting the completed pattern for whatever use
he chose to make of it.

"Action Stations closed up, sir!" he called out. Then he
dropped back to his own charge, the asdic set: the killing
instrument itself, if one were needed. . . . Underneath
them, as if conscious of her weight of tensed and ready men,
Compass Rose began to tremble.

Ericson was watching the radar screen. His call for Action
Stations had been not much more than an impulse: he could
even admit that it might have been prompted by irritation, by
the feeling that, if he himself had to be awake, then no one
else on board was going to go on sleeping. But certainly they
had picked up an odd-looking echo, one of the most promis-

ing so far: it was possible that this time they were really on to something, and in that case the full readiness of *Compass Rose* was a solid comfort. Momentarily he raised his binoculars and peered ahead, but the morning mist lay all round the horizon and there was nothing to be seen. He looked down at the radar screen again, and then bent to the voice-pipe.

"Report your target."

Sellars gave the range and the bearing of the contact. Whatever it was, it was still moving at the slow convoy speed, and they were overhauling it rapidly.

"It's gaining strength a bit, sir," he concluded. "Same size, but a firmer echo. Must be something pretty solid."

That was what the picture on the radar screen showed. The whole convoy had emerged now: a compact square of ships, with the outlying escorts showing clearly, and the small stranger swimming along behind. . . . Ericson had begun to believe in it; for the first time, he felt he was watching a U-boat behaving according to the book—trailing a convoy just out of sight, perhaps after an abortive night attack, and waiting for dusk to come again before moving up for another attempt. But what this U-boat *didn't* know about was the straggling escort left behind, the ship outside the picture which was hurrying in to spoil it. If they could just get within range before they were spotted. . . .

Compass Rose ran on; the whole ship was expectant, pointing toward her target, racing to find out what it was, hoping for the legal quarry. If it were a U-boat, then they were building up toward the best chance of the war so far: it was the thing they had been waiting for, the point of all their endurance; the next hour could make sense of everything. All over the upper deck, the men standing-to were cheerful in their hope: the word had gone round that they were chasing something definite, and a steady leakage of information from the radar room kept them up-to-date and fed their expectation. And on the bridge, every man who had a pair of glasses—the Captain, Wells, the two look-outs—strained toward the horizon, and the promise that might break from it at any moment.

Compass Rose ran on: the bow wave creamed under her forefoot, the boiling wake spread behind her, whipping against the wind with rough impatience as she drove towards her prey. The sun was over the horizon now, a pale sun that melted the mist and set the waves sparkling for ten and fifteen miles ahead: a pale sun, a strengthening sun, a cheerful sun which was on their side and had come up to help them. The rigging began to whine: the trembling of the bow plating as it thrust and divided the water could be felt all over the upper deck: by the depth-charge rails, the pulse of the screw against the racing sea made the whole afterpart vibrate, on a broad monotone singing-note like a statement of intention in some formidable work of music. "Chief must be giving it stick," thought Ericson with a grin of satisfaction: "That'll wake up those loafing stokers, that'll shake a bit of soot down the funnel. . . ." After last night's protracted helplessness, it was good to reverse the roles and to be launched on this swift stalking hunt.

Compass Rose ran on. "Report your target!" said Ericson, for the fifth or sixth time: from below, Sellars's voice, excited and jubilant, confirmed the dwindling range, the certainty of a lively rendezvous. For Ericson, it was as if the whole ship were gathering herself together under his hand, getting wound up taut for the spring: it was a fanciful thought, such as he sometimes had when he was very tired or very tense: he felt the ship under him as the rider feels the horse, and he felt glad and proud of her ready response. It was for this that they had waited so long and sweated so hard. . . . He crossed to the compass platform, took an exact bearing from the last radar report, raised his glasses, and stared along the line.

Almost immediately he saw it.

It was a square speck of black on the horizon: it was the conning tower of a U-boat. Even as he looked at it, it lifted to the long swell, and he saw at its base a plume of white—the wash thrown off by the submerged hull. Far ahead of it, to complete the picture, there were some stray wisps of smoke, the telltale marks of the convoy that was betraying itself from over twenty miles away. Two targets, two hunters—he straightened up with a jerk, and whipped to the front of the bridge.

"Morell!" he snapped.

Morell looked up. "Sir?"

"There's a U-boat on the surface, dead ahead. Far out of range at the moment. But be ready. We want to get a couple of shots in before she dives—if we can get near enough." Ericson half-turned, toward Lockhart: as he did so, Wells, who was standing by his side and staring through his binoculars, called out:

"I can see it, sir—dead ahead!" His voice was high with excitement, but almost immediately his professional sense pulled him back to normal again. "Shall we send a sighting report, sir?"

"Yes. W/T signal. Warn the office." He gathered his thoughts together. "Take this down: 'Admiralty, repeated to *Viperous*. Submarine on surface ten miles astern of Convoy TG104. Course 345, speed five knots. Am engaging.' " He turned round again, toward Lockhart in the asdic cabinet. "Number One! There's a—"

Lockhart put his head out of the small window, smiling widely. "I kind of overheard, sir," he answered. "Too far away for me, at the moment."

Ericson smiled in answer. "We'll need that damned box of tricks before very long. You can stand by for the quickest crash-dive in history, as soon as they see us."

"Sir," said Lockhart, "let's make the most of it while their trousers are down."

All over the ship, the next few minutes were intense and crowded. The warning of immediate action was passed to Ferraby on the depth charges aft, and then to the engine room. "Crack it on, Chief!" said Ericson crisply, down the voice-pipe: "We've only got a certain amount of time to play with." *Compass Rose* began to romp across the sea toward her target: under pressure from the last few pounds of steam, she seemed to be spurning the water in a desperate attempt to close the range before she was discovered.

Through Ericson's glasses, the square speck of the conning tower was bigger now: it had gained in detail, it had a variety of light and shade, it even had the head and shoulders of a man—a man silhouetted against the hard horizon, a man gazing stolidly ahead, ludicrously intent on his arc of duty. "All unconscious of their fate, the little victims play," thought Lockhart, who could now see the U-boat with his naked eye, without effort: it was still too far away for an asdic contact, but at this rate, by God, they could do a straightforward ramming job, without calling on the blessings of science. . . . The distance shortened: Sellars's voice rose steadily up the scale as he reported the closing range: presently a totally unfamiliar bell rang on the bridge—the bell from the four-inch gun—and Morell, with the air of a man presenting his compliments on some purely speculative occasion, said:

"I think I could reach him now, sir."

The range was four sea miles: eight thousand yards. It was a long shot for a small gun, it might spoil the whole thing; but surely, thought Ericson, that stolid man in the conning tower *must* turn round, and see them, and say either "Donnerwetter!" or "Gott in Himmel!" and take the U-boat in a steep dive down to safety. . . . He delayed for a moment longer, weighing the chances of discovery against the limitations of the valiant pop-gun that was their main armament; then he leaned over the front of the bridge, and nodded permission to Morell.

The roar of the gun could hardly have followed more swiftly: Morell's finger must have been hovering very near the trigger. . . .

It was a good shot, even with the help of radar to do the range-finding, but it was not good enough for their crucial circumstances; the spout of grey-white water that leapt skyward was thirty yards ahead of the U-boat—the best alarm-signal she could ever have had. The man in the conning tower turned as if he could hardly credit his senses, like a lover who has been given a positive guarantee that the husband is overseas and now hears his voice in the hall; then he ducked down, as if plucked from below, and the conning tower was empty. In the expectant silence, their gun roared again: Ericson swore aloud as this time the shot fell short, and the tall column of water unsighted them. When it fell back into the sea, and their vision cleared, the U-boat was already going down, at a steep angle, in a fluster of disturbed water.

Whatever the state of her look-outs, she must have had her crash-diving routine worked out to perfection. In a matter of seconds, the hull and most of the conning tower were submerged: Morell got in a third shot before the surface of the sea was blank, but in the flurry of her dive it was difficult to spot its exact fall. It seemed to land close alongside: it might have hit her. She was moving to the right as she disappeared.

Ericson shouted: "She's down, Lockhart!"

Almost immediately, Lockhart's tense voice answered: "In contact. . . ."

The pinging echo of the asdic contact was loud and clear, audible all over the bridge: Lockhart watched in extreme nervous excitement as the operator settled down to hold onto it: they could not lose it now, when the U-boat had been right before their eyes a few seconds ago. . . . *Compass Rose* was moving very fast, and he had to prompt the operator once as the U-boat seemed to be slipping out of the asdic beam: the man was sweating with excitement, pounding with his fist on one edge of his chair. "Moving quickly right, sir!" Lockhart called out, and nodded to himself as Ericson laid a course to cut the corner and intercept. He rang the warning bell to the depth charges aft: they were now very near, and the sound of the contact was getting blurred, merging with the noise of the transmission. This was the moment when luck could take a hand: if the U-boat chose her moment rightly, and made a violent alteration of her course, she might slip out of the lethal area of the coming explosion. There were a few more seconds of waiting, while they covered the last remaining yards of the attack; then Lockhart pressed the firing-bell, and a moment later the depth charges went down. The whole surface of the sea jumped as the pattern exploded: Ferraby, busy over the reloading and harassed by the knowledge that there was a U-boat within a few yards of them, jumped with it, startled out of his wits by the noise so close to him. The columns of water shot high into the air: it seemed to all of them unfair—scarcely believable, in fact—that the shattered U-boat did not shoot up at the same time, so sure were they that they must have hit her. . . . As *Compass Rose* ran on, and the shocked sea subsided, they were left staring, voiceless with expectation, at the great patch of discoloured water that marked the explosion area: they were waiting for the U-boat to break surface and surrender.

Nothing happened: the ripples began to subside, and with them their foolish hopes: in anger and amazement they realized that the attack had been a failure. "But God damn it!" swore Lockhart, speaking for the whole ship, "we *must* have got her. The damned thing was *there*. . . ." "Get back on that search," said Ericson shortly. "We haven't finished yet." Lockhart flushed at the rebuke, which could not have been more public: he felt raw enough already, without the Captain giving the wound an extra scrape. He said: "Search sixty degrees across the stern," and bent to the asdic set again: almost immediately, they regained the contact, fifty yards from where they had dropped the pattern of depth charges.

Compass Rose turned under full helm, and raced in for her second attack. This time it was simpler: perhaps they *had* done some damage after all, because the U-boat did not seem to be moving or making any attempt at evasion. "Target stationary, sir!" reported Lockhart as they completed their turn, and he repeated the words, at intervals, right down to the very end of their run-in. Once more the depth charges went down, once more the enormous crack of the explosion shook the whole ship, once more they waited for success or failure to crown their efforts.

Someone on the bridge said: "Any minute now. . . ."

The U-boat rose in their wake like a huge unwieldy fish, black and gleaming in the sunlight.

A great roar went up from the men on the upper deck, a

howl of triumph. The U-boat came up bows first at an extraordinary angle, blown right out of her proper trim by the
force of the explosion: clearly she was, for the moment, beyond control. The water sluiced and poured from her casings
as she rose: great bubbles burst round her conning tower:
gouts of oil spread outward from the crushed plating amidships. "Open fire!" shouted Ericson—and for a few moments it was Baker's chance, and his alone: the two-pounder
pom-pom, set just behind the funnel, was the only gun that
could be brought to bear. The staccato force of its firing
shook the still air, and with a noise and a chain of shock like
the punch! punch! punch! of a trip-hammer the red glowing
tracer shells began to chase each other low across the water
toward the U-boat. She had now fallen back on a level keel,
and for the moment she rode at her proper trim: it was odd,
and infinitely disgusting, suddenly to see this wicked object,
the loathsome cause of a hundred nights of fear and disaster,
so close to them, so innocently exposed. It was like seeing
some criminal, who had outraged honour and society, and
had long been shunned, taking his ease at one's own fireside.

The two-pounder was beginning to score hits: bright
flashes came from the U-boat's bows, and small yellow
mushrooms of cordite smoke followed them: the shells were
light, but the repeated blows were ripping through her pres-
sure-hull and finding her vitals. As *Compass Rose* came round
again, listing sharply under full helm, the machine-guns on
her bridge and her signal deck joined in, with an immense
clatter. The U-boat settled a little lower, and men began
to clamber and pour out of her conning tower. Most of them
ran forward, stumbling over the uneven deck, their hands
above their heads, waving and shouting at *Compass Rose*; but
one man, more angry or more valiant than the rest, opened
fire with a small gun from the shelter of the conning tower,
and a spatter of machine-gun bullets hit *Compass Rose* amidships. Then the counter-firing ceased suddenly, as the brave
man with the gun slumped forward over the edge of the
conning tower: the rest of the crew started jumping overboard—or falling, for *Compass Rose's* guns were still blazing

away and still scoring hits on men and steel. Blood overran
the U-boat's wet deck, and sluiced down through the scuppers, darkly and agreeably red against the hated grey hull:
she began to slide down, stern first, in a great upheaval of
oil and air bubbles and the smoke and smell of cordite. A
man climbed halfway out of the conning tower, throwing
a weighted sack into the water as he did so: for a moment he
wrestled to get his body clear, but the dead gunner must
have jammed the escape hatch, for the U-boat disappeared
before he could free himself. A final explosion from below
drove a cascade of oily water upwards: then there was silence. "Cease fire," said Ericson, when the sea began to
close in again and the surface flattened under a spreading
film of oil. "Wheel amidships. Stop engines. And stand by
with those scrambling-nets."

The wonderful moment was over.

For one man aboard *Compass Rose* it had been over for some
little time. A young seaman, one of the victorious pom-pom's
crew, had been killed outright by the lone machine-gunner
on the U-boat; the small group of men bending over his
body, in compassion and concern, was out of sight behind
the gun-mounting, but they made a private world of grief
none the less authentic for being completely at variance with
the rest of the ship. They were, however, truly private: no
one else could see them: and no one else had eyes for anything but the remnants of the U-boat's crew as they swam
toward the safety of *Compass Rose*. Many of these, in an
extremity of fear or exhaustion, were gasping and crying for
help: still exalted by their triumph, the men aboard *Compass
Rose* began to cheer them ironically, unable to take seriously
the plight of people who they knew instinctively had been,
a few minutes before, staunch apostles of total warfare. . . .
"These are my favourite kind of survivors," said Morell
suddenly, to no one in particular: "they invented the whole
idea themselves. I want to see how they perform."

They performed as did all the other survivors whom *Compass Rose* had picked out of the water: some cried for help,
some swam in sensible silence towards their rescuers, some

The Cruel Sea

sank before they could be reached. There was one exception, a notable individualist who might well have sabotaged the whole affair. This was a man who, swimming strongly toward the scrambling-net that hung down over the ship's side, suddenly looked up at his rescuers, raised his right arm, and roared out: "Heil Hitler!" There was a swift and immediate growl of rage from aboard *Compass Rose*, and a sudden disinclination to put any heart into the heaving and hauling that was necessary to bring the survivors on board. "Cocky lot of bastards," said Wainwright, the torpedoman, sullenly: "we ought to leave them in to soak. . . ."

Lockhart, who was standing on the iron deck overseeing the rescue work, felt a sudden spurt of rage as he watched the incident. He felt like agreeing with Wainwright, out loud: he felt that the Captain would be justified in ringing "Full ahead" and leaving these men to splash around until they sank. But that was only a single impulse of emotion. "Hurry up!" he called out, affecting not to notice the mood of the men round him. "We haven't got all day. . . ." One by one the swimmers were hauled out of the water: the man who had shouted was the last to be lifted out, and he had his bare foot so severely trodden on by Leading Seaman Tonbridge, not a light-treading character, that he now gave a shout of a very different sort.

"Less noise there!" said Lockhart curtly, his face expressionless. "You're out of danger now. . . . Fall them in," he added to Tonbridge: and the prisoners were marshalled into a rough line. There were fourteen of them, with one dead man lying at their feet: the crew of *Compass Rose* stood round in a rough semicircle, staring at their captives. They seemed an insignificant and unexciting lot: water dripped from their hands and feet onto the deck, and above their nondescript and sodden clothes their faces were at once woebegone and relieved, like very bad comedians who have at least got through their act without violence from the audience. No heroes, these: deprived of their ship, they were indeed hardly men at all. The crew of *Compass Rose* felt disappointed, al-

270

most tricked, by the quality of those whom they had first defeated and then salvaged from defeat. Was this, they thought, really all that was meant by a U-boat's crew?

But there was still something about them, something that attacked the senses and spread discomfort and unease, like an infected limb in a sound body. . . . They were strangers, and their presence on board was disgusting, like the appearance of the U-boat on the surface of the sea. They were people from another and infinitely abhorrent world—not just Germans, but U-boat Germans, doubly revolting. As quickly as possible, they were searched, and listed, and hidden below.

Ericson had ordered the German captain, who was among the prisoners, to be put in his own cabin, with a sentry on the door as a formal precaution; and later that morning, when they were within sight of the convoy and steaming up to report to *Viperous*, he went below to meet his opposite number. That was how he phrased it, in his mood of triumph and satisfaction: *Compass Rose* had really done very well, she had brought off something that had cost two years of hard effort, and he was ready to meet anyone halfway, in the interests of good humour. But after the testing excitement of the morning, his mood was a matter of careful balance: he was not prepared for the sort of man he found in his cabin, and he experienced, during the interview, the swiftest change of feeling he had ever known.

The German captain was standing in the middle of the cabin, peering somewhat forlornly out of the porthole: he turned as Ericson came in, and seemed to collect himself into some accustomed pattern, the only one that the world deserved to see. He was tall, dead-blond, and young—nearly young enough to be Ericson's son; but thank God he was not, thought Ericson suddenly, noting the pale and slightly mad eyes, the contempt that twitched his lips and nostrils, the sneer against life and the hatred of his capture by an inferior. He was young, but his face was old with some derivative disease of power. "There's nothing we can do with these people," thought Ericson with sombre insight: "they are not curable. We can only shoot them, and hope for a better crop next time."

"Heil Hitler!" began the German crisply. "I wish to—"

"No," said Ericson grimly, "I don't think we'll start like that. What's your name?"

The German glared. "Von Hellmuth. Kapitän-Leutnant von Hellmuth. You are also the captain? What is yours?"

"Ericson."

"Ah, a good German name!" exclaimed von Hellmuth, raising his yellow eyebrows, as at some evidence of gentility in a tramp.

"Certainly not!" snapped Ericson. "And stop throwing your weight about. You're a prisoner. You're confined here. Just behave yourself."

The German frowned at this breach of decorum: there was bitter hostility in his whole expression, even in the set of his shoulders. "You took my ship by surprise, Captain," he said sourly. "Otherwise. . . ."

His tone hinted at treachery, unfair tactics, a course of conduct outrageous to German honour: suitable only for Englishmen, Poles, Negroes. "And what the hell have you been doing all these months," Ericson thought, "except taking people by surprise, stalking them, giving them no chance." But that idea would not have registered. Instead he smiled ironically, and said:

"It is war. I am sorry if it is too hard for you."

Von Hellmuth gave him a furious glance, but he did not answer the remark: he saw, too late, that by complaining of his method of defeat he had confessed to weakness. His glance went round the cabin, and changed to a sneer.

"This is a poor cabin," he said. "I am not accustomed—"

Ericson stepped up to him, suddenly shaking with anger. In the back of his mind he thought: "If I had a revolver I'd shoot you here and now." That was what these bloody people did to you: that was how the evil disease multiplied and bred in the heart. . . . When he spoke his voice was clipped and violent.

"Be quiet!" he snapped out. "If you say another word, I shall have you put down in one of the provision lockers. . . ." He turned suddenly toward the door. "Sentry!"

The leading seaman on duty, a revolver in his belt, appeared in the doorway. "Sir?"

"This prisoner is dangerous," said Ericson tautly. "If he makes any sort of move to leave the cabin, shoot him."

The man's face was expressionless: only his eyes, moving suddenly from the Captain to von Hellmuth, gave a startled flicker of interest. "Aye, aye, sir!" He disappeared again.

Von Hellmuth's expression hovered between contempt and anxiety. "I am an officer of the German Navy—" he began.

"You're a bastard in any language," Ericson interrupted curtly. He felt another violent surge of anger. I could do it, he thought, in amazement at his wild feeling: I could do it now, as easily as snapping my fingers. . . . "I'm not particularly interested in getting you back to England," he said, slowly and carefully. "We could bury you this afternoon, if I felt like it. . . . Just watch it, that's all—just watch it!"

He turned and strode from the cabin. Outside, he wondered why he was not ashamed of himself.

[*11*]

The two bodies lay side by side on the quarterdeck, neatly tucked in under the two ensigns. Ericson, clearing his throat to start reading the burial service, found his eye held almost hypnotically by the twin splashes of colour. "There are two sailors under there," he thought: "They lie there indistinguishable, except that ours was killed outright and theirs died of wounds and exhaustion: and there's not much to choose between the two flags either, in the use they are now put to" —though perhaps the boldly marked swastika made a smarter shroud than the white ensign. . . . He cleared his throat again, irritated and surprised at his thoughts.

273

"Man that is born of woman hath but a short time to live," he began, hardly looking at the book: he knew the service by heart. But the gentle words affected him: as he read, he thought of the dead, and of the young seaman who was *Compass Rose's* first casualty. He found that sad: and the German captain, standing free of escort a yard from him, found his own role sad also. His proud face was working, he was emotionally shocked out of the arrogant mould: he admitted bereavement. . . . It was probably the swastika, Ericson reflected: the dead sailor from his crew would not bother him, but the "gesture of honour" implied by the burial party and the enemy ensign would knock him out.

At Lockhart's signal to the bridge, the engine stopped: *Compass Rose* fell silent, save for the water sucking and gurgling under her counter. *"We do now commit their bodies to the deep,"* said Ericson, and paused. The pipes shrilled, the planks tipped, the neat canvas parcels slid from under the ensigns and went over the side, disappearing without trace. Close by him, he heard and felt the German captain tremble. "Yes," thought Ericson, "it *is* sad, after all."

He put on his cap, and saluted. The German captain, watching him, did the same. When they faced each other, Ericson saw tears glittering in the pale eyes. He nodded, and looked away.

"Thank you, Captain," said the German. "I appreciate all you have done." He held out his hand awkwardly. "I would like—"

Ericson shook his hand without saying anything. He was shy of his emotion, and of the thirty-odd members of *Compass Rose's* crew who must be watching them.

The German captain said suddenly: "Comrades of the sea. . . ." Did he mean the two men they had just buried, Ericson wondered, or themselves, the two captains who were sharing the same experience? Perhaps it did not matter. . . . He nodded again, and began to walk forward, leaving Lockhart to see to the prisoner.

But as he walked, he lost the mood of emotion and sorrow: it suddenly became false. This was no special occasion: there had been so many burials from *Compass Rose:* eighteen in one day was the record so far—eighteen before breakfast. Two was nothing: two was hardly worth turning out for. . . . "Those bloody Germans!" he thought as he began the climb up the bridge: first they made you lose your temper, then they made you cry. It was unsettling, it was spurious; there was something totally wrong in having them on board. One lost strength and virtue through the mere association. "Prisoners are a mistake," he thought crudely: "We should have used them for target practice in the water, we should have steamed away and left them whining." They would spoil *any* ship, destroy any settled habit of mind. . . .

Subconsciously he knew that even this atrocious thought— the shooting of survivors in the water—had its origin in the presence of the prisoners on board, in the way in which von Hellmuth had twice thrown him off balance.

He sat down in his chair on the bridge, and began a conscious effort to get back to normal. He realized that he was very tired.

[12]

The tiredness and the revulsion of feeling meant that he hardly talked at all about the sinking of the U-boat: after the first excitement, he became taciturn, and Lockhart, who suggested a drink in the wardroom to celebrate, found himself virtually snubbed when Ericson said: "I don't think we ought to start drinking at sea." But Ericson was hugging close to him his pride and pleasure in their triumph: indeed, it was the first time he had ever understood this phrase "hugging close," and he found that it brought almost physical warmth. He did not share in the immense and uproarious excitement that pervaded the whole ship and could initiate a ragged burst of cheering from the mess-decks at any hour of the day; but in the back of his mind, as in the minds of every man on board, was a clear sense of achievement—achievement crowning 1941, crowning two whole years of trial and effort, and making up for every hated minute of them. They had worked very hard for that U-boat, they had endured every extreme of fatigue, boredom, eyestrain, cold, and crude discomfort: now, at a stroke, the slate seemed to be wiped clean, the account squared. But for Ericson, it was a private account: he did not want to share his new solvency with anyone.

Only once did he emerge from his emotional retreat. Later in the voyage, when they were near home, chance took them close alongside *Viperous*, and the flood of congratulations that came over the loud-hailer seemed to release some spring within him, unloosing a boyish sense of well-being and cheerfulness. He picked up the microphone.

"Would you like to see some Germans?" he asked *Viperous*, across twenty yards of water that separated them. "They're just about due for an airing. . . . Dig them out, Number One," he added aside to Lockhart. "Fall them in on the fo'c's'le."

Presently the first of the file of prisoners began to mount the ladder.

"They're a scruffy looking lot," Ericson called out apologetically, as the men shambled into view, peering about them like mice leaving the shelter of the wainscot. "I think we ought to win the war, don't you?"

PART FOUR

1942: *Fighting*

[*1*]

The old year, triumphant only at its close, had achieved a level of violence and disaster that set the tone for the new. Just before Christmas, two Allied countries had sustained naval losses of shocking dimensions: Britain had lost two great ships—*Prince of Wales* and *Repulse*—in a single bombing attack, and America, at Pearl Harbor, had suffered a crippling blow that robbed her of half her effective fleet at one stroke. ("Proper uproar, it must have been," Lockhart overheard someone in the mess-decks say; and another anonymous voice answered: "Biggest surprise since Ma caught 'er tits in the mangle. . . .") The attack brought America into the war, an ally coming to the rescue at a most crucial moment: but her principal war was never the Atlantic —that lifeline remained, from beginning to end, the ward of the British and the Canadian navies. America turned her eyes to the Pacific, where she had much to do to stem the furious tide of the Japanese advance: in the Atlantic, the battle of escort against U-boat still saw the same contestants in the ring, now coming up for the fourth round, the bloodiest so far.

For now the battle was in spate, now the wild and vicious blows of both sides were storming toward a climax. The U-boats had a clear ascendancy, and they used it with the utmost skill and complete ruthlessness. Germany started that year with a total of 260 of them: she added to it at the rate of

277

twenty a month—a swelling fleet that made it possible for her to keep a hundred U-boats at sea in the Atlantic at the same time. Spread in a long line across the convoy routes, they intercepted and reported convoys as a matter of the simplest routine: this interception was combined with a perfected system of pack-attack, by which twenty or more U-boats were "homed" onto a convoy and fell upon it, as one team, with a series of repeated blows, until its remnants reached safety. In the face of this crushing opposition, the Allied efforts seemed puny, and their countermeasures like the futile gestures of one slow wrestler caged in a ring with a dozen tormenting opponents.

In the single month of March, 94 ships were sunk: in May, 125: in June, 144—nearly five a day: the appalling rate of loss continued around the 100 mark every month for the rest of the year. It was the nadir of the war at sea: it was, in fact, a tempo of destruction that would mean defeat for the Allies within a measurable period of time, if it were allowed to continue. The escorts did their best, aided by new offensive weapons and by the inclusion of small aircraft-carriers— converted merchantmen—accompanying the convoys: in addition, they initiated a scheme of "support groups," self-contained striking forces of six or eight escorts which were kept continuously at sea, ready to go to the help of hard-pressed convoys. These combined efforts showed results that were the best of the war so far: in the first seven months of the year, 42 U-boats were sunk, and in the best month of all, November, 16 of them were destroyed: this was double the rate of destruction of the previous year, but then the U-boats were doubling their successes as well. . . . On balance, the honours—if that was the right word for so inhuman and treacherous a struggle—were going overwhelmingly to the enemy; unless that tide could be stemmed, and turned backward, the battle of the Atlantic was going to decide the whole war; and the Allied cause, squeezed and throttled by starvation and the denial of war materials, would collapse in ruins.

"It is," said Mr. Churchill at one point, "a war of groping

278

and drowning, of ambuscade and stratagem, of science and seamanship."

It was all that. And sometimes the thing was in terms still cruder: sometimes the blood was thicker than the water.

[*2*]

For *Compass Rose*, there were special times that stuck in the memory, like insects of some unusually disgusting shape or colour, transfixed for ever in a dirty web that no cleansing element could reach.

There was the time of the Dead Helmsman (all these occasions had distinctive labels, given them either when they happened, or on later recollection. It simplified the pleasure of reminiscence.) This particular incident had a touch of operatic fantasy about it that prompted Morell to say, at the end: "I think we must have strayed into the Flying Dutchman country": it was a cold-blooded dismissal, but that was the way that all their thoughts and feelings were moving now.

The ship's lifeboat was first seen by Baker, during the forenoon watch: it was sailing boldly through the convoy, giving way to no man, and pursued by a formidable chorus of sirens as, one after another, the ships had to alter course to avoid collision. The Captain, summoned to the bridge, stared at it through his glasses: he could see that it must have been adrift for many days—the hull was blistered, and the sail, tattered and discoloured, had been strained out of shape and spilled half the wind. But in the stern the single figure of the helmsman, hunched over the tiller, held his course confidently: according to the strict rule of the road he had, as a sailing ship, the right of way, though it took a brave man to put the matter to the test without, at least, paying some attention to the result.

It seemed that he was steering for *Compass Rose*, which was a sensible thing to do, even if it did give several ship's captains heart failure in the process: the escorts were better equipped for dealing with survivors, and he probably realized it. Ericson stopped his ship, and waited for the small boat to approach: it held its course steadily, and then, at the last moment, veered with a gust of wind and passed close under *Compass Rose's* stern. A seaman standing on the depth-charge rails threw a heaving-line, and they all shouted: the man, so far from making any effort to reach them, did not even look up, and the boat sailed past and began to draw away.

"He must be deaf," said Baker, in a puzzled voice. "But he can't be blind as well. . . ."

"He's the deafest man you'll ever meet," said Ericson, suddenly grim. He put *Compass Rose* to Slow Ahead again, and brought her round on the same course the boat was taking. Slowly they overhauled it, stealing the wind so that presently it came to a stop: someone in the waist of the ship threw a grappling-hook across, and the boat was drawn alongside.

The man still sat there patiently, seeming unaware of them.

The boat rocked gently as Leading Seaman Phillips jumped down into it. He smiled at the helmsman: "Now then, chum!" he called out encouragingly—and then, puzzled by some curious air of vacancy in the face opposite, he bent closer, and put out his hand. When he straightened up again, he was grey with shock and disgust.

He looked up at Lockhart, waiting above him in the waist of the ship.

"Sir," he began. Then he flung himself across and vomited over the side of the boat.

It was as Ericson had guessed. The man must have been dead for many days: the bare feet splayed on the floorboards were paper-thin, the hand gripping the tiller was not much more than a claw. The eyes that had seemed to stare so boldly ahead were empty sockets—some sea-bird's plunder: the face was burnt black by a hundred suns, pinched and shrivelled by a hundred bitter nights.

1942: *Fighting*

The boat had no compass, and no chart: the water barrel was empty, and yawning at the seams. It was impossible to guess how long he had been sailing on that senseless voyage —alone, hopeful in death as in life, but steering directly away from the land, which was already a thousand miles astern.

There was the time of the Bombed Ship, which was the finest exercise in patience they ever had.

It started, in mid-ocean, with a corrupt wireless message, of which the only readable parts were the prefix "S.O.S." and a position, in latitude and longitude, about four hundred miles to the north of their convoy. The rest was a jumble of code groups that, even when "reconstructed," did not yield much beyond the words "bomb," "fire," and "abandon." It must have been difficult for *Viperous* to decide whether it was worth detaching an escort for this forlorn effort of detection: there was no reason to suppose that the position given was accurate, and they could ill spare a ship for a long search; and this quite apart from the fact that the message might be false—the result of a light-hearted wireless operator amusing himself, or an attempted decoy by a U-boat, both of which had happened before. But evidently *Viperous* decided that it was worth a chance: her next signal was addressed to *Compass Rose*, and read: "Search in accordance with S.O.S. timed 1300 today." A little later she re-opened R/T communication to add: "Good-bye."

The first part of the assignment was easy: it boiled down to turning ninety degrees to port, increasing to fifteen knots, and holding that course and speed for twenty-six hours on end. It was the sort of run they all enjoyed, like a dog let off a leash normally in the grasp of the slowest old lady in the world: now there was no restraint on them, no convoy to worry about, no Senior Officer to wake from his siesta and ask them what on earth they were doing. *Compass Rose* raced on, with a rising wind and sea on her quarter sometimes making her sheer widely, till the quartermaster could haul her back on her course again: she was alone, like a ship in a picture, crossing cold grey waves towards an untenanted horizon.

She ran all through the night, and all next morning: not a stick, not a sail, not a smudge of smoke did she see: it was a continuous reminder of how vast this ocean was, how formidable a hiding place. There were hundreds of ships at sea in the Atlantic all the time, and yet *Compass Rose* seemed to have it to herself, with nothing to show that she was not, suddenly, the last ship left afloat in the world.

But when they had run the distance and reached the likely search-area, the phrase "hiding place" returned again, this time to mock them. It was mid-afternoon of a brisk, lowering February day, with darkness due to fall within three hours: they were looking for a ship that might have been bombed, might have been sunk, might have been playing the fool, might be in a different longitude altogether, and halfway round the world from this one. On a sheet of squared tracing-paper Ericson plotted out a "box search"—a course for *Compass Rose* consisting of a series of squares, gradually extending down wind in the direction the ship should have drifted. Its sides were each seven miles long: every two hours, the area shifted another seven miles to the northeastward. Then he laid it off on the chart, so as to keep a check on their final position, and they settled down to quarter the ocean according to this pattern.

It was very cold. Darkness came down, and with it the first drift of snow: as hour succeeded hour, with nothing sighted and no hint of a contact on the radar screen, they began to lose the immediate sense of quest and to be preoccupied only with the weather. The wind was keen, the snow was penetratingly cold, the water racing past was wild and noisy: these were the realities, and the early feeling of urgency in their search was progressively blunted, progressively forgotten. Hours before, it seemed, there *had* been something about a carefully worked-out, meticulous investigation of this area; but this was a very long time ago, and the bombed ship (if she existed) and her crew (if they still lived) were probably somewhere quite different, and in the meantime it was excruciatingly cold and unpleasant. . . . At midnight, the snow was a whirling blizzard: at four a.m., when Lockhart came on watch, it was to a bitter, pitch-black darkness that stung his face to the marrow when he had scarcely mounted the bridge.

"Any sign of them?" he shouted to Morell.

"Nothing. . . . If they're adrift in this, God help them."

It was "nothing" all that watch, and "nothing" when daylight came, and "nothing" all the morning: at midday the wind fell light and the snow diminished to an occasional drift, wafting gently past them as if hoping to be included in a Christmas card. Individually, without sharing their doubts, they began to wonder if the thing had not gone on long enough: the search had taken two days already, and during the last twenty-four hours they had "swept" nearly six hundred square miles of water. The contract could not call for very much more. . . . "I've just remembered it's St. Valentine's Day," said Ferraby suddenly to Baker, during the idle hours of the afternoon watch. "Put it down in the log," growled Ericson, overhearing. "There won't be any other entries. . . ." It was unusual for him to admit openly to any sort of doubt or hesitation: they felt free now to question the situation themselves, even to give up and turn back and forget about it.

The solid echo presently reported on the radar hardly broke through to their attention at first.

But it was the ship all right, the ship they had been sent to find. They came upon her suddenly: she was masked until the last moment by the gently whirling snow, and then suddenly she emerged and lay before them—a small untidy freighter with Swedish funnel-markings. She was derelict, drifting down-wind like some wretched tramp sagging his way through a crowd: she listed heavily, her bridge and fore-part were blistered and fire-blackened, and her fore-bridge itself, which seemed to have taken a direct hit from a bomb or a shell, looked like a twisted metal cage from which something violent and strong had ripped a way to freedom. One lifeboat was missing, the other hung down from the falls, half-overturned and empty. There was nothing else in the picture.

Compass Rose circled slowly, alert for any development, but there was no sound, no movement save the snow falling lightly on the deserted upper deck. They sounded their siren, they fired a blank shot: nothing stirred. Presently they stopped, and lowered a boat: Morell was in charge, and with him were Rose, the young signalman, Leading Seaman Tonbridge, and a stoker named Evans. As they pulled away from *Compass Rose*, Ericson leant over the side of the bridge, megaphone in hand.

"We'll have to keep moving," he called out. "This ship is too much of an attraction. . . . Don't worry if you lose sight of us."

Morell waved, but did not answer. He was no longer thinking about *Compass Rose*: he was thinking, with a prickling of his scalp, of what he was going to find when he boarded the derelict.

"I am no good at this," he thought as they pulled across the short stretch of water that separated the two ships: "no good at bombs, no good at blood, no good at the brutal elements of disaster. . . ." When Leading Seaman Tonbridge jumped onto the sloping deck with the painter, and made the boat fast, it was all Morell could do to follow him over the side: "*You* go," his subconscious voice was saying to Tonbridge: "I'll wait here, while you take a look." It was not that he was afraid, within the normal meaning of the word: simply that he doubted his ability to deal with the disgusting unknown.

In silence he climbed up and stood on the deck: a tall grave young man in a yellow duffle coat and sea boots, looking through falling snow toward the outline of the shattered bridge. He said to Stoker Evans: "Have a look below—see how deep she's flooded," and to Tonbridge: "Stay by the boat," and to Signalman Rose: "Come with me." Then they began to walk forward: their feet rang loudly on the iron deck, their tracks in the snow were fresh, like children's in a garden before breakfast: round them was complete silence, complete empty stillness, such as no ship that was not fundamentally cursed would ever show.

It was not as bad as Morell had expected—in the sense that he did not faint, or vomit, or disgrace himself: the actual details were horrifying. The bridge had taken the full force of a direct hit by a bomb: there had been a small fire started, and a larger one further forward, between the well-deck and the fo'c's'le. It was difficult to determine exactly how many people had been on the bridge when it was hit: none of the bodies was complete, and the scattered fragments seemed at a first glance to add up to a whole vanished regiment of men. There must have been about six of them: now they were in dissolution, and their remnants hung like some appalling tapestry round the bulkheads, gleaming here and there with the dull gleam of half-dried paint. The whole gory enclosure seemed to have been decorated with blood and tissue: " 'When father papered the parlour,' " hummed Morell to himself, "he never thought of this. . . ." The helmsman's hand was still clutching the wheel—but it was only a hand, it grew out of the air: tatters of uniforms, of entrails, tufts of hair, met the eye at every turn: on one flat surface the imprint of a skull in profile, impressed into the paintwork, stood out like a revolting street-corner caricature, stencilled in human skin and fragments of bone. "You died with your mouth open," said Morell, looking at this last with eyes that seemed to have lost their capacity to communicate sensation to the brain. "I hope you were saying something polite."

He walked to the open side of the bridge, high above the water, and looked out. The snow still fell gently and lazily, dusting the surface of the sea for a moment before it melted. There was nothing round them except anonymous greyness: the afternoon light was failing: *Compass Rose* came into view momentarily, and then vanished. He turned back to Rose who stood waiting with his signal-lamp, and they stared at each other across the space of the bridge: each of their faces had the same serious concentration, the same wish to accept this charnel-house and be unmoved by it. It was part of their war, the sort of thing they were trained for, the sort of thing they now took in their stride—sometimes without effort, sometimes with. . . . "I suppose Rose has looked at all this, and looked away again," thought Morell: "I suppose he is waiting for me to say something, or to take him down the ladder and away from the bridge. That would be my own choice too. . . ." He cleared his throat.

"We'll see what Evans has to say, and then send a signal."

The ship could not be got going again, but she was fit to be towed: though the engine room and one hold were deeply flooded, the water was no longer coming in and she might remain afloat indefinitely. That was the outline of the signal Rose presently sent across to *Compass Rose:* reading it, Ericson had to make up his mind whether to start the towing straight away, or to cast around for the missing boat and its survivors. After two nights adrift in this bitter weather, there was little chance of their being alive; but if the bombed ship would remain afloat, it would not matter spending another day or so on the search. Perhaps Morell had better stay where he was, though: he could keep an eye on things, and there must be a lot of tidying up to do.

"Remain on board," he signalled to Morell finally. "I am going to search for the lifeboat, and return tomorrow morning." Something made him add: "Are you quite happy about being left?"

Happy, thought Morell: now *there* was a word. . . . It was now nearly nightfall: they were to be left alone in this floating coffin for over twelve hours of darkness, with the snow to stare at, the sea to listen to, and a bridgeful of corpses for company. " 'Happiness is relative,' " he began dictating to Rose, and then he changed his mind. The moment did not really deserve humour. "Reply: 'Quite all right,' " he said shortly. Then he called Tonbridge and Evans, and took them back with him to the bridge. That was where a start must be made.

Morell was never to forget that night. They used the remains of daylight for cleaning up: the increasing gloom was a blessing, making just tolerable this disgusting operation. They worked in silence, hard-breathing, not looking closely at what they were doing: the things they had to dispose of disappeared steadily over the side, and were hidden by the merciful sea. Only once was the silence broken, by Leading Seaman Tonbridge. "Pity we haven't got a hose, sir," he said, straightening up from a corner of the bridge which had kept him busy for some minutes. Morell did not answer him: no one did. The place where they stood, though blurred now by shadow, was eloquent enough.

They made a meal off the emergency rations in the boat, and boiled some tea on the spirit-stove they found in the galley; then they settled down for the night, in the cramped chartroom behind the bridge. There were mattresses and blankets, and a lamp to give them some warmth: it was good enough for one night on board, if they did not start thinking.

Morell started thinking: his thoughts destroyed the hope of sleep, and drove him outside onto the upper deck—there was no comfort in the sleeping men close to him, only anger at the relief they had found: he felt that if he stayed he would have to invent some pretext for waking them up. He made his footfalls soft as he went down the ladder, he made his breathing imperceptible as he crossed the well-deck: the hand that pushed aside the canvas curtain screening the fo'c's'le was the hand of a conspirator. He took a step forward, and felt in front of him a hollow emptiness: he struck a match, and found that he was in a large mess-hall, full of shadows, full of its own deserted silence. The match flared: he saw a long table, with plates set out on it—plates with half-eaten helpings of stew, crumbled squares of bread, knives and forks set down hurriedly at the moment of crisis. None of those meals would ever be finished now: all the men who had set down the knives and forks were almost certainly dead. "I am thinking in clichés," he thought, as the match spluttered and went out. But clichés were as effective as thoughts freshly minted, when the reality they clothed pressed in so closely and was backed by such a weight of crude fact.

Pursued by ghosts, he walked aft along the snow-covered upper deck. The wind whined on a strange note in the rigging: the water gurgled close under his feet: the ship was restless, needing to fight the sea all the time. There was no comfort to be found under the open sky: the deck held too many shadows, the unfamiliar shape of it had too many surprises. And suppose there were *other* surprises: suppose the ship were not deserted, suppose a mad seaman with an axe rushed him from the next blind corner: suppose he found fresh footprints in the snow, where none of them had trodden.

At the base of the mast a shadow moved. Morell gripped the pockets of his duffle coat, his nerves screaming. The shadow moved again, sliding away from him.

He roared out: "Stop!"

The cat mewed, and fled.

Morning came, and with it *Compass Rose*. She had nothing to report—no boats, no survivors—and Morell, in a sense, had nothing to report either. A heaving-line was passed from *Compass Rose*, and then a light grass-rope, and then the heavy towing-hawser: there was no windlass to haul this on board the bombed ship, and Morell's party had to manhandle it in foot by foot, straining against a dead weight of wire, which at times seemed as if it would never reach them. But finally they made it fast, and gave the signal, and the tow started.

They made less than three knots, even in good weather: it took them ten days of crawling to finish the journey. Each morning, as soon as it was light, Morell waved a greeting to Lockhart: each evening, as Darken Ship was piped, Lockhart waved good-bye to Morell. Day after day, night after night, the two ships crept over the water, both useless save for this single purpose, both doomed by their umbilical tie to be any U-boat's sitting shot. When, at the mouth of the Mersey, they parted at last and Morell came aboard, it was like waking from a nightmare that one had despaired of surviving.

"Sorry to leave?" asked Lockhart ironically, as Morell came up to the bridge.

"No," answered Morell, fingering his ten days' growth of beard, "no, I'm not." He looked at the ship astern of them, now in the charge of two harbour tugs. "I may say that the

idea of the convict missing his chains is purely a novelist's
conception of life."

There was the time that was rather difficult to label: they
mostly knew it as the time of the Captain's Meeting.

This time was on a Gibraltar convoy, a convoy in the same
bad tradition as most of the Gibraltar runs: there had been a
steady wastage of ships all the way southward, and although
they were now within two days of the end of the trip the
U-boat pack was still with them. Ericson seemed to be showing particular interest in a ship in the front line of the convoy:
often he would train his glasses on her for minutes at a time,
and she was the one he always looked for first as soon as daylight came up. She survived until the last day; and then, when
dawn broke after a night of disaster, she was no longer in her
station, and her place in the van of the convoy had been taken
by the next ship astern.

At first light the customary signal came from *Viperous:*
"Following ships were sunk last night: *Fort James, Eriskay,
Bulstrode Manor, Glen MacCurtain.* Amend convoy lists ac-
cordingly."

There was something in Ericson's manner as he read this
signal which discouraged comment. He remained on the
bridge for a full hour, staring silently at the convoy, before
saying suddenly to Wells:

"Take a signal. . . . 'To escorts in company, from
Compass Rose. Please report any survivors you may have from
Glen MacCurtain.' "

The answering signals came in very slowly: they did not
make cheerful reading. *Viperous* and two other escorts sent
"Nil" reports. The corvette in the rear position signalled:
"Two seamen, one Chinese fireman." The rescue ship detailed to look after survivors sent: "First officer, two seamen, one fireman, five Lascars."

They waited, but that seemed to be all. *Glen MacCurtain*
must have gone down quickly. Ferraby, who had the watch,
said tentatively:

"Not many picked up, sir?"

"No," said Ericson. "Not many." He looked toward the horizon astern of them, and then walked to his chair and sat down heavily.

Presently a merchant ship in the rear of the convoy started flashing to them. Wells took the signal, muttering impatiently to himself: evidently the operating was not up to acceptable Naval standards.

"Message from that Polish packet, sir," he said to Ericson. "It's a bit rocky. . . . 'We did see your signal by mistake,' he read out, his voice slightly disparaging. " 'We have one man from that ship.' "

"Ask them who it was," said Ericson. His voice was quiet, but there was such acute tension in it that everyone on the bridge stared at him.

Wells began to flash the question, signalling very slowly, with frequent pauses and repetitions. There was a long wait; then the Polish ship began to answer. Wells read it out as it came across:

" 'The man is fourth officer,' " he began. Then he started to spell, letter by letter: " 'E-R-I-C-S-O-N.' " Wells looked up from the signal-lamp. "Ericson. . . . Same name as yours, sir."

"Yes," said Ericson. "Thank you, Wells."

There was a time, a personal time for Lockhart, which he knew as the time of the Burnt Man.

Ordinarily, he did not concern himself a great deal with looking after survivors: Crowther, the sick-berth attendant, had proved himself sensible and competent, and unless there were more cases than one man could cope with, Lockhart left him to get on with his work alone. But now and again, as the bad year progressed, there was an overflow of injured or exhausted men who needed immediate attention; and it was on one of these occasions, when the night had yielded nearly forty survivors from two ships, that Lockhart found himself back again at his old job of ship's doctor.

The small, two-berth sick-bay was already filled: the work to be done was, as in the old days, waiting for him in the fo'c's'le. As he stepped into the crowded, badly lit space, he no longer felt the primitive revulsion of two years ago, when all this was new and harassing; but there was nothing changed in the dismal picture, nothing was any the less crude or moving or repellent. There were the same rows of sur-vivors—wet through, dirt-streaked, shivering: the same reek of oil and sea water: the same relief on one face, the same remembered terror on another. There were the same people drinking tea or retching their stomachs up or telling their story to anyone who would listen. Crowther had marshalled the men needing attention in one corner, and here again the picture was the same: wounded men, exhausted men, men in pain afraid to die, men in a worse agony hoping not to live.

Crowther was bending over one of these last, a seaman whose filthy overalls had been cut away to reveal a splintered knee-cap: as soon as he looked the rest of the casualties over, Lockhart knew at once which one of them had the first priority.

He picked his way across the fo'c's'le and stood over the man, who was being gently held by two of his shipmates. It seemed incredible that he was still conscious, still able to ad-vertise his agony: by rights he should have been dead—not moaning, not trying to pluck something from his breast. . . . He had sustained deep and cruel first-degree burns, from his throat to his waist: the whole raw surface had been flayed and roasted, as if he had been caught too long on a spit that had stopped turning: he now gave out, appropriately, a kitchen smell indescribably horrible. What the first touch of salt water on his body must have felt like passed imagination.

"He got copped by a flash-back from the boiler," said one of the men holding him. "Burning oil. Can you fix him?"

"Fix him," thought Lockhart: "I wish I could fix him in his coffin right now. . . ." He forced himself to bend down and draw close to this sickening object: above the scored and shrivelled flesh the man's face, bereft of eyelashes, eyebrows, and the front portion of his scalp, looked expressionless and foolish. But there was no lack of expression in the eyes, which were liquid with pain and surprise. If the man could have bent his head and looked at his own chest, thought Lockhart, he would give up worrying and ask for a revolver straight away. . . . He turned and called across to Crowther:

"What have you got for burns?"

Crowther rummaged in his first-aid satchel. "This, sir," he said, and passed something across. A dozen willing hands relayed it to Lockhart, as if it were the elixir of life itself. It was in fact a small tube of ointment, about the size of a toothpaste tube. On the label was the picture of a smiling child, and the inscription: "For the Relief of Burns. Use Sparingly."

"Use sparingly," thought Lockhart; "if I used it as if it were platinum dust, I'd still need about two tons of it." He held the small tube in his hand and looked down again at the survivor. One of the men holding him said: "Here's the doctor. He'll fix you up right away," and the fringeless eyes came slowly round and settled on Lockhart's face as if he were the ministering Christ himself.

Lockhart took a swab of cotton wool, put some of the ointment on it, swallowed a deep revulsion, and started to stroke, very gently, the area of the burnt chest. Just before he began he said: "It's a soothing ointment."

"I suppose it's natural that he should scream," thought Lockhart presently, shutting his ears: all the old-fashioned pictures showed a man screaming as soon as the barber-surgeon started to operate, while his friends plied the patient with rum or knocked him out with a mallet. . . . The trouble was that the man was still so horrifyingly alive: he pulled and wrenched at the two men holding him, while Lockhart, stroking and swabbing with a mother's tenderness, removed layer after layer of his flesh. For the *other* trouble was that however gently he was touched, the raw tissue went on and on coming away with the cotton wool.

Lockhart was aware that the ring of men who were watching had fallen silent: he felt rather than saw their faces contract with pity and disgust as he swabbed the ointment deeper and deeper, and the flesh still flaked off like blistered paint-work. "I wonder how long this can go on," he thought, as he saw, without surprise, that at one point he had laid bare a rib that gleamed with an astonishing cleanness and astrin-gency. "I don't think this is any good," he thought again, as the man fainted at last, and the two sailors holding him turned their eyes toward Lockhart in question and disbelief. The ointment was almost finished: the raw chest now gaped at him like the foundation of some rotten building. "Die!" he thought, almost aloud, as he sponged once more, near the throat, and a new layer of sinew came into view, laid bare like a lecturer's diagram. "Please give up, and die. I can't go on doing this, and I can't stop while you're still alive."

He heard a dozen men behind him draw in their breath sharply as a fresh area of skin suddenly crumbled under his most gentle hand and adhered to the cotton wool. Crowther, attracted by the focus of interest and now kneeling by his side, said: "Any good, sir?" and he shook his head. "I'm doing wonders," he thought: "They'll give me a job in a canning factory. . . ." Some blood flowed over the rib he had laid bare, and he swabbed it off almost apologetically. "Sorry," he thought: "that was probably my fault"—and then again: "Die! Please die! I'm making a fool of myself, and certainly of you. You'll never be any use now. And we'll give you a lovely funeral, well out of sight. . . ."

Suddenly and momentarily, the man opened his eyes, and looked up at Lockhart with a deeper, more fundamental sur-prise, as if he had intercepted the thought and was now aware that a traitor and not a friend was touching him. He twisted his body, and a rippling spasm ran across the scorched flesh. "Steady, Jock!" said one of his friends, and: "Die!" thought Lockhart yet again, squeezing the last smear of ointment from the tube and touching with it a shoulder muscle that immediately gave way and parted from its ligament. "Die. Do us all a favour. Die!"

Aloud, he repeated, with the utmost foolishness: "It's a

soothing ointment." But: "Die now!" his lips formed. "Don't be obstinate. No one wants you. You wouldn't want yourself if you could take a look. Please die!"

Presently, obediently, but far too late, the man died.

There was the time of the Skeletons.

It happened when *Compass Rose* was in a hurry, late one summer afternoon when she had been delayed for nearly half a day by a search for an aircraft reported down in the sea, a long way south of the convoy. She had not found the aircraft, nor any trace of it: *Viperous* had wirelessed: "Rejoin forthwith," and she was now hurrying to catch up before nightfall. The sea was glassy smooth, the sky a pale and perfect blue: the hands lounging on the upper deck were mostly stripped to the waist, enjoying the last hour of hot sunshine. It was a day for doing nothing elegantly, for going nowhere at half speed: it seemed a pity that they had to force the pace, and even more of a pity when the radar operator got a "suspicious contact" several miles off their course, and they had to turn aside to investigate.

"It's a very small echo," said the operator apologetically. "Sort of muzzy, too."

"Better take a look," said Ericson to Morell, who had called him to the bridge. "You never know. . . ." He grinned. "What does small and muzzy suggest to you?"

To Morell, it suggested an undersized man tacking up Regent Street after a thick night, but he glossed over the thought, and said instead:

"It might be wreckage, sir. Or a submarine, just awash."

"Or porpoises," said Ericson, who seemed in a better humour than he usually was after being woken. "Or seaweed with very big sand-fleas hopping about on top. . . . It's a damned nuisance, anyway: I didn't want to waste time."

In the event, it wasted very little of their time, for *Compass Rose* ran the distance swiftly, and what they found did not delay them. It was Wells—the best pair of eyes in the ship—who first sighted the specks on the surface, specks that gradually grew until, a mile or so away, they had become heads and shoulders—a cluster of men floating in the water.

"Survivors, by God!" exclaimed Ericson. "I wonder how long they've been there."

They were soon to know. *Compass Rose* ran on, the hands crowding to the rail to look at the men ahead of them. Momentarily Ericson recalled that other occasion when they had sped toward men in the water, only to destroy them out of hand. Not this time, he thought as he reduced speed: now he could make amends.

He need not have bothered to slow down: he might well have ploughed through, the same as last time. He had thought it odd that the men did not wave or shout to *Compass Rose*, as they usually did: he had thought it odd that they did not swim even a little way towards the ship, to close the gap between death and life. Now he saw, through his glasses, that there was no gap to be closed: for the men, riding high out of the water, held upright by their life-jackets, were featureless, bony images—skeletons now for many a long day and night.

There was something infinitely obscene in the collection of lolling corpses, with bleached faces and white hairless heads, clustered together like men waiting for a bus that had gone by twenty years before. There were nine of them in that close corporation; they rode the water not more than four or five yards from each other: here and there a couple had come together as if embracing. *Compass Rose* circled, starting a wash that set the dead men bobbing and bowing to each other, like performers in some infernal dance. Nine of them, thought Morell in horror: what is the correct noun of association? A school of skeletons? A corps?

Then he saw—they all saw—that the men were roped together. A frayed and slimy strand of rope linked each one of them, tied round the waist and trailing languidly in the water: when the ripples of the ship's wash drove two of the men apart, the rope between them tightened with a jerk and a splash. The other men swayed and bowed, as if approving this evidence of comradeship. . . . But this is crazy, thought

Ericson: this is the sort of thing you hope not to dream about. *Compass Rose* still circled, as he looked down at the company of dead men. They must have been there for months. There was not an ounce of flesh under the yellow skins, not a single reminder of warmth or manhood. They had perished, and they had gone on perishing, beyond the grave, beyond the moment when the last man alive found rest.

He was hesitating about picking them up, but he knew that he would not. *Compass Rose* was in a hurry. There was nothing to be gained by fishing them out, sewing them up, and putting them back again. And anyway . . .

"But why roped together?" asked Morell, puzzled, as the ship completed her last circle, and drew away, and left the men behind. "It doesn't make sense."

Ericson had been thinking. "It might," he said, in a voice infinitely subdued. "If they were in a lifeboat, and the boat was being swamped, they might tie themselves together so as not to lose touch during the night. It would give them a better chance of being picked up."

"And they weren't," said Morell after a pause.

"And they weren't. I wonder how long—" but he did not finish that sentence, except in his thoughts.

He was wondering how long it had taken the nine men to die: and what it was like for the others when the first man died: and what it was like when half of them had gone: and what it was like for the last man left alive, roped to his tail of eight dead shipmates, still hopeful, but surely feeling himself doomed by their company.

Perhaps, thought Ericson, he went mad in the end, and started to swim away, and towed them all after him, shouting, until he lost his strength as well as his wits, and gave up, and turned back to join the majority.

Quite a story.

There was the time that was the worst time of all, the time that seemed to synthesize the whole corpse-ridden ocean; the time of the Burning Tanker.

Aboard *Compass Rose*, as in every escort that crossed the

Atlantic, there had developed an unstinting admiration of the men who sailed in oil tankers. They lived, for an entire voyage of three or four weeks, as a man living on top of a keg of gunpowder: the stuff they carried—the life blood of the whole war—was the most treacherous cargo of all; a single torpedo, a single small bomb, even a stray shot from a machine-gun, could transform their ship into a torch. Many times this had happened, in *Compass Rose's* convoys: many times they had had to watch these men die, or pick up the tiny remnants of a tanker's crew—men who seemed to display not the slightest hesitation at the prospect of signing on again, for the same job, as soon as they reached harbour. It was these expendable seaman who were the real "petrol coupons"—the things one could wangle from the garage on the corner: and whenever sailors saw or read of petrol being wasted or stolen, they saw the cost in lives as well, peeping from behind the headline or the music-hall joke, feeding their anger and disgust.

Appropriately, it was an oil tanker that gave the men in *Compass Rose*, as spectators, the most hideous hour of the whole war.

She was an oil-tanker they had grown rather fond of: she was the only tanker in a homeward-bound convoy of fifty ships which had run into trouble, and they had been cherishing her, as they sometimes cherished ships they recognized from former convoys, or ships with queer funnels, or ships that told lies about their capacity to keep up with the rest of the fleet. On this occasion, she had won their affection by being obviously the number one target of the attacking U-boats: on three successive nights they had sunk the ship ahead of her, the ship astern, and the corresponding ship in the next column; and as the shelter of land approached it became of supreme importance to see her through to the end of the voyage. But her luck did not hold: on their last day of the open sea, with the Scottish hills only just over the horizon, the attackers found their mark, and she was mortally struck.

She was torpedoed in broad daylight on a lovely sunny

afternoon: there had been the usual scare, the usual waiting, the usual noise of an underwater explosion, and then, from this ship they had been trying to guard, a colossal pillar of smoke and flame came billowing, and in a minute the long shapely hull was on fire almost from end to end.

The ships on either side of her, and the ships astern, fanned outwards, like men stepping past a hole in the road: *Compass Rose* cut in towards her, intent on bringing help. But no help had yet been devised that could be of any use to a ship so stricken. Already the oil that had been thrown skyward by the explosion had bathed the ship in flame: and now, as more and more oil came gushing out of the hull and spread over the water all round her, she became the centre-piece of a huge conflagration. There was still one gap in the solid wall of fire, near her bows, and above this, on the fo'c's'le, her crew began to collect—small figures, running and stumbling in furious haste towards the only chance they had for their lives. They could be seen waving, shouting, hesitating before they jumped; and *Compass Rose* crept in a little closer, as much as she dared, and called back to them to take the chance. It was dangerously, unbearably hot, even at this distance: and the shouting, and the men waving their arms, backed by the flaming roaring ship with her curtain of smoke and burning oil closing round her, completed an authentic picture of hell.

There were about twenty men on the fo'c's'le: if they were going to jump, they would have to jump soon. . . . And then, in ones and twos, hesitating, changing their minds, they did begin to jump: successive splashes showed suddenly white against the dark grey of the hull, and soon all twenty of them were down, and on their way across. From the bridge of *Compass Rose*, and from the men thronging her rail, came encouraging shouts as the gap of water between them narrowed.

Then they noticed that the oil, spreading over the surface of the water and catching fire as it spread, was moving faster than any of the men could swim. They noticed it before the swimmers, but soon the swimmers noticed it too. They began to scream as they swam, and to look back over their shoulders, and thrash and claw their way through the water as if suddenly insane.

But one by one they were caught. The older ones went first, and then the men who couldn't swim fast because of their life-jackets, and then the strong swimmers, without life-jackets, last of all. But perhaps it was better not to be a strong swimmer on that day, because none of them was strong enough: one by one they were overtaken, and licked by flame, and fried, and left behind.

Compass Rose could not lessen the gap, even for the last few who nearly made it. Black and filthy clouds of smoke were now coursing across the sky overhead, darkening the sun: the men on the upper deck were pouring with sweat. With their own load of fuel oil and their ammunition, they could go no closer, even for these frying men whose faces were inhumanly ugly with fear and who screamed at them for help; soon, indeed, they had to give ground to the stifling heat, and back away, and desert the few that were left, defeated by the mortal risk to themselves.

Waiting a little way off, they were entirely helpless: they stood on the bridge, and did nothing, and said nothing. One of the look-outs, a young seaman of not more than seventeen, was crying as he looked towards the fire: he made no sound, but the tears were streaming down his face. It was not easy to say what sort of tears they were—of rage, of pity, of the bitterness of watching the men dying so cruelly, and not being able to do a thing about it.

Compass Rose stayed till they were all gone, and the area of sea with the ship and the men inside it was burning steadily and remorselessly, and then she sailed on. Looking back, as they did quite often, they could see the pillar of smoke from nearly fifty miles away: at nightfall, there was still a glow and sometimes a flicker on the far horizon. But the men of course were not there any more: only the monstrous funeral pyre remained.

[3]

The time for their long leave came round again.

Each leave was different from the last one, a development or a stultification of what had gone before. In war, nothing stood still, in any part of the field; in this war, the years were passing, eating up not only men and treasure but bearing swiftly onward the normal tide of life as well. Nothing stood still: nothing waited for peacetime before moving on to the next chapter. The men grew older: the women loved them more, or less, or fell in love again; babies were born, cooking deteriorated, mortgages fell due, uncle died and left that funny will, mother came to live, the paint flaked off the bathroom ceiling. And sometimes, with distance and separation, it was difficult to do anything about the paint or the baby or the loving more or less: the men just had to hope, and trust, and be reassured or betrayed, and take whatever they found when they got back. Distances were too great, and the thread sometimes too tenuous, for them to play an effective part at home as well as at sea; and the sea had the priority, whether they liked it or not.

Able Seaman Gregg's baby was not a success. He had been prepared to shut his mind to its suspect parentage: this might have been possible if the child had been attractive, or cheerful, or just plain healthy, but as it was none of these things he could not help seeing, behind the sickly and squalling infant, the image of a large man called Walter something who had got away with murder. He had been looking forward to this spell of leave, and the chance of being with Edith and getting to know the child; but now he knew the child too well—a pale, underdeveloped, and undeniably dirty child that filled the house with its crying and the larger part of the kitchen with its soiled napkins. And Edith—he was now not sure whether he really knew anything about Edith at all.

1942: *Fighting*

He had been brought face to face with this doubt one evening when, returning to the house after a shopping expedition, he had passed a stranger on the way out—a middle-aged woman in W.V.S. uniform who had given him first a questioning glance and then a grudging smile as he stood aside to let her go by. He had watched her doubtfully as she went off down the street, and then gone through to the kitchen. The scene was as usual—the hearth and the clothes rack were strung with drying baby-clothes, the child whimpered in its cot; amid a smell compounded of food, urine, and scorched napkins, Edith sat by the fireside reading a film magazine.

He threw in his cap on the table. "Who was that?" he asked.

Edith looked up. "Who?"

"The woman."

"Oh, her. . . ." Edith shrugged elaborately. "Some old Nosy Parker from the welfare."

"What welfare?"

"The Borough Council. They send them round. Nothing better to do, I suppose."

Gregg found himself, for once, wanting to sort the matter out. He sat down opposite her. "But how did she come here, in the first place?"

Edith yawned, not looking at him. "She started coming. To see the baby. Kind of welfare work."

"But what did she say?"

"She said to look after it."

"Feed it, you mean?"

"Yes. And stay with it all the time."

"But you do stay with it, don't you?"

"Course I do. Don't go on so, Tom. I tell you, she's just poking her nose. All that about a summons . . . Cheeky old bitch—I bet no one ever tried to give *her* a baby."

"A summons . . ." Gregg stood up again, frowning. "Here, what's it all about?"

"There was a report," said Edith sulkily, after a pause. "The baby was crying one night."

"Well, what about it?"

"They thought I'd left it alone in the house. But I was asleep, Tom, honest I was. I just didn't hear it, that's all. And someone reported it."

"Why didn't you tell me?" he asked.

"What's there to worry about?" she said jauntily. "They can't do anything to you. It's a lot of sauce."

"But you don't want that sort of thing . . ." He wondered, as many times before, how much to believe; he could only guess and grope at what went on while he was away, he could only go by the probabilities. . . . He walked over and looked down at the baby, which was sucking a wooden spoon. Its face was small and pinched: there were sores round its mouth: its legs were like small pale sticks on the soiled and tumbled bedclothes. "I wish it could talk," he thought, not for the first time. He turned back to his wife.

"You don't leave it by itself, Edith, do you? Or go out nights."

"Course not."

"Wonder why you didn't hear it crying."

"You know me when I'm asleep."

Lockhart, also in London, did four things, and then seemed to come to a dead stop. He went to a concert: he called on an editor for whom he had written before the war, and sold him an article on corvettes—subject to Admiralty approval: he had a Turkish bath: and he ordered a new uniform, adorned with the small oak-leaf emblem which signified that he had been mentioned in dispatches. That was a two-day program: when it was completed, he was aware that he was looking round for more, and that nothing was in prospect. It was not that he was bored—no Londoner could be bored in London; it was simply that, when he was on leave, his life seemed to lack human significance altogether. His living world was *Compass Rose*, and nothing else; away from her, he felt as if he were held in suspension, waiting for the time when he could leave the trivial shadow-life and return to hard fact.

It was all wrong, of course: he ought to have been able to

profit from his holiday. But there was something missing ashore: something to make sense of the necessary interlude. It would have been nice, for example, to have someone to say good-bye to, at the end. . . .

Later, however, when he caught his train at Euston, and watched the leave-takers on No. 13 Platform, he was not so sure. There was something in the universal good-bye atmosphere that seemed likely to spoil both the past and the future: the kisses, the tears, the hungry mouths groping for each other for the last time—all these must surely mean that the leave period had been sad, with this parting in view all the time, and that the future was going to be lonely and unhappy on both sides, for the same reason. It was not difficult to see what this sadness did to a man, in terms of his contentment and his efficiency: it was a necessary part of war, but it impeded it at the same time. For sailors, there should be no ties with the land at all, if they were to produce their best when the need came to show it: the recurrent dream of home could only stand in the way, getting in a man's heart and eyes when both of these had to be purposeful and clear.

"If I were in love with someone, like *that*—" thought Lockhart, watching out of the corner of his eye one of *Compass Rose's* leading stokers, whose dejection at saying good-bye to his wife was matched by the unselfconscious misery written in her face: "if I felt like *that*, every time I came back to the ship, what sort of a job would I do in the morning? . . ." But even as the thought struck him, he became aware of its inherent smugness; and presently, as the train drew out of Euston and headed for the north, he began to wonder if any rule of this sort could be applied in general terms. One man might need the tenderness of a love affair or a happy married life, to dilute the ordeal of war: it might, indeed, be the only thing that would keep him going and make his wartime life endurable. Another might only be devitalized or distracted by any break in the hard routine, and would be compelled to sign on for a sort of monastic dedication, if he were to be any use in war at all.

He himself—but even there he was not entirely sure. He had grown used to the company of women, before the war: he certainly appeared to have "given them up" for the duration. . . . Until now, it seemed to have been working out admirably. But just lately he had found himself wondering if some concession to humanity might not pay a dividend.

For instance, he thought, as he settled himself for the uncomfortable night-journey, there was a fair-haired W.A.A.F. sitting opposite to him, whose entrancing legs no dull grey stockings could spoil: whose shoulders would feel very square under his hand: and whose eyes, agreeably ready to flicker in his direction even under these unpromising circumstances, might well have widened and softened, to a really heart-breaking extent, on a pillow.

The sensual day-dream merged gradually into a drowsy night-time version, which lasted a long way north.

For Ericson, there were no day-dreams, and few night ones: he had found himself very tired by the time his leave came round, and he wanted to do nothing except sleep, and relax, and potter about the house until he had to return to the ship. It was a program Grace understood, and could adapt herself to; but the third member of the household, her mother, seemed unable to take it at its face value. It was clear that she interpreted his laziness, in some odd way, as a reflection on Grace, or on herself, or even on the quality of the housekeeping. The old woman had aged, becoming querulous in the process: from her permanent stronghold by the fireside ("Used to be my chair," thought Ericson) she issued comment, criticism, and an undertone of discord that cut right across his need for a quiet life.

"He ought to take you out more," was one theme that was always good for a triangular half-hour of discomfort when the three of them were together. "Is he ashamed of you, or what?"

It always annoyed Ericson that she spoke as if he were a small boy allowed, on sufferance, to listen in to the grown-ups.

"I don't want to go out, Mother," Grace would say. "It's quite comfortable here, thank you."

"Of course you want to go out! You're still a young woman. What's the good of him winning all these medals if he never stirs outside the house?"

Ericson, on whose chest the blue-and-white ribbon of the D.S.C. stood out in solitary splendour, lowered his newspaper.

"You've got it mixed up," he said tolerantly. "They gave me a medal for the U-boat, not for parading up and down Lord Street with Grace."

The old woman sniffed. "It's not natural. . . . He ought to take you down to the ship, too. He's the captain, isn't he?"

"Mother!" said Grace warningly.

"She's refitting," put in Ericson shortly.

"They can still give you a nice dinner, I shouldn't wonder. It'd make a change for Grace."

"I don't want a change," said Grace.

"If I'm going to eat corned beef," said Ericson, "I'd rather eat it here than in a stone-cold wardroom."

"What's the matter with corned beef, I'd like to know?" asked the old woman pregnantly. "I'm sure Grace does her best to make things nice for you. Slaving away in the kitchen all day, with never a chance to go anywhere. . . . When your father was alive," she said to Grace, "he used to take me out twice a week."

"Poor old bastard," thought Ericson, raising his newspaper again: "that's probably what killed him off so quickly. . . ." It had, as usual, been a mistake to join in the conversation: it never got them anywhere, and the old woman could twist and turn and shift her ground like something in the zoo. But later, when he was alone with Grace, he returned to a point that had worried him momentarily, and he asked:

"*Do* you want to go out in the evenings, instead of staying at home?"

She smiled comfortably. "I want to do what you want. And I know you're tired when you come back."

He squeezed her arm, with a rare gesture of affection. "I

don't know what I'd do without you, Grace. . . . But your mother makes me angry sometimes, always complaining, whatever we do or don't do."

"She's getting old, George."

"We're all getting old," he said irritably. "I'm getting damned old myself. It doesn't mean I have to keep nagging away all the time, just to show I'm still alive."

"You're different."

"So are you."

She smiled again. "They say that daughters always grow up to be like their mothers, in the end."

"Then God help me, twenty years from now!"

"Now, George . . . What are you going to do this afternoon?"

"Sleep." He caught her eye, and laughed. "I suppose you'd really like to dress up and go out calling."

"No," she said seriously. "You have your sleep. You've earned it. We'll go calling when all this is over."

Tallow and Watts sat side by side in a Lime Street pub, drinking beer and watching the dart players. The two Chief Petty Officer's caps lay peak-to-peak on the table in front of them: their two square-cut uniforms, with the gold buttons and badges catching the light, seemed far too smart and businesslike for their surroundings. The place was crowded, dingy, and uncomfortable: a near-miss in one of the big raids had removed every square foot of glass, and the windows were permanently boarded up, so that even at high noon the lights had to be burning, the air stale. Every time the door swung open, loosing a vicious draught round their ankles, a rather drunk man at the end of the counter called out: "Mind the lights—you'll have us all blown to bits!" He had been saying this virtually every night for the past year: it had involved him in arguments and fights a few times, but usually people grinned at him and said nothing. The door was on an automatic spring, and heavily curtained, in any case: it completed the pub's air of makeshift inferiority.

Tallow and Watts had spent every evening of their leave

there: it was as good as any other pub in the district, and it was the one nearest to the Y.M.C.A. hostel where they were staying. Though they did not voice their thoughts, they were both in mourning for the past, and for the comfort and cheer-fulness of the house in Dock Road. Then, there had been some point in going ashore, some sense in the way they spent their time: now there was just this sort of place, and a shake-down in a glorified doss-house, and a cup of tea and a meat pie at the corner café. It was a break with the past which they still had not got used to.

For Watts there was another break, which after the first weeks he had never mentioned again: the way that Gladys Tallow had been killed, just when things seemed to be com-ing out well for them. He could not pretend, even to himself, that the bomb falling on 29 Dock Road had destroyed any wild and colourful romance; but it would have been a com-fortable sort of marriage, it would have been what he wanted. . . . He mourned her death in the same way that Tallow had mourned when *Repulse*, his old ship, had been sunk: it had destroyed a more promising, more significant past, it was a senseless waste, it left a blank where no blank should be.

The pub door swung open, the draught stirred the sawdust on the floor, the man at the bar said: "Mind the light—you'll have us all blown to bits!"

"Bloody fool," said Tallow morosely.

"Round the bend," said Watts.

They returned to their silence: drinking, not talking, watching a small man in a cloth cap placing his darts wher-ever he pleased, with an easy skill that brought a murmur of appreciation from the other players. Presently Watts said: "He must have played before." Then he stood up, and col-lected their empty glasses for another pint.

Ferraby played in the garden with the baby, but the baby was different, and Ferraby was different too.

The little girl was now eighteen months old, and starting to talk: she was also starting to have an expressive will of her own, and the will seemed to be directed against himself. It was as if the tension and the jitters, which he could not now shake off, communicated themselves to the child as soon as he touched her: it was to her mother she ran now, whenever she wanted comfort or companionship, never to him, and if he took her in his arms she would wriggle free within a few moments, and then keep a careful space between them. She would watch him, and in the small lively face would be the beginning of fear; and even as he grieved, he wondered at it. How could she sense his terrible unease? What could a shaking hand mean to a child? How was it that, as soon as they were close to each other, the small mind could feel the brush of his disquiet, the chaos of his thoughts?

He admitted the chaos; he knew, though he could not control, the nightmare direction that his mind was taking, the total preoccupation with violent death. He kept seeing, in the child's smooth and soft limbs, other bodies neither soft nor smooth—crushed bodies, burnt bodies, bodies that came apart as soon as they were lifted from the water. Under the brown curls he saw a bleached skull: under the pretty shoulders he saw a watery skeleton. He imagined death in his child, and he imagined things more terrible still in his wife.

For many weeks now he had been unable to make love to Mavis, because of an insane fear of a happening that he saw in acute detail: the fear that he might do something terrible to her body, and it would prove to be rotten, and rip apart from the crotch upward, and never come together again.

Now, in the quiet garden, the little girl said: "Leaf," and pointed to the tree above their heads. Ferraby said: "Leaf— that's right," and reached out and gently squeezed her leg. She said: "No," immediately, and drew away and then stood watching him—serious, withdrawn, on guard. He said: "I won't hurt you, love," and she hesitated, and took a step— but it was a step backward; and before he could help himself she had turned into a different picture altogether, and was lost to him.

He saw, in the bare pointing foot, a bony splinter sticking out from under a blanket; and in the finger that went up to her mouth he saw the finger of a man trying to make himself vomit, to rid his stomach of the oil that was poisoning him.

He turned away, and lay down, and felt his body tremble against the earth.

Morell was washing his hands in the cloakroom of a night club when he overheard some R.A.F. officers talking about his wife. As a result of this, when he finally took Elaine home they had a furious quarrel which lasted for several days and was still unresolved—except in the fatal sense of surrender and defeat for himself—when his leave came to an end.

The two R.A.F. officers were moderately drunk: they had come into the cloakroom a few minutes after Morell, and had not seen him as he bent over the wash-basin. But the thick speech was clear enough for him to hear every word.

"That's a lot better," said the first voice.

"Mine's pure gin, old boy," said the other.

"Better tell the quack in the morning."

"He knows already. . . . Who's the tarty-looking number in the red dress?"

"Actress type, old boy. Elaine Swainson."

"Oh, her. . . . Know her?"

"Used to. She aims a bit higher these days. The hat on the bedpost has to have a ton of brass on it."

"Nice take-off?"

"They say. . . . Try your luck if you want to. She might feel like slumming."

"Isn't she married?"

"Not all that amount. Got marital thrombosis."

"What's that, old boy?"

"Got a clot for a husband."

There was a sound of laughter. "That's bloody good, old boy."

"Think I'll write a book about it. . . . Are you going to have a crack at her?"

"Maybe." There was another laugh, of a different sort. "Lend me a quid, old boy."

"A quid?" A snort of derision. "More like a tenner, and don't expect any change."

"Commercial type, huh?"

"There's a safe-deposit box under the bed. . . . Come on —let's look over the stable again."

Morell carried that conversation back to sea with him. He could remember every word, every inflexion of it: he could remember the exact smell of the antiseptic, and the look of servile discontent on the attendant's face as he slipped out without tipping him. But as well as the conversation, there was the quarrel with Elaine; and the quarrel was worst of all.

It started in the taxi on the way home, it continued at the flat; it drove him to sleep alone, on the sofa, and to suffer the most fearful night of his life. In the morning, there was no truce, and no respite for his thoughts either: she would excuse nothing, she would admit nothing, she would not even give a straightforward denial to his suspicions. It was clear that she did not give a damn either way; in the music-hall phrase, he knew what he could do with it.

The trouble was that he did not know at all. He could believe, or he could disbelieve, that she was faithful to him; but he could not say truly whether he wanted Elaine on any terms, or only on honest ones.

She knew this; it gave her a whip in either hand.

"You can think what you like," she said disdainfully, later next morning. "I'm sick of all this questioning, all this drama every time you come home."

"Darling, it isn't drama." He looked at her as she stood by the window, in her green flowered dressing-gown, with the edge of her nightdress showing above the patterned mules: after the night spent apart from her, she was specially lovely, specially desirable: her body beckoned to him, her set face overrode the beckoning. "But can't you see how I feel? It's natural for me to be jealous, when I hear people talking about you like that."

"You could give me the benefit of the doubt."

"There shouldn't be any doubt."

"Oh, God!" She gestured impatiently: he had seen her duplicate it a hundred times on the stage. "This is such tripe. . . . Do you expect me to stay home every night, just to make you happy?"

"You would if you loved me. . . . Do you love me?"

She said: "When you behave. But I won't be told what I'm allowed to do. I won't be taken for granted."

"You can take *me* for granted."

She nodded to that. At first she said nothing: it was as if he had produced some cliché that had hardly been fresh the first time she heard it. Then she said: "That may not be what I want."

He thought, in surprise: "But darling, you *married* me. . . ."

There was something here that no longer added up. He shut his mind to what it was: he had no weapons anyway, and he had to bring her back, he could not lose her. . . . When he gave in, and asked for her forgiveness and appealed for her continuing love, she allowed him no more than a perfunctory acquiescence. It was clear to him—except when he blinded himself with emotion or sentiment or hope—that she did not give a damn about that either. She was in the strongest position in the world: the loved woman who needs only love when she chooses, and who, at the slightest crossing of her will, reverts to natural ice.

He wanted to kiss her, he wanted to take her in his arms, and then back to bed. But he did not know what the answer would be—not now, not any more. He looked away from her, and round the softly furnished room with its overflow of cushions, its feminine accent and promise. He remembered suddenly the bridge of the bombed ship, adorned with blood and scraps of dead men. He thought: "This is a slaughter-house, just like that was."

Baker, for the first time, did not spend his leave at home. He did not even tell his mother that leave was due again: he wrote that *Compass Rose* was in port for a bit, and then, when his fortnight's spell of freedom arrived, he booked a room at a small downtown hotel, and settled in there. He had no clear idea of what he was going to do, except for one point, one action—the thing he had dreamt and thought about for so long.

This leave, he *must* do it. The time for dreaming was past. Everyone else slept with women, and talked about it, and took it for granted. He had overheard a mess-deck phrase that pricked his imagination: "She gave me a slice on the mat." He wanted a slice on the mat—not the next time they were in harbour, but this time.

On the first night of his leave he stood by the tram stop outside Central Station, looking about him, and wondering. He realized that he knew nothing at all about what he meant to do: now that it had come to the point, he was in a panic of indecision. He ought to have asked someone, he ought to have listened properly when people were talking about it, instead of pursuing his own day-dreams. . . . How did you pick up a woman? What did you *do?* How did you tell a prostitute from an ordinary woman, anyway? And then, did you give them the money first, or did you say nothing, and leave it on the dressing-table afterwards? Would it be expensive? Did they tell you how much it was, before you started? Did they understand how not to have babies? Could you be arrested if they found you doing it? What was it like, how did you begin, how long did it go on for?

Confused with doubt, sweating a little, but desperately determined, he started to walk slowly along the street towards the Adelphi Hotel, looking at the women as they came towards him. He had twenty-five pounds in his pocket: he wanted to be on the safe side.

When the members of the wardroom reassembled, on the last night of the refit leave, and were sharing a rather silent after-dinner drink, Lockhart said suddenly:

"I've been looking at some figures."

"I'm sure you have," said Morell suavely, glancing up from his newspaper. "Please spare us the details."

"Please don't," said Baker.

"These are the other kind," said Lockhart, "and they've taken me the best part of a day to work out, from the old deck-logs. Do you know that tomorrow's convoy is the thirty-first that we've done, and that we've now put in four hundred and ninety days at sea—nearly a year and a half?"

A glum silence greeted the intelligence. Then:

"I didn't know," said Morell. "Now I do. Tell me some more."

Lockhart looked at the piece of paper in his hand. "We've steamed ninety-eight thousand miles. We've picked up six hundred and forty survivors."

"How many have we buried?" asked Ferraby.

"I left that out. . . . We've each kept about a thousand watches—"

"And we've got one solitary U-boat, out of the whole thing," interrupted Morell. "Are you trying to break our hearts?" He stood up, and stretched: his face was pale and rather drawn, as if he had either had a very good leave or a very bad one. "And tomorrow we start another convoy— and then another, and another. . . . I wonder what we'll die of, in the end."

"Excitement," said Baker.

"Old age," said Ferraby.

"Food poisoning," said Lockhart, who had over-eaten.

"None of those things. . . ." Morell yawned again. "One day someone will ring a bell and say the war's over and we can go home, and we'll all die of surprise."

Lockhart smiled. "In the circumstances, not a bad death."

Morell nodded to him. "Not a bad death at all. But I don't think it will happen tomorrow."

[4]

Waiting on the fo'c's'le, with the two lines of men on either side and the petty officers facing him, Lockhart wondered why Ericson had decided to have Sunday Divisions, when *Compass Rose* was due to sail at eleven that morning. Usually he skipped Divisions if they were sailing on a Sunday—there was too much to do, and it was a nuisance for the hands to dress up in their clean rig when they had to get back into their working clothes immediately afterward. But possibly he wanted to smarten the ship's company up a bit, the day after their long leave ended: a formal parade, with a church service at the end, was a good way of taking a fresh tug at discipline, a method of pointing out, in simple terms, the difference between life ashore and life afloat. And perhaps, thought Lockhart, he might as well point a bit of it out himself.

"Lieutenant Morell!" he called out sharply.

"Sir?" said Morell.

"Stop those men in your division talking."

"Aye, aye, sir."

By agreement, Lockhart looked exceedingly bleak, and Morell unusually attentive, during this exchange, which was a purely formal expression of reproof within the Naval hierarchy. His seniority over Morell was just under three weeks: enough to preserve the chain of command, not enough to make his position as First Lieutenant any sort of dividing line between them.

He heard Morell administering a rocket to the offender, and he turned away toward the bows of the ship, glancing as he did so down the lines of men whom he had just inspected. Leave or no leave, they looked smart enough: clean, polished up, fundamentally tidy and seamanlike. There was a breeze whipping across the dock, setting the signal-halyards rattling, ruffling the men's collars here and there: a cold breeze, a sharp breeze, promising a brisk start to their convoy. He wondered how many of the hands would be seasick tonight, after their spell ashore: it was going to be lively enough, as soon as they left the shelter of the river.

Ericson's head appeared at the top of the ladder. Lockhart called out: "Divisions! 'Tenshun!" and saluted, formally presenting the ship's company for the Captain's inspection.

Ericson took his time as he walked up and down the lines:

it was a smart turn-out, he saw immediately, and he wanted, as usual, to make it seem worth while by giving it careful attention. (He remembered overhearing a rating off another ship complaining: "Divisions? Skipper runs past like a bloody ferret and then dives down to the gin again. . . .") *Compass Rose* had been lucky in the way she had kept her ship's company together, for though it was getting on for three years since they commissioned, there had been remarkably few changes. As he walked slowly round, Ericson was reminded of this passage of time, and the movements up the scale that had taken place within the family: Wells, for instance, was now a yeoman of signals again, Leading Seaman Phillips and Carslake, the leading steward, were both petty officers, Wainwright a leading torpedoman. "God knows they've earned it," he thought as he reached Ferraby's communications division, and the latter saluted: they had made of *Compass Rose* one of the best ships in the flotilla, the one that *Viperous* seemed to choose automatically when there was anything out of the ordinary to be done. (That cut both ways, of course: it was one thing to earn the limelight by sinking a U-boat, but quite another to qualify, on that account, for all the odd jobs, all the towing and rescuing and searching that were liable to keep a ship at sea for a couple of extra nights at the end of a convoy.) These were the men, anyway, who had made *Compass Rose* what she was; the process had meant, for them, nearly three years of training and practice and learning at first hand, three years of sweating it out in wretched surroundings, three years of cruel weather, cruel dangers, cruel sights to remember.

Life in corvettes had claimed them altogether: there were times when each man was, for days and weeks at a stretch, reduced (or perhaps exalted) to nothing more than a pair of strained eyes, a pair of sea boots anchoring him to the deck, and a life-belt snugly clamped round his waist. These were the essentials, these were what a man had to become. . . . The thing Ericson still found amazing was that the great majority of his crew, who had taken on this astonishing transformation, were amateurs: they had volunteered or been conscripted from a dozen different jobs, without a hint of the sea in them; and the original stiffening from the "old Navy" no longer stood out at all in the general picture.

"The sea in their blood," he thought, as he acknowledged Baker's salute and turned to his division of stokers: the phrase meant something after all: it was not just a romantic notion left over from Nelson, it was not just a baritone rendering of *Heart of Oak*, with manly emphasis on "Jolly tars are our men." "The sea in their blood" meant that you could pour Englishmen—any Englishmen—into a ship, and they made that ship work and fight as if they had been doing it all their lives, catching up, overtaking, and leaving behind the professionals of any other nation. It was the basic virtue of living on an island.

He was proud of them.

He completed his inspection of this last division, walked back to his place in the centre of the square, took off his cap, and after a pause began to read the Morning Service.

The noises of departure began, sounding all over the ship like repeated calls to action.

Ericson, sitting in his cabin and listening to the familiar activity intensifying as their sailing time drew near, could follow its progress in detail. He heard the pipe for the hands to fall in: he heard them begin to move about the deck, making fast all the spare gear, getting out the fenders, running back with the wires as they were cast off from the dockside. Another pipe sounded close by him, and with it the quartermaster's voice: "Testing alarm bells! Testing alarm bells!": presently the bells themselves sounded, clanging for a full minute throughout the ship and giving him, in spite of the preliminary warning, a twinge of discomfort somewhere under his heart. Muffled in the background, Chief E.R.A. Watts's contribution began to make itself heard: the windlass clanked as it was turned over, the steering engine ran backward and forward through the full arc of the rudder, and a gentle pulsing indicated that the main shaft was moving slowly, at five or ten revolutions a minute, in preparation for its long task. It would never stop turning, for the next four hundred hours at least. . . . Just over Ericson's head, the telegraph bells rang in the wheelhouse, and were faintly answered from the engine room; and then, after a pause, came the last pipe of all: "Hands to stations for leaving harbour! Special sea-duty men—close up!"

Lockhart appeared at the door of his cabin, his cap under his arm, and said: "Ready to proceed, sir."

Ericson took his binoculars from the shelf over his bunk, buttoned up his greatcoat, and made for the bridge ladder.

Down-river, to seaward of the Bar Light Vessel, the convoy assembled.

There were forty-four ships, ranging from a ten-thousand-ton tanker to what looked like the oldest refrigerator ship in the world: another six would join them south of the Isle of Man, and another eight off the Firth of Clyde: and Baker, checking the names and numbers of the Liverpool portion from the convoy list on the chart-table, found himself wondering, not for the first time, at the immense complexity of organization that lay behind all these convoys. There might be a dozen of them at sea at the same time, comprising upward of five hundred ships: these individual ships would come from a score of different ports all round the coast of England: they would have to be manned, and loaded at a prescribed date, railage and docking difficulties notwithstanding: they would each have to receive identical convoy-instructions, and their masters would have to attend sailing conferences for last-minute orders: they would have to rendezvous at a set time and place, with pilots made available for them; and their readiness for sea had to coincide with that of an escort group to accompany them, which itself needed the same preparation and the same careful routing. Dock space had to be waiting for them, and men to load and unload: a hundred factories had to meet a fixed dispatch-date on their account: a railway shunter falling asleep at Birmingham or Clapham could spoil the whole thing, a third mate getting drunk on Tuesday instead of Monday could wreck a dozen carefully laid plans, a single air-raid out of the hundreds that had harassed the harbours of Britain could halve a convoy and make it not worth the trouble of sending across the Atlantic.

Yet the ships always seemed to turn up: as usual, here they were, on this bright cold afternoon. . . . Baker, ticking off their names as Wells called them out, wondered idly who was behind the organization: was it one superman, or a committee, or hundreds of civil servants all telephoning each other at once?

Thank God it wasn't *his* worry, anyway. He had a particular worry of his own.

The convoy was "north-about"—that is, it was routed past the coast of Scotland, between the Isle of Lewis and the mainland, through the troubled, tide-ridden water of the Minches, and then westward from Cape Wrath toward the open sea.

They sailed past the Isle of Man, and the smug neutrals of Ireland, and the Lowland Scottish hills: the Bristol portion of the convoy joined them, and then the Clyde contingent: a day and a night passed, and they were steaming northward through the last of the sheltered water before they made their turn westward. But "sheltered" did not mean much, where the Minches were concerned: this stretch of narrow sea between Stornaway and the Scottish coast was one of the wildest anywhere round Britain, an uneasy area with swirling currents, violent overfalls, and, at the northern end, the ceaseless swell of the Atlantic coiling in to set up a wicked cross-sea at any state of the tide. Ships here were never still, sailors here were never easy: *Compass Rose*, with her convoy, was moving past one of the loveliest meeting-places of sea, sky, and land in the world—past a brave seacoast with the sunlight sparkling on its fringe of breakers, past whitewashed cottages at the heads of lochs, and lighthouses and beacons standing guard at their entrance, past royal purple hills with the first snow of winter already lying on their

peaks: *Compass Rose* had this to look at, this to enjoy, and all
that her company could think about was the prospect that the
ship, harried by this wilful sea, would roll so far in one direction that she would be unable to make a recovery towards the
other.

It had never happened yet; but they had already learned
that, in war, there was a first time for everything.

Presently however, when towards evening they came level
with Cape Wrath, the awkward motion subsided, and the
noise of their passage changed to a steady threshing as
Compass Rose turned westward with the convoy and headed
for the main Atlantic. Just before nightfall, a rain squall
blotted out the craggy and forbidding cliff that would be their
last sight of land for many days.

Now they were setting out again: leaving the Island, and
facing the tiredness, the nerve-strain, the huge question-mark
of the journey: taking it all on again, confronting once more,
with a possessive hatred, the things they had got used to, the
ordeal they understood.

It was very cold within sight of Iceland: *Compass Rose*,
running southwestward past the frozen coastline after delivering four ships independently to Reykjavík, had a rime of
bitter frost all over her upper-works. The watch on deck,
stamping their feet and blowing through numbed lips, stared
indifferently at this strange island, on which the pale afternoon sun glinted as upon an iced cake left by the kitchen
windowsill. It looked just as Iceland ought to look—no more,
no less: it had plenty of snow, it had black cliffs and white
mountains and a broad glacier. It did not seem to repay them
for the many extra degrees of cold involved in approaching
near enough to take a peep.

At four o'clock, Ericson came up to the bridge, checked
their position, and rang down for increased speed. The diversion had put them a long way astern of the main body of the
convoy, and he wanted to catch up before midnight, if possible.

It grew colder still as night fell.

[5]

The torpedo struck *Compass Rose* as she was moving at almost her full speed: she was therefore mortally torn by the sea as well as by the violence of the enemy. She was hit squarely about twelve feet from her bows: there was one slamming explosion, and the noise of ripping and tearing metal, and the fatal sound of sea water flooding in under great pressure: a blast of heat from the stricken fo'c's'le rose to the bridge like a hideous waft of incense. *Compass Rose* veered wildly from her course, and came to a shaking stop, like a dog with a bloody muzzle: her bows were very nearly blown off, and her stern was already starting to cant in the air, almost before the way was off the ship.

At the moment of disaster, Ericson was on the bridge, and Lockhart, and Wells: the same incredulous shock hit them all like a sickening body-blow. They were masked and confused by the pitch-dark night, and they could not believe that *Compass Rose* had been struck. But the ugly angle of the deck must have only one meaning, and the noise of things sliding about below their feet confirmed it. There was another noise, too, a noise that momentarily paralyzed Ericson's brain and prevented him thinking at all: it came from a voice-pipe connecting the fo'c's'le with the bridge—an agonized animal howling, like a hundred dogs going mad in a pit. It was the men caught by the explosion, which must have jammed their only escape: up the voice-pipe came their shouts, their crazy hammering, their screams for help. But there was no help for them: with an executioner's hand, Ericson snapped the voice-pipe cover shut, cutting off the noise.

To Wells he said: "Call *Viperous* on R/T. Plain language. Say—" he did an almost violent sum in his brain; "Say: 'Torpedoed in position oh-five-oh degrees, thirty miles astern of you.' "

To Lockhart he said: "Clear away boats and rafts. But wait for the word."

The deck started to tilt more acutely still. There was a crash from below as something heavy broke adrift and slid down the slope. Steam began to roar out of the safety valve alongside the funnel.

Ericson thought: "God, she's going down already, like *Sorrel*."

Wells said: "The R/T's smashed, sir."

Down in the wardroom, the noise and shock had been appalling: the explosion was in the very next compartment, and the bulkhead had buckled and sagged toward them, just above the table they were eating at. They all leapt to their feet, and jumped for the doorway: for a moment there were five men at the foot of the ladder leading to the upper deck— Morell, Ferraby, Baker, Carslake, and Tomlinson, the second steward. They seemed to be mobbing each other: Baker was shouting: "My life-belt—I've left my life-belt!" Ferraby was being lifted off his feet by the rush, Tomlinson was waving a dishcloth, Carslake had reached out above their heads and grabbed the hand-rail. As the group struggled, it had an ugly illusion of panic, though it was in fact no more than the swift reaction to danger. Someone had to lead the way up the ladder: by the compulsion of their peril, they had all got there at the same time.

Morell suddenly turned back against the fierce rush, buffeted his way through, and darted into his cabin. Above his bunk was a photograph of his wife: he seized it, and thrust it inside his jacket. He looked round swiftly, but there seemed nothing else he wanted.

He ran out again, and found himself already alone: the others had all got clear away, even during the few seconds of his absence. He wondered which one of them had given way. . . . Just as he reached the foot of the ladder there was an enormous cracking noise behind him: foolishly he turned, and through the wardroom door he saw the bulkhead split asunder and the water burst in. It flooded toward him like a cataract: quickly though he moved up the ladder, he was waist-deep before he reached the top step, and the water seemed to suck greedily at his thighs as he threw himself clear. He looked down at the swirling chaos that now covered everything—the wardroom, the cabins, all their clothes and small possessions. There was one light still burning under water, illuminating the dark green, treacherous torrent that had so nearly trapped him. He shook himself, in fear and relief, and ran out into the open, where in the freezing night air the shouting was already wild, the deck already steep under his feet.

The open space between the boats was a dark shambles. Men blundered to and fro, cursing wildly, cannoning into each other, slipping on the unaccustomed slope of the deck: above their heads the steam from the safety valve was reaching a crescendo of noise, as if the ship, pouring out her vitals, was screaming her rage and defiance at the same time. One of the boats was useless—it could not be launched at the angle *Compass Rose* had now reached: the other had jammed in its chocks, and no effort, however violent, could move it. Tonbridge, who was in charge, hammered and punched at it: the dozen men with him strove desperately to lift it clear: it stuck there as if pegged to the deck, it was immovable. Tonbridge said, for the fourth or fifth time: "Come on, lads—heave!" He had to roar to make himself heard; but roaring was no use, and heaving was no use either. Gregg, who was by his shoulder, straining at the gunwale, gasped: "It's no bloody good, Ted. . . . She's fast. . . . It's the list . . ." and Tonbridge called out: "The rafts, then— clear the rafts!"

The men left the boat, which in their mortal need had failed them and wasted precious minutes, and made for the Carley floats: they blundered into each other once more, and ran full tilt into the funnel guys, and shouted fresh curses at the confusion. Tonbridge started them lifting the raft that was on the high side of the ship, and bringing it across to the other rail; in the dark, with half a dozen fear-driven men heaving and wrenching at it, it was as if they were already fighting each other for the safety it promised. Then he stood back,

looking up at the bridge where the next order—the last order of all—must come from. The bridge was crooked against the sky. He fingered his life-jacket, and tightened the straps. He said, not bothering to make his voice audible:
"It's going to be cold, lads."

Down in the engine room, three minutes after the explosion, Watts and E.R.A. Broughton were alone, waiting for the order of release from the bridge. They knew it ought to come, they trusted that it would. . . . Watts had been "on the plate" when the torpedo struck home: on his own initiative, he had stopped the engine, and then, as the angle of their list increased, he had opened the safety valve and let the pressure off the boilers. He had followed what was happening from the noise outside, and it was easy enough to follow. The series of crashes from forward were the bulkheads going, the trampling overhead was the boats being cleared away: the wicked downhill angle of the ship was their doom. Now they waited, side by side in the deserted engine-room: the old E.R.A. and the young apprentice. Watts noticed that Broughton was crossing himself, and remembered he was a Roman Catholic. Good luck to him tonight.
. . . The bell from the bridge rang sharply, and he put his mouth to the voice-pipe:
"Engine room!" he called.
"Chief," said the Captain's far-away voice.
"Sir?"
"Leave it, and come up."
That was all—and it was enough. "Up you go, lad!" he said to Broughton. "We're finished here."
"Is she sinking?" asked Broughton uncertainly.
"Not with me on board. . . . Jump to it!"

H plus four minutes. . . . Peace had already come to the fo'c's'le; the hammering had ceased, the wild voices were choked and stilled. The torpedo had struck at a bad moment —for many people, the worst and last moment of their lives. Thirty-seven men of the port watch, seamen and stokers, had been in the mess-decks at the time of the explosion: sitting about, or eating, or sleeping, or reading, or playing cards or dominoes; and doing all these things in snug warmth, behind the single closed watertight door. None of them had got out alive: most had been killed instantly, but a few, lucky or unlucky, had raced or crawled for the door, to find it warped and buckled by the explosion, and hopelessly jammed. There was no other way out, except the gaping hole through which the water was now bursting in a broad and furious jet.

The shambles that followed were mercifully brief; but until the water quenched the last screams and uncurled the last clawing hands, it was as Ericson had heard it through the voice-pipe—a paroxysm of despair, terror, and convulsive violence, all in full and dreadful flood, an extreme corner of the human zoo for which there should be no witnesses.

At the other end of the ship, one peaceful and determined man had gone to his post and set about the job assigned to him under Abandon Ship Stations. This was Wainwright, the leading torpedoman, who, perched high in the stern which had now begun to tower over the rest of the ship, was withdrawing the primers from the depth charges, so that they could not explode when the ship went down.

He went about the task methodically. Unscrew, pull, throw away—unscrew, pull, throw away. He whistled as he worked, a tuneless version of *Roll Out the Barrel*. Each primer took him between ten and fifteen seconds to dispose of: he had thirty depth-charges to see to: he reckoned that there would just about be time to finish. . . . Under his feet, the stern was steadily lifting, like one end of a gigantic seesaw: there was enough light in the gloom for him to follow the line of the ship, down the steep slope that now led straight into the sea. He could hear the steam blowing off, and the voices of the men shouting further along the upper deck. "Noisy bastards," he thought, dispassionately. Pity they hadn't got anything better to do.

Alone and purposeful, he worked on. There was an obscure enjoyment in throwing over the side the equipment that had plagued him for nearly three years. The bloody things all had numbers, and special boxes, and checklists, and history-sheets; now they were just splashes in the dark, and even these need not be counted.

Someone loomed up near by, climbing the slope with painful effort, and bumped into him. He recognized an officer's uniform, and then Ferraby.

Ferraby said: "Who's that?" in a strangled voice.

"The L.T., sir. I'm just chucking away the primers."

He went on with the job, without waiting for a comment. Ferraby was staring about him as if he were lost in some terrible dream, but presently he crossed to the other depth-charge rail and began, awkwardly, to deal with the depth charges on that side. They worked steadily, back to back, braced against the slope of the deck. At first they were silent; then Wainwright started to whistle again, and Ferraby, as he dropped one of the primers, to sob. The ship gave a violent lurch under their feet, and the stern rose higher still, enthroning them above the sea.

H plus seven. . . . Ericson realized that she was going, and that nothing could stop her. The bridge now hung over the sea at an acute forward angle, the stern was lifting, the bows deep in the water, the stem itself just awash. The ship they had spent so much time and care on, their own *Compass Rose*, was poised for her dive, and she would not be poised much longer.

He was tormented by what he had not been able to do: the signal to *Viperous*, the clearing of the boats, the shoring-up of the wardroom bulkhead, which might conceivably have been caught in time. He thought: the Admiral at Ardnacraish was right—we ought to have practised this more. . . . But it had all happened too quickly for them: perhaps *nothing* could have saved her, perhaps she was too vulnerable, perhaps the odds were too great, and he could clear his conscience.

Wells, alert at his elbow, said: "Shall I ditch the books, sir?"

Ericson jerked his head up. Throwing overboard the confidential signal books and ciphers, in their weighted bag, was the last thing of all for them to do, before they went down: it was the final signal for their dissolution. He remembered having watched the man in the U-boat do it—losing his life doing it, in fact. For a moment he held back from the order, in fear and foreboding.

. He looked once more down the length of his ship. She was quieter already, fatally past the turmoil and the furious endeavour of the first few minutes: they had all done their best, and it didn't seem to have been any use: now they were simply sweating out the last brief pause, before they started swimming. He thought momentarily of their position, thirty miles astern of the convoy, and wondered whether any of the stern escorts would have seen *Compass Rose* catching up on their radar, and then noticed that she had faded out, and guessed what had happened. That was their only chance, on this deadly cold night.

He said: "Yes, Wells, throw them over." Then he turned to another figure waiting at the back of the bridge, and called out: "Coxswain."

"Sir?" said Tallow.

"Pipe: 'Abandon Ship.' "

He followed Tallow down the ladder, and along the steep iron deck, hearing his voice bawling "Abandon ship! Abandon ship!" ahead of him. There was a crowd of men collected, milling around in silence, edging towards the high stern: below them, on the black water, the two Carley floats had been launched and lay in wretched attendance on their peril. A handful of Tonbridge's party, having disposed of the Carleys, had turned back to wrestle afresh with the boat, but it had become locked still more securely as their list increased. When Ericson was among his men, he was recognized; the words "The Skipper—the Skipper" exploded in a small hissing murmur all round him, and one of the men asked: "What's the chances, sir?"

1942: *Fighting*

Compass Rose trembled under their feet, and slid further forward.

A man by the rails shouted: "I'm off, lads," and jumped headlong into the sea.

Ericson said: "It's time to go. Good luck to you all."

Now fear took hold. Some men jumped straight away, and struck out from the ship, panting with the cold and calling to their comrades to follow them: others held back, and crowded further towards the stern, on the high side away from the water; when at last they jumped, many of them slid and scraped their way down the barnacled hull, and their clothes and then the softer projections of their bodies—sometimes their faces, sometimes their genitals—were torn to ribbons by the rough plating. The sea began to sprout bobbing red lights as the safety lamps were switched on: the men struck out and away, and then crowded together, shouting and calling encouragement to each other, and turned to watch *Compass Rose*. High out of the water, she seemed to be considering the plunge before she took it: the propeller, bared against the night sky, looked foolish and indecent, the canted mast was like an admonishing finger, bidding them all behave in her absence.

She did not long delay thus: she could not. As they watched, the stern rose higher still: the last man left on board, standing on the tip of the after-rail, now plunged down with a yell of fear. The noise seemed to unloose another: there was a rending crash as the whole load of depth charges broke loose from their lashings and ploughed wildly down the length of the upper deck, and splashed into the water.

From a dozen constricted throats came the same words: "She's going."

There was a muffled explosion, which they could each feel like a giant hand squeezing their stomachs, and *Compass Rose* began to slide down. Now she went quickly, as if glad to be quit of her misery: the mast snapped in a ruin of rigging as she fell. When the stern dipped beneath the surface, a tumult of water leapt upward: then the smell of oil came thick and strong towards them. It was a smell they had got used to, on many convoys: they had never thought that *Compass Rose* would ever exude the same disgusting stench.

The sea flattened, the oil spread, their ship was plainly gone: a matter of minutes had wiped out a matter of years. Now the biting cold, forgotten before the huge disaster of their loss, began to return. They were bereaved and left alone in the darkness; fifty men, two rafts, misery, fear, and the sea.

There was not room for them all on the two Carleys: there never had been room. Some sat or lay on them, some gripped the ratlines that hung down from their sides, some swam round in hopeful circles, or clung to other luckier men who had found a place. The bobbing red lights converged on the rafts: as the men swam, they gasped with fear and cold, and icy waves hit them in the face, and oil went up their nostrils and down their throats. Their hands were quickly numbed, and then their legs, and then the cold probed deep within them, searching for the main blood of their body. They thrashed about wildly, they tried to shoulder a place at the rafts, and were pushed away again: they swam round and round in the darkness, calling out, cursing their comrades, crying for help, slobbering their prayers.

Some of those gripping the ratlines found that they could do so no longer, and drifted away. Some of those who had swallowed fuel oil developed a paralyzing cramp, and began to retch up what was poisoning them. Some of those who had torn their bodies against the ship's side were attacked by a deadly and congealing chill.

Some of those on the rafts grew sleepy as the bitter night progressed; and others lost heart as they peered round them at the black and hopeless darkness, and listened to the sea and the wind, and smelt the oil, and heard their comrades giving way before this extremity of fear and cold.

Presently, men began to die.

• • •

1942: *Fighting*

Some men died well: Chief Petty Officer Tallow, Leading Seaman Tonbridge, Leading Torpedoman Wainwright, Yeoman of Signals Wells; and many others. These were the men who did all things well, automatically; in death, the trick did not desert them.

Tallow died looking after people: it had always been his main job aboard *Compass Rose*, and he practised it to the last. He gave up his place on Number One Carley to a young seaman who had no life-belt: when he saw the man's plight, Tallow first reprimanded him for disobeying standing orders, and then slipped down off the raft and shouldered the other man up. But once in the water, a fierce cramp attacked him, and he could not hold onto the ratlines; even as the man he had rescued was grumbling about the "bloody coxswain never giving them any peace," Tallow drifted away and presently died of cold, alone.

Tonbridge overspent his strength trying to round up people and guide them towards the Carleys. He had already brought in half a dozen men who were too far gone to think or act for themselves, when he heard another choking cry from the further darkness, another man on the point of drowning. He set off, for the seventh time, to help, and did not come back.

Wainwright, having decided that it would be better if the two Carleys kept close together, set himself the job of steering and pushing one towards the other. But it was heavier than he thought, and he was not as strong as he hoped; he soon lost his temper with the sea that kept forcing the rafts apart, and the cold that robbed him of his strength, and he wrestled with the task to the point of exhaustion, and died in a fierce rage.

Wells died making lists. He had been making lists nearly all his sea-going life: lists of signals, lists of ships in convoy, lists of code-flags. Now it seemed to him essential to find out how many men had got away from *Compass Rose*, and how many were left alive: the Captain was sure to ask him, and he didn't want to be caught out. He swam round, counting

329

heads, for more than an hour; he got up to forty-seven, and then he began to be afraid that some of the men he had counted might have died in the meantime, and he started to go round again.

It was much slower work, this second time, and presently, as he swam towards a dark figure in the water, a figure who would not answer his hail, the man seemed to draw away instead of coming nearer. Wells approached him very slowly, unable to manage more than one stroke at a time, resting for long pauses in between; and within a few moments of finding that the man was dead, he died himself, calling out a total that was now far from accurate.

Some men died badly: Chief Engine-Room Artificer Watts, Able Seaman Gregg, Petty Officer Steward Carslake; and many others. These were the men whose nature or whose past life had made them selfish, or afraid, or so eager to live that they destroyed themselves with hope.

Watts died badly: perhaps it was unfair to expect him to do anything else. He was old, and tired, and terrified; he should have been by the fire with his grandchildren, and instead he was thrashing about in oily water, bumping in the darkness against men he knew well, men already dead. He never stopped crying out, and calling for help, from the moment he jumped from *Compass Rose*: he clung to other men, he fought wildly to get onto one of the Carleys which was already crammed with people, he got deeper and deeper into the grip of an insane fear. It was fear that killed him, more than anything else: he became convinced that he could stand no more, and that unless he were rescued immediately he would perish. At this, a last constricting terror began to bind his weak limbs and pinch the brittle arteries of his blood, until abject death itself came to rescue him. It had nothing about it that the death of an old pensioner should have had, and both his service and his normal spirit deserved far better than the last prayerful wailing that saw him out. But that was true of many other people, at this fearful ending to their lives.

Gregg died badly, because he clung to life with ferocious hope; and on this account he met death in a curious way. Just before the ship sailed, Gregg had got another letter from his friend in the Army. "Dear Tom," it said, "You asked me to keep an eye on Edith when I got home on leave. Well . . ." Gregg found it hard to believe that his wife could have gone straight off the rails again, the moment he had left her and returned to his ship; but even if it were true, he felt sure that he could fix it all up in a couple of days. "Just let me get back to her," he thought: "She's only a kid, all she needs is a good talking-to, all she needs is me to make love to her. . . ." For that reason, he felt that he could not die: it was a feeling shared by many of his shipmates, and the competition to stay alive was, in out-of-the-way corners, spiteful and violent.

It took Gregg an exhausting hour to jostle and force his way to a place alongside one of the Carleys: he saw that it was hopeless to try to get on top of it, but his immense determination drove him to do all he could to see that he did not lose his place. He finally squeezed his body between the side of the Carley and the ratline that ran round it, so that he was fastened to the raft like a small parcel tied to a larger one; and there, securely anchored, he aimed to pass the whole night, dreaming of home and the wife who must surely love him again as soon as he got back. . . . But he had been too greedy for his life: as the night progressed, and he weakened and grew sleepy with cold, the rope slipped from his shoulders to his neck—the rope that ran, through loops, all the way round the raft, and was being drawn tight by a score of desperate men clinging to it. He woke suddenly, to find it pressing hard on his neck; before he could struggle free, the raft lurched upwards as a man on top fell from one side to the other, and the rope bit deep under his chin and lifted him from the water. It was too dark for the others to see what was happening, and by that time, Gregg's strangled cries might have been any other strangled cries, the ordinary humdrum sounds of drowning. His wild struggles only shortened the time it took him to hang himself.

331

Carslake died a murderer's death. The small baulk of wood which floated near him during the darkest hour of the night was only big enough for one man, and one man was on it already, a telegraphist named Rollestone. Rollestone was small, bespectacled, and afraid; Carslake matched him in fear, but in nothing else, and the fact that he had not been able to get a place at one of the Carleys had inflamed in him a vindictive frenzy to preserve his life. He saw Rollestone's figure, prone on the plank of wood, and he swam over slowly, and pulled at one end of it so that it went under water. Rollestone raised his head.

"Look out," he said fearfully. "You'll have me over."

"There's room for both of us," said Carslake roughly, and pulled the wood under water again.

"There isn't. . . . Leave me alone. . . . Find another piece."

It was the darkest hour of the night. Carslake swam slowly round to the other end of the plank, and went to work with his hands to loosen Rollestone's grip.

"What are you doing?" whimpered Rollestone.

"I saw this first," said Carslake, panting with the effort to dislodge him.

"But I was *on* it," said Rollestone, nearly crying with fear and anger. "It's mine."

Carslake pulled at him again, clawing at his fingers. The plank tipped and rocked dangerously. Rollestone began to shout for help, and Carslake, shifting his grip, raised an arm and hit him in the mouth. He fell off the plank, but immediately started to scramble back onto it, kicking out at Carslake as he did so. Carslake waited until Rollestone's head was clearly outlined against the dark sky, and then raised both hands, locked together, and struck hard, again and again. Rollestone only had time to shout once more before he was silenced for ever. It was the darkest hour of the night.

But the murderous effort seemed to weaken Carslake. His body, hot for the moment of killing, now grew very cold; when he tried to climb onto the plank, he found that he was too heavy and too awkward in his movements, and he could not balance properly. Presently he rolled off it, and sank back into the water, breathing slowly and painfully. The plank floated away again, ownerless.

Some men just died: Sub-Lieutenant Baker, Stoker Evans, Lieutenant Morell; and many others. These were the men who had nothing particular to live for, or who had made so fundamental a mess of their lives that it was a relief to forfeit them.

Baker, for example, found in death no terror that he had not already suffered, in full measure, during the past week. Ever since *Compass Rose* sailed, he had been wandering round the ship under a morbid load of guilt, alone with a shameful fear that the passing days had disgustingly confirmed. He knew nothing about venereal infection, and he had no one to turn to; indeed, he was only guessing when he diagnosed the swollen and painful organs, and the soiled underwear, as symptoms of what, in the happy past, he had learned to call a "dose"—the cheerful joke of the cheerful man-of-the-world. . . . But as the days went by, he could no longer be in any doubt of what had happened to him; it had meant a week of trying to avoid human contact, a week of increasing pain, a week of infinite degradation and terror. On the night that *Compass Rose* had been hit, he had already been prepared to end his life by his own hand.

In the abandoning of the ship, he had swum about for some minutes and then found a place on Number Two Carley; but the slow drying of his body after he had climbed out of the water was horribly painful. He had fidgeted and altered his position continuously, without relief, for several hours, and finally, driven to desperation, he had slipped off the raft and into the sea again. The icy water was agreeably numbing. . . . He had begun to welcome the increasing cold as it ate into his groin, and the feeling that this loathsome and hated part of his body was at last being brought under control. He died as quickly as would any other man who welcomed the cold, at a moment when a single degree of temperature, one way or the other, could make the difference between a bloodstream moving and a bloodstream brought to a dead stop.

Stoker Evans also died for love: indeed, there had been so much of it, in one form or another, in his life, that it had long got out of hand. By this stage of the war, Evans had acquired two nagging wives—one in London, the other in Glasgow: he had a depressed young woman in Liverpool, and a hopeful widow in Londonderry: there was a girl in Manchester who was nursing one of his children, and a girl in Greenock who was expecting another. If the ship went to Gibraltar, there would be a couple of Spanish women gesticulating on the quay: if it went to Iceland or Halifax or St. John's, Newfoundland, some sort of loving or threatening message would arrive on board within the hour. All his money went to meet half a dozen different lots of housekeeping bills, or to satisfy affiliation orders: all his spare time in harbour was spent in writing letters. He was rarely inclined to go ashore, in any event: the infuriated husbands or brothers or fathers who were sure to be waiting for him outside the dock gates were not the sort of welcome-home he relished.

Evans had arrived at this deplorable situation by a fatal process of enterprise. He was not in the least good-looking; it was just that he could never take "No" for an answer.

But recently there had been a new and more serious development. Just before *Compass Rose* had sailed, the two official "wives" had found out about each other: the ship had in fact only just cleared harbour in time for him to escape. But he could guess what would happen now. The wives would combine against the other women, and rout them: they would then combine again, this time against himself. He saw himself in the police court for breach of promise, in the dock for seduction, in prison for debt, in jail for bigamy: he could imagine no future that was not black and complicated, and no way out of it, of any sort.

When, toward three o'clock in the morning, the time came for him to fight for his life against the cold, he felt only lassitude and despair. It seemed to him, in a moment of insight, that he had had a good run—too good a run to continue indefinitely—and that the moment had come for him to pay for it. If he did not pay for it now—in the darkness, in the cold oily water, in private—then he would have to meet a much harsher reckoning when he got home.

He did not exactly surrender to the sea, but he stopped caring much whether he lived or died; and on this night, an ambiguous will was not enough. Evans did not struggle for the favour of life with anything like the requisite desperation; and that potent region of his body which had got him into the most trouble seemed, curiously, the least determined of all in this final wooing. Indeed, the swift chill spreading from his loins was like a derisive snub from headquarters; as if life itself were somehow, for the first and last time, shaking its head and crossing its legs.

Morell died, as it happened, in French, which was his grandmother's tongue: and he died, as he had lately lived, alone. He had spent much of the bitter night outside the main cluster of survivors, floating motionless in his kapok life-jacket, watching the bobbing red lights, listening to the sounds of men in terror and despair. As so often during the past, he felt aloof from what was going on around him; it did not seem to be a party one was really required to join—death would find him here, thirty yards off, if death were coming for him, and in the meantime the remnant of his life was still a private matter.

He thought a great deal about Elaine: his thoughts of her lasted, as he himself did, till nearly daylight. But there came a time, toward five o'clock, when his cold body and his tired brain seemed to compass a full circle and meet at the same point of futility and exhaustion. He saw now that he had been utterly foolish, where Elaine was concerned: foolish, and ineffective. He had run an antic course of protest and persuasion: latterly he had behaved like any harassed stage-husband, stalking the boards in some grotesque mask of cuckoldry, while the lovers peeped from the wings and winked at the huge audience. Nothing he had done, he realized now, had served any useful purpose: no words, no appeals, no protests could ever have had an ounce of weight. Elaine either loved him or did not, wanted him or could do without, remained faithful or betrayed him. If her love were strong enough, she would stay his: if not, he could not recall her, could not talk her into love again.

It was, of course, now crystal clear that for a long time she had not given a finger-snap for him, one way or the other.

The bleak thought brought a bleaker chill to his body, a fatal hesitation in the tide of life. A long time passed, with no more thoughts at all, and when he woke to this he realized that it was the onset of sleep, and of death. It did not matter now. With calm despair, he stirred himself to sum up what was in his mind, what was in his life. It took him a long and labouring time; but presently he muttered, aloud:

"*Il y en a toujours l'un qui baise, et l'un qui tourne la joue.*"

He put his head on one side, as if considering whether this could be improved on. No improvement offered itself, and his slow thoughts petered to nothing again; but his head stayed where it was, and presently the angle of inquiry became the congealing angle of death.

Some—a few—did not die: Lieutenant-Commander Ericson, Lieutenant Lockhart, Leading Radar Mechanic Sellars, Sick-Berth Attendant Crowther, Sub-Lieutenant Ferraby, Petty Officer Phillips, Leading Stoker Gracey, Stoker Grey, Stoker Spurway, Telegraphist Widdowes, Ordinary Seaman Tewson. Eleven men, on the two rafts; no others were left alive by morning.

It reminded Lockhart of the way a party ashore gradually thinned out and died away, as time and quarrelling and stupor and sleepiness took their toll. At one stage it had been, almost, a manageable affair: the two Carleys, with their load of a dozen men each and their cluster of hangers-on, had paddled toward each other across the oily heaving sea, and he had taken some kind of rough roll-call, and found that there were over thirty men still alive. But that had been a lot earlier on, when the party was a comparative success. . . .

As the long endless night progressed, men slipped out of life

without warning, shivering and freezing to death almost between sentences: the strict account of dead and living got out
of hand, lost its authority and became meaningless. Indeed,
the score was hardly worth the keeping, when within a little
while—unless the night ended and the sun came up to warm
them—it might add up to total disaster.

On the rafts, in the whispering misery of the night that
would not end, men were either voices or silences: if they
were silences for too many minutes, it meant that they need
no longer be counted in, and their places might be taken by
others who still had a margin of life and warmth in their
bodies.

"Christ, it's cold. . . ."

"How far away was the convoy?"

"About thirty miles."

"Shorty. . . ."

"Did anyone see Jameson?"

"He was in the fo'c's'le."

"None of *them* got out."

"Lucky bastards. . . . Better than this, any road."

"We've got a chance still."

"It's getting lighter."

"That's the moon."

"Shorty. . . . Wake up. . . ."

"She must 've gone down inside of five minutes."

"Like *Sorrel*."

"Thirty miles off, they should have got us on the radar."

"If they were watching out properly."

"Who was stern escort?"

"*Trefoil*."

"Shorty. . . ."

"How many on the other raft?"

"Same as us, I reckon."

"Christ, it's cold."

"Wind's getting up, too."

"I'd like to meet the bastard that put us here."

"Once is enough for me."

"Shorty. . . . What's the matter with you?"

337

"Must be pretty near Iceland."

"We don't need telling that."

"*Trefoil's* all right. They ought to have seen us on the radar."

"Not with some half-asleep sod of an operator on watch."

"Shorty. . . ."

"Stop saying that! . . . Can't you see he's finished?"

"But he was talking to me."

"That was an hour ago, you dope."

"Wilson's dead, sir."

"Sure?"

"Yes. Stone cold."

"Tip him over, then. . . . Who's coming up next?"

"Any more for the Skylark?"

"What's the use? It's no warmer up on the raft."

"Christ, it's cold. . . ."

At one point during the night, the thin crescent moon came through the ragged clouds, and illuminated for a few moments the desperate scene below. It shone on a waste of water, growing choppy with the biting wind: it shone on the silhouettes of men hunched together on the rafts, and the shadows of men clinging to them, and the blurred outlines of men in the outer ring, where the corpses wallowed and heaved, and the red lights burned and burned aimlessly on the breasts of those who, hours before, had switched them on in hope and confidence. For a few minutes the moon put this cold sheen upon the face of the water, and upon the foreheads of the men whose heads were still upright; and then it withdrew, veiling itself abruptly as if, in pity and amazement, it had seen enough, and knew that men in this extremity deserved only the decent mercy of darkness.

Ferraby did not die: but toward dawn it seemed to him that he *did* die, as he held Rose, the young signalman, in his arms, and Rose died for him. Throughout the night Rose had been sitting next to him on the raft, and sometimes they had talked and sometimes fallen silent: it had recalled that other night of long ago, their first night at sea, when he and Rose had chatted to each other and, urged on by the darkness and

loneliness of their new surroundings, had drawn close together. Now the need for closeness was more compelling
still, and they had turned to each other again, in an unspoken
hunger for comfort so young and unashamed that presently
they found that they were holding hands. . . . But in the
end Rose had fallen silent, and had not answered his questions, and had sagged against him as if he had gone to sleep:
Ferraby had put his arm round him and, when he slipped
down further still, had held him on his knees.

After waiting, afraid to put it to the test, he said: "Are
you all right, Rose?" There was no answer. He bent down
and touched the face that was close under his own. By some
instinct of compassion, it was with his lips that he touched it,
and his lips came away icy and trembling. Now he was alone.
. . . The tears ran down Ferraby's cheeks, and fell on the
open up-turned eyes. In mourning and in mortal fear, he sat
on, with the cold stiffening body of his friend like a dead
child under his heart.

Lockhart did not die, though many times during that night
there seemed to him little reason why this should be so. He
had spent most of the dark hours in the water alongside
Number Two Carley, of which he was in charge: only towards morning, when there was room and to spare, did he
climb onto it. From this slightly higher vantage point he
looked round him, and felt the cold and smelt the oil, and
saw the other raft near by, and the troubled water in between; and he pondered the dark shadows that were dead
men, and the clouds racing across the sky, and the single star
overhead, and the sound of the bitter wind; and then, with
all this to daunt him and drain him of hope, he took a last
grip on himself, and on the handful of men on the raft, and
set himself to stay alive till daylight, and to take them along
with him.

He made them sing, he made them move their arms and
legs, he made them talk, he made them keep awake. He
slapped their faces, he kicked them, he rocked the raft till
they were forced to rouse themselves and cling on: he dug
deep into his repertoire of filthy stories and produced a selec-

tion so pointless and so disgusting that he would have blushed to tell them, if the extra blood had been available. He made them act "Underneath the Spreading Chestnut Tree," and play guessing games: he roused Ferraby from his dejected silence, and made him repeat all the poetry he knew: he imitated all the characters of "Itma," and forced the others to join in. He set them to paddling the raft round in circles, and singing the "Volga Boatman": recalling a childhood game, he divided them into three parties, and detailed them to shout "Russia," "Prussia," and "Austria" at the same moment—a manœuvre designed to sound like a giant and appropriate sneeze. . . . The men on his raft loathed him, and the sound of his voice, and his appalling optimism: they cursed him openly, and he answered them back in the same language, and promised them a liberal dose of detention as soon as they got back to harbour.

For all this, he drew on an unknown reserve of strength and energy, which now came to his rescue. When he climbed out of the water, he had felt miserably stiff and cold: the wild and foolish activity, the clownish antics, soon restored him, and some of it communicated itself to some of the men with him, and some of them caught the point of it and became foolish and clownish and energetic in their turn, and so some of them saved their lives.

Sellars, Crowther, Gracey, and Tewson did not die. They were on Number Two Carley with Lockhart and Ferraby, and they were all that were left alive by morning, despite these frenzied efforts to keep at bay the lure and the sweetness of sleep. It was Tewson's first ship, and his first voyage: he was a cheerful young Cockney, and now and again during the night he had made them laugh by asking cheekily: "Does this sort of thing happen *every* trip?" It was a pretty small joke, but (as Lockhart realized) it was the sort of contribution they had to have. . . . There were other contributions: Sellars sang an interminable version of *The Harlot of Jerusalem*, Crowther (the sick-berth attendant who had been a vet) imitated animal noises, Gracey gave an exhibition of shadow-boxing which nearly overturned the raft. They did, in fact, the best they could; and their best was just good enough to save their lives.

Phillips, Grey, Spurway, and Widdowes did not die. They were the survivors of Number One Carley, with the Captain; and they owed their lives to him. Ericson, like Lockhart, had realized that sleep had to be fought continuously and relentlessly, if anyone were to be left alive in the morning: he had therefore spent the greater part of the night putting the men on his raft through an examination for their next highest rating. He made a round-game of it, half serious, half childish: he asked each man upwards of thirty questions: if the answer were correct all the others had to clap, if not, they had to boo at the tops of their voices, and the culprit had to perform some vigorous kind of forfeit. . . . His authority carried many of the men along for several hours: it was only toward dawn, when he felt his own brain lagging with the effort of concentration, that the competitors began to thin out, and the clapping and shouting to fade to a ghostly mutter of sound: to a moaning like the wind, and a rustling like the cold waves curling and slopping against the raft, the waves that trustfully waited to swallow them all.

The Captain did not die: it was as if, after *Compass Rose* went down, he had nothing left to die with. The night's "examination" effort had been necessary, and so he had made it, automatically—but only as the Captain, in charge of a raftful of men who had always been owed his utmost care and skill: the effort had had no part of his heart in it. That heart seemed to have shrivelled, in the few terrible minutes between the striking of his ship and her sinking: he had loved *Compass Rose*, not sentimentally, but with the pride and the strong attachment that the past three years had inevitably brought, and to see her thus contemptuously destroyed before his eyes had been an appalling shock. There was no word and no reaction appropriate to this wicked night: it drained him of all feeling. But still he had not died, because he was forty-seven, and a sailor, and tough and strong, and he understood—though now he hated—the sea.

All his men had longed for daylight: Ericson merely noted

341

that it was now at hand, and that the poor remnants of his crew might yet survive. When the first grey light from the eastward began to creep across the water, he roused himself and his men, and set them to paddling towards the other raft, which had drifted a full mile away. The light, gaining in strength, seeped round them as if borne by the bitter wind itself, and fell without pity upon the terrible pale sea, and the great streaks of oil, and the floating bundles that had been living men. As the two rafts drew together, the figures on them waved to each other, jerkily, like people who could scarcely believe that they were not alone: when they were within earshot, there was a croaking hail from a man on Lockhart's raft, and Phillips, on the Captain's, made a vague noise in his throat, in reply.

No one said anything more until the rafts met, and touched; and then they all looked at each other, in horror and in fear.

The two rafts were much alike. On each of them was the same handful of filthy oil-soaked men who still sat upright, while other men lay stiffly in their arms or sprawled like dogs at their feet. Round them, in the water, were the same attendant figures—a horrifying fringe of bobbing corpses, with their meaningless faces blank to the sky and their hands frozen to the ratlines.

Between the dead and the living was no sharp dividing line. The men upright on the rafts seemed to blur with the dead men they nursed, and with the derelict men in the water, as part of the same vague and pitiful design.

Ericson counted the figures still alive on the other Carley. There were four of them, and Lockhart, and Ferraby: they had the same fearful aspect as the men on his own raft: blackened, shivering, their cheeks and temples sunken with the cold, their limbs bloodless; men who, escaping death during the dark hours, still crouched stricken in its shadow when morning came. And the whole total was eleven. . . . He rubbed his hand across his frozen lips, and cleared his throat, and said:

"Well, Number One. . . ."

"Well, sir. . . ."

Lockhart stared back at Ericson for a moment, and then looked away. There could be nothing more, nothing to ease the unbearable moment.

The wind blew chill in their faces, the water slopped and broke in small ice-cold waves against the rafts, the harnessed fringe of dead men swayed like dancers. The sun was coming up now, to add dreadful detail: it showed the rafts, horrible in themselves, to be only single items in a whole waste of cruel water, on which countless bodies rolled and laboured amid countless bits of wreckage, adrift under the bleak sky. All round them, on the oily, fouled surface, the wretched flotsam, all that was left of *Compass Rose*, hurt and shamed the eye.

The picture of the year, thought Lockhart: *Morning, with Corpses*.

So *Viperous* found them.

343

PART FIVE

1943: *The Moment of Balance*

[1]

Three out of the fourteen mirrors that lined the walls of the smoothest bar in London gave Lockhart three versions of himself to choose from. There was the looking-straight-at, and the looking-sideways-to-the-right, and the looking-sideways-to-the-left: having nothing better to do, while he waited for Ericson to keep their midday appointment, he studied, with a certain speculative interest, these three different aspects of the lean young naval officer relaxing from the fatigue of active service. The uniform was immaculate: the face was thin, but not without a significant determination: the smudges under the eyes were an understandable tribute to the rigours of the past. . . . Against the background of this enormously sophisticated room, with its thick carpet, shiny furniture, and general air of luxury, the face and figure were perhaps a trifle on the functional side: though there were other officers, from all three services, lined up at the bar or seated at the flanking tables, they were hardly warlike—in fact they looked as though they had been sitting where they were since the beginning of hostilities; and the women they escorted had, to an even greater degree, this same air of permanent availability. But he did not appear wholly out of place, Lockhart decided; if he could not attain the easy self-confidence of the habitués, at least he brought to his corner of the room an authoritative look, a dark-blue consequence that matched the carpet. And one more pink gin would come near to putting him in the habitué class, in any case. . . . He glanced around him.

"Waiter!"

"Sir?" The waiter, a very old man in a soft frilled shirt, appeared by his side.

"Another pink gin, please."

"Pink gin, sir."

"And, waiter—"

"Yes, sir?"

Lockhart pointed to the water jug on his table. "This water has some dust on it."

The old waiter clicked his tongue. "I'm sorry, sir." He lifted the jug, examined it for a moment, and then put it on his tray. "I'll have it changed immediately, sir." He bent forward. "I'm sorry, sir," he repeated. "It's the war, I'm afraid."

"Oh, dear," said Lockhart. "In that case I don't want to make too much out of it."

The old waiter shook his head. "You've no idea what it's like now, sir. Cracked glasses—not enough ice—bits of cork in the sherry. . . ." He bent forward again. "We had a cockroach in the potato chips, just the other day."

Lockhart swallowed. "Should you be telling me this?"

"I thought I'd just mention it, sir. It's not at all what we like to give our customers, but what can we do? We just can't get the supplies like we used to. There was an American officer here only last week, complaining about the soda-water being warm."

"Warm soda-water is a terrible thing," said Lockhart dreamily.

"It spoils everything, sir."

"Yes, indeed. Horrible to swim in, too."

"I beg your pardon, sir?"

"Nothing," said Lockhart. "I was just thinking of something."

"Pink gin, then, sir?"

"Yes, and make it a big one." He looked up suddenly, and caught sight of Ericson standing at the entrance to the bar.

After staring at him closely for a moment, he added: "Make it two big ones, in fact. I think we have something to celebrate."

Ericson caught his eye, and began to twist his way through the crowded room toward the table. There was a certain faint self-consciousness about the big figure, which Lockhart noticed, understood, and indubitably loved. This was a man to go through the war with. . . . When Ericson reached his table, Lockhart stood up, and smiled broadly.

"Sir," he said, "congratulations."

Ericson looked down, a trifle shyly, at the cap he was carrying under his arm. The shining gold braid on its peak proclaimed a very new promotion. "Thanks, Number One," he said. "They only told me last week. The passage of time, of course."

"Nothing else," said Lockhart equably. "But here's to it, all the same." He drank off the last quarter-inch of liquid in his glass, and looked towards the bar. "I ordered you a large pink gin."

"That," said Ericson, "will do for a start."

The drinks arrived. As Ericson nodded and raised his glass, Lockhart glanced down once again at the gold braid on the peak of the cap. He was now feeling a trifle shy himself: he had not seen the Captain for over two months, and their last dockside parting—a strange blend of formality, raw emotion, and mutual astonishment at their survival—was not a thing to be recalled, in these or indeed in any surroundings.

"I doubt if I shall ever be a commander," he said finally. "The passage of time won't be enough—at least, I hope not—and nothing else will operate in my case."

"Don't be too sure," said Ericson. He paused. "I was at the Admiralty most of yesterday. Things are starting to move again."

Lockhart was suddenly attacked by a spasm of the nervousness, the near-terror, that he had not yet learned to subdue. If things were "starting to move again," he himself must move with them: it meant the end of the hard-won in-

346

terval, the end of relaxation and recovery: it meant taking
the whole thing on again. He knew that Ericson must have
been settling his future, or at least suggesting to the Admiralty the line it might take; and he was almost afraid to
learn what that future was going to be. For him, the balance
between control and surrender was delicate still: his nerves,
tautened and laid bare under the shock of *Compass Rose*,
seemed ready to treat any change as if it were the end of the
whole world. Even Ericson's brass hat came into this category: it was like a secret signal, dismissing all he knew and
trusted, promising nothing but change and complication. It
could mean anything: it could mean loneliness, strange difficulties, good-bye. . . . Aware of how odd it must sound, he
switched the subject abruptly, and asked:

"What else have you been doing? Did you go and see
Morell's wife?"

Ericson, who seemed content to follow his lead for the
moment, nodded. "Yes. I've just come from her flat."

"How was she?"

"She was in bed."

"Oh. . . . Is she taking it badly?"

"I think she was taking it very well," said Ericson grimly.
"There was someone there with her."

For a moment the two men's eyes met.

"Damn the war," said Lockhart.

"Yes," said Ericson. "To hell with it."

For some queer reason Lockhart suddenly felt relieved.
Sex, he thought: the universal cure. . . . "Tell me all," he
said: "omit nothing. . . . She hasn't wasted much time, has
she?"

"I shouldn't say she ever has," answered Ericson. "But
you shall be the judge. . . . When I got to the flat, some
sort of maid or charwoman opened the door. She said straight
away that Mrs. Morell couldn't talk to anyone. I didn't want
to have the journey for nothing, so I said: 'Will you tell her
that the captain of her husband's old ship would like to see
her for a few minutes.' She said she'd ask, and went off."
He paused. "It's queer, you know: I didn't imagine for a

moment that anything funny was going on, even though I
had to wait for a very long time. I should have guessed,
really: the place smelt like a brothel, from the start."

"I wouldn't know," said Lockhart primly.

"I'll give you the address, if you like. . . . Well, after a
bit, Mrs. Morell came into the room where I was." Ericson
paused again.

"Pretty?" asked Lockhart.

"Very. . . . She had a dressing-gown on, but she looked
quite tidy otherwise, and damned attractive. She apologized
for keeping me waiting, and sat down, and waited for me to
start. I said how sorry I was about her husband, and how
much we'd all liked him—the usual thing."

"But true," said Lockhart.

"But true. . . . Then I waited, in case she wanted to say
something, but she just sat there looking at me. So I said,
would she like to hear about the torpedoing, and what probably happened to Morell." He paused. "She said: 'No—I
don't think I'm terribly keen to hear about that. Those things
are all the same, aren't they?' "

"Oh," said Lockhart inadequately.

Ericson nodded. "By this time I was feeling rather a fool.
There she was, having obviously just got out of bed, lounging on the sofa to the very best advantage—and I must say
she had a wonderful figure: not a line or a shadow on her
face, beautifully made up, and about as much in mourning as
the man that sank us. . . . It was all so unreal, when you
remember what Morell was like." He laughed shortly. "As a
matter of fact, I'd had a sentence ready in case she was too
upset—something to the effect that though it was terribly
sad now, later on she could be proud of the way he died and
the job he was doing—but by God! that was one sentence
I didn't use. . . . After a bit I'd had enough, so I stood up
to go. I said: 'If there's anything I can do, please let me
know,' and she—she gave me a great big smile and said:
'That's swell—and if you'd like a couple of tickets for the
show, I'll leave your name at the box office. And mind you
come round afterwards.' "

Ericson sipped his drink. After a moment he continued:

"I'm not sure how I answered that one, but anyway I didn't take up the offer. . . . I said good-bye, and she followed me out into the hall; and just as she was opening the front door there was a lot of noise from behind us, a sort of thumping. I heard a door being opened, and then a man's voice, rather drunk, called out: 'For Christ's sake throw that sailor out and come back to bed!' By that time I was in the corridor outside the flat, and as I turned back she said 'Good-bye' very quickly, and shut the front door between us, and after a moment I heard her on the other side."

"Talking?" asked Lockhart.

"No—starting to laugh."

The ordinary sounds of the bar, which had been somehow held at bay during Ericson's recital, now seemed to break in upon them. Voices sprouted here and there: glasses rattled on the tabletops: a man and a woman giggled in chorus. Lockhart sighed gently: the sigh covered many things, many futile and conflicting thoughts: but all he said was:

"I wonder if Morell knew about it."

Ericson raised his head. "She didn't strike me as the sort of woman who would bother to keep it a secret, if she saw anything she wanted."

"Poor old bastard. . . . What a waste of a good man."

"It's a waste of a good man, quite apart from her. In fact if you relate his death to her at all, you poison the whole thing."

Lockhart nodded. "True. . . ." He raised his glass. "Absent friends."

"Absent friends."

Immediately they had drunk, and set down their glasses, Lockhart squared his shoulders, and said: "And the Admiralty?"

Ericson sat back, and rubbed his hands together, as if at last ready to share a pleasing prospect. "Now then. . . . It's a new ship, Number One: new job, new everything. They're giving me a frigate—that's the latest type of escort. They've given me *that*—" he pointed to the gold peak of his cap "—so that we'll be in charge of the escort group. And they're giving you a half-stripe."

Lockhart, genuinely startled, sat up in his chair. "Good Lord! Lieutenant-commander? What will they do next?"

"There's a new Fleet Order, just come out," answered Ericson. "You're the right age, and you've done enough time as First Lieutenant, and you've got the necessary recommendation."

Lockhart smiled. "That's you, I suppose?"

Ericson smiled back. "That's me. . . . But there's a snag. Or rather, there could be, as far as I'm concerned." He paused. "I'll be senior officer of the group, as I said. They agreed that I could have a lieutenant-commander as First Lieutenant, to keep an eye on the rest of the group as well as my own ship. The job's worth the step-up in rank. They said that I could have you, if I wanted. I said I didn't know."

Lockhart waited, not sure what was behind Ericson's last phrase. Was it doubt as to whether he could handle the job—or had Ericson noticed that his nerves were still shaky—or was it something else?

It was something else, something quite different. "Listen," said Ericson, "I'll be quite honest with you. You could have your own command if you wanted it—command of a corvette, that is. They're moving up one or two First Lieutenants already, and you could do the job on your head. I could give you *that* recommendation too." He was looking, once more, a trifle shy. "I don't know how you feel about it. If you stay with me, it'll postpone your command for at least a year, or you might even miss it altogether. Sometimes these things have to happen with a rush, just at the right moment, or they don't happen at all. The job with me—senior First Lieutenant of the group—is a good one, and I'd very much like to have you with me; but it's not the top job for you, and I can't pretend it is." He laughed suddenly. "This is all slightly embarrassing. You'll have to make up your own mind about it. I won't make any comment, either way."

Lockhart's thoughts, in that moment of decision, were

swift and undelaying. A or B, he thought: the crossroads of the career, the choice (maybe) between fame and obscurity, living and dying. Then he thought: "This is all nonsense—I don't have to weigh it up at all. We're a good team—none better—and it's a blessing that we're going to be allowed to continue. Why fool about with it, why invent a dilemma where none exists?" He smiled afresh, and sat back, nursing his drink, and said: "Tell me about the new ship."

Ericson's glance was the full equivalent of the comment he had promised not to make: he had no need to enlarge upon it. Instead he said:

"It's a new class—frigates—and they're really something. . . . Same size and shape as a destroyer: eight or nine officers, about a hundred and sixty men. It's got everything, Number One: turbines, twin screws, three big guns, new asdics, new radar. The group will probably be three frigates and four or five corvettes, so we'll have plenty to do, playing round with them and keeping them up to the mark. Ours is still building, by the way; she's on the Clyde, and we'll be commissioning her in a couple of months' time."

"What's she called?"

"*Saltash*. They're all called after rivers."

"*Saltash*. . . ." Lockhart rolled it round his tongue. It was going to be strange, getting used to a new name. "It has a nice sound," he said, "but I can't say I ever heard of it, as a river."

"It's a very small and obscure river in Northumberland," answered Ericson. "I looked it up. It flows into the Tyne. It's not on the map."

"Well, it is now," said Lockhart, almost belligerently. He snapped his fingers. "Waiter! Bring a lot more pink gin. . . . *Saltash*," he said again. "Yes, I think we might make something out of her. . . ."

"It rhymes with 'hash,'" said Ericson tentatively.

"True," said Lockhart. "I'll bear that in mind all the time."

They lunched well and, toward the end, hilariously. Once

committed to a new and definite course, Lockhart felt very much better; and Ericson seemed to catch his mood and to turn, with him, away from the dark past, and to bend every hope on what was to come. Indeed, it was with something like a holiday cheerfulness that they arranged a meeting, in Glasgow, later in the month, as a preliminary to the first look at the new ship. There was much that they had left unsaid concerning the fact that they would be together again; but it seemed that they were both taking it for granted that nothing else, however promising, would have seemed wholly right, and that something in the past had already shaped the future.

"If we are both content," thought Lockhart, looking across at Ericson as he drew gingerly on an unaccustomed cigar, "then we are both lucky, and we can leave it so. War won't offer us much more than that. . . . There's a lot of gin in that thought," he said to himself wisely, "and a lot of claret too; but it's a good thought, all the same, a rare thought."

"Sir," he said, "I've had a rare thought."

"So have I," said Ericson. "Brandy or Benedictine?"

But later that week, alone, Lockhart found that the past still lived, and was not to be exorcized by the simple act of thinking and planning their next step. Caught off his guard, he was tricked into a last, inadvertent, backward glance at *Compass Rose* which was acutely moving.

He had gone to the National Gallery in Trafalgar Square, to hear one of the "lunch-time concerts" that were just beginning to draw the London crowds. He found the big gathering somewhat intimidating, and he sat down well at the back of the gallery, half-hidden behind a pillar. Myra Hess was playing the piano, and playing Chopin; in the perfect stillness that the audience accorded her, the lovely notes dropped like jewels, exquisitely shaped and strung, sculptured and liquid at the same time, falling straight upon the heart.

He listened unguardedly, surrendering to the music, keeping no reserve and no awareness of the outside world. She played two gentle nocturnes, and then one of the studies, one with a repeated descending passage that sounded like a terrible lament. Lockhart sat back, and the music carried him, like a child, from note to note and phrase to phrase. He drew a long breath, and suddenly he found that he was crying.

He knew, without doubt, why. He was crying, uncontrollably, for the many things he had hoped to have forgotten. It was not only because of the weakness, the nervous frailty that was still with him, two months after the appalling ordeal: the tears were drawn from him by *Compass Rose* herself, and the wasted love and effort, and the many dead. And by others besides the dead. . . . Earlier in the month, he had gone to see Ferraby, who was still detained in hospital. Looking down at him as he lay in bed, Lockhart had wondered, indeed, whether he would ever come out of it. Ferraby was now a ruin of a young man, thin, wasted, intolerably nervous: the face on the pillow was like a damp skull. Tied round one of his wrists was a piece of string. "It's my string," said Ferraby, embarrassed, and began to play with it. Then. more confidently: "They gave it to me. It's for my nerves, They said I was to play with it whenever I felt I had to do something." As he spoke, the hooked fingers wrenched and pulled at the string, and knotted it, and twisted it, and set it swinging like a pendulum. Then Ferraby said: "I'm much better now, though," and turned over on his pillow and began to cry.

He had cried as Lockhart was crying now: perhaps with the same tears, perhaps with others. Many tears could flow for *Compass Rose*: too many to be stanched, or swallowed, or ignored. Lockhart turned aside in his chair, and tried to control his moving face and lips. The music ceased: the applause filled the hall. Near by, a girl stared at him, and then whispered to her companion. Under their prying gaze he got up, awkwardly, and walked through into one of the empty galleries. His throat was aching, but the tears, ceasing to fall, were drying on his cheeks.

"All right, I was crying," he thought: "what of it? Some-

353

one should cry for *Compass Rose*: she deserved it. I don't mind its being me: not with that music, not with all those people dead and the ship wasted. The music released the crying, but the crying was due anyway: I would rather cry to Chopin than to a silence, or to a drink, or to a woman. I was hearing that sad and lovely music: underneath it I must have been thinking of all those men, and Morell and Ferraby, and Tallow giving up his place on the raft: I could not help the tears. But they're finished now, and better now: it was a thing to happen once, and it is over, costing nothing, spoiling nothing, proving nothing except that the past is sad and wasteful, and that sometimes music can point directly at it and say so."

The ache in his throat eased, and he walked back, and stood in the entrance to the music gallery, leaning against a pillar. When, after an interval, the notes of the piano started again, he found that their power to unman was gone, and that he could listen, and not be moved. He found also, later, that this was for him the last moment of mourning.

[*2*]

The Clyde shipyards again. . . . They were far busier now, Ericson realized, remembering the slow, gearing-up days of 1939, when the Clyde was just getting into its war stride, and there was room to move and time to spare. Now things were very different: from Renfrew down to Gourock, the banks seemed to be lined and crammed with ships at every stage of construction, and the men working on them had a purposeful air, a strained eagerness to be quit of one ship and get started on the next, which had altered the whole tempo of the river. The rate of sinkings in the Atlantic had served as a progressive challenge: air raids had sharpened the will to hit back: the news that now came out of Africa, of an army no longer barely holding its own but romping

354

forward to victory, had been a heartening tonic, prompting the wish to join in that advance and finish the business once and for all. Now the Clyde was on its mettle: after nearly four years of it, the men toiling up and down its banks to meet the needs of the war at sea might be just about ready for a rest, but if that showed anywhere it showed in impatience and haste, not in any slackening of the output of work. That was constant, intensive, and admirable.

Saltash, the nearly finished product of their care and skill, lay at the fitting-out wharf opposite John Brown's yard. Seen close to, the frigate appeared enormous: to Ericson and Lockhart, as they stared up from the dockside, she seemed to symbolize, dauntingly, the size and weight of what they now had to take on afresh. "Looks like a block of flats," said Ericson, letting his eyes move slowly from the outward sheer of the bows towering over them, past the tall super-structure of the bridge, and along the sweep of the iron deck to the square-cut stern; and indeed there was something big, solid, and ponderous about *Saltash* which seemed to match, in permanence, the long sheds that lined the wharf. Somehow, presumably, they would have to take this lot to sea. . . . Viewed from the dockside, she exhibited the usual, half-bedevilled air of a ship that was not yet free of the land. Her first coat of Naval grey was marred and spotted by red lead: her upper decks were grimy, and littered with the sweepings of weeks of fitting-out work: the shattering noise made by the riveters, still busy on the fo'c's'lehead, was the signature tune of the whole disorder.

She was thus dirty, noisy, and confused: to the casual passer-by she seemed hardly worth looking at yet. But Ericson could no more have walked past at that moment than he could have quit the sea itself.

He led the way on board, crossing the rough gangplank and stepping down onto a deck cluttered with packing-cases and empty oil-drums. Now the impression of size and complexity increased: even allowing for the confusion of fitting-out, there was clearly going to be an enormous amount to take in and to master. *Saltash* was over three hundred feet long, and she seemed to rise in mounting tiers, building up steeply in a line that climbed by way of the quarterdeck, fo'c's'le, flag-deck, bridge, upper-bridge, and crow's-nest, to the wireless aerial that crowned the tip of the mast. At all levels, she was already crowded with equipment, and there were indications of much more to come: there was stowage for a huge outfit of depth charges, there was any number of rafts and life-nets, there were dozens of ready-use ammunition lockers to serve the guns. Guns, thought Ericson appreciatively: lots of guns, not just a gun-and-a-half like the corvettes carried: here there were three big ones, and a four-barrelled pom-pom, and a dozen Oerlikons stuck all over the upper deck like sprigs of holly. There was also, by way of refinement, a power-operated hoist from the main magazine, to keep all these weapons blazing away merrily, with no awkward pauses. . . . Two big motorboats: direction-finding apparatus: a very new weapon that threw a positive spray of small depth-charges over the side: echo-sounding gear: some equipment for dealing with acoustic torpedoes: these were what even a cursory glance found time to take in. They promised complication, and a lot of new things to learn; but they promised a formidable ship also, as soon as they were in practised use.

Ericson left Lockhart staring at some minesweeping equipment that was entirely novel to both of them, and made his way down to the engine room. The succession of steep ladders that led to the lowest level of the ship became progressively more oily and dirty: by the time he had reached the engine room itself, badly lit by makeshift "shore lighting," Ericson's hands and the sleeves of his coat were much the worse for wear. The place, full of shadows, seemed to be a tangle of unrelated equipment: it was also cold and damp. A group of men were working on part of the oil feed, and on the other side from them a man in white overalls and a naval cap was examining the main switchboard with the help of a torch. He turned as he heard Ericson's step behind him, and Ericson looked at him more closely. He was a small man of about forty, with thin greying hair above a solid brown face:

he had an air of energy and competence, with something else added to it, a sort of ingrained deference which came immediately to the surface as soon as he saw the brass hat and the three gold rings, and the D.S.C. ribbon on Ericson's shoulder.

"I'm the Captain," said Ericson after a pause. "Are you my engineer officer?"

"Yes, sir," said the other man, somewhat warily. "Johnson. Commissioned engineer."

"How do you do, Chief?" Ericson held out his hand. "What's the state of things down here?"

Johnson swept his arm round. "All the main machinery's in, sir. I've been here three weeks now, and of course they were working on the fitting-out long before that. They're doing the fans and dynamos now. They reckon another month before she's ready for trials."

"What's the quality of the work, generally?"

Johnson shrugged his shoulders. "It's a bit austerity, sir. Fourth year of the war. . . . But the turbines are all right—lovely job. They say they'll give us twenty-five knots."

"Sounds promising. . . . What was your last ship, Chief?"

"*Manacle*, sir. Destroyer. In the Med., mostly."

"Is this your first time in charge?"

"Yes, sir." He hesitated. "As an officer, that is. I've just come up from E.R.A."

Ericson nodded to himself, in satisfaction. A youngish commissioned engineer, newly promoted from engine-room artificer, and ex-destroyers, sounded a likely proposition. It was probable that none of his skill would be wasted in the new job. A twin-turbine ship of two thousand tons was no longer in the "simple" class, as *Compass Rose* had been: she was a complicated mass of machinery which would need a high degree of attention for most of its working life. . . . He saw Johnson glancing uncertainly at his hands, and he smiled and said:

"I got a bit dirty on the way down here."

"I'll find you a pair of gauntlets if you like, sir." Johnson

357

was quickly apologetic, and ready to help. "She's very dirty all over, I'm afraid. These dockies don't seem to care what they do to her."

Ericson nodded again. "You can't do much about keeping her clean at this stage, I know. Yes, get me a pair of gauntlets, and some overalls too, if you can. I'll be doing a lot of climbing about, the next few weeks."

"Do you want to look round here now, sir?"

"Not yet, Chief. I'll leave it till things are a bit more shipshape."

He paused, before ending the interview, and Johnson, hesitating, asked:

"What was *your* last ship, sir?"

"A corvette. *Compass Rose.*"

Immediately an alert look came over Johnson's face. Ericson thought: "He's heard about *Compass Rose*, he probably remembers the exact details—that she went down in seven minutes, that we lost eighty men out of ninety-one. He knows all about it, like everyone else in the Navy, whether they're in destroyers in the Mediterranean or attached to the base at Scapa Flow: it's part of the linked feeling, part of the fact of family bereavement. Thousands of sailors felt personally sad when they read about her loss; Johnson was one of them, though he'd never been within a thousand miles of *Compass Rose* and had never heard her name before."

He became conscious that Johnson was still staring at him, and he said, with an effort:

"She was torpedoed."

Johnson said: "Yes, I know, sir."

That was all there was for either of them to say.

When he left the engine room, Ericson went up to the bridge: he had been saving it until the last, and this seemed to be the moment. . . . It was deserted, and his feet left fresh tracks in the frosty rime that covered the planking: he was struck, first, by the amount of space there was, and then by the array of equipment that lined it. There were rows of telephones, there were batteries of voice-pipes; there were special radar-repeaters, and a big chartroom at the back, and gunnery-control instruments, and a really tremendous asdic set. There was an illuminated plotting-table that recorded the ship's movements electrically: there was a wide flag-deck with a pair of outsize signalling lamps. They would need a lot of men up here at sea, he realized presently: two officers-of-the-watch, two signalmen, two look-outs, two asdic operators, a bridge-messenger—nine at least, even at normal cruising stations. But from this centre of control, command could be fittingly exercised. . . . And then, as he walked slowly to the front of the bridge and looked down at the fo'c's'le with its two hooded guns, a feeling of futility suddenly attacked him. Certainly he could command the ship, from this wide high platform with its mass of technical aids: but what was the point of it? Look what happened to the last lot. . . . He shivered involuntarily in the raw morning air, and gripped the steel plating at his chest-level as if steadying himself against the shock of a breaking wave: below him, the black and greasy Clyde, meandering past their hull, was an uncomfortable reminder of the sea lying in wait outside. There had been many thoughts like this, during the past two months, and he had hoped that he had begun to be free of them: he had not guessed that they would return so strongly, as soon as he stood on the bridge of another ship.

He *must* be free of them—and there was only one cure. . . . He straightened up, and walked across the bridge and down the ladder towards his own quarters. On the way he met Lockhart.

"Collect all the plans, and whatever else the Chief has, Number One," he said briskly. "We'd better learn the complete layout, for a start."

The job must begin all over again.

The next officer to arrive, a few days later, gave Lockhart a singular shock. He was sitting in the small dock-office that had been set aside for their use, working out a rough watch-bill from the scheme of complement, when the door opened behind him, and a voice said:

"Say—is this right for *Saltash*?"

That tone, that accent . . . Lockhart spun round in his chair, and then relaxed again. It was *not* Bennett, their old Australian First Lieutenant, but the two voices could not have been more alike: the one he heard now had the same broad twang, the same sharpened vowel-sounds, recalling Heaven-knew-what annoyance and dislike from the past. The newcomer was a lanky, fresh-faced lieutenant, in a uniform of a curious light-blue serge: he stood in the doorway with a confident air, and then as his eye fell on Lockhart's sleeve he straightened up promptly and said:

"Sorry to interrupt, sir. I'm looking for *Saltash*."

Lockhart, listening in fascination to his voice, gathered himself together.

"This is the right place—she's the one over there." He pointed out of the window, toward the untidy grey hull. "Who are you?"

"Allingham, sir. Gunnery Officer."

"Australian?"

"Yes. R.A.N.V.R." He looked down at Lockhart's two-and-a-half rings again. "Are you the Captain, sir?"

"No—First Lieutenant. The Captain's a commander."

Allingham abandoned formality again, with perceptible readiness. "Big stuff. . . . But why so much brass?"

"We're going to be in charge of the escort group," said Lockhart, somewhat austerely. Hearing the loathed accent, he was ready to dislike on sight, and readier still to resent any kind of uppishness. "So I'll be senior First Lieutenant."

Allingham nodded. "Fair enough. What's the ship like?"

"Still in a mess," said Lockhart. "But she's going to be good." He relaxed a trifle: "There are lots of guns for you to play with."

"Good-oh!"

Once more the accent and the expression stabbed Lockhart's memory, an authentic, arrow-swift echo from the past, and he could not resist remarking on it.

"We used to have an Australian First Lieutenant in my first ship. His name was Bennett."

"Not Jim Bennett?"

"I expect so."

Allingham whistled. "Say—he was a bit of a success up here, wasn't he?"

"No," said Lockhart. "I wouldn't say that."

Allingham put his cap and gas mask down on the table. "But if it's the same man, he certainly was. I heard him lecturing back in Australia."

"Lecturing?" said Lockhart blankly.

"Yes. He's ashore now, you know. Didn't he have a nervous breakdown after sinking those submarines?"

"I don't know," said Lockhart. "You tell me."

"Oh, he's famous, back home. Quite a character. It seems he was in this ship called *Compass Rose*, and the skipper got sick, and Bennett took her out on a convoy, and they got two submarines after a four-day battle. But he had to be on the bridge the whole time, and he cracked up after it." Allingham paused. "Between you and me, there was a bit of a stink in some of the papers because he didn't get a medal out of it. . . . *Is* it the same man?"

"None other." Lockhart collected his wits. "And he goes round lecturing about all that?"

"Sure. They had him on a recruiting drive. And talking in the factories—all that sort of bull. They say it stimulates production."

"It stimulates me," said Lockhart equably. "The last I saw of Bennett, he'd succumbed to a duodenal ulcer through eating tinned sausages too fast, and he left *Compass Rose* and went ashore to a hospital."

"No submarines?" asked Allingham, surprised. "No nervous strain?"

Lockhart shook his head. "The submarine, like the nervous strain, was all ours."

Allingham laughed. "Good old Jim Bennett. He certainly could tell the tale."

"He was a bastard," said Lockhart succinctly. "I loathed him and everything he stood for."

Something in his tone caught Allingham's attention. He hesitated, and then said with a certain emphasis:

"They're not all like that, where I come from."

"I'm beginning to appreciate that." Lockhart smiled, and the other man met his smile, and relaxed, turning his back on the dangerous ground. "They couldn't be," Lockhart continued, "or Australia would have fallen to bits long ago. . . ." He stood up. "Let's forget it. Come and look at the ship."

Saltash's complement of officers was eight: besides Ericson, Lockhart, Johnson, and Allingham, they had been allocated a surgeon-lieutenant, two sub-lieutenants (one of them a navigating specialist), and a midshipman who was to act as the Captain's secretary. It was their first formal meeting in the big wardroom which brought, to Ericson, the most vivid reminder of the past: there was, particularly among the younger men, the same reserve, the same wariness, as he remembered in the Lockhart and Ferraby of long ago, when he had watched them feeling their way in new surroundings, trying to guess what would be popular and what would not. But there, he realized as he looked at them sitting round the table, there the resemblance ended: for these were no green hands—with the exception of the midshipman, they had all been to sea before, and they knew the best and the worst of convoy work. Clearly, he wouldn't be taking *this* ship to sea with a couple of brand-new subs who had never yet stood a watch, and a First Lieutenant of Bennett's peculiar calibre. . . . He waited until they were all settled in their places, and then he tapped on the table.

"I've collected you all here," he began, "so that I can meet you properly, and also get an idea of what you've been doing before you joined *Saltash*." He looked round the ring of watchful faces. "Some of it I know already: the First

Lieutenant was with me in another ship, and—" he smiled
at Johnson "—the Chief I've talked to before. As far as the
rest of you are concerned, all I've got is your names." He
looked down at the list in front of him. "Let's start with you,
Guns—you seem to have made the longest journey to join
us. What were you doing before this?"

"Minesweeping, sir," said Allingham promptly, as if well
used to being singled out on an occasion like this. "Round
the north coast of Australia, based on Darwin mostly. Then
I got a bit browned off with that, because nothing was happening and it didn't look as if the Japs would get down our
way after all, so I put in for a transfer up here."

"Was there any mine-laying in that area?"

Allingham shook his head. "We put up two in three
years."

"And you've taken a gunnery course here?"

"Yes, sir. I've just come from Whale Island."

"Did they make you run about much?"

Allingham grinned. "I don't think we ever stopped, from
the time we stepped inside the gates. I must have lost pounds,
myself."

There was a ripple of laughter round the table. Whale
Island, the Royal Navy gunnery school, had a reputation for
tough, everything-at-the-double discipline that no one who
had taken a course there ever troubled to deny.

"Well, you've got plenty of guns to practise with. . . ."
He looked for the next name on his list, and read: "Raikes,
Sub-Lieutenant." He turned inquiringly to the young man at
the bottom of the table. "Where have you come from, Sub?"

"East coast, sir," answered Raikes, the sub-lieutenant who
was to be navigating officer. He was a brisk young man with
a precise, rather high-pressure manner: Ericson got the impression that his peacetime job had probably involved selling
some slightly unpopular household gadget, and that he had
carried the necessary tricks of speech and habit with him
into the war.

"Whereabouts? Harwich?"

"Yes, sir. We did convoys from there up to the Humber."

"What sort of ship?"

"Corvette, sir. The prewar type. Twin screw."

"I remember them. . . . You must have had plenty of practice in coastal navigation."

"Yes, sir." Raikes hesitated, not knowing how much Ericson knew about the east coast, or wanted to know. "There's a swept channel for the convoys, with a buoy every five miles or so. If you miss one of them, you probably run aground, or end up in a mine field."

"How many times did that happen to you?"

"It didn't, sir."

Ericson smiled at the forthright answer. "Well, you'll have to rub up on the other sort of navigation now. How long is it since you used a sextant?"

"Not since the training course, sir—a couple of years. There was never any need on the east coast. But I've been practising a lot lately."

"Good. I did most of it myself in my last ship, but I'll want you to take it over."

The next officer on Ericson's list was the doctor. "Surgeon-Lieutenant Scott-Brown," he read, and found no difficulty in identifying him, even without the bright red rings on his sleeve. Scott-Brown reminded him of Morell: he had the same assured, slightly *dégagé* air, as if, without in the least disparaging the present, he felt all the time that his real background, the structure of his competent life, was elsewhere. He was large and fair: he sat solidly in his chair, giving the impression that it was he who was conducting the interview, and that Ericson was the patient whose duty it was to reveal everything. "But that doesn't matter," thought Ericson: "All we want is a good doctor."

He said: "Where do you come from, Scott-Brown?"

Scott-Brown said, somewhat surprisingly: "Harley Street, sir."

"Oh. . . . This is your first ship?"

Scott-Brown nodded. "I was in practice, sir, and then I was doing research work for Guy's Hospital, and then there were the big raids on London. They've only just released me." He said this with no apologetic air, as if it were beyond dispute that he had not been wasting his time, before his late arrival in the Navy.

"You're something of a luxury," said Ericson. "We've never had a doctor before."

"Who did the doctoring for you?"

"I did," said Lockhart. He had been watching Scott-Brown, and he too had been reminded, like Ericson, of Morell. This man seemed patently sure of himself and of his skill, in just the same way, but the fact was a comfort, not an irritant. "No more first-aid for me," thought Lockhart thankfully: "not unless things go very wrong. . . ."

Scott-Brown turned in his direction. "How did you learn the job?"

"As I went along. . . . I'm afraid I must have killed a lot more patients than you have."

A brief smile showed itself on Scott-Brown's face. "That's a very large assumption," he answered slowly. "I've been in practice nearly eight years."

Once more the ripple of laughter round the table linked them all together. This might be rather a good wardroom, thought Ericson: plenty of variety, plenty of common sense, something solid and confident about it.

"We could have kept you pretty busy during the last two years," he said: "I don't know what it's going to be like now. . . ."

There were two more names on the paper in front of him, those of the second sub-lieutenant and the midshipman. Out of the corner of his eye he had been watching the latter, a tall, slim, and wonderfully innocent-looking young man who was at present fidgeting with an ash-tray in the nervousness of waiting for his turn. "He's almost a schoolboy," thought Ericson: in fact, that was probably exactly what he was, until a few weeks ago. Perhaps one so young could afford to wait a little longer. . . . He looked at the other man, the sub-lieutenant, who sat at his side.

"Vincent," he said. "Haven't I seen you somewhere before?"

Vincent was small, dark, and rather shy: before he spoke, he seemed to be gathering himself together, and making a tangible effort to arrange his words properly.

"I was in the same group as you, sir," he brought out finally. "In *Trefoil*."

Ericson nodded slowly. "I thought it was something like that." His voice was normal, but within himself he had been startled by the familiar name. *Trefoil* had been a sister ship of *Compass Rose*, for nearly two years: she had been the stern escort on that last convoy, and it was she who, blessedly wide-awake, had noticed *Compass Rose* appear and then disappear on the radar screen, and had reported the fact to *Viperous*. It was probable that he and Lockhart owed their lives to *Trefoil*, it was even possible that this small shy sub-lieutenant had had a direct hand in it. But he did not want to raise the subject now: it would keep for a more private occasion.

"Then we know all about each other," he said pleasantly, "and you know what the job entails. . . . That leaves you, Holt," he said suddenly to the midshipman. "How have you been spending your time lately?"

The ash-tray fell off the table with a clatter. Midshipman Holt blushed vividly: the colour rose in his clear face, producing an enviable air of youth and health. "Heavens!" thought Ericson: "He must be about seventeen. I could be his father—in fact I could damned nearly be his grandfather."

"Sorry, sir," said Holt. He collected himself manfully. "I've just finished the course at *King Alfred*."

"And before that?"

"Er—Eton, sir."

"Oh." Ericson caught Johnson's eye, and was amused to see in it a perceptible degree of deference. Certainly Eton gave the wardroom a touch of class, a leavening of distinction for the rough sailormen. . . . He took another look at Holt, and saw that, in gaining confidence, his face had taken on a lively intelligence and humour. Perhaps it wasn't simply the Eton label that they would come to remember him by.

"Did they teach you anything about the sea there?" he asked.

"Oh no, sir," said Holt, in surprise. "It was a very *narrow* sort of education."

For the third time a small laugh went round the table, and again Ericson welcomed it. "As soon as this kid finds his feet," he thought, "he'll keep us all young—and God knows we need it. . . ." A pause intervened, while Ericson looked at them each in turn, and tried to sum up what he and they had learnt. "Now we know where we all come from, anyway," he thought: "We come from the Atlantic, the Mediterranean, the east coast of England, North Australia, Harley Street, and Eton." But the assorted backgrounds had given them a valuable range of experience: *Saltash*, providing them all with plenty to do and plenty to learn, would have a substantial fund of skill and energy to draw on.

He cleared his throat. "Well, that will do for a start," he said. "We'll have a lot of hard work, getting the ship ready for sea, but I know I can rely on all of you to do your best. The First Lieutenant will be allocating the various jobs to you, as far as divisional work is concerned, and of course you have your own departments already: that is"—he looked down again—"Allingham—gunnery: Raikes—navigation: Vincent—depth charges: and Holt—correspondence. I don't expect we'll be ready for trials for another three weeks, so you'll have plenty of time to get things in running order." He stood up, and signed to Lockhart to come with him. At the door he turned and said:

"We can have a less formal meeting at six this evening, if the gin's arrived."

When the door shut behind them, a silence fell on the wardroom. Johnson was studying an engineering manual that had been open on the table in front of him: Scott-Brown, the doctor, and Raikes were lighting cigarettes: Holt was picking up, as unobtrusively as possible, the fallen ash-tray. Finally, after a long pause, Allingham looked across at Vincent, the sub-lieutenant who had been in *Trefoil*, and said:

"What happened to the Skipper's last ship? She was torpedoed, wasn't she?"

Vincent nodded, searching for the right words again. "Yes.

367

She was catching up the convoy after taking a couple of ships to Iceland; we got her on the radar, just after midnight, a long way astern of us, and then she faded out. We waited a bit, but nothing happened, so we reported it to *Viperous*— she was senior officer of the escort—and *Viperous* went back and found the rafts in the morning."

"It was damned lucky someone noticed them on the radar," said Allingham.

"Yes," said Vincent non-committally.

Scott-Brown looked at him. "Was that you?"

Vincent said: "I was Officer-of-the-Watch, yes."

"Nice work," said Allingham. "How many of them were picked up?"

"Ten, I think. Ten or eleven."

Allingham whistled. "Not so hot."

"What's that medal he's wearing?" asked Scott-Brown.

"The D.S.C.," said Holt, the midshipman, readily. "And the First Lieutenant's got a mention."

"I wonder what they were for."

Johnson looked up from his book. "They sank a submarine, coming back from Gibraltar. About a year ago. Took a lot of prisoners, too."

Scott-Brown smiled. "You've got an accurate memory, Chief."

"She was a good ship, *Compass Rose*," answered Johnson seriously. "One of the best."

"Jolly bad luck, losing all those chaps," said Holt. His young voice and "London" accent were a curious contrast with Johnson's rough north-country tone. "I wonder what it's really like, being torpedoed."

"Don't you bother with it," said Raikes succinctly. "They say it's not worth finding out."

"I'm not in the least inquisitive myself," commented Scott-Brown.

"Me neither," said Allingham. "I just want to see Australia again."

"What a curious thing to want," said Holt innocently.

Allingham looked at him for a moment, and then said: "Young fellow, you want to buck your ideas up a bit. Didn't they teach you about Australia at that slap-up school of yours?"

"Oh yes," said Holt. "Convicts and rabbits."

"Now see here—" began Allingham energetically.

"I think," said Scott-Brown, intervening, "that your leg is being pulled, in the best Etonian manner."

"Oh. . . ." Allingham finally achieved a smile. "Isn't there some system of flogging midshipmen in the British Navy?"

Johnson looked up again. "It went out a long time ago."

"I'm an old-fashioned sort of joker," said Allingham. "I'm thinking of bringing it in again."

In the captain's cabin, Ericson was saying:

"They're not a bad lot at all, Number One. They've had a good deal of experience, anyway—about two-hundred-per-cent more than *Compass Rose* started with, I should say."

Lockhart smiled. "Don't rub it in, sir."

"I remember you and Ferraby coming into that dockside hut, looking like a couple of white mice. . . . You know, it's funny to have an Australian in the ship again. Reminds me of Bennett."

"Yes," said Lockhart. "Horrible, isn't it?"

[3]

It was Holt who normally made the twice-a-week journey into Glasgow, to collect their secret signals from Operations and to see to the other odd jobs that attended the progress of *Saltash* toward her readiness for sea. After a couple of weeks, however, Lockhart found himself growing restless, as if he had spent long enough on board at one stretch and needed to move outside the atmosphere of routine and detail which was his particular and unending share of that progress. For a fortnight he had been wrestling with stores lists, alterations lists, accommodation lists, and the various complicated schemes that would keep *Saltash* in running order at sea and in harbour: he was finding it dry work, and he felt that he needed a break. He was also curious to learn what was going on in the outside world, the world that lay beyond the mouth of the Clyde, which was still their closest contact with the sea: he had been away from the Atlantic for nearly four months, and the personal interest, the feeling almost of responsibility for the whole ocean, which had retreated under the deep hurt of *Compass Rose*, was now returning. It was time to be drawn into the swim again, time to find out what was going on and how the battle was faring; particularly so as they would be returning to that battle, with their brand-new contribution, in a matter of a few weeks.

At breakfast one morning, therefore, Lockhart said to Holt: "I'll do the Glasgow trip today, Mid. I want some fresh air."

Scott-Brown looked at him over the top of his newspaper. "That's the one thing you won't find in Glasgow."

Lockhart smiled. "I want a change, anyway."

"Sir?" said Holt. Lockhart turned to him inquiringly. "Sir, there's a commissioned lovely in Operations—"

"There's a *what?*"

"A Wren officer, sir."

"I prefer that version. . . . What about her?"

"They say she's the prettiest girl in the Wrens. She's got everyone at Operations tied up in knots."

"I don't think that it's a Wren who's responsible for that. . . . What about her, anyway?"

"I just thought I'd mention it, sir."

Lockhart inclined his head gravely. "Thank you. . . . Where can one see this paragon?"

"In the Ops Room itself, sir. She practically runs the place."

"What were you doing in Ops Room, when the signal section is miles away, and on a different floor?"

The midshipman smiled engagingly. "Just keeping in touch, sir."

Scott-Brown looked at him. "How old are you, midshipman?"

"Nearly eighteen."

"I can't help feeling that you've got plenty of time ahead of you for this sort of thing."

"Don't rush it," agreed Raikes. "Leave a little for when you come of age."

"In Australia," said Allingham, "he'd be married by now."

"I dare say he would be in England, if there were any justice." That was Scott-Brown again, precise and authoritative as usual. "But there are people who can evade their responsibilities almost indefinitely."

"One law for the rich," said Raikes.

"I'm not rich," interrupted Holt.

"You are doubtless well-endowed," said Lockhart. "It's better, really."

"Certainly," said Scott-Brown. "Some say that those are the only true riches."

Lockhart nodded. "A lot of women think so."

"Particularly the rather older ones, of independent means already."

"This conversation is beyond me," said Holt.

"Then there's hope for you yet." Lockhart stretched. "Well, I shall be seeing your pretty Wren, as it happens, because I'm going to Ops Room to find out who's winning the war."

"H'm," said Scott-Brown.

"H'm," said Holt, on a more meaning note still.

"Cough your fill," said Lockhart, preparing to leave. "I've got a great deal of leeway to make up."

A barrage of coughing from the entire wardroom followed him down the passage to his cabin.

. . .

371

On this bleak March morning, the grey town was infinitely drab. "Spring must come to Glasgow some time," thought Lockhart, as he made his slow way down Argyll Street through the crowds of apathetic shoppers and the depressed hang-dog men waiting for the pubs to open; "but it's not happening yet, it simply hasn't got anything to work on. . . ." He remembered the weeks he had spent in Glasgow, more than three years ago, when he and Ferraby were sharing a hotel room, and, in their time off from *Compass Rose*, had walked round the town doing their best to feel that they were gay young blades giving the place a treat. Glasgow had not suited that part, any more than it now suited the idea and the promise of spring; today it had the same dour unimpressionable aspect, the same futureless air, that he remembered from 1939. Presumably something had been happening in the meantime: babies must have been born, love must have been made, money must have been lost and won; but it did not show on the grimy wet pavements, or in the desolate, half-empty shops, and all the inward-looking pallid faces he passed in the streets denied it utterly.

"One is on one's own here," he thought, staring momentarily into the window of a cheap jeweller's shop, where tray upon tray of weddings rings waited for the customers that never came, the sparks that were never kindled. If a man did not carry, within his breast, the urgency, the flicker of risky life, the touch of wilful self-conceit that turned a body into a person, then he would never catch it anywhere in these ten square miles.

But perhaps it was the war. . . . At the Naval Headquarters he collected a bundle of signals and some sealed envelopes, and then went down two floors and walked along a dark echoing corridor until he came to a room labelled STAFF OFFICER, OPERATIONS. He knocked and opened the door.

One desk was empty: at the other was a girl. She was telephoning as Lockhart came in, and for a full half-minute, as she listened, her eyes rested on his face. He was very glad to have the enjoyment of them for so long, without interruption: they were large eyes, with long lashes, and they were the principal feature in a face of extraordinary distinction. This was not "the prettiest girl in the Wrens," as the midshipman had phrased it—anyone could have *that* title. She was lovely: there were those eyes, and an oval face with high cheek-bones, and dark hair swept upward, and a pale and flawless skin. "What have you *not* got?" wondered Lockhart, as he came nearer, and saw that the eyes were grey and that her hands were slim and beautifully kept. He looked down and away, not yet prepared to hold her glance indefinitely. There was a card on her desk, with SECOND OFFICER HALLAM printed on it, and underneath, S.O.O.2. "S.O.O.2.," he thought, without the least surprise: second staff-officer in charge of operations: she must be good. But what else could she be, looking like that, lovely, intelligent, her trim tailored uniform as becoming as any ball-dress ever made? "I'm building this up," he thought, a trifle wildly, "but by God I'm not inventing it. . . ." She said: "Send it to me, please," into the telephone, put down the receiver, made a note on a pad in front of her, and looked up again. Then she said: "Yes?"

Lockhart swallowed. "If it's not illegal," he began uncertainly, "I wanted to have a look at the plot, and see what's going on in the Western Approaches."

"Oh." She did not bother to look doubtful: she was simply cool and unimpressed. Probably she got a lot of people coming in here, on any damned silly excuse. . . . "I don't think I can let you do that," she said after a moment. "There's a security ban on the whole thing."

Her voice was low, the words musically pronounced as if each one were worth saying and not swallowing.

"I know that," answered Lockhart. "But you see . . . I was in it for the last three years, and now I've been ashore for nearly four months, commissioning a new ship, and I wanted to catch up with what's been happening."

He might have resented having to give this long explanation, if she had not been so clearly the kind of person who was entitled to an explanation for everything. Her grey eyes now rested firmly on his, without any hesitation. "Somewhere behind all this there's a woman," thought Lockhart: "there must be. But she isn't on view today. Not for me, anyway."

After a moment she said:

"Which ship are you?"

"*Saltash.*"

"Oh yes, the new frigate." She smiled momentarily: the movement gave to her mouth an opening softness that made Lockhart tremble. "It's because I haven't seen a girl like this for so long," he thought, and then: "Hell! there's got to be *some* explanation." After a moment he heard her continue: "Haven't you got a young man called Gavin Holt on board?"

"Yes, indeed. Our midshipman. He practically sent his love to you."

"I practically return it. . . ." But that might be too close an approach, Lockhart realized immediately; in a minute she wasn't going to like him at all. However, she went on, amiably enough: "Who's your captain? Or is it you?"

"No. Commander Ericson."

"Oh yes. He's rather a star, isn't he?"

"Yes."

Her eyes went down to the rings on his sleeves. "Are you the First Lieutenant, then?"

He nodded. "Yes."

She frowned, for a swift moment. "Isn't that a bit unusual? Why not a command of your own?"

"I wanted to stay with Ericson," answered Lockhart, somewhat rebelliously.

The eyebrows moved again, a fractional and intolerable lifting. "Scared of it?"

Lockhart flushed suddenly. "Now we throw it all away," he thought. "If I were scared of having a command," he said, "I'm damned if I'd tell *you* about it."

After a moment's silence, the smile began to break in her face again, and now it reached her eyes, which were frankly drawing his.

"Sorry," she said. The voice was soft, and a little laughing. "*Really* sorry. . . . Look—if you worked in this building, with a lot of peculiar young men all scheming for a rise in rank without a rise in the amount of work they're doing, you'd become a bit suspicious yourself."

"It isn't like that," said Lockhart inadequately.

"I'm sure. Because I've just remembered who you are." There was a genuine, an exquisite contrition in her face now. "You and he were in *Compass Rose* together, weren't you?"

"Yes," said Lockhart. "How did you know that?"

"Someone was talking about it the other night. . . . You got a submarine, too. Do I apologize again?"

"Never again. . . . But does it increase my chance of seeing the plot and hearing the news?"

She nodded readily. "I think it guarantees it. What can we tell you?"

They talked, with some degree of technicality, for nearly ten minutes: from it, Lockhart gathered a confused impression that things in the Atlantic were slightly on the upgrade, after a bad Christmastime, that Second Officer Hallam had held her present job for four months, and that her eyes were dark rather than light grey. But he could not enjoy those eyes and that lovely face and voice for ever, and presently she said: "I expect you're very busy with commissioning," which was clearly her method of saying that she herself was busy anyway. He took the hint without any resentment. Once again, she was that sort of person.

And in a way, he realized, he was only living on borrowed good-humour: if she had not been over-disdainful in the first place, mistaking his quality, she would not now be making these charming amends, she might never have taken as much as a single step toward him.

Even so, their leave-taking was vaguely depressing. As Lockhart got up to go, a young R.N. lieutenant put his head round the door and said: "Are we lunching, Julie?" She smiled, and answered: "Yes, Edward. In about five minutes." "Julie," thought Lockhart, on his way down the gloomy corridor. "Now there's a nice name." Further down, he

375

thought: "I can't say I've ever cared very much for 'Edward,' though."

Certainly Lockhart was very busy with commissioning—all of them were. The crew—the west country crew from Devonport Barracks—had arrived: there were now 172 men living aboard *Saltash*, and the task of fitting them in and organizing them into their watches was a complex and rather dull job that needed a lot of patience. At this stage, most of it devolved upon Lockhart and on the coxswain, Chief Petty Officer Barnard. Barnard was the very antithesis of Tallow: Tallow had been rather slow-moving and solid, something like the north-country accent he talked with: Barnard was small, energetic, quick-witted, and the west-country drawl in his speech seemed almost out of character, as if he were a brittle drawing-room actor playing, for fun, a country farmer's part. He had, also, a small yellow beard; and Lockhart, looking at it for the first time, had thought to himself: "I wonder whether we ought to have that beard off—it's almost too like Captain Kettle. . . ." But the beard was not just another bit of theatrical nonsense: it was a genuine Western Approaches beard, nourished in the cold-weather, non-shaving routine of convoy escort: when one got used to it, it seemed an essential part of this brisk and capable man. Barnard was obviously a disciplinarian, with a frosty eye for defaulters; but he had an engaging humanity as well, and his contribution, during those first few weeks, in binding a new and somewhat raw crew together, was invaluable.

All the wardroom was busy: some of its activity was inescapable, to be met and heard all over the ship, some of it patient and unobtrusive. The largest quota of noise and movement was undoubtedly made by Allingham, who had set to work to instil into his guns' crews something of the fiery discipline he had just picked up at Whale Island. The broad Australian voice might be heard at any hour of the day, anywhere on the upper deck, going through the loading or the firing drill: there would be a harsh series of commands, then the click and clang of machinery, then another spate of words, usually either discontented or threatening. But there was something about Allingham's manner, a sort of fierce gusto, which made him popular with the crew in spite of his badgering tactics: the words and phrases he used might, in Bennett's mouth, have been actively unpleasant, but here there could be no resentment—Allingham was so obviously efficient, and so obviously ready to jump in and do the job himself, any time of the day, that he carried his men along with him without a hitch.

His manner was a direct contrast with that of Vincent, the sub-lieutenant who was working up the depth-charge crews. Vincent knew his job well enough, after two or three years in corvettes, but he was extremely diffident about giving the necessary orders, and his way of supervising a practice run recalled a rather young governess whose only effective weapon was an appeal to nursery good-will. "I'm afraid that wasn't very successful," Vincent would say mildly: "try to hurry it up a little, next time"; while within earshot —there were few places on board where he was *not* within earshot—Allingham was bawling: "If you jokers are trying to break my heart by waddling round the deck like a flock of old whores on a picnic, you'll have to try a long long time. NOW GET CRACKING!"

Only the future could show which of these methods of instruction was the more effective. . . . Between the two extremes, like a man keeping his head in a foreign country, Johnson was often to be seen striding round the upper deck, silent, purposeful, followed by gangs of filthy and forbidding-looking stokers, intent on rounding up the spare engine-room stores and getting them below. Sometimes he would pause to listen to Allingham, sometimes he would watch Vincent; then he would frown, and turn away, and say something brief and incomprehensible to one of his strange followers; and they would gather round whatever it was they had discovered—a drum of oil, or a set of spares—and lumber into action, claiming their own with the heavy gestures of men for whom one idea at a time was saturation-point.

In the wardroom itself, a holy calm reigned during most of the working day. Three people were permanently installed there: Scott-Brown, who was checking over his medical equipment item by item; Raikes, the navigator, bringing the charts up to date; and Midshipman Holt, who was listing the confidential books and codes. Lockhart, putting his head round the door one morning, was struck by their industrious air: the only movement was the scratch of a pen, the rustle of a sheet of paper. Then Holt looked up, and caught his glance.

"The backroom boys, sir," he said. There was a thunderous clatter overhead, where Allingham was doing something very noisy at high speed, time and time again. Holt raised his eyes theatrically. "All the brains of the ship are here, and yet we don't make a sound."

"Quiet!" said Scott-Brown vaguely, without looking up from his lists.

"Me?" asked the midshipman, astonished.

"Yes, you," said Raikes. "If you've got time to talk, you've got time to help me with these charts."

"I couldn't be busier," said the midshipman promptly. "I'm working my trousers to the bone. . . ." He sighed a deep sigh, and bent to his task again. There was another roar from overhead as Allingham started to reason with his men. The bearded coxswain appeared at the doorway, and said briskly to Lockhart: "Requestmen ready, sir." An encouraging odour of coffee came from the wardroom pantry.

Saltash was getting into her stride.

The Captain himself was away: he had, in fact, gone back to school.

For a fortnight he had been at Liverpool, caught deep in the toils of something which, innocently labelled "Commanding Officers' Tactical Course," had proved an ordeal of the most daunting kind. The course was intended to illustrate the latest developments of the war in the Atlantic, and to provide a practice ground for close study of them: there was a series of lectures, and then, each afternoon, the officers under instruction were installed in a large empty room, on the floor of which was a "plot," with models to illustrate the convoy, the escort, and the threatening enemy. The "convoy game" began: "sighting reports" came in, bad weather was laid on, ships were sunk: U-boats crowded round, and the escorts had to work out their counter-tactics, and put them into effect, as they would do at sea. A formidable R.N. captain was in charge: and large numbers of patient Wrens stood by, moving the ship models, bringing the latest "signals," and sometimes discreetly advising the next course of action. Rather unfairly, they seemed to know all about everything.

Even with the intensive lecturing, Ericson found a lot of it extraordinarily difficult to grasp. Things had moved on in the Atlantic, during the four months he had been ashore: there were new weapons, new dangers, new schemes of counter-attack about which he knew very little. He found that he was out of practice, too, and out of tune with the feel of command: there was so much to think about, and to guard against, as soon as a crisis blew up: often he could hardly remember the correct helm-orders, or how to draft an intelligible signal. . . . By reason of his rank, he was usually chosen to be Senior Officer of the escort, when they played the convoy game; and whenever he made mistakes, he could not help remembering that in a few weeks he was going to be leading his own escort group to sea, and that if he made these mistakes in a real battle they would carry a heavy price: more ships sunk, more men drowned: perhaps another burning tanker, perhaps another *Compass Rose*—and all now to be laid directly at his door and on his conscience.

Sometimes these errors were so elementary that they appalled him. There was one occasion that remained in his memory for a long time afterward. He had been detailed, as usual, to act as the Senior Officer of the escort: it was an action at night, and to initiate it he was given two "sighting reports," coming in the form of two urgent signals within a minute of each other.

"Radar contact bearing 300 degrees, three miles."

"Asdic contact bearing 360 degrees, one mile."

That meant, presumably, two submarines, some distance apart but both on the same side of the convoy. He thought for a moment: then he sent signals to two of his wing escorts, telling them to investigate the contacts. When he had done so, he tried to think of what should follow, he tried to translate the picture on the floor into the reality of a convoy at sea, with danger threatening and a hundred ships to guard. Nothing happened in his brain, nothing occurred to him. The minutes went by. Presently the Wren by his side shook her head, solemn and reproachful.

"Sir," she said, "you *must* remember to bring up another escort, to close the gap on the starboard side."

"The gap," thought Ericson, with a feeling of extreme guilt: "Yes, we've had that gap before. . . ." He looked at the girl, who was not more than twenty years old, and the sight of her young, thoughtful, and intelligent face suddenly stabbed him with a sense of his inadequacy. "I must be slipping," he thought, and then: "*Perhaps I have slipped. . . .*" Here was a kid of twenty, who had remembered the correct move: he himself was forty-eight, and he had not. Possibly that was the whole fatal point: he was forty-eight, and there had been nearly four years of this: it might be that he was now permanently stale, permanently beyond the flexibility of mind that the job demanded. Perhaps he had had his war, as far as a front-rank contribution was concerned.

He had shaken his head at the ugly thought, but it had stayed with him, even when, toward the end of the course, he started to get the hang of things and had improved his record. He had not been able to rid himself of this depression, he had remained puzzled and daunted by the prospect of the future. It would have been bad enough anyway, after *Compass Rose*, to make the fresh start and get geared up again; but now the new tactics, the larger responsibility, and the complex problems had multiplied beyond belief the range of effort needed. Clearly there was an immense amount to learn; clearly he might be past the learning stage. And what sort of a Senior

Officer was he going to be, when he made mistakes that, a year ago, he would not have made in his sleep?

He allowed none of this doubt to show, when he returned to *Saltash*; and indeed, as soon as he stepped aboard the ship and felt the solid deck under his feet, he began to feel that some of his misgivings had been foolish and exaggerated. At forty-eight, he could not really be past the effort of command. . . . Lockhart had met him at the gangway, and Ericson had been further heartened, as they walked round the ship together, by the progress she had made while he was away. It was half past four, and the first libertymen were just falling in on the quarterdeck: the inspection of them, before they went ashore, was efficiently and properly handled by Raikes, and the men themselves looked trim and alert. *Saltash* herself seemed almost ready to go to work: the upper deck was clear, the paintwork clean: one need no longer pick one's way through strange and encumbered territory— she had emerged as an organized ship, easy to recognize, familiar in every part. After Lockhart had given him a detailed progress-report, the two of them went down below to have tea in the wardroom, where the rest of the officers were gathered; and Ericson found it good to relax in this young company, and to join in talk that, where he was concerned, had just enough formality in it to mark him out as the Captain, and just enough freedom to show that here the others were off duty, and on their own ground. It was a delicate and entirely natural balance, which both sides understood perfectly.

"How was the course, sir?" asked Allingham, as soon as he had settled in an armchair. "Tough?"

Ericson nodded. "They didn't exactly make us run about, but there was everything else. I haven't worked so hard for a long time."

"Are there any new horrors in the way of weapons?" asked Raikes.

"Well . . ." Ericson considered. "They've perfected

those acoustic torpedoes that chase you up the tail, but that's rather old stuff by now. Then there's a rumour of some sort of underwater breathing apparatus for U-boats—" he broke off, and looked round the wardroom "—this is not to be talked about, by the way—a long tube or pipe which allows them to stay submerged indefinitely."

"Bastards," said Raikes, without rancour.

"We'll just have to try a little harder, that's all. . . ." He turned to Johnson. "We shall be starting trials in about ten days' time, Chief. Down river to the Tail-of-the-Bank, and we'll stay there till we go up to Ardnacraish."

"I seem to have heard that program before," said Lockhart.

"Me too," said Vincent. "I wonder how that fierce old character at Ardnacraish is getting on."

"Who is that?" asked Scott-Brown.

"The Admiral in charge of working up all the escort ships. He's done a terrific job, right through the war, but he's not exactly an angel of compassion."

"The position doesn't really call for one. . . ." Ericson pondered the prospect of the future. "How about a farewell party, before we leave here?"

"It's provisionally arranged, sir," said Lockhart. "At the end of next week, if that's all right with you. Chief is going to rig up a bit of fancy lighting for us, and we thought of having drinks and then some sort of supper afterwards."

"Do we know enough people for a big party?"

Scott-Brown laughed. "The present invitation list is about sixty."

"Sixty?" Ericson raised his eyebrows. "What have you all been doing while I've been away?"

"You know how wardroom visitors add up, sir," said Johnson, with the morose air of a man with a small bank-balance and no social ambitions at all. "This place has been a proper hotel, sometimes."

"Oh, there are quite a lot of deserving characters as well," said Scott-Brown. "We owe a good deal of hospitality, really. There are officers from the two other ships in the yard. And the builders. And people from the base. And lots of Wrens. I've got a rough list here."

He dug it out of his pocket, and passed it over to Ericson.

"Will the Admiral come?" asked Ericson, looking at the name at the top of the paper.

"His flag-lieutenant says, yes, he loves parties and wouldn't miss this one for the world."

"Good." Ericson went further down the list. "I suppose all these mysterious men with Scottish names are from the shipyard. . . . Who's Second Officer Hallam?"

"A glamour-pants from Ops," said Holt.

"A what?" asked Ericson, startled.

The midshipman blushed. "Er—she's a Wren from Operations, sir. The First Lieutenant asked her."

"Pretty?"

"Absolute smash hit, sir."

Ericson looked quizzically at Lockhart, who to his own surprise was conscious of a shade of embarrassment. "I hope you're not weakening, Number One."

"In no sense, sir," answered Lockhart. "I thought we ought to have as many people as possible from the base. They've been rather good to us."

"Is Second Officer Hallam in that category?"

"Yes, I think so."

"She hasn't been good to me," murmured the midshipman, not quite under his breath.

"Holt!" said Lockhart, in a voice accustomed to command.

"Sir?" said Holt.

"That will just about do."

"Sorry, sir," said Holt, not in the least put out. "I thought you'd be glad to know."

Lockhart opened his mouth to speak, and then wisely decided to leave it. Ericson looked at him again. "Well, well," he thought: "so that's how it is. About time, too. I hope she's nice."

Lockhart had not really expected Julie Hallam to accept the invitation to their party; and watching her installed in one corner of the rapidly filling wardroom, he was not sure that it was a good idea, for his own peace of mind. She really was alarmingly attractive: he had not seen her since their first meeting, and everything about her—her hair, the shape of her face, her clear skin and large grey eyes—came as a new and delicious shock. He had met her at the head of the gangway, and taken her down to the wardroom, almost in silence; and there he had had to surrender her—there were still plenty of minor things for him to see to, and he wanted to be on hand to greet the Admiral. When he returned to the wardroom, he knew at once that he would never get close to her, in any effective sense.

She was sitting on the arm of a chair, and her corner of the room seemed to be everyone's favourite choice. At her side, Scott-Brown was exerting his formidable charm: there were a number of base-officers who had a clear and undeserved priority: Ericson, doing the rounds of his guests, delayed near her for a long time, talking and making her laugh. Holt was constantly attentive: the Admiral's flag-lieutenant hung over her like a decorated cliff: even the stewards, circulating with drinks and oddments to eat, seemed to reduce to Dead Slow when they were within the orbit. . . . "I can't blame anyone," thought Lockhart: "not with her looking like that. But damn it, all the same. . . ." The party, crowded and noisy, made him remember *Compass Rose's* modest start, with not more than a dozen people in the wardroom, and Bennett walking in with some horrible woman or other. "I wonder where Julie Hallam was then," he thought: "it's getting on for four years ago—she must have met lots of people in four years: how does she manage to look lovely, beckoning, and proud at the same time? . . ." He shook his head, and turned away, and began conscientiously to talk to people.

The Admiral, a genial and popular character, made conversation on the royal pattern: there was a series of adroit questions, two minutes' exchange of pleasantries, and then a move on to someone else. To Lockhart he said:

"Is this your first job as First Lieutenant?"

"No, sir," said Lockhart. "I was in another ship with Commander Ericson. *Compass Rose.*"

"Oh yes." The Admiral, who had a royal memory as well, sheered away from what was evidently not a party topic. "You've been in the Western Approaches all the time, haven't you?"

"Yes, sir. Over three years."

"A long stretch. . . . Is your commissioning going all right?"

"Yes, sir."

"I hope my people are looking after you properly."

"They've been very helpful, sir."

"Good." He nodded, and moved away. Presently Lockhart heard him ask Allingham: "Is this your first job as Gunnery Officer?" He caught sight of Johnson standing by himself in one corner of the room, and made his way across.

"Enjoying yourself, Chief?"

Johnson nodded. Then he said, somewhat hesitatingly: "This is all a bit new to me, Number One."

That was something which Lockhart specially liked about Johnson: a few weeks ago he had been in the petty-officers' mess of a destroyer, and he was entirely honest about the novelty of his promotion. He said: "If you get bored, Chief, you can always blow the fuses and finish the party."

Johnson smiled. "I'll remember that."

Lockhart took a small tray of food from one of the stewards, and began to go round with it, talking to people on the way. The room was now very crowded: in Julie Hallam's corner, the attendant circle was thickest of all. Like vultures, he thought ruefully, and then: no, like courtiers, with the best excuse in the world for their loyal attendance. . . . He had a momentary glimpse of the shapely head, with its crown of dark hair, bending forward to listen to something that Holt was saying: then she vanished, and he went back to work, wishing, for the first time in the war, that he could be a good-looking seventeen-year-old midshipman without a care in the world.

He talked to a woman in a very large hat, who said:

"What I don't understand is, how you know where you're going when you're in the middle of the sea."

He talked to a man in a raincoat, who said: "We've put a lot of work into this ship. Hope you take care of her."

He talked to a rather plain Wren who said: "I've seen you in a restaurant somewhere." He talked to the harbourmaster, and handed round some more food, and saw the Admiral off, and went out onto the upper deck to look at the blackout: then he wrote up the Night Order Book, and had a word with Chief Petty Officer Barnard, and came back and talked to the Deputy Provost of Glasgow. Time passed: there were no signs of the crowd thinning out. Then he found himself next to the First Lieutenant of another new frigate, who said:

"I've just arrived. One of our libertymen fell into the river. Who's that incredibly good-looking girl over there?"

Lockhart's eyes went round, for the first time for nearly two hours, to Julie Hallam, and by chance she raised her head at the same moment. Across the dozen people between them, across the nodding faces and bent backs that were nearest to her, their eyes met. She smiled directly for him, and he smiled back, and then made a comical grimace of despair, indicating the close containing circle around her. He saw her hesitate: then she said something to the people nearest to her, broke away from them, and came toward him. He moved at the same moment, and they met under the lamp in the middle of the room, a rather hard lamp that made her hair shine and still could not rob her face of an atom of its loveliness. To be close to her suddenly was like a dagger in the heart, a melting dagger that turned on the instant to tender warmth. The smile still lingered round her mouth and eyes when she looked up and said:

"As my official escort, you haven't done terribly well for yourself, have you?"

He laughed, liking the word 'escort.' "Such competition . . ."

"And you've been busy, like a good First Lieutenant." She glanced down at her watch. "I must go soon, I'm afraid. We have to be back at ten."

"Oh. . . . I haven't spoken to you at all."

She smiled once more, letting her eyes move frankly over his face. After a moment she said, with a trace of shyness:

"You wouldn't believe how many people have been told that you're seeing me home."

In the darkness, their footsteps were slow: spinning out the deserted streets, cherishing the black pavement as if it were a measure of fleeting time itself.

"That seems a very cheerful sort of wardroom you have there," she said presently. "I like Allingham, and your doctor too. And of course the midshipman is terribly sweet."

"He makes me feel about ninety, sometimes. But it's good to have someone really young and cheerful about the place."

"It can be infectious. . . . You must be very fond of Ericson."

"I feel I want to finish the war with him, and with no one else. It's as strong as that."

The blur of her face turned towards him, and he saw her smile. "That's almost exactly what he said about you."

"David and Jonathan," he said. "Does it sound silly?"

"I'm jealous." He heard her laugh. "I don't mean *jealous*. I mean that women don't often have that relationship, and if they do there aren't many first-rate things it can be applied to, like running a ship or fighting a war."

"It's about the only personal relationship that should be allowed to operate in wartime."

"Marriage, surely?"

He shook his head. "No. That's a side-tracking element, a distraction. There was a girl I was talking to tonight, one of your Wrens. Joan something."

"Joan Warrender. Yes, she's getting married quite soon."

"To a Naval officer. The captain of a destroyer, in fact."

"Well?" She sounded rather puzzled.

"I wondered how getting married fitted in with being a destroyer captain during a war."

There was silence, while they traversed a cross-street and came into the shadow of a building again.

"You're rather a Puritan, aren't you?" she said reflectively.

"In that respect, yes. War has to be a matter of dedication: anything else gets in the way. You have to be single-minded, free of distraction, tough, un-tender—all the words that don't go with marriage. Otherwise you'll fail, and war will weed you out. It might even do worse: it might take your life, because you're not attending properly."

"How did you get like this?" she asked after a moment. "You're not a professional—you don't have to crucify yourself. . . . What *were* you before the war?"

"Journalist. . . . It's just something that grew. Perhaps it's only true for me. But there was a man in my last ship who was being torn to bits by a bad marriage—and I think one could be sapped by a good one, in the same way. It's too dangerous, too much of a hostage to give away. Better to be on your own. You've got to reach that professional standard, anyway. Muddling through at half-speed just won't do."

Inconsequently she said: "You're very thin."

"That was *Compass Rose*, mostly. And worry, and less sleep than usual, for a long time." But he did not want to talk about any of that. He said: "You're not thin."

After a moment she smiled, and said: "You might at least qualify that."

"I mean, you're not harassed or over-driven, although you're doing a harassing job. What were *you* before the war?"

"I was on *Vogue*."

"Oh." He glanced round at her figure in its austere, unfeminine uniform, and they both laughed, making the dark night a companionable cloak shared between them. He said suddenly: "And now you're S.O.O.2., and you look the way you do. You have everything, really, haven't you?"

He wondered how she would answer that, or whether she would become, in any degree, coy or disclaiming. He need not have bothered.

"It's not a particularly successful combination." Once more he was struck by the low clarity, the beauty of her voice in the darkness. Their steps slowed again, willingly matching each other's, as he listened to it, and to her. "Look," she said, "I have this face, and I have a brain, and I can talk. But people don't really like the arrangement: they prefer things one at a time. Women are afraid of the mixture, men don't want it—they don't even know what to do with it."

"Surely they do. Look at the droves of courtiers tonight."

"But what did the courtiers want? Me as a woman, solely, not as an individual."

"They enjoy talking to you as well."

"And all the time they think: 'Chat, chat, chat—doesn't she know that a mouth is for kissing?' True?"

He laughed. "Maybe truc. You wouldn't want yourself changed though."

Her head went up, challenging him and the dark night as well. "Not I. . . . I wouldn't pretend to change, either. I won't pretend to be a plain girl with brains, to suit the women, or a pretty one without them, for you people."

"Count me out," he said. "I have a weakness for organized perfection."

After a moment, she stopped before a tall gloomy building, and said: "This is where I live."

He did not know how to say good-bye. He remembered her phrase, "a mouth is for kissing," but the moment was not that moment. He said: "The walk made the party. Thank you for it."

A shaded light falling on her face showed it serious, and heartbreakingly lovely at the same time. Its shape held him in a spell he could have prolonged for ever: its nearness transfixed him. But this was still farewell: the night that had embraced must now divide them.

"The walk was a good idea," she said. "Mine, too. . . . Would you have asked me?"

He shook his head.

She said: "Why? Dedication to war?"

He shook his head again. "I just thought the answer would be 'No.'"

"Next time—" she began, and stopped.

There was a long pause, while they eyed each other: she hesitant, even discomposed, he diverted. Finally:

"I just thought I'd leave you in the air for a moment," he said. "Next time, I'll certainly take a chance and stake the earliest possible claim."

"It will be very embarrassing if you don't," she answered, restored to her grave serenity. "Even with Puritans, one can't make the running every day of the week."

"My turn next," he agreed. "Good night."

She nodded and was gone, walking quickly up some steps and through a curtained doorway. Lockhart stared for a moment at the place where she had been standing; and then he turned and went slowly down the street again. His footsteps made an endless hollow ring on the lonely pavement, but the man within him had never been further from loneliness.

[4]

Vice-Admiral Sir Vincent Murray-Forbes, K.C.B., D.S.O., came down to the quay at Ardnacraish as soon as *Saltash* was signalled, and put off in his barge almost before she was secured to the buoy. *Saltash* would be the five-hundred-and-twenty-first ship to pass through his hands, and she received exactly the same welcome as the previous five hundred and twenty: if the enormous amount of work that this number entailed weighed heavily on the Admiral, it did not show either in his face, which was alert and attentive as usual, or in his scramble up the ladder, which was as energetic as it had ever been. Tremendous in gold braid, he acknowledged the piping and the salutes of Ericson and his officers, who were drawn up in a respectful semicircle on the quarterdeck; then he walked a pace or two forward, glared round him, turned back to Ericson, and said:

"She's bigger than I thought."

Ericson, working it out rapidly, came to the right answer and put on an expression of interest.

1943: *The Moment of Balance*

"Is this the first frigate to arrive here, sir?"

"Yes. Yours was the first corvette, too, back in 1939. Strange. Long time since then. Introduce me to your officers."

The Admiral went quickly round the assembled ring. To Lockhart he said: "You met me without a cap, last time," and to Vincent: "You were in *Trefoil*"; the rest of them received a nod and a straight glance from under his bushy eyebrows. After that he toured the ship at a brisk pace, and then descended to Ericson's cabin, where he sat down, accepted a glass of their best sherry, and said:

"They seem a good class of ship, these frigates. We want something bigger and tougher in the Atlantic, though the corvettes have done a good job, a first-rate job." He looked at Ericson. "You lost *Compass Rose*."

"Yes, sir," said Ericson.

"It's a long war," said the Admiral, looking as though he were ready to begin the whole thing over again if necessary. "A damned long war. But the Huns are running, by God, they're running! Or they will be soon. This is the beginning of the end of it." His manner changed. "You're here for three weeks, Ericson. I needn't tell you anything about the training course, or what I want you to do. You know the sort of standard I expect." He looked out of the porthole. "You'll find it a bit bleak here, as usual. We've got a cinema ashore now, and a better canteen, but that's about all there is."

Ericson ventured a smile. "As far as I remember, sir, there won't be much spare time anyway."

"I should think not, by God! It's still the middle of the war. . . . How's that First Lieutenant of yours? Better than the last one you had?"

"He's first class, sir. We've been together a long time."

"Remarkable what these R.N.V.R. fellows have done. I wouldn't have believed it, at the beginning." He drained his sherry, refused a second glass, and stood up again. "Time for me to be moving. . . . You must dine with me one night. I want to hear about that U-boat."

"How does he do it," wondered Ericson, ushering him out

onto the upper deck: "Is it a prodigious memory—or just good briefing. . . ." By the ladder, the piping party came to attention, headed by the coxswain. "I've seen you before," said the Admiral, looking at the yellow beard rather than the man. "Barnard, sir," said the coxswain, his west-country accent very prominent: "coxswain of the *Tangerine* when she was up here." The Admiral nodded, satisfied. "No beard then," he said to Ericson, "but it takes more than a beard to hide a man. Knew him straight away."

The pipes shrilled, and the Admiral saluted and climbed over the side, all in one agile movement. With his head at a level with the rail, he said gruffly: "You start your sea exercises at half past five tomorrow morning." Then he disappeared down the ladder, and presently the sleek and spotless barge shot out from the side of the ship and sped towards the shore. On the way it started signalling to *Saltash* with a handlamp. "All guns should be trained fore-and-aft in harbour," came the message. Lockhart looked round swiftly, and saw, alas, that "X" gun was trained approximately ten degrees out of the true. He walked heavily aft, calling for Allingham as he went.

Three weeks, the Admiral had said, and three weeks it was, with every hour counting. The time went more quickly now: for all of them except Holt, there was less to learn, more to practise and to perfect: they were simply picking up again the outlines of a known job, on a bigger and broader scale than ever before. *Saltash* steamed faster, fired more guns, detected U-boats at a greater range, and dropped more depth charges; in the matter of degree, they were breaking new ground, in the matter of anti-submarine warfare they were not. It was the same task it had been for the last three years; they now had better weapons to help them in it, but its essentials never altered. They must accept A, they must guard against B—and A and B were the same old characters, the weather and the enemy, waiting in the wings for yet another scene from the longest play in the world.

The days passed: the ship shook together and started to

work: the men smartened up, and the time taken for each operation—for firing a gun, dropping a depth charge, sending a signal, lowering a boat, rigging a hose—decreased gradually as the seconds were pared off. *Saltash* began to fulfil the picture in the Admiral's mind—and in Ericson's as well. A bigger and better *Compass Rose*, Ericson wanted her to be; in moments of introspection and memory, it did not seem a particularly happy thing to be aiming at, but it was the whole point of being given a new ship and more men to man her. He and Lockhart were alike in mourning the past, and in turning their backs upon it; it was made easier by a ship that came readily to hand, and by the intensive and demanding future they knew they must prepare for.

In a ship of this size, both of them were far more remote from the crew than had been the case in *Compass Rose*; the working day was no longer a matter of dealing with personalities at close range, it was simply a question of the allocation of numbers—twenty seamen to do a job on the fo'c's'le, sixteen stokers to practise oiling at sea. All that mattered was that there should be enough men available at any given moment, with a petty officer to detail them off by name, using his closer knowledge of their capabilities. *Saltash's* crew was almost double the size of *Compass Rose's*, and sometimes it seemed that they were twice the distance away as well, and twice as anonymous. There was no one like Gregg, the seaman with the unfaithful wife, there was no one like Wainwright to cherish the depth charges, there was no one like Yeoman Wells who looked after the signalmen with a father's care; or if there *were* these characters on board, as there must still have been, they did not meet the eye, they had the permanent disguise of being names on a watch bill or a pay list, not individuals whose foibles had to be remembered. Perhaps it was a gain, perhaps it was a loss; when he took Hands Fall In each morning, and looked down a long double line of eighty seamen whom he barely knew by sight and would not have recognized ashore, Lockhart sometimes regretted the intimate past, and the feeling, which he had had in *Compass Rose*, that this was a family matter, not a parade. But possibly the gain was in efficiency, which was always liable to be a cold-blooded matter.

"I just want the whaler lowered," thought Lockhart to himself on one occasion, when he could not avoid noticing that one or two of the hands were still miserable with seasickness, after a day outside. "I need twelve men to do it. I don't want to bother about whether they've got hang-overs this morning, or whether their wives are due to have babies tomorrow, or whether they're in debt or in despair. I just want the whaler on the water. Twelve men, that's all I need. Bodies. . . . Coxswain!"

It was he who dealt mostly in this principle of numbers, not people; and he could not help being aware of the change. He could even feel guilty about it, like a man forced by circumstances to replace twelve trusted workmen with twelve mechanical grabs. The answer, of course, lay in the extra amount of work the grabs could do; but that did not salve the general wound to humanity. . . . Without doubt, however, that was the way the war was going; the individual had to retreat or submerge, the simple unfeeling pair of hands must come to the fore. The emphasis was now on the tireless machine of war; men were parts of this machine, and so they must remain, till they fulfilled their function or wore out. If, in the process, they did wear out, it was bad luck on the men —but not bad luck on the war, which had had its money's worth out of them. The hateful struggle, to be effective, demanded one hundred per cent from many millions of individual people; death was in this category of demand, and, lower down the list, the cancellation of humanity was an essential element in the total price.

They were all together in the wardroom, after dinner, when their sailing signal arrived, marking the end of their stay at Ardnacraish. Earlier, the Admiral's report had come through; he was satisfied—no more, no less—and *Saltash* could go. The signal that translated this into action was short and to the point.

1943: *The Moment of Balance*

"H.M.S. *Saltash* sails for Greenock 0600 hours April 15, and will be attached to Clyde Escort Force."

"Damn," said Vincent as he read the message. "I wanted to be at Liverpool again."

"The Clyde will do for me," said Johnson.

"Anything will do for me," said Holt. "I want to see the world."

"I must say," remarked Scott-Brown, "that there are worse places than Glasgow in the spring."

"We may not see much of it," said Lockhart, carefully non-committal. The midshipman's bright and speculative eye was on him, but he avoided meeting it. Julie, he thought: it wasn't good-bye after all. . . . "But Glasgow is certainly something to have in the background."

So, once more, they went to war.

The war to which they went, toward the middle of 1943, had reached a hard and hopeful moment. Since the new year, the escorts and convoys in the Atlantic had been neither winning nor losing: the moment of balance was at hand, with the escorts cutting back the long start that the U-boats had gained, and attaining, with tremendous effort, some sort of parity in terms of sinkings. They were still stretched thin—sometimes there were seven hundred ships at sea at one time, and a hundred escorts, which meant a huge choice of targets for the U-boats; but the thin weapon was sharp, and try as they would, the U-boats could no longer break through in any decisive sense, could not hold the bloody advantage they had gained during the past three years.

Certainly they tried desperately hard, certainly they tried everything. The wolf-pack attacks were now reaching their zenith, and occasionally they brought off a surprise and brutal success, as when seven tankers out of a total convoy of nine were sunk in a two-night battle in the South Atlantic. The enemy could now regularly keep over a hundred U-boats at sea at the same time, and the packs themselves, concentrating in any given area, could always muster anything up to twenty. Early in the year, their successes had begun to mount again, to a peak point in March when they sank a hundred and eight ships. The new acoustic torpedoes, which automatically "homed" themselves onto the noise of a propeller, claimed many victims. But then the tide began to turn: March saw fifteen U-boats sunk, April sixteen, and May the huge total of forty-five. At this stage, evidently, the German High Command began to think it over, for the U-boats now started to withdraw from the North Atlantic convoy routes, and to disperse to other and softer areas. The attack, at long last, was running down.

It was running down because the pace was too hot: the escorts, as well as the U-boats, had been steadily crowding onto the scene, and they had at last got the full measure of what they had to deal with. They could now go all the way across the Atlantic, thanks to the new technique of oiling at sea: there were enough ships available to provide many roving escort-groups, independent of any specific convoy, and coming to the help of the ones that were hardest pressed. Above all, the escorts were learning how to find, stalk, and kill the enemy, with the smallest possible margin for failure.

It was now a very skilful war. Nothing was left to chance: gone forever were the makeshift days when untrained and under-armed escorts put to sea with a handful of depth charges and a couple of Lewis guns and, hoping for the best, ran straight into slaughter. Science was now king in the Atlantic: science, and skilled men to make use of it. Radar and asdics had become phenomenally accurate: a system of interception of wireless signals from U-boats made it possible to foresee an attack almost before it had been planned: aircraft carriers accompanied many of the convoys, to give, all the way across, the air cover that had been so long and so fatally absent from the black stretch of water that marked and marred the centre.

Counter-attacks on U-boats had now reached a high degree of skill and co-ordination: practice and training during the time spent in harbour, carried out in concert by teams from each ship in the group, ensured that escorts knew what to do, no matter what happened, and knew also exactly what all the other ships would be doing at the same moment. There was no more improvisation, no more of the slapdash "it'll-be-all-right-on-the-night" feeling that had cost so many ships and men in the past. Now it was a streamlined job, a smooth essay in destruction; and the ships that went to sea to carry it out had strong and highly organized backing from the naval bases ashore, which sent them out well-equipped, well worked-up, ready for anything.

They dispatched them fully armoured to a war where convoy losses were no longer inevitable, where the total frustration of an attack, and even the sinking of a U-boat, were beginning to be nothing out of the ordinary. With the tide starting at last to flow in the escorts' favour, there could have been no better moment to rejoin the battle.

Ericson had summoned a last conference aboard *Saltash*, at ten o'clock on the morning of their sailing day, so that he could give the captains of the seven other ships under his command a final run through their sailing orders, a final briefing on the way the escort screen was to be organized. The whole group, comprising three frigates and five corvettes, lay at anchor off the Tail-of-the-Bank; swinging to their shortened cables in the brisk tideway, enjoying a bright blustering April morning that promised them lively movement as soon as they left the shelter of the Clyde. The three frigates—*Saltash*, and the two others that, fresh off the stocks, had later joined her at Ardnacraish—were brand-new; the five corvettes were old stagers, and they looked it, as did most corvettes nowadays: they had an air of shabby sufficiency, a salt-stained rusty competence impossible to counterfeit. At a quarter to ten, motorboats began to put off from each ship in turn, all bearing, besides their coxswain and bowman, a solitary figure in the stern; and Lockhart, waiting at the head of the ladder to greet the various captains and pipe them aboard, saw them converging on *Saltash* like chickens rallying to the man with the dinner-pail.

They had to pick their way through a crowded anchorage;

within his view were upward of forty naval escorts—destroyers, sloops, frigates, corvettes, and trawlers: a battleship, a cruiser, and two small aircraft-carriers lay in an outer ring, as if to endorse the evidence of power and plenty; and further down the river the vast concourse of merchant ships in the convoy anchorage completed a picture of concentrated naval might.

It was, indeed, a brave sight, a promise of success coming at last within reach. But it recalled, inevitably, the stringencies of the past. "I wish we'd had some of these ships available, a couple of years ago," said Lockhart, indicating the escorts to Raikes, who as Officer-of-the-Day was waiting on deck with him. "It might have saved us a few rough nights."

"Muddle through," answered Raikes, in tones of brisk cynicism. "If we'd had these ships then, there would have been something wrong with them, for certain—they wouldn't have floated in salt water, or something. Better to wait for nature to take its course."

"We're not muddling through now," said Lockhart coldly, summoning his decided views on the point. "We weren't then, really, either. We just hadn't got the machinery for building escorts quickly, that's all."

"Which was part of the muddle, surely," said Raikes, uncertain whether he ought to argue about it. Lockhart, he knew, had a definite viewpoint on the subject, whereas he himself had only a vague civilian disparagement of the whole conduct of the war, summed up now and again in the words: "If this thing was run on competitive business lines, the Navy wouldn't last a fortnight."

"We hadn't got the ships," he continued, "because we were caught with our pants down."

"That's the difference," said Lockhart, "between thinking war's a good thing, and thinking it's horrible. We delayed getting ready for it as long as we possibly could, because we thought it was thoroughly bad, and could somehow be avoided. We're only just catching up now."

"Boat coming alongside, sir," said the quartermaster, a

bored eavesdropper in this conversation. He intercepted, and acknowledged, a covert signal from the coxswain of the approaching motorboat. "Captain of *Harmer*, sir."

"Stand by to pipe," said Lockhart. *Harmer* was the senior frigate, after *Saltash*, and her captain was a notorious stickler for the utmost limits of naval etiquette. Lockhart could see him now, peering up out of the corner of his eye to confirm that he was going to be properly piped aboard. On the last day of the war, he thought, they might consider piping him aboard with a mouth-organ—playing, preferably: "*I'll Be Glad When You're Dead, You Rascal, You!*" He realized that he was thinking on the lines of the cynical, the determinedly amateur Raikes, and he came to an especially stiff salute as the captain of *Harmer* started to climb on board. The latter might have a weakness, amounting almost to fetishism, for the ceremonial aspect of command, but he ran a good ship at the same time; and that, in war, excused nearly everything, from bad temper to sodomy.

Something like the same thought presently struck Ericson, as he sat at the head of the wardroom table and surveyed his assembled captains. These were the sort of men he wanted: two of them, he knew for certain, drank far more than they ought to, one was invariably unpleasant to his officers—but their methods got results, their ships *worked*. . . . There were seven of them, ranging from the captain of *Harmer*, an old lieutenant-commander nearer sixty than fifty, to the young, the positively baby-faced two-ringer in charge of *Petal*, the junior corvette. But in spite of a wide variety in age, in looks, in accent and upbringing, they all had the same aura of responsibility, the same air of knowing what it was all about: their faces—the lined, over-accented faces of men who had often been exhausted in the past and would often be so again—their faces all bore, in a greater or less degree, the harsh stamp of command in war.

"Perhaps I look like that myself," thought Ericson; and indeed, he had only to recall the face that met him in his shaving-mirror every morning to be damned certain that he did. . . . But the hard lines had been hardly earned, the look of undue and continued tension was excusable. He himself, with the men round the table, made up a handful of the principals in a private fight that all the participants knew, perforce, in exhaustive detail. They were men who had become dedicated to a single theme of war, like the Eighth Army men in the desert who had slept for years under the same stars, grown to love the same comrades, and fought two and three and four times over the same stretch of arid, precarious coastline. Like these desert fighters, the men of the Atlantic had become remarkably expert, astonishingly specialist, with no eyes for any theatre of war except their own. For them, even the cleansing of that other disputed ocean, the Mediterranean, was a different sort of job from this one; it was being carried out by another group of sailors who, though brothers, had no connection with their own single-emblem firm. *Their* firm was the Atlantic, and their job was the unspectacular, year-to-year passing of ships to and fro between the New World and the Old: an aspect of war that was hardly war at all, but more like a rescue operation on an enormous scale—rescue of ships in peril, rescue of men in the water, rescue of troops who needed arms and of aircraft that needed petrol; rescue of the forty-million garrison of Britain who had to have food and clothing to keep them alive, as they confronted, year after year, the hostile coast of Europe.

When the newspapers called it "the lifeline," for once the newspapers were right; and the men who had tended that lifeline for nearly four years, who had watched it being almost throttled and at last saw it easing, included, as of right, the men who now sat round the table in the wardroom of *Saltash*—men who were hopeful and cynical at the same time, tired but not too tired, ready for surprises and wielding counter-surprises of their own.

On the table before them were the tools of their trade: the convoy lists, the sailing orders, the charts, signal-codes, lists of R/T call-signs, screening diagrams, schemes of search, tables of fuel endurance. In this self-contained circle, these were as familiar as the alphabet or the sound of their own ship's bell; for months and years on end, these things had been the interior decoration of their lives, the frieze that ran round the inside of the head. . . . Ericson looked down at the list of his ships: it read like a banner whose staff was clasped in his own hands:

"*Saltash, Harmer, Streamer, Vista, Rockery, Rose Arbour, Pergola*, and *Petal.*"

But was the staff truly and firmly in his hands? Reading the list, knowing what it meant in terms of effort and effectiveness, he was conscious, as he had been on the tactical course at Liverpool, of a certain inadequacy. There had been an undeniable break in his training, a break that the men round him had not suffered: no one else at the table had been stuck on shore for four months, no one else had had a chance to become rusty, no one else (though this was a private whisper) came fresh from losing his ship and nearly all his men. . . . But that was something which was *not* to show. He cleared his throat.

"You've all got the screening diagram in front of you," he began formally. "You see how the escort is to be stationed, on the outward journey at least: two frigates in front of the convoy—that's myself and *Harmer*: two corvettes on either side—*Vista* and *Pergola* to starboard, *Rockery* and *Rose Arbour* to port. The third frigate, *Streamer*, is in position K, and the other corvette, *Petal*, is astern of the whole outfit."

"Tail-end Charlie, as usual," said the captain of *Petal*, a young man entirely undaunted by his lack of seniority. "One day I'm going to find out what the *bows* of a merchant ship look like."

"You'd better ask *Rockery* about that," remarked the captain of *Harmer* caustically, and there was a general laugh round the table. A few weeks previously, *Rockery* had been squarely rammed by a straggling merchantman whom she was trying to chivvy into greater activity, wrapping herself round the bows of the bigger ship and remaining there for some hours, as neatly centred and as prominent as a handlebar moustache: she had only just come out of the repair dock after the encounter.

"It wasn't my fault," said the captain of *Rockery* rebelliously. He had the air of a man who had been repeating the phrase, at very short intervals, for a very long time, and had still to make his first convert. "She came straight at me, and I couldn't dodge."

"Sounds like a girl in Piccadilly," said the captain of *Petal*.

"The result was the same, too," said *Streamer's* captain, the one whom Ericson had earlier recalled as being unpleasant to his officers. "He had to go into dock for repairs."

There was another laugh round the table, a further loosening of the atmosphere of purpose which had been present at the beginning. "Now just a minute," thought Ericson to himself: "This is all very well, but it isn't to be this sort of meeting and I'm not going to run it like this at all; here is where we end the chatter, here is where I take a good sharp pull. . . ." He rapped on the table suddenly.

"That's enough gossip for today," he said, as coldly as he could. "I want to get through this as quickly as possible, because I'm sure you all have as much to do in your own ships as I have in mine." Disregarding the swift chilling of the atmosphere, meeting no one's eye, he continued: "We're going all the way across this time, to St. John's, Newfoundland: there'll be the usual procedure for oiling at sea—that is, you will make a 'fuel remaining' signal each morning, and I will choose the time for refuelling, and the order in which you're to come alongside the tanker." "I'm laying this on a bit thick," he thought suddenly, "but it's their own fault for chattering like a lot of bloody women. . . ." He looked up, to find the captain of *Harmer* staring at him with an expression of active dislike; and after a moment the latter said:

"So far, we've always made our own decisions about oiling."

There was a silence, while the others waited for his answer: it was clear that none of them had liked his exercise of discipline, the first essay in the strict control of the group, and were ready, if not to defy him, at least to nibble at his authority in any way they could. It was not a sulky or a disgruntled reaction, it was just that they were all conscious of knowing their jobs just as well as Ericson did—otherwise they would not have achieved their commands—and they resented any hint to the contrary. "All right," thought Ericson instantly: "if that's the way you want it, I'll be tough with you—the group is mine, and if it makes any mistakes, the blame is mine as well. . . ." He suddenly put up one hand, and touched, lightly, the three broad rings on his other sleeve: he saw the eyes of every one at the table follow the gesture, which could not have been clearer, or, indeed, more offensively pointed. Then he looked directly at *Harmer*, and said, in a voice he hardly recognized and with an entirely novel feeling of challenge:

"Then that is one of the things I want to change."

The sentence, undisputed, set the tone for the rest of the session, and, though he had really had no intention of making so crude a declaration of authority, Ericson did not try to improve on it. Instead, he dealt brusquely with all he had to deal with: the signal routines, the procedure in case of attack, the half-dozen different points that had to be settled at the start of every convoy. No one at the table said anything, except to agree with him; it was as if they had decided to leave things where they were, to suspend judgement and see how the new scheme of close control worked out. But they gave no ground in the way of good humour, either; when, at the end, Ericson relaxed his formal manner and said: "I'll see you all later, then—probably in some frightful hotel at St. John's," no one smiled or tried to meet him in any way. They too were clearly saying to themselves: "If you want to be a bastard, go ahead and see how it works. . . ."

When they had gone, and he surveyed the empty wardroom, he had a moment of doubt as to how he had handled the meeting. He began to wonder why he had behaved like that— and then, consciously, he stopped himself wondering, and stood up, and gathered his papers together. All that he wanted, all that the situation at sea demanded, was an efficient, tightly organized escort group: if he became unpopular in the process of getting it, it did not matter in the least.

. . .

403

They sailed on the last day of April, under a ragged sky that soon clouded over to form a lowering barrier to the westward; and that first convoy—free of attack, but rough and slow and tiring—was the start of a four-months' routine, all spent on the run to and from St. John's, Newfoundland. Neither Ericson nor Lockhart had ever been there before, though most of the other ships had: it was an area continually menaced by fog, and occasionally—if they were routed far northward—by the threat of ice; and the Newfoundland coastline, with its black crags endlessly battered by the shock and surge of the Western Atlantic, was forbidding in the extreme. The entrance to St. John's was a difficult one, not much more than a hole in the rocks, a narrow passage between tall cliffs with a strong tide sluicing past on the seaward side: the approach had to be at speed, and speed, with a few yards to spare on either side of the ship as she threaded her way through the gap, added a hair-raising risk to normal navigation. Ericson had never heard of a ship piling up in the narrows, in spite of the scores that went in and out every week, and certainly *Saltash* never came to any harm; but the ordeal of the entrance waited for him at the end of each trip westward, and again when they left St. John's homeward bound—a recurrent hazard, a sting in the tail of every convoy, which might one day find its mark.

Once inside the landlocked harbour they were snug enough, though St. John's had little to give in the way of material comfort. It had the air of being the last outpost of civilization in a wild continent: the quays were crowded with tough, salty fishing-schooners, the streets were steep and narrow, and, though it was late spring, only just free of snow: the townsfolk still trudged round in snow-boots and jerkins, fur caps and lumberjack shirts. In nearly every shop window was a placard advertising that the wares were "just landed" or "just unpacked"—frontier phrases that were still appropriate here: many of the buildings and houses had a makeshift, impermanent air, as if it were even now uncertain whether the inhabitants could cling to the small haven they had wrestled from nature. Moving against this crude back-

cloth, the men in naval uniform from the British and Canadian escorts that thronged the harbour had a curious over-
dressed look about them, an insistence on formality which the
natives were surely entitled to laugh at. . . . There was
really nothing to do in St. John's except to go ship-visiting
and wait for the return journey: it was no more than a pause,
in rough and simple terms, before making the outward passage of the narrows and rounding up the convoy again for
its three-thousand-mile gauntlet, with the enemy ahead preparing new snares, brewing new poisons for their ruin.

For Ericson, not only the harbour entrance was difficult
and trying. Falling into the old routine, getting geared up
again to the heavy rhythm of sea-going in war, would have
been hard enough in any case, after so long ashore and with
the imprint of *Compass Rose* so fresh and cruel upon the memory; but for him it was complicated by a dozen new tasks,
a dozen additional items that went with the job of Senior
Officer Escort. He had to handle his group at sea, he had to
supervise them when they were docked: he had to keep an
eye on the commodore, on the moon, on stragglers and ships
out of station, on U-boat signals, on the fuel position, on the
routing of the different components of the convoy: he had
also to continue nagging at his ships in harbour, where the
emptying of the dust-bins by the guard-corvette seemed just
as important to higher authority as the posting of *Streamer*
to the danger side of the convoy, whenever they were on
passage.

It meant that there was something to think about all the
time, it meant that he could never relax his grip; and the
tactical side of it, when they were in convoy, put the whole
concept of escort into a higher category altogether. One
ship—a big, new ship, still at the exploratory stage—would
have been sufficient responsibility already: but now he had
eight of them, to be handled as a single weapon, a single
shield for what he had to guard: it meant that he must carry
in his brain, not the manageable plan of his own command,
but another bigger picture altogether—a picture with eight
arms, eight different possibilities, eight assorted points of

strength or weakness. All of them must be considered and remembered, none must be wasted or ignored.

Each day and night of each trip could bring its own problems, and no problem could ever be left to solve itself. If there were a suspicious radar contact to be investigated, for example, he might detach *Streamer*, the third frigate which was usually given these roving commissions. Detaching *Streamer* meant putting one of the corvettes in her place— *Pergola* for choice, the best of the five. That made a gap on the port side, and the port side was the moonless side, the point of danger. It must be filled immediately: *Petal* must come up from astern. But that left the straggling merchant-man, which *Petal* had been shepherding, without any protection. Was that to be accepted? Or should he reduce the convoy speed, to let the straggler catch up? And supposing there were a threat of attack, should he bring *Streamer* back again to the close screen?—or was she doing more useful work, possibly intercepting another U-boat before it was in touch with the convoy? But suppose *Streamer's* contact were an independent merchant ship in difficulties: the job might delay her for two or three days: should he then tell her to proceed independently, knowing that she might run short of fuel and would need to rendezvous with the tanker that travelled with them? Could he spare her from the screen, in any case? Was it worth leaving his own station, *now at this moment*, to investigate a woolly asdic contact that had just been reported ahead? If it were a U-boat, and if it attacked, and if it scored a hit, there might be survivors: could a corvette be spared, to pick them up? If so, which wing of the convoy was it safer to weaken? And was that a star-shell, low on the horizon to starboard? And if so, was it from *Streamer*? And if so, did she need help? And if so, who was to give it?

Sometimes the questions seemed to come like a storm of insects, pricking and stinging him from a dozen different directions at once. But they had to be handled on this personal plane: there had to be one co-ordinating brain, no matter how overloaded it became, and one authoritative voice, even though it might have to speak swiftly and continuously for hours on end. Now, in retrospect, Ericson forgave *Viperous* every complaint or query, every testy signal, every bit of interference that *Compass Rose* had ever suffered from her: he forgave, and he copied the pattern thankfully. For if complete control had to be exercised, it could only be done on this basis of the all-seeing eye, the voice of Jove from the clouds, the thunder-clap that allowed no back answer. There was no room for hurt feelings: in fact there was little room for feelings of any sort.

It was a regime he found himself applying, within his own group; nothing else would serve, whether the rest of them liked it or not. He was aware that he was still unpopular with the other captains, or, at best, regarded warily as a man likely to stick a surprise oar in, any time of the day or night. It did not matter: it was a small price to pay for efficiency and confidence. If the relationship, within the group, was businesslike and nothing more, at least it was effective, and it was showing results.

That, at least, was obvious to them all. *Saltash* was now becoming the nucleus of a strong team that, welded together gradually and exercised to the point of exhaustion, was achieving a solid sort of partnership, an improving standard. Fewer mistakes were made, fewer foolish signals sent, less time wasted. It had tangible successes to its credit, too. In May, *Harmer* shot down a reconnaissance aircraft over the Clyde estuary: a month later, two of the corvettes, *Vista* and *Rose Arbour*, shared a U-boat between them, a quick mid-ocean kill that may have surprised both sides. It was good to chalk up this official evidence of something they all knew— that the group was an effective force, and that all the effort and the patience did not go to waste.

Other groups were doing as well, some of them better: for that was the sort of place the Atlantic was becoming, toward the turn of that crucial year. The new ships were proving themselves, the new weapons were flattering their designers; the small aircraft-carriers that were now available for many convoys were playing a steady part in spotting U-boats before they became actively dangerous. And in

August of that year came a piece of news that stirred a thousand hearts, afloat and ashore; for during that month, more U-boats were destroyed than merchant ships were sunk. For the first time in the war, the astonishing balance was struck.

It was heartening, it was wonderful—but perhaps, on reflection, it was no more than was to be expected. If it *didn't* happen at some point, if the two lines on the graph *didn't* cross, that was the time to start worrying. . . . For now they were beginning to be cool in killing, now nothing surprised them: winning as well as losing, they were ready to take it in their stride. In Ericson's group, as with the rest of the Clyde Escort Force, and the Liverpool contingent, and the strange fellows who sometimes came round from Rosyth on the east coast, the Atlantic had become a profession; if the Royal Navy were rising to the top of it, that was hardly a matter for comment—it would really have been extremely odd if anything else had happened.

Aboard *Saltash*, when they weighed anchor at the start of a fresh convoy, and set off down-river, with the rest of the group tailing along behind them at the regulation five cables' distance—aboard *Saltash*, the gramophone that was connected to the loudspeakers on the upper deck always played the same tune. The tune was that jaunty trifle, *We're Off to See the Wizard, the Wonderful Wizard of Oz*. Lockhart had initiated its playing, as something between a joke and a tonic— but somehow the tune was serious, and the words were true. It was as if they were really going off to search a strange sea-lair, to seek once more a passage of arms with a cunning enemy who sometimes used magic. . . . But it was their own lair as well, and their own familiar wizard, no longer veiled, no longer fearful: now they knew him, and all about him, from the tip of his watery whiskers to the cold green gleam in his eye.

"Starboard ten."

"Starboard ten, sir."

"Steer one-three-five."

"Steer one-three-five, sir."

Saltash came round slowly in the gloom, preparing for the long leg across the front of the convoy. Lockhart, watching the dim compass-card edging away to the left, tried to work out the diameter of their turning-circle, and then gave up the calculation. Must be about a thousand yards. . . . A mile astern of them, he could just see the leading ship of the port column—or rather, he could see a vague smudge, darker than the grey night, and a thin white bow-wave that occasionally caught the moon: in between them, *Saltash's* phosphorescent wake boiled and spread and faded to nothing in the calm darkness.

Within a minute or so the leader of the next column came into view on their quarter, and then the next, and the next, a whole rank of shadows, admirably disciplined and stationed; as it ploughed towards the homeward horizon, escaping notice for the fifteenth night in succession, the whole convoy was on its best behaviour. The look-out called: "Ship fine on the starboard bow, sir!" but he called softly, for the ship was *Harmer*, keeping her distance on a parallel zigzag, and the look-out knew it, and Lockhart knew it as well. Then the helmsman said: "Course one-three-five, sir." Then there was silence again, and the crisp threshing of their bow-wave, and the ghostly shadows of a score of ships slipping past under their lee, as they made their starboard leg across the van, their precise act of guardianship. Smoothly, steadily, like these shadows, the summer night with the convoy slid by.

Presently Lockhart became aware that Ericson had come up to the bridge and was standing some paces behind him, accustoming his eyes to the darkness. As usual, he waited a few moments, while the Captain glanced up at the sky, and bent to the compass-bowl, and stared at the nearest ships, and raised his glasses and looked at *Harmer*; then Lockhart turned, and said:

"Good morning, sir."

"Morning, Number One." The gruff voice, the phrase a thousand times used, were as much a part of Lockhart's watch as the sound of that bow-wave breaking below them. Ericson moved up to his side, leaning over the front of the bridge, and stared down at the fo'c's'le, and the seven attendant shadows that were the figures of B-gun's crew.

"Cocoa, sir? It's just been made."

"Thanks." Ericson took the cup from the bridge-messenger, and sipped it cautiously. "What's the time?"

"About half past four, sir. Did you sleep?"

"A little. . . . Anything I haven't seen in the signals?"

"A routine one about a change of ciphers. And *Petal* came through on R/T. One of the ships was showing a stern light."

Ericson lowered his cup, and Lockhart felt rather than saw that he had stiffened to attention.

"When was this?" he asked curtly.

"Just after I came on watch, sir. *Petal* hailed them, and they switched it out."

"Why didn't you tell me?" The tone, infinitely cold, was no longer a novelty to anyone on board.

Lockhart frowned in the darkness. "It solved itself, sir. I didn't want to wake you for nothing."

"You know my standing orders, Number One."

"I'm sorry, sir."

With anyone else, Lockhart knew, Ericson would have already been in a rage: even now, the margin between control and anger was paper-thin. "Anything," said Ericson, with extraordinary force, "*anything* that happens at sea—to an escort, to a ship in convoy, to this ship—is to be reported to me straight away. You understand that perfectly well."

"Yes, sir," said Lockhart formally, and waited. He knew that there would be two more sentences, in the same raw tone of reproof, and that Ericson would then let it go. It was not that he was becoming set in any offensive mould; but he really did feel that he should be told of every conceivable development, no matter how trivial, and the idea that Lockhart might try to stand between him and petty interruptions —and was, indeed, perfectly capable of doing so on many occasions—was still unacceptable, and still provoked him.

The taut shadow at Lockhart's side spoke again. "If anything goes wrong, it is my responsibility."

"Yes, sir."

"And I expect you, as First Lieutenant, to set an example to the other officers."

"Yes, sir."

"There will be a pause now," thought Lockhart, "and then he will relax: and after a bit he will remember that he often does trust me to an extraordinary degree, and he will want to bring all this back to normal again, and he will do so —though perhaps obliquely." The Captain would never apologize, Lockhart knew, because there was no warrant for it. He *was* allowed to make any rules he liked, in the interests of the ship or the group; the order that he was always to be called, if they sighted as much as a single smudge of smoke thirty miles away, was a perfectly legitimate one, and he was entitled to give it, and to see that it was obeyed. But behind all this there were other things, threads of a different weaving that were just as strong—the past years, the imponderables of their friendship, *Compass Rose*, the two rafts. . . . Ericson set down his cup, and straightened up again, and looking ahead towards the horizon said:

"It's getting to be a different kind of war, now."

Lockhart smiled to himself, sensing the first proffering of the olive branch, though he could not yet accurately divine the form that it would take. But all that it was proper for him to say was:

"In what way do you mean, sir?"

Ericson gestured vaguely, like a man groping toward an idea whose outline was still blurred.

"It's so much less personal than it was at the beginning," he said slowly. "There doesn't seem to be any room for— for individual people any more."

"I suppose not, sir."

"At the beginning, there was time for all sorts of things— making allowances for people, and joking, and treating people like sensitive human beings, and wondering whether they were happy, and whether they—they liked you or not."

Ericson drew in his breath, as if his ideas, cloaked by darkness, were running away with him. "But now, now the war doesn't seem to be a matter of men any more, it's just weapons and toughness. There's no margin for humanity left—humanity takes up too much room, it gets in the way of things."

"Yes, sir."

"It used to be a family sort of job, this. Christian names, lots of parties, week-ends off if your wife could get up to see you—" he gestured "—all that sort of thing. People could still afford to be people—in fact they felt offended if you didn't allow them to be. That was specially true of a small ship, like *Compass Rose*. It was a very cheerful sort of wardroom we had there, wasn't it? From time to time it was serious, but mostly it wasn't, it was just a lot of friends doing the best they could with the job, and shrugging their shoulders if it went wrong, and laughing it off together. It was friendly —human—but it's certainly finished now. It finished with *Compass Rose*, in fact."

"Port ten," said Lockhart.

"Port ten, sir."

"Steer oh-six-five."

"Steer oh-six-five, sir."

Ericson waited, while *Saltash* came round in a wide circle, and settled down on her new course. Then:

"I don't mean that *Compass Rose* was a bad sort of ship, or that that was a bad way to fight the war, at that stage. Far from it. I just mean that it's out-of-date now. The war has squeezed out everything except the essentials. You can't make any allowances now, you can't forgive a mistake. The price may be too high."

"Yes, sir," said Lockhart.

"Do you remember," said the Captain reflectively, "that kid Gregg—able seaman—whose wife was playing him up, and who broke ship and went home to try to fix things up. That's almost two years ago now, and two years ago I could afford to let him off with a hell of a lecture, and a caution." He shook his head in the darkness. "Not now, by God! If

412

Gregg came up before me now, I wouldn't listen to any of that damned rigmarole about his wife. I'd give him three months in prison for desertion, and take very good care that he stayed an able seaman for the rest of the war. We can't afford wives and domestic trouble and sympathetic understanding, any more. That sort of thing is finished with."

"Yes, sir."

"It's just the way the war has gone, that's all. It's too serious now for anything except a hundred-per-cent effort." He thought for a moment. "A hundred-per-cent toughness, too. I remember when we sank that U-boat, and I had the German captain in my cabin. He was rude to me—damned insolent, in fact—and I remember thinking that if I got just a little bit angrier, I'd probably pull out a gun and shoot him." He drew a long breath again. "If that happened now, I wouldn't wait, I wouldn't count ten and think it over. This time, I'd plug him, and chuck him overboard afterwards—and anyone else who was inclined to argue the toss about it."

"Yes, sir."

"I know that that isn't the sort of thing we're fighting for—but we've got to win, before we can pick or choose about moral issues. Get this thing over, and I'll be as sweet as you like to anyone, whether it's a German captain, or Able Seaman Gregg, or—" Lockhart felt him smiling as he came at last to the point "—or you."

"I'll remember that, sir."

"I suppose you think, Number One, that this is all wrong, and that you should never allow yourself to be deteriorated by war."

"Yes, sir."

"But you've become dedicated to it yourself, surely? You believe in that hundred-per-cent idea, don't you? No room for mistakes, no room for mercy—no room for love or gentleness, either."

"Yes, I suppose so. . . . Difficult, isn't it?"

Saltash ploughed on, and the convoy with her, creeping steadily across the dark sea. Ahead of them, on the far eastern horizon, it was already lighter, already a whole night and a quarter of a day nearer home. Home, thought Lockhart. The Clyde again, the anchorage, calm and rest. Julie Hallam.

[5]

"Julie Hallam," said Lockhart distantly, "I thought you were high up in the Wrens, I thought you were the strictest Wren in the world."

"So I am," said Julie. "I terrorize all the others. Tell me more."

"Then what about the feet, the toes . . . ?" He pointed. "What could be less official, less strict? How can you justify that sort of thing?"

Julie glanced over the side of the dinghy, where her bare toes trailed in the gently passing water. She raised one foot, and the shining drops, catching the sunlight, chased each other down her leg and fell inboard. She looked up at him again.

"Do I have to justify?" Her voice was slow, rather dreamy, as though, at this happy moment, she was hardly listening to what she was saying, and trusted him not to take advantage of it. "What regulation am I breaking?"

He waved his hand vaguely, releasing the tiller for a moment to do so. The small boat yawed, and he pulled it back on its course again. "Oh—good order and Naval discipline generally. You're a Wren—fully Naval, subject to the Articles of War. And they lay it down clearly that you must *not* dabble your toes in the water, while in any ship under my command."

The foot splashed over the side again, and the boat rocked momentarily. "You're rather sweet," she said, "when you're talking nonsense. . . . On the contrary, I've suspended all the Articles of War for at least five hours. I'm on a picnic, far out of reach of the Naval tentacles. I'm in very shabby slacks. My hair is down—literally. Dabbling my toes fits in perfectly with all that. Nelson would approve."

He looked at her. "Nelson would not approve. But your hair is very pretty that way."

It was true. As he looked at her, half-sitting and half-lying on the middle thwart of the dinghy, he was deeply conscious that she had foregone nothing by assuming a holiday air. Enjoying his leisurely scrutiny, he presently decided that it was the shape of her face which was the continuing focus of her loveliness: the dark hair down nearly to her shoulders could not detract from its distinction, any more than the slacks and the yellow shirt could alter the rest of her. Rather did they proclaim it louder, as if her beauty were free to say: "I am available in any version—take your choice!" She was elegant still, without the groomed hair, and wearing washed-out blue denim slacks instead of a tailored skirt: if the elegance were now on a totally different plane, it did not make any difference. Nor could he decide whether, thus relaxed, she was nearer to the natural Julie Hallam, or further away. It was difficult to decide her true *métier*, and it was not in the least important, when she filled all of them so well. And, beyond all this, to have her exclusive company, at any level, in any circumstances, was still a rapturous surprise, disarming completely the subtleties of preference.

They were picnicking, as she had said by way of excuse: the boat was a borrowed sailing-dinghy, which was taking them, before a light breeze, from Hunter's Quay to the head of Holy Loch. The early September afternoon could not have been lovelier: as sometimes happened in these bleak northern waters, the relenting sun shone down with spring-like fervour, warming the water, bathing the whole estuary of the Clyde in a comforting glow. Their tiny boat ran between brown and purple hills, leaving far astern the busy anchorage, making for the peace and solitude promised them at the head of the loch. Lapped in a lazy quiet, they seemed to be deserting the normal world, whose demands they knew too well, for a private realm that they could fashion to their own liking. He was proud to be taking her there—proud, and happy, and something else as well, something gently

415

beckoning, which he could not define, and did not want to.
The occasion had, he could not help realizing, all the elements of a "party": she was a beautiful girl in a boat, they
were alone on a picnic, he was already much aware of her as
a woman. But like that first time, when he had not kissed
her, so now the moment was not necessarily that moment,
and need not become so. What they shared between them—
the boat, the ripples that chattered under their prow, the
sunshine, the hills—were clearly enough for her, and were
thus enough for him.

Presently, breaking the companionable silence, she said:
"About Nelson."

He smiled, recognizing in her a wayward but questing
attention, and in himself a delight to be talking to her, on any
subject under the sun, so long as her voice still linked him
to her by its lovely clarity.

"About Nelson," he repeated after her.

She leaned back on the thwart, and the drops of water
from her leg fell inboard again. "I should say," she remarked
thoughtfully, "that he would have liked my hair, whether it
was officially approved or not. He would have made any
allowances for a woman, surely? Look at Lady Hamilton."

Lockhart stiffened, in spite of himself, in spite of the moment. "What about Lady Hamilton?"

Julie was glancing up at the sail, whose shadow had just
touched her face as the boat heeled. "Didn't he come rather
near to giving up everything for her—or at least, neglecting
a lot of things which were really a great deal more important?"

"Nelson?" Lockhart drew in his breath. "He would never
have done anything of the sort, never in his life." There was
something in his tone that made her turn and look at him,
and something in his face that surprised her when she saw it.
"He wouldn't have done so for anyone," Lockhart repeated.
"He loved three things—the Navy, England, and Lady
Hamilton. He loved them all very much—overwhelmingly,
sometimes—but he always loved them in that order."

"Oh. . . ." Julie smiled, still watching him. "I only

asked. . . ." But her curiosity continued. "I didn't know he was a hero of yours. In fact I didn't know you had such things as heroes."

He smiled back at her. "Certainly. I like dogs, too. And football matches, and beer, and life insurance. Every Sunday we put the nippers in the sidecar—"

She held up her hand, rather firmly. "Just you go back a bit."

"Yes, ma'am. . . . He's very much a hero of mine, as a matter of fact: a wonderful seaman, a wonderful leader, a kind man, a brave man, a lover whose mistress was perfectly content to bear his child, in or out of wedlock." Lockhart, in his turn, looked up at the sail, as if he might find there the words he wanted to use. "You know, there was a time when he held all England in the palm of his hand, and all Europe too: a single mistake at Trafalgar—the difference between saying "port" and "starboard"—might have been the difference between winning and losing, and could have changed the map of the world—and he knew it, and he was equal to it. He didn't lose sight of that, and he didn't lose sight of the rules he fought by, either." Lockhart paused. "If I were to give you the words of his last prayer, would you laugh at me?"

She shook her head. "Tell."

" 'May the great God whom I worship grant to my country and for the benefit of Europe in general, a great and glorious victory: and may no misconduct in anyone tarnish it; and may humanity after victory be the predominant feature of the British Fleet.' "

Now she nodded. "That really covers everything, doesn't it? Right up-to-date, too. Were those the last words he wrote?"

"No. As far as I remember, he wrote to Lady Hamilton the last thing of all, just before Trafalgar, when he knew the French fleet was coming out and was going to fight. At least, he started the letter, and then stopped and said that he hoped to be able to finish it after the battle."

"What was it about?"

"He just sent his love."

After a moment, Julie said: "She must have been beautiful."

He shook his head. "Not even that. Most people loathed her on sight: she had a lot of enemies—partly jealousy, partly because she was rather too candid and downright; and she was an easy person to sneer at—even her friends agreed that she wasn't attractive to the eye, by the time she met Nelson. Undistinguished, fat, rather blowsy."

"What, then?"

Lockhart shrugged. "She had something for him. She was the other half of him, emotionally, the person he had to have, to make up for the difficulty and strain of what he was doing. You know, it doesn't really matter what a woman looks like, where a loving relationship is concerned. She's either desirable, or she is not: if she is, her looks and her manners don't matter, and if she isn't, no amount of small talk and smart-aleck stuff will make any difference."

"Pity," said Julie despondently.

"You should complain. . . ."

"But if he was so exceptional a person," she said, "I wonder why he needed a woman, anyway. People like that are usually entirely self-sufficient."

"I think it's reasonable," said Lockhart after a moment. "He was a complete man—a man of action, a man of imagination, a man capable of love. England provided half of what he needed to fulfil himself, she gave him the other half."

"And they never overlapped, or got in the way of each other?"

"No. That was the admirable part. He was dedicated to both, and there was room for both." Then he paused, and frowned. "I've an idea," he said after a moment, "that all this contradicts completely something I've said to you already."

She nodded, and smiled, and sat up suddenly. "But I'm certainly not going to remind you, on this lovely day. . . . Are we nearly there?"

They were nearly there; and presently the boat grounded

on the rough shingle beach, and slid forward a few feet, and came gently to rest. As they lowered and stowed the sail, they looked about them at the strange secret world they had reached. They were five miles up the still water of the loch, and almost out of sight of its entrance; they, and the boat, were dwarfed by what lay all round them, but it was a benevolent dwarfing, as if they were held within some capacious natural embrace that would never press too hard on them, never fail to cherish. Behind them was the deserted stretch of water, before them a curved beach, a single pine tree, and a ring of silent hills; the sun was warm on their faces, the whole air enchanted. Their voices when they spoke seemed to fall into deep silence, challenging it for a moment, and then becoming lost for ever.

They slipped over the side of the boat, and paddled ashore. He might have carried her, he thought suddenly, but it did not seem a necessary thing to do: her body that he had never touched, her perfume that he knew only faintly, were not appropriate to the innocent moment they were sharing. But perhaps this thought of his had also reached her, for when they had spread their rugs and unpacked the picnic basket, and settled down side by side, there was an unusual constraint between them. It was the first time that their isolation had been so complete, so unguarded: it was the first time, also, that they had seen each other out of uniform, and the simple clothes they were wearing somehow made it easier for them to think of each other as a man and a woman, bringing nearer to the surface a sensual awareness of their proximity, associating, for the very first time and with the utmost significance, her loveliness, his masculinity.

They talked desultorily, but it had no flow, no ease: they lay silent, enjoying the sun, but it was a restless enjoyment: they looked fleetingly at each other, but the looks were complicated and unreal. At last she frowned, and sat up straight, and said:

"This is quite different from any other time. Why is that?"

He might have guessed that she would thus present the

problem for their joint inspection, promptly and candidly.
. . . He said:

"It's being alone, I think. In complete isolation. It hasn't happened to us before."

"But surely—" she paused, and frowned again "—why should we be shy, or ill at ease, over that? It's not as if we were babies."

"Babies," he thought—"why have I now only one image when she says 'babies' like that? What is happening to us so quickly?—or is it only to me? . . ." He spoke almost at random:

"Julie, we've met five or six times, in the past eight months. Each time we come to know each other a little better, and I think we enjoy it a little more." She nodded in agreement. "It's been a process of exploration—very sweet, too. But it's been progressive all the time."

"So it should be. That's been the best part of it."

He was becoming shy now, and, he noted with faint alarm, rather breathless. Surely he should be past that sort of nervousness. . . . "I want her," he thought in confusion, looking at her breast and shoulders under the thin shirt: "I knew that I would, but it isn't as simple as that, after all—I want her in so many different ways, apart from the breast, the mouth that promises to be soft. I want her and must have her, on any terms she chooses. But the more closely bound, the better. . . ." He drew an uneven breath.

"It's still progressive," he said with difficulty, "but now we've come to the point when—you're so lovely—I am a man—"

She said: "Oh!" suddenly, and then: "I know very well that you are a man." He was aware of tension in her manner also: she was looking away, she might even have coloured slightly. Presently she asked: "Couldn't that be postponed a little longer?"

"It doesn't feel like it."

"No, it doesn't, does it?"

"You know that I love you."

She nodded her head. "Now I do."

"And you?"

"Wait for a few moments." She was staring at the water, undecided, troubled as he had never seen her before. But already the air was lighter, the honest day more beautiful, because of what they had said. Now they knew, at least, where the margin of their delight was set.

She was silent a long time, while the small waves lapped the beach and the sun blessed them; but when she spoke, it was in a happier, more confident voice, as if she too were glad that the plain words and thoughts were now before them.

"I wish," she said, turning toward him, "that there could be a straightforward 'yes' to that question, but it wouldn't be an accurate answer. We share a lot, don't we?—that's been true from the very beginning: we've seen it and we've felt it happening, and parts of it have been lovely." Her eyes, grave and tender, were now regarding him with every sort of honesty. "It began during that very first walk home from your party, when we came together at last after having to be apart for the whole evening. Probably we knew that this was the way it would go. You said—" she smiled vividly "—'the walk made the party,' and then we said good night."

"I thought of kissing you, and then I thought not."

"That was the first thought we shared. . . . Now we are here, suddenly peaceful in the middle of a war: you love and want me, and I—" She paused, and afterwards her voice was stronger. "Look," she said, "people are always asking me to marry them, or sleep with them." From her, in that firm and honest tone, it did not sound crude or awkward. "In a war, in my job, surrounded by lots of people, it's bound to happen: no special merit is attached. Sometimes I think about the proposition, quite seriously, and then there is a false note, or the man is too quick, or the day is too dull, and I walk away from it again." For some reason, she leaned forward at that moment, and touched his bare arm: her soft fingers were immensely comforting, so that the bleak and terrible thoughts of other men making love to her, which had started to devour his brain, melted away on the instant. "Now there is you," she went on, "and you are none of those bad things.

There have been no false notes, you have matched my own pace, my own will, and no day with you is dull."

He covered her hand with his own, and felt it move slightly. He looked up, and said: "As long as we *both* tremble a little, I don't think we need tell anybody about it."

"Oh, I can tremble for you. . . . Look," she said again, "with you I am on the edge of love, the very edge. There are things about you I like, things about you I respect, things that I love already, other things that are surprising. This afternoon, we've discovered something else—or almost discovered it."

As she paused again, he nodded, and said: "A new thing, but in line with the rest. The senses, the first stirring. It has been sweet."

"It has been frightening. . . . I don't mean that I've been afraid of suddenly looking up and finding you lying on top of me: I mean that it is altogether a new thing, and I have never felt it so strongly before."

"And with all that?"

"With all that, the edge of love still."

He got up, crossed the two paces between them on the rugs, and deliberately sat down again, close to her.

"You mean, I spoke too soon?"

"Not quite—it had to be said." She leaned towards him. "When you are near to me, I *know* it had to be said. But as far as my answer is concerned, perhaps it *is* too soon—perhaps one single meeting too soon."

"When you are near me," he said unsteadily, "I have to say: 'May I kiss you?' "

"And I," she answered, not hesitating, "have to say: 'Oh yes, the situation certainly covers *that.*' "

Her lips were wonderfully soft, her cheek and hair fragrant, her body as compliant and as ravishing to his senses as he had known it would be. He murmured: "Julie. . . ." between two kisses, and he felt a trembling of her lower lip which might have been nervousness, could have been desire. The sky seemed to turn over as he opened his eyes again, to find her looking at him with a gentle, delighted surprise.

She said: "You have all the talents."

Smiling, taking from her the cue for a cooler moment, he asked: "The edge of love, still?"

She nodded, laughing with him now. "But the edge is nice, too." She leaned forward, kissed him briefly and assuredly once again, and then said, with infinite composure: "Were you asking me to marry you?"

He stared at her. "What else?"

"Kissing you put all sorts of other things into my mind."

He realized that she had suddenly been made immensely happy, and deeply moved at the same time, and he wanted to match that mood with his own. He said, slowly:

"I was asking you for that, too. . . . Of course I want you, in all the ways there are, including being your lover as soon as possible. But marriage seemed the way for us."

"And dedication? The war?"

"Sweet," he said—the first endearment between them seemed to constrict his throat—"I just don't know the answer to that, any more. The war's still there to be fought, and we both still have to fight it. Long ago, it seemed to me that one could only do that by concentrating all the time, and excluding every other distraction. Now that seems—long ago."

"We'll talk," she said, watching his face. "It doesn't matter now. The edge of love," she murmured. "How patient are you?"

"With hope, very patient."

"No hurry for an answer?"

"No hurry in the world."

"But you said 'Lovers as soon as possible.' "

"That was because I'd just kissed you. Kissing you means wanting you, on the instant. There were indications that—I don't think there's any polite way of putting this—it seemed to me that you were turning me into a very effective lover, just with two kisses and an arm round my shoulder."

She smiled faintly, colouring again. "I felt something like that, too."

"It's all right for you," he grumbled. "No one can tell."

She laughed. "I suddenly know you very well. It's a tremendous relief."

"How lovely," he said, touching her cheek, "to have someone who always understands what I'm talking about. . . . And now I *really* want a drink."

They held hands all the way back. Sometimes he said "Julie," sometimes he leaned over and kissed her: she seemed, on that slow return journey, to be exquisitely tender and near to him, as if they had already become lovers. At the foot of the loch they turned and set course for Hunter's Quay; and there, coming through the boom, a reminder of something not yet resolved, was a line of escorts—two frigates, four corvettes—punching the tide as they hurried for home after delivering their convoy. The two of them watched the ships in silence: they passed quite close, and the successive waves of their wash set the little dinghy dancing. When they were past, Julie said:

"You are thinking: 'There is *Allendale's* group,' and I am thinking: 'There is the war again.' "

"We've managed to escape it for a long time." He pressed her shoulder. "Never leave me, Julie."

As if she had not heard him, she said: "I know where you're going tomorrow. Take care of yourself."

Surprised, he asked: "Something special?"

She inclined her head, very slowly. "It's said to be the coldest journey in the world." And she said again, her eyes on his face: "Take care of yourself."

[6]

North Russia. . . . Chief Petty Officer Barnard, the bearded coxswain of *Saltash*, surveying the shoddy waterfront of Murmansk, decided that this place was right in line with most of the other places he had visited during the war—

424

it was not worth the trip. A pale sun, peering like a froggy, myopic eye from the lustreless sky, picked out the length of the wooden quay, and the snow continually trodden to dirty slush, and the jumble of rooftops that lined the harbour. Murmansk—from this viewpoint, at least—was simply another harbour, with its equipment a little less efficient, its armed sentries a little more obtrusive, and its air a damned sight colder; and to get there, they had endured everything that the enemy had to offer in the way of attack, and had lost, in the process, a dozen ships, three escorts, and upwards of twenty planes from their carriers. They had made, in fact, an expensive, tiring, and extremely noisy excursion, and it was to be hoped that the Russians were duly grateful for the effort.

Barnard stirred inside his thick hairy duffle coat, and beat his gloved hands together, and stamped his feet on the iron deck. Murmansk was unspeakably cold—he had never been more glad of his beard—but then, the whole of the trip had been like Murmansk in that respect, inflicting on them a seeping searing sort of cold that found its way everywhere. The convoy, "evasively routed" as usual, had coasted past the thick pack-ice round Bear Island and North Cape: in these Arctic wastes, there was no night, no real darkness at all, and over them, all the time, was the same cold grey light, falling on a flat sea also cold and grey. *Saltash*, and her fellow escorts, and the convoy, might have been a selection of scale models, placed, for further effect, on a false glass ocean decorated with falling snow. All the drama had come from the enemy, and it had come thick and fast, in every imaginable and vicious form.

Presumably these convoys had to go to Russia, thought Barnard: but by God the price was a stinger! Jerry had tried everything on this trip, and it had paid him a classy sort of dividend. They'd had U-boats, they'd had torpedo-bombers and dive-bombers, they'd had a destroyer sortie from one of the Norwegian fiords, they'd had swarms of E-boats—and it was damned cheek *them* joining in the Battle of the Atlantic. At one time there had even been a threat that the

Scharnhorst would come out of hiding and add to the fun. Of course, there had been bags of escorts round the convoy—three groups altogether, with *Saltash* in charge of the lot. The skipper must have had something to carry in his head, all right. . . . And there had been a big-ship escort as well, three cruisers and a battleship, mooching about to the north of them, ready for trouble. But imagine the *Scharnhorst*, with four turrets of fourteen-inch guns, getting in among the merchant ships, before their own battleship could come within range. The German destroyers had been quite bad enough, when it came to ships being outgunned by other ships.

Perhaps, thought Barnard, the destroyers had been worst of all. They'd come roaring down from the northeastward, three of them in line ahead, big as bloody cruisers, and then turned outward and begun to pour hell into the ships nearest to them. One of the corvettes had bought it straight away—she'd steamed straight toward the leading destroyer, plucky little bastard, and been blown out of the water for her trouble, before she even got within range. There was nothing that corvettes could do about destroyers, and nothing much that frigates could do either—though *Saltash* had come streaking across to join in, with everyone on board soiling their pants on the way. Destroyers—six-inch guns. . . . Luckily the skipper must have sent a signal straight away, as soon as the destroyers were sighted, because before anything else could happen, two of the cruisers had popped up over the horizon, and the destroyers had mucked off, without waiting to be told. They'd done enough damage, anyway—a corvette sunk, and three merchant ships set on fire; but it might have been a lot worse, and they didn't come back for more, on that or any other day.

Perhaps, thought Barnard, the destroyers weren't as bad as the torpedo-bombers: they were both new weapons to *Saltash*, as well as to everyone else, but the bombers came over every day, for eleven days at a stretch, and in the end it got you down. Sometimes it was ordinary bombing, with the planes high up, and nothing much happening until the bombs arrived and the whole sea jumped, and the ships went up in smoke; sometimes it was dive-bombing, and the planes came screaming down, pointing straight at you, and flattening out at the very last moment; but usually it was torpedoes. The torpedo-planes were the hardest of all to spot; they came in low over the water, little specks of things hard to see in the grey light: then they started weaving, so that you couldn't keep them in the gunsights, and then they dropped their torpedoes, almost within touching distance, so that there was no time to dodge, and then they got to hell out of it, while you were still waiting for the bang. . . . *Saltash* had shot one of them down with her two-pounder, but one plane hardly made a dent; because the torpedo attack went on for eleven days, and it happened four times a day—just as quickly as the planes could nip back to Norway and refuel—and they came over in droves from every bloody angle in the compass, twelve of them, twenty of them at a time, dropping their fish all round the convoy so they were bound to hit something. And when the ships were hit, and went down, there wasn't much chance for the poor sods on board, because of the cold.

Perhaps, thought Barnard, the cold was worse than the destroyers and the torpedo-bombers put together. The cold was everywhere, inside the ship as well as out: you *couldn't* get warm, not if you stretched yourself out on top of the galley stove. They must have shovelled tons of snow off the upper deck: they must have thawed out the guns a dozen times, using a steam-hose that damned nearly got frozen up itself. Near to the ice, when *Saltash* was level with North Cape, and a bit of wind got up, the cold was like a scraper running over your raw face. One of the seamen, taking off his gauntlets to open an ammunition locker, had torn off the whole of the skin of one palm, and left it stuck to the locker like half a bloody glove, with him staring at it as if it was something hanging up in a shop. But that wasn't as bad as what happened to the poor bastards that got dropped into the drink.

There, you couldn't last more than a few minutes—the cold got you as soon as the water touched your body. There was one time that Barnard remembered specially, because it topped the level for the whole trip. One of the Seafires from a carrier, trying to intercept some high-level bombing, had got into trouble, and the pilot had to bail out ahead of the convoy. While the parachute was still in the air, *Saltash* had her whaler down and rowing toward the spot where he was going to fall—about a mile away. But even a mile had been too far, in that sort of weather. The pilot had waved when he landed in the water, and the coxswain of the whaler had waved back: it took them not more than three minutes to get to him, but in those three minutes he was stone-cold dead —frozen as stiff as a bloody plank. That was how you could die, up in these parts—in three minutes, between waving and rescue, between a smile and a fixed-for-ever grin.

Barnard, lost in his not-too-happy dream, became aware of a movement by his side, and found that he had been joined at the rail by Lieutenant Allingham, the Gunnery Officer. The two were good friends, and they smiled at each other, and then without a word ranged themselves side by side, leaning over the taut wire rail of the fo'c's'le, staring down at the quay. Below them, a Russian sentry, bristling with weapons, came to a halt at the end of his beat, turned, and met their gaze unblinkingly, his hand on the butt of his revolver—an armed man in an ambiguous trance, a man standing stock-still at the tip of a fabulous continent, tethered to the end of his tracks in the snow. . . . They both watched him for a moment: then Allingham sighed, and straightened up a little, and said:

"Looking at Russia, coxswain?"

Barnard nodded. "That's just about it, sir. And Russia's looking at me, as usual." He indicated the armed sentry, who still eyed them fixedly from under his strange steel helmet, as if daring them to come ashore, or to move *Saltash* one inch nearer the fatherland. Barnard, bored with that stare, waved to the man, who fingered his rifle instead of answering. "Cheer up, *tovarich!*" called out Barnard, not to be rebuffed. The man below them looked to the right, then to the left, then jerked his head up again. "Churchill!" he answered, conspiratorially. But he still did not smile.

"Churchill!" repeated Barnard, with great readiness. But then he shook his head. "They're a queer lot, sir. Can't get on with them at all. Some of the lads have had rows already, over at the canteen. They just don't want to know. . . ."

"It's nothing like what I thought it would be," said Allingham non-committally. He too had developed some strong views on Russia during the past few days, but the need for Allied solidarity, prominently featured in confidential directives from the Admiralty, had to be borne in mind. "You can't really expect them to be the same as us, though."

Barnard nodded. "Long way from home. . . . Specially from your home, sir."

"I'll say. . . . Think of coming all this way, just to get a lot of dirty looks and an air raid every morning and evening."

"*And* what we ran into on the way here." Barnard drew in his breath sharply. "I reckon the skipper must be just about clapped out."

"I could have slept for a week myself. In fact, if it weren't for these bloody air-raids all the time, that's just what I'd be doing."

"I hope we don't have to do too many of these trips." The sentry frowned up at them, as if he had been able to tune in to this disparaging thought. "Do you honestly think they're worth it, sir?"

"I reckon so. The Russians need the material, and they're putting up the hell of a fight, you know. It's the only country, so far, where the Germans are really taking a knock." Allingham waved his arm round, embracing the trodden slush of the quay, the mean ice-bound town, the single man watchful in the snow. "It's difficult to realize it, looking at this little scrap-heap. But down there—" he pointed vaguely southward "—all sorts of big things are going on. If the Russians can stage a few more Stalingrads, and if we can help them via the back door here, then the war will start to peter out. That's worth a few trips like this one."

"As long as they realize what these convoys have to go through, to get here. I wonder what it is makes them so cagey." He pointed once more to the snow-bound sentry. "Look at that chap. He either hates our guts, or he's scared stiff of being caught fraternizing. And they've all been like that. Whichever way you look at it, it's not much of a welcome."

"Perhaps it's because they *are* fighting so hard, and what we've done so far doesn't show on the map. The only thing they want to hear is that we've started our second front, and until they read about that in the newspapers, they're inclined to think we're loafing."

"But still. . . ." Barnard frowned. "They're a queer lot, sir," he repeated. "Remember how we wanted to shift that wire, when we first came alongside? They wouldn't even let us land a couple of seamen, before one of their officers had been aboard to check up. Bloody cheek, considering the sort of trip we'd made to get here."

Allingham nodded, in spite of himself. "Yeah, it's queer. . . . If these chaps landed up in Sydney, we wouldn't exactly kiss them, but at least we'd say hello, and ask them along for a drink."

"What do they drink in Sydney, then?"

"Beer, and plenty of it."

"Tried the vodka yet, sir?"

"Yes—anything once. Perhaps it's no wonder these chaps are so bad-tempered."

The air-raid sirens sounded, for the third time since daylight, *Saltash's* own alarm-bells followed a moment later, and the ship sprang to life, forfeiting, as on so many other days, her afternoon siesta. The man on the quay retreated to a small sand-bagged sentry-box a few yards away, but he continued to watch them warily, alert for sabotage or the display of secret weapons. Near to, some guns started firing, and from the grey lowering sky came the steady beat of aircraft engines. As usual, they would have to fight an extra round with the enemy, when they should have been in shelter and at peace.

"Murmansk!" said Allingham disgustedly. "No sleep on the way up, and no sleep when we get here. The sooner we start back, the better I'll like it."

"But we can't do it twice without a rest in the middle," said Barnard, grinning.

"Coxswain," said Allingham, completing the joke, "that's what all the girls say. . . ." Then, the edge of laughter still in his voice, he began to marshal his guns' crews and bring them to readiness, while the man on the quay watched and listened to these antics from another world, and guarded closely his own.

Lockhart had already been in collision a number of times with the Russian interpreter, a small fiery individual who seemed to regard every request for stores or facilities as yet another example of the top-hatted capitalists milking the simple proletariat. On their last morning, an hour before sailing, there developed between them a row so furious and so all-embracing that it was difficult to remember that it had started with a complaint about the quality of the fresh meat supplied to *Saltash* for her return journey. When it had ranged widely, from a comparison of the Russian and the British standards of living, to an analysis of their respective war efforts, and fists had been shaken on both sides—for Lockhart found this habit of emphasis infectious—the interpreter took a stormy departure. At the head of the gangway he turned, for a final blistering farewell.

"You English," he said, in thunderous accents and with extraordinary venom, "think we know damn nothing—*but I tell you we know damn all.*"

Scene Two: A Storm at Sea. Enter a Ship, hard-driven, labouring. . . . But even that simple directive could not be obeyed, because no ship could enter, no ship could make a foot of headway onto any stage like this. The storm scene itself would have to move to meet the ship—and that, thought Ericson, when the fifth dawn in succession found his ship still fighting a fantastic battle to force her way even as

431

far south as Iceland, that reversal of nature was not impossible; for here must be the worst weather of the war, the worst weather in the world.

It was more than a full gale at sea, it was nearer to a great roaring battlefield with ships blowing across it like scraps of newspaper. The convoy no longer had the shape of a convoy, and indeed a ship was scarcely a ship, trapped and hounded in this howling wilderness. The tumult of that southerly gale, increasing in fury from day to day, had a staggering malice from which there was no escape: it was as if each ship were some desperate fugitive, sentenced to be lynched by a mob whose movements had progressed from clumsy ill-humour to sightless rage.

Huge waves, a mile from crest to crest, roared down upon the pigmies that were to be their prey; sometimes the entire surface of the water would be blown bodily away, and any ship that stood in the path of the onslaught shook and staggered as tons of green sea smote her upper deck and raced in a torrent down her whole length. Boats were smashed, funnels were buckled, bridges and deck-houses were crushed out of shape: men disappeared overboard without trace and without a cry, sponged out of life like figures wiped from a blackboard at a single imperious stroke. Even when the green seas withheld their blows for a moment, the wind, screaming and clawing at the rigging, struck fear into every heart; for if deck gear and canvas screens could vanish, perhaps even men could be whipped away by its furious strength. . . . For the crew of *Saltash*, there was no convoy, and no other ships save their own; and she, and they, were caught in a mesh of fearful days and nights, which might defeat them by their sheer brutal force. Normally a good sea boat, *Saltash* had ridden out many storms and had often had strength to spare for other ships that might be in difficulties; now, entirely on her own, she laboured to stay afloat, wearily performing, for hour after hour and day after day, the ugly antics of a ship that refused, under the most desperate compulsion, to stand on her head.

Throughout it all, the ship's relay-loudspeaker system,

monotonously fed by a satirical hand, boomed out a tune called *Someone's Rocking My Dream-Boat*.

Each of them in the wardroom had problems of a special sort to cope with, over and above the ones they shared with the rest of the crew—the problem of eating without having food flung in their faces, of sleeping without being thrown out of their bunks, of getting warm and dry again after the misery of a four-hour watch: above all, the problem of staying unhurt.

Scott-Brown, the doctor, was kept busy with this human wreckage of the storm, treating from hour to hour the cuts, the cracked ribs, the seasickness that could exhaust a man beyond the wish to live. His worst casualty, the one that would have needed all his skill and patience even if he had been able to deal with it in a quiet, fully equipped operating-theatre ashore, was a man who, thrown bodily from one side of the mess-deck to the other, had landed on his knee-cap and smashed it into a dozen bloody fragments.

Johnson, the engineer officer, had a problem calling for endless watchfulness—the drunken movements of the ship, which brought her stern high out of the water with every second wave, and could set the screws racing and tearing the shaft to bits, unless the throttle were clamped down straight away.

Raikes, in charge of navigation, was confronted by a truly hopeless job. For days on end there had been no sun to shoot, no stars to be seen, no set speed to give him even a rough D.R. position: where *Saltash* had got to, after five days and nights of chaos, was a matter of pure guesswork that any second-class stoker, pin in hand, could have done just as well as he. Ill-balanced on the Arctic Circle, sixty-something north by nothing west—that was the nearest he could get to it: *Saltash* lay somewhere inside these ragged limits, drifting slowly backward within the wild triangle of Iceland, Jan Mayen Island, and Norway.

The ship's organization was, as usual, Lockhart's responsibility; and the ship's organization had become a wicked sort of joke. Between decks, *Saltash* was in chaos—the wardroom uninhabitable, the mess-decks a shambles: there could be no hot food, no way of drying clothes, no comfort for anyone under the ceaseless battering of the storm. Deck gear worked loose, boats jumped their chocks and battered themselves to bits, water fell in solid tons on every part of the ship: after facing with hope a thousand dawns, Lockhart now dreaded what might meet his eye at the end of his watch, when daylight pierced the wild and lowering sky and showed him the ship again. An upper deck swept clean, a whole watch of thirty seamen vanished overboard—these were the outlines of a waking nightmare that might, with a single turn of fortune, come hideously true.

As *Saltash* laboured, as *Saltash* faltered and groaned, as *Saltash* found each tortured dawn no better than the last, he, along with the rest, could only endure, and curse the cruel sea.

No one cursed it with more cause and with less public demonstration than Ericson, who, self-locked into one corner of the bridge, was fulfilling once more his traditional role of holding the whole thing together. After five days and nights of storm, he was so exhausted that the feeling of exhaustion had virtually disappeared: anchored to the deck by lead-like legs and soaked sea boots, clamped to the bridge rail by weary half-frozen arms, he seemed to have become a part of the ship herself—a fixed pair of eyes, a watchful brain welded into the fabric of *Saltash*. All the way north to Murmansk he had had to perform the mental acrobatics necessary to the control of twenty escorts and the repelling of three or four different kinds of attack: now the physical harassing of this monstrous gale was battering at his body in turn, sapping at a lifetime's endurance that had never had so testing a call made upon it, had never had to cope with an ordeal on this scale.

Assaulted by noise, bruised and punished by frenzied movement, thrown about endlessly, he had to watch and feel the same things happening to his ship.

The scene from the bridge of *Saltash* never lost an outline of senseless violence. By day it showed a square mile of tormented water, with huge waves flooding in like mountains sliding down the surface of the earth: with a haze of spray and spume scudding across it continually: with gulfs opening before the ship as if the whole ocean were avid to swallow her. Outlined against a livid sky, the mast plunged and rocked through a wild arc of space, flinging the aerials and the signal-halyards about as if to whip the sea for its wickedness. Night added the terrible unknown; night was pitch-black, unpierceable to the eye, inhabited by fearful noises and sudden treacherous surprises: by waves that crashed down from nowhere, by stinging spray that tore into a man's face and eyes before he could duck for shelter. Isolated in the blackness, *Saltash* suffered every assault: she pitched, she rolled, she laboured: she met the shock of a breaking wave with a jar that shook her from end to end, she dived shuddering into a deep trough, shipping tons of water with a noise like a collapsing house, and then rose with infinite slowness, infinite pain, to shoulder the mass of water aside, and shake herself free, and prepare herself for the next blow.

Ericson watched and suffered with her, and felt it all in his own body: felt especially the agony of that slow rise under the crushing weight of the sea, felt often the enormous doubt as to whether she would rise at all. Ships had foundered without trace in this sort of weather: ships could give up, and lie down under punishment, just as could human beings: here, in this high corner of the world where the weather had started to scream insanely, and the sea to boil, here could be murder: here, where some of *Compass Rose's* corpses might still be wandering, here he might join them, with yet another ship's company in his train.

He stayed where he was on the bridge, and waited for it to happen, or not to happen. He was a pair of red eyes, inflamed by wind and salt water: he was a brain, tired, fluttering, but forced into a channel of watchfulness: he was sometimes a voice, shouting to the helmsman below to prepare for another threatening blow from the sea. He was a core of fear and of control, clipped small and tight into a body he had first ill-treated, and then begun, perforce, to disregard.

. . .

No gale of this force could last forever, or the very fabric of the globe would long ago have been torn to bits; and presently, as a grudging act of grace, the weather took a turn for the better. The sea was still jumbled and violent, but it was no longer on the attack: the wind still sang on a high note, but it had lost its venom: the ship still rolled and staggered, but she could, at least, now steer a single fixed course. There came a day when the upper deck began to dry off, and a start could be made toward cleaning up the shambles below: when a hot meal could be cooked and eaten in comfort: when a man could climb from the fo'c's'le to the bridge without running a gauntlet of green seas that might toss him into the scuppers, or straight overboard: when the Captain could leave the bridge for more than half a watch, and sleep for more than an hour at a stretch. . . . The sun pierced the clouds, for the first time for many days, and set the grey water gleaming: it warmed the shoulders of their duffle coats, and sent up a small haze of steam from the drying decks. It also showed them exactly three ships in sight, over a space of a hundred square miles of ocean which should have held fifty-four vessels in orderly convoy formation.

But perhaps that was too much to expect. . . . The process of rounding up the convoy took *Saltash* nearly forty-eight hours, steaming all the time at an average of twenty knots on a dozen different schemes of search; it was not eased by the fact that all the escorts were doing this same thing simultaneously, trying to marshal whatever merchantmen were in their immediate area, and that there were at one time six of these small convoys, of half a dozen ships each, all trying to attract fresh customers to the only true fold, and all steering different courses. On one occasion, *Saltash*, coming across the frigate *Streamer* with five ships in company, signalled to her: "The convoy is 200 degrees, fourteen miles from you," only to receive the answer: "The convoy is here." It was, for a tired Senior Officer on the edge of irritation, a pregnant moment that Ericson longed to exploit.

But for him there could be no such delaying luxury: the

crisp orders that went to *Streamer* were neither brutal nor
sarcastic, simply explicit and not to be argued. They formed
a pattern with all the other crisp orders of the last two days,
and presently, as a result, things were under control again;
presently, *Saltash* could station herself at the van of what
really looked something like a convoy—straggling, woefully
battered, but still a body of ships that could be honestly reported to their Lordships as Convoy RC 17. Ericson made
this report, and disposed of his escorts in their night positions, and handed over to Allingham, who was Officer-of-
the-Watch; and then, with a drugged thankfulness, he took
his aching body down the ladder, in search of the shelter of
his cabin, and of longed-for rest.

The weather was still wild; but with the convoy intact and
the main chaos retrieved, the hours ahead seemed bearable
and hopeful, and above all suitable for oblivion.

Then, not a mile astern of *Saltash*, a ship was torpedoed.

Ericson had just passed the first sweet margin of sleep
when the alarm bells clanged: for a moment he could not
really believe that they were ringing, and then, as he felt the
loathed sound drilling deep into his brain, he had such a
violent upsurge of rage and disappointment that he came near
to childish tears. It was too much altogether, it wasn't fair.
. . . He heaved himself out of his bunk, and followed the
many other running feet up the ladder again, conscious only
of an enormous weariness, and a brain suddenly and brutally
robbed of the sleep it craved. How could a man, or a ship,
cope with this? How could they be expected to fight anything except the weather?

It seemed that they would have to: it seemed that, as soon
as the weather gave a foot of ground, the other enemy, ready
in the wings, stepped in with fresh violence, fresh treachery.
The scene that greeted Ericson had a pattern made familiar
by a hundred convoys: it showed the ships in station, the
dusk gathering round them, the heaving sea, and then the
ugly deformity that meant disaster—the single winged ship
sagging away out of line, already listing mortally, already

437

doomed. She was a small ship: she must, as a prelude to her defeat, have had to endure a special form of hell during the last week of storm. . . . Ericson looked at Allingham.

"What happened, Guns?"

"She just went, sir." The Australian accent, as usual in moments of excitement, was thick and somehow reassuring. "Fired a distress rocket, about a minute ago. But how the hell could they hit her, in this sort of weather?"

"M'm," Ericson grunted. The astonishing question had already occurred to him, but it was useless to speculate. Probably there was yet another new weapon: probably U-boats could now fire a torpedo vertically from the bed of the ocean, and hit a ship plumb in its guts. One could think of a nice expressive name for it. But it was no use being surprised at anything in this bloody, this immensely long war. . . . "Who's the wing escort?"

"*Pergola*, sir. She's making a sweep to starboard."

Ericson grunted again. That was all that could be done, at the moment: *Pergola* could sweep the suspect area, the stern escort could pick up the bits, *Saltash* could plod along at the head of the convoy, he himself could think it all out, with cutting logic, using an ice-cold brain. . . . He saw Allingham looking at him with a rough sort of compassion in his glance, taking in his inflamed eyes, half sunk in sleep, his swollen face, the twitching on his cheek-bone—all the marks of exhaustion which Ericson was aware of himself and which could not be disguised. He smiled ruefully.

"I'd just got my head down."

"Bad luck, sir." Allingham paused. "Shall I go along to the fo'c's'le, sir? Or stay up here?"

Ericson smiled again, acknowledging the line of thought. "You go down, Guns. I've got the ship."

When he had gone, there was silence among the men now gathered at action stations on the bridge. Ericson watched the convoy, Lockhart watched the sinking ship, Holt and the signalmen watched *Pergola*, the look-outs watched their appointed arcs, the bridge messenger watched Ericson. It was a closed circle, of men in danger doing nothing at a moment

438

when active movement would have been a relief, carried in a ship that might herself be doing the wrong thing for want of a single clue. When Ericson said, suddenly and aloud: "We'll wait," it was as much to bridge the dubious pause in his own mind as to inform the men round him.

But the pause was not long. There was an exclamation from Holt, the midshipman, and then he said excitedly:

"*Pergola's* got a signal hoisted!" He stared through his glasses at the corvette, rooting away to starboard like a questing terrier. "Large flag, sir."

The yeoman of signals called out: "*Pergola* in contact, sir."

"I wonder," thought Ericson; but he did not say it aloud. *Pergola*, young and enthusiastic, was always ready to depth-charge anything, from a clump of sea-weed to a shoal of sardines, but he did not want to discourage her. Depth charges were cheap, ships and men were not. . . . Now all of them, save the stolid look-outs dedicated to their arcs of vision, turned to watch *Pergola*. Three miles to starboard, she was steering obliquely away from the convoy: she was rolling and pitching drunkenly, and her increased speed sent the spray in great clouds over her bridge. "Steaming full ahead," thought Ericson appraisingly: "she must be going to drop some for luck." And as he thought it, and wished that *Saltash* might have an excuse for doing the same, another flag fluttered up to *Pergola's* cross-trees, and the yeoman of signals called out:

"*Pergola* attacking, sir."

Now they all watched with fresh attention, wondering how good the asdic contact was, knowing with professional insight just how difficult it must be for *Pergola* to get her depth charges cleared away and ready for dropping, while steaming full ahead in this immensely troubled sea. *Compass Rose* used to do this sort of thing, thought Lockhart, as *Pergola* gave an especially vicious lurch and shipped a green sea on her quarter: *Compass Rose* used to sweep into action balanced inelegantly on one ear and one leg, while poor old Ferraby danced a jig round the depth-charge rails as he tried to get his charges ready, with a bunch of ham-handed stokers to help him, and plenty of caustic comment from the bridge. It was nice to have graduated from corvettes. . . . Lockhart watched *Pergola* reminiscently: Holt and the signalmen watched her with a professional eye to her signals: below on the plotting-table, Raikes the navigator watched her with the searching beam of the radar set; and Ericson watched her with a proprietary interest. For him, she was simply an extension of his own armament, a probing steel finger sent out from *Saltash* to find and hit the enemy. The torpedoed ship had been his, and *Pergola* was his too: if the one balanced the account of the other, it would not be so bad, it would justify the escort screen, it would appease the sense of failure that nagged his tired brain. It would let him sleep once more.

Pergola went in like an express train somehow diverted onto a switch-back railway. They saw her charges go down, they saw her sweep round to port as soon as they were dropped: then, after a few moments, the huge columns of grey-green water were tossed into the air by the explosion. When the spray settled, they waited again, their glasses trained on the place of execution; but the surface of the sea was innocent, the expected black shape did not appear. *Pergola*, now at half speed, headed back toward the explosion area, uncertainly, like a small boy who has made far too much noise in his mother's drawing-room and wishes he were safely and anonymously back in the nursery. There was a pause, and then a third flag went up from her bridge.

"From *Pergola*, sir," said the yeoman of signals promptly. " 'Lost contact.' "

"Call her up," said Ericson. "Make: 'Continue to search your area. Report nature of original contact.' "

The lamps flickered between the two ships.

"Contact was firm, moving left, classified as U-boat," came *Pergola's* answer.

"What is your estimate now?" was Ericson's next signal.

"I still think it was a U-boat," said *Pergola* manfully. Then she added, as if with an ingenuous smile: "It was where a U-boat ought to have been."

440

"Now there," thought Ericson, "there I agree with you." The attack had certainly come from that side, the U-boat would naturally have tried to move away to starboard, she would have been steering the course that *Pergola* indicated; she might well have been just about where *Pergola* had dropped her depth charges. That being so, it was worth while *Pergola* staying where she was, and continuing the hunt: in fact, he thought with sudden vehemence, it was worth while staying there himself, and organizing the hunt on a two-ship basis. He would be taking a chance if he detached two escorts from the screen; but it was very unlikely that the U-boat was one of a pack: in this weather, the convoy could only have been sighted by chance, from close to, and there would have been no time to assemble other craft for a concerted attack. She was therefore a lone wolf, sinking her fangs once, swiftly, and then slinking off into the forest again. Lone wolves of this sort deserved special attention, special treatment. The chance was worth taking.

The pattern of action emerged new-minted from his brain, as if, however tired he were, he had only to press a button marked *Detach Two Escorts for Independent Search* in order to produce a typed schedule of operational orders. The necessary directions were dictated in a smooth series that kept all three signalmen busy at the same time. Signals went to the Admiralty and the commodore of the convoy, to tell them what was happening: to *Harmer*, to take over as Senior Officer: to *Pergola*, to continue her search until *Saltash* joined her; to *Rose Arbour*, to take *Pergola's* place on the screen: to *Streamer*, to dispatch the sinking merchantman by gunfire, and then rejoin: and to the other escorts, to station themselves according to the new diagram. Then Ericson summoned Lockhart and Johnson, the engineer officer, to the bridge, to explain what he proposed to do: he conferred, lengthily and technically, with Raikes at the plotting-table; and then he took *Saltash* round in a wide sweep to starboard, and, coming up on *Pergola's* quarter, started sending a final long signal beginning: "We will organize our search in accordance with two alternative possibilities."

Lockhart had never admired the Captain more than during the twelve hours that followed. In the end, he thought, for all these new machines and scientific stuff, war depends on men. . . . He knew that Ericson must have been desperately tired, even before the new crisis arrived: if the exacting trip northbound to Murmansk, and the last five days of battering weather, did not suggest it, then his grey lined face and humped shoulders supplied a reliable clue. And yet there was in all his actions, both now, and during the subsequent long, intricate, and determined hunt for the submarine, no trace of tiredness or of readiness to compromise: he rose to the moment, and kept at the required pitch of alertness, as if he had come to the task fresh from a six weeks' holiday; and the result, in addition to being a remarkable physical effort, was, in the realm of submarine detection, a tactical master-piece as well.

Ericson must have been very sure, thought Lockhart, that the submarine was there, and that *Pergola*—the happy-go-lucky *Pergola*—had for once been on the right track and might well have damaged her: he must have conquered his tiredness with this knowledge that the quarry was immedi-ately to hand. For it was not enough to keep in mind that a ship had been sunk, and men killed in the process: that was a commonplace of the Atlantic, and the revengeful energy it bred soon petered out. It was the professional sense that was now the mainspring of every sustained effort of will: the feeling, present all the time, that senior officers of escorts were specifically hired to sink U-boats, and that for this reason U-boats must never be allowed to go to waste.

Certainly, Ericson clung onto his quarry, or the hope of it, as if he would have been personally ashamed to forfeit the chance of a kill. . . . It was six o'clock in the evening when *Saltash* and *Pergola* separated, to start their different schemes of search: it was midnight before any results rewarded either of them. Earlier, down in *Saltash's* plotting-room, Ericson and Raikes had made a detailed appreciation of the prospects, involving three different suppositions. Firstly, the U-boat might have been slightly damaged by *Pergola's* attack, in which case she would dive deep and stay there, in the hope of fooling the pursuit and patching herself up in the meantime. Alternatively, she might have been badly damaged, and would need to start creeping for the shelter of the nearest home-port as soon as she could. Lastly, she might have escaped damage altogether—or have been outside the area of attack in the first place: she would then probably decide, after the initial scare, to follow the convoy at a distance and come in for a second helping later that night. There were variations latent in all these possibilities; but thus the broad outlines had confronted Ericson as he started his reasoned, highly technical guesswork on the plotting-table.

The last possibility—that the U-boat would continue to follow the convoy—was something that *Saltash* must now disregard: if the U-boat were going to try again, *Harmer* and the rest of the escort screen must cope with it themselves. That left the other two alternatives: the lurking in the deep, or the immediate creep for home. Lurking meant, for the hunting escort, a long and patient period of waiting up above: it might involve circling the area slowly for as long as twenty-four hours, all the time on the alert for any sign of a break-out. If, on the other hand, the U-boat had already started for home, the journey might be eastward towards Norway, or southeast to the German coast, or due south to one of the Biscay ports: it meant in any case a rapidly extending range of search, becoming more like a needle-in-the-haystack proposition with every hour that passed.

Of the two, Ericson finally chose for himself the patient, stalking wait, above the spot where the U-boat ought to be: it was the one he thought most likely, and *Saltash's* superior asdic and radar would give her a decided advantage, if the U-boat tried to run for it. The other—the cast for home, in an ever widening arc—was a somewhat forlorn venture: in assigning it to *Pergola*, he tried not to feel that he was giving the junior ship a dubious chance of distinguishing herself. . . . Something of the sort must have occurred to the irrepressible *Pergola*, who, on taking her leave, signalled:

"Don't forget it was originally my bird."

Ericson, hovering between the alternative answers "We'll go fifty-fifty on the medals," and "Confine your signals to essential traffic," finally sent none at all. All that he really wanted to say to *Pergola*, as she drew away and the darkness thickened between them, was that she carried his blessings with her. But there was really no official version of this.

The next six hours had not the smallest excitement for anyone aboard *Saltash*: they had, in fact, a deadly sameness, an unrewarding monotony, the hardest thing of all for tired men to support. Ericson remained on the bridge the whole time, hunched in his chair, wide awake, while *Saltash* quartered the suspect area at half speed; for hour after hour her asdic recorded nothing at all, and her radar simply the diminishing speck of light that was *Pergola* sweeping deeper and deeper to the southeast. Ericson ate a scratch meal at eight o'clock: relays of cocoa reached him at hourly intervals: the moon came up, and then left them again: the sea flattened as the wind died. It was cold: the cold attacked not only the body, it chilled the mind as well, so that to keep alert, to believe that what one was doing was right, became more and more difficult.

At times Ericson's thoughts wandered so far that the effort to bring them back was like a physical ordeal, a cruel tug on some stretched sinew of the brain. "I am very tired," he thought: "I have this pain of tiredness in my legs and across my shoulders and under my heart: that thing inside my head is starting to flutter again. This search may go on for hours, this search may go on for ever: we are probably doing the wrong thing, we have probably guessed wrong in every respect, from the very beginning: there was probably a pack of six or eight U-boats in this area all the time, and they are preparing to fall upon the convoy at this moment, while we fool about, fifty miles astern of it. I have weakened the escort screen at this crucial time, I have taken away two ships out of eight, I have been, by one quarter, unforgivably stupid and rash, I am ripe for a court-martial. . . ." The asdic pinged away, like a nagging insect: the tick-tick of the motor on the plotting-table reached Ericson continually up the voice-pipe, like some infernal metronome reminding him that everything he did was out of joint. The hours crept past, and the change of course which came every fifteen minutes seemed a futile break in a pattern already futile.

Now and again he spoke to Raikes, the navigator, who had the first watch; and Raikes answered him quietly, unhurriedly, without turning from his place at the front of the bridge. But these exchanges never contained what Ericson really wanted to say, and never what he wanted to hear, either: they simply featured a comment on the weather, a query about the distance run, a neutral remark on any neutral subject that occurred to him. For his own comfort, his own hunger, he wanted to say: "Do you think we are right, do you think we are wasting our time: is the U-boat here at all, or have I, in diluting the escort screen by a quarter, made what may turn out to be a murderous mistake?" But none of these were captain's questions, and so they remained unasked, prisoners in the brain, while *Saltash* covered the same square of ocean once every hour, and *Pergola* gradually faded out of range, and the black and empty sea, deserted even by the moon, offered to *Saltash* only a cold derisive hissing as she passed.

But the change of watch at midnight marked a change of fortune as well; Allingham and Vincent had hardly taken over from Raikes—indeed, Raikes was still writing up his meagre entry in the deck-log—when the pattern of the night quickly flowered, in the only way that could bring any pleasure to the senses. The asdic repeater, which could be heard all over the bridge, and which had been sounding an identical, damnable note for six hours on end, suddenly produced an astonishing variation—a solid echo, an iron contact in a featureless ocean. . . . Ericson jumped when he heard it, as did everyone else within earshot: the bridge sprang to life as if the darkness had become charged with an electric fervour that reached them all instantly.

"Sir!" began Allingham.

"Bridge!" called the asdic rating.

445

"Captain, sir!" said the yeoman of signals.

"All right," said Ericson, slipping down off his chair. "I heard it. . . . What a nice noise. . . . Hold on to it. . . . Sound Action Stations. . . . Yeoman!"

"Sir?" said the yeoman of signals.

"Make to *Pergola*: 'Return to me with all dispatch.' "

That's a guess, he thought as he said it—but the echo, loud and clear, confirmed him in the belief that this, the blank stretch of ocean which had suddenly blossomed, was now the place for all available hunting escorts to be. Only U-boats sounded like that, only U-boats could produce that beautiful metallic ring; and this U-boat, which had struck once and then lain in hiding for so long, must now be finally cornered. It would take *Pergola* over two hours to get back from her search, even "with all dispatch"—the Navy's most urgent order; but she deserved to be in at the kill, and she could play a useful supporting role if the U-boat were elusive. . . . The asdic echo sharpened: Lockhart, now stationed on the set, called out: "Target moving slowly right": Vincent, from aft, reported his depth charges ready: *Saltash* began to tremble as the revolutions mounted, and the range shortened down to striking distance.

But this was to be no swift kill: perhaps, indeed, it was to be no kill at all. During the next hour, *Saltash* dropped a total of sixty-eight depth charges without, apparently, the slightest effect: the echo remained constant, the U-boat still twisted and turned and doubled back, with limitless cunning. It seemed as if no attack, however carefully calculated, was sufficiently accurate to bring her up short; they might have been launching snowballs into the fire, they might have been dropping cotton-wool bombs on the nursery floor, for all the difference their efforts made. Time and again *Saltash* swept in for the assault: the depth charges went down, the surface of the sea leapt and boiled astern of her; but when she came round again, in a tight circle, she found that her searchlight still shone on a blank sea, and presently she would pick up the contact again—always there, always solid, but never to be grasped, and seemingly unaffected by the fury of the at-

446

tack. "Sixty-eight depth-charges," thought Ericson wearily: "most of them had been pretty close: the men down there in the U-boat must be going through hell: why doesn't something happen, why doesn't it *work?* . . ." He shaped up for yet another attack, on a contact that was as firm as ever; and then he suddenly lifted his head, and sniffed.

"Number One!" he called out.

"Sir?" said Lockhart.

"Smell anything?"

After a pause: "Yes—oil," said Lockhart.

Oil. The hateful smell, which to them had always meant a sinking ship, could now mean a sinking U-boat instead. . . . Ericson, walking to the wing of the bridge, sniffed violently again, and the smell of oil came thick and strong to his nostrils: taken at its face value, it meant damage, it meant, at least, a crushed and leaking bulkhead inside the U-boat, and it could mean total. success. He ordered the searchlight to be trained right ahead, and there, where they had dropped their last charges, they presently saw the patch of oil itself—glistening, sluggish, reflecting the light most prettily, and spreading outwards in a heartening circle. They dropped another pattern of depth charges as they rode over the area; and then, as they turned in again, the asdic faded, and Lockhart reported: "Lost contact."

The silence that fell on the bridge seemed to be a self-congratulatory one, but it was not so for Ericson. He would have liked to believe in that patch of oil, and that fading contact which everyone else took to be the U-boat slowly sinking beneath the beam of the asdic; but he suddenly found that he could not. Oil, for his private satisfaction, was not nearly enough: he wanted wreckage, woodwork, an underwater explosion, bits of men weaving gently to the surface. Oil could come from a minor leak, oil could even be a subterfuge; the U-boat might have released some on purpose, and then crept away, leaving the feeble English sailors to celebrate their kill in feeble English beer. Oil, like wine, could be a mocker. . . . "She has gone deep again," he thought, with sudden, illogical conviction: "maybe she is damaged, but she is not

447

yet done to death: she will wait, and then come up again. We will wait too," he told himself grimly, with a new access of determination which must have come from the very core of his brain; and then, aloud to Lockhart, he called out:

"Carry out lost-contact procedure. I'm going to go on with the attack."

To his tautened nerves, it seemed as if the bridge personnel and indeed the whole tired ship had sighed as he said the words. "I do not care how sick of it you are," he said, almost aloud, instantly angry: "if I am the last man to keep awake in this ship, if I am the last man left alive, I will still drive her, and you, and myself, for just as long as I want to. . . ." But no one had sighed, and no one had spoken, save Lockhart who repeated: "Lost-contact procedure" to his asdic operator; and *Saltash*, settling down to her steady half-speed progress, began again her interminable search, as if the past six hours now counted for nothing, and they were starting again from the beginning.

The trouble was that, ludicrously, there was nothing to start on. For the second time the U-boat, with her leak or her oil-decoy, with her shaken or exultant crew, with her dubious amount of damage, had vanished.

Surveying the fact dispassionately, Ericson found it hard to believe: continuing to survey it, his dispassion gave way to the beginnings of a blind rage. When Lockhart had reported "Lost contact," he imagined that it was because of the disturbed state of the water, and that they would pick the U-boat up again in a matter of minutes, as had happened before; but when those minutes went by, and added up to five, and then ten, and then twenty, without a single trace of an echo on the asdic, he found himself face to face with the fact that they might have lost her. After seven hours of trying, after nearly eighty depth charges, after this enormous and sustained effort which was eating into the last reserves of his endurance. . . . He stood over the two operators at the asdic set, and looked down at the backs of their stupid doltish heads, and wanted above all else to take a revolver from the rack and put a bullet through the pair of them. *This could not happen to him*—the U-boat was *there*—they had had her almost in their hands, and now Lockhart and his two bloody fools of operators and his rotten set had let her slip away again. . . . When Lockhart reported, for the tenth time: "No contact," and added: "She could have been sunk, don't you think, sir?" Ericson, with a spurt of anger, answered: "I wish to Christ you'd mind your own business and get on with your job!" and strode out of the asdic compartment as if he could bear the infected air no longer.

But: "I should not have said that," he thought immediately, leaning against the front of the bridge: "it comes of being tired, it comes of losing the U-boat when we were so close. . . ." He turned round.

"Number One!"

Lockhart came out of the asdic hut, and walked toward him in the darkness. "Sir?" he said, with extreme formality.

"Sorry I said that," grunted Ericson. "Forget it."

"That's all right, sir," said Lockhart, who could rarely resist an apology, and certainly not one so promptly offered.

"I don't think she was sunk," went on Ericson. "Not enough evidence for it."

"No, sir," answered Lockhart. He did not agree, but this was not the moment to say so.

"I'm going back to that square search again. We'll keep at Action Stations."

"Aye, aye, sir."

"Not Action Stations, but sleep," thought Lockhart, returning to the set: "That's what I want, that's what he wants, that's what we all want: and we're none of us going to get it, because the obstinate old bastard won't listen to reason. . . ." He was quite sure, as was his leading asdic-rating, that the U-boat had been destroyed, crushed or battered to bits by the cumulative effect of seventy or eighty near-misses: she had probably collapsed, and was going down slowly, leaving that trail of oil which had so cheered him when he caught sight of it. But since it seemed that the

449

slightest hint to this effect was enough to start a riot, it was better to carry on, without comment. . . . He shut the door of the asdic compartment, and said, in a non-committal voice:

"Normal sweep. We're doing a box search again."

The senior rating on the set repeated: "Normal sweep, sir," and then sucked his teeth in unmistakable reproach.

"Don't make that filthy noise!" snapped Lockhart. "Without comment" covered that sort of thing as well.

"Hollow tooth, sir," said the man rebelliously.

"Get on with your work."

The rating, now breathing heavily, bent over the set and made an adjustment to it, as noisily as he could. They were all of them a bit short-tempered, thought Lockhart: it's catching, it's an inevitable product of tiredness. He smiled to himself as he looked at the asdic rating, who was normally one of his favourites: he could have quoted with reasonable accuracy most of the thoughts and phrases that were going through the man's head. (*All you get is threats and abuse.* . . . *The skipper gives him a rocket and he passes it on to me.* . . . *Bloody officers.* . . . *Roll on my twelve.* . . .) With just enough friendliness in his voice to bring things back to normal without surrendering his point, Lockhart said:

"We'd better have another brew of cocoa. This is going to take a long time."

It took a very long time indeed; and as the hours went by, without change, without significance, it began to seem as if the futile hunt might well continue to the end of time itself—or until, for some reason unrelated to their private effort, the war came to a finish, one side was declared the winner and the other not, and *Saltash*, receiving a postcard about the result, would be able to set course for home, in reasonable time to claim her old age pension. . . . *Pergola* joined them at three o'clock, coming up from the southeast at a speed that seemed to spurn the wasted hours of her diversion: her arrival enabled Ericson to extend the scope of the search, to guard the back door as well as the front, but she was no more successful than *Saltash* in picking up the scent again. The watch changed at four, the sky began to lighten from the eastward, illuminating a sea as grey and flat and worthless as a washed-out water-colour: it showed also the two ships, five miles apart, seemingly intent but scarcely convincing—in fact, plodding to and fro like a couple of myopic old women making the rounds of the dust-bins, not knowing that these had been emptied hours before.

To Ericson, the dawn, and the outlines of his ship, and the grey faces of the men on the bridge, brought a sudden bleak doubt. He could be wrong, he could be wasting his time, for two reasons that now began to appeal irresistibly: the U-boat might be many miles away, or she might have been sunk by their original attack. At this, the lowest hour dividing night and day, when *Saltash* had been hunting for eleven hours on end, and he himself had been on the bridge the entire time, he was assailed by the most wretched sense of futility he had ever known; the temptation to call the thing off, to take the oil patch at its face value and claim a victory that no one would seriously deny them—this nagged at him like a cat mewing endlessly outside a door, his own door, which sooner or later he would have to open. It would stop the noise; it would please the neighbours. And it would bring, for his own relief, the prospect of sleep. . . .

He was aware that all round him were men who had long ago made up their minds on these very lines: that Lockhart thought the U-boat had been sunk, that the hard-driven asdic operators were sulky and sullen for the same reason; that *Pergola*, reading the report he had given her, to bring her up to date when she arrived, must have wondered why on earth they had not packed up and joined the convoy hours before, signalling a definite kill to the Admiralty as they did so.

The doubt and uncertainty increased his weariness: slumping in his chair, with nothing to break the monotony and no glimmer of success to sustain him, he found himself in mortal fear of falling asleep. He felt his whole brain and body being lulled into a delicious weary doze by the sounds round him— the noise of the asdic, the slice-slice of *Saltash's* bow wave, the men washing down the upper deck: even the movement each half hour, as the look-outs changed and the helmsman was relieved, could be strung together as part of the same sleep-inducing chain. To resist it was agony, not to resist it gave him a feeling of sick foreboding: if he stayed awake he would begin to weep, if he slept he would fall off his chair, and then they would all think he was cracking up, and it would be true. . . .

Lockhart, who now had the watch, came out of the asdic hut, for the twentieth time, and said:

"Nothing on the recorder, sir."

Involuntarily, Ericson's nerves began to jump. "What about it?"

Lockhart stared. "Nothing, sir. Routine report. It's the end of another sweep."

"What do you mean, *another* sweep?"

Lockhart swallowed, as he had had to do many times during the past twelve hours. "I thought you said, sir—"

"Jesus Christ, Number One—" began Ericson, and then stopped. His heart was thudding, his brain felt like a box with a little bird fluttering about inside it. He thought: "This won't do at all—I really will crack up, I'll be shooting somebody in a minute. . . ." He stood up, and flexed his shoulders, sharpening and then easing the pain that lay across them. His head swam with the effort. But he knew now what he had to do next.

Two minutes later, down in his cabin, he confronted Scott-Brown, the doctor. The latter, routed out of his sleep as a matter of urgency by a startled bridge-messenger, was dressed in a pair of pyjama trousers and an inflated life-belt; he still maintained, unimpaired, his Harley Street air of complete dependability. He took one look at the Captain, and said, in a tone of reproof which Ericson did not mind:

"Time you turned in, sir."

"I know, Doc. But I can't."

"How long have you been up on the bridge?"

"Since that ship went down."

"It's too long."

"I know," repeated Ericson. "But I've got to stay there. Can you fix me up with something?"

Scott-Brown frowned at him. "Is it necessary? What's this all about?"

Ericson flared: "Christ, don't *you* start—" and then, his heart thudding again, he sat down suddenly. "There's a U-boat here," he said quietly, trying to conserve every effort, every urge of feeling. "I know damned well there is, and I'm going to get her. I want something to keep me awake while I'm doing it."

"How long for?"

"Another night, maybe. . . . Can you do it?"

"Oh, I can do it all right. It's just a question of—"

Ericson's nerves were starting to jump again. "Well, do it then," he interrupted roughly. "What does it involve? An injection?"

Scott-Brown smiled, recognizing the point where medical prudence succumbed to the lash of discipline. "Just a pill or two. Benzedrine. You'll feel like a spring lamb."

"How long will it last?"

"We'll start with twenty-four hours." The doctor smiled again, turning for the door. "After that you'll go out like a light, and wake up with the hell of a hangover."

"Is that all?"

"Probably. How old are you, sir?"

"Forty-eight."

Scott-Brown wrinkled his nose. "Benzedrine isn't a thing to play about with, you know."

"I wasn't intending to make a habit of it," said Ericson sourly. "This is a special occasion."

Another two minutes, and Scott-Brown was back again, with two grey pills and a glass of water. Ericson had disposed of the first one, and had the second poised upon his tongue, when the bell at the head of his bunk began to ring.

He bent to the voice-pipe, swallowing as he did so, and called out:

"Captain."

"Bridge, sir!" came Lockhart's voice, off-key with excitement. "*Pergola's* got a contact."

He felt like saying: "I told you so," he felt like shouting "Nuts to all of you. . . ." He caught Scott-Brown's eye, expectant, slightly amused: he said: "Thanks, Doc," and started for the door. Behind him, the doctor said: "In theory, you ought to lie down for ten minutes, and then—" and then the measured voice was lost as he turned the corner of the passageway and began to race up the bridge ladder.

Whether it was the benzedrine, or the feeling of eleventh-hour reprieve, or *Pergola's* activity, or the heartening effect of full daylight, he felt like a king when he stood on the bridge again, and looked round him. Now it was a different sort of scene. . . . Five miles away across the flat sea, *Pergola* was turning under full helm and at full speed: the water creamed at her bow as, coming obliquely towards *Saltash*, she roared in for her attack. She flew the two flags which meant: "I have an underwater contact," and: "I am attacking": she looked everything that a corvette, viewed at dawn after a long and exhausting night, should look. . . . Ericson called to Lockhart in the asdic hut: "Have you got anything?" and then there was a pause, and Lockhart answered suddenly: "In contact—starboard bow—bearing one-nine-oh!" and the asdic repeater began to produce a loud clear singing echo, on a cross-bearing that could only be the U-boat *Pergola* was attacking.

Pergola's charges exploded half a mile ahead of them: *Saltash*, weaving in at right angles to complete a lethal tapestry, dropped her own not more than twenty yards from the discoloured, still frothing patch of water. Then the two ships turned together, heading back towards the fatal area, ready to do it all again, but this time, this time there was no need. There came a sudden dull underwater explosion, clearly audible all over the ship: a great gout of oily water burst upward from the heart of the sea, and it was followed by other things—bits of wood, bits of clothing, bits of things that might later need a very close analysis. . . . Ericson called for Stop Engines, and *Saltash* came to a standstill, surrounded now by a bloody chaplet of wreckage; the crew crowded to the rails, the curious debris thickened and spread, a working-party aft got busy with buckets and grappling-hooks. This was a victory that called for trophies. . . . "It took us twelve hours," thought Ericson, leaning against the front of the bridge, hugely exultant, "but we did it, she *was* there all the time, I was right. . . ." He turned and caught Lockhart's eye—Lockhart, whose last attack must have been accurate to within five yards—and Lockhart smiled ruefully and said: "Sorry, sir!" to cover the past night of disbelief, and the bad judgement that had prompted it. But it did not matter now, and Ericson sat down in his chair, himself sorry for only one thing—the benzedrine which he need not have taken, which he should have saved for a really exhausting occasion. . . .

The bell rang from the quarterdeck aft, and Vincent said, in the voice of a man facing grisly reality rather too early in the morning:

"We've got lots of woodwork, sir, and some clothes, and some other things as well. Two buckets full."

"What other things, Sub?"

After a pause: "The doctor says, sir, they're clearly in his department."

The ring of men standing around the two slopping buckets, sipping cocoa and staring, were talkative in victory.

"What's the skipper want with this lot? Bloody-minded old bastard!"

"It's evidence. Got to take it home with us. They won't believe us otherwise."

"Only kind of a Jerry I ever want to see."

"Looks more like tripe and onions."

"Don't let on to the cook, for Christ's sake."

"Must be a month's meat ration there. Wait till I tell the wife."

"Coxswain," said Ericson, later that day, "where are those buckets stowed?"

"In the galley, sir."

Ericson swallowed. "I think we'll have them in the sick-bay for the rest of the trip."

"Sir," said Lockhart, "That looks like the Admiral waiting on the quay."

"Oh." Ericson, who was much preoccupied with bringing *Saltash* alongside, against a breeze blowing her offshore and a brisk tide under her stern, merely grunted. Then he said: "Stop starboard, slow astern port," and then: "I wonder what brings him here."

"It could be us."

"Stop port," said Ericson. "Hurry up those heaving-lines, or she'll blow out into the stream again. . . ." He took a quick look through his glasses at the quayside, and nodded. "Yes, it is us," he said. "That's really very nice of him. . . . Slow ahead port. . . . I hope we don't do any damage as we come alongside."

"Stern-wire ashore, sir. . . . I think he'd be prepared to forgive us, in the circumstances."

The water between the quay and the ship began to boil as it was squeezed outward: the wash of their screws surged and sucked at the oily wooden piles. *Saltash* edged nearer, cheating the wind, using the tide skilfully; the windlass on the fo'c's'le started a solid clanking as the head-ropes came in. The Admiral, catching sight of Ericson on the bridge, waved cheerfully, and Ericson saluted.

"Better have a piping party, Number One," said Ericson. "This looks official."

"Will you meet him, sir?"

"Yes. In fact I'll go down now, in case he does something athletic without waiting for the gangway. Take over here, and finish it off." He smiled. "Don't disgrace me, will you?"

It was a good ten minutes before *Saltash* was securely berthed, and Lockhart could give the crossed-hands signal that meant "Wrap up your mooring wires," and then ring off the engines. He delayed some moments longer on the bridge, savouring the fact of homecoming; watching the signalmen stowing away their flags and books, and the men on *Saltash's* fo'c's'le talking to other men on the quay, and the tide running past their hull, and the fair estuary of the Clyde which they had not seen for six long weeks. It was nice of the Admiral to come down to meet them, though after the rough convoy, and the U-boat at the end of it, they did perhaps deserve a little cherishing. Lockhart had watched the Admiral come aboard, while the pipes shrilled, and had seen him shake Ericson's hand, and talk smilingly for a moment, and then go below with him; he himself might be sent for presently, to share in the congratulations, but it did not matter either way—they had their U-boat, they were home again, *Saltash* was secured alongside after yet another convoy, they were due for a boiler-clean. . . . He called down to the quartermaster, still in the wheelhouse: "Pipe leave to the port watch from seventeen hundred to oh-eight-double-oh," and then he gathered his belongings together and made his way down the succession of ladders to his cabin. He was tired, and there was an ache in his legs, and he felt grimy and unshaven; but a hot bath and a couple of quick gins would cure most of that, and there was, at last, the blessed night for sleep.

From the passageway he saw a shadow move within his cabin, and he thought: "Oh God, what is it now?" and he pulled aside the curtain, and there, standing by his desk, was Julie Hallam.

They looked at each other for a long moment, he smiling, she grave and shy. Finally she said:

"Your steward is shocked. But he let me in."

He took her hand and pressed it. "Of course he did. No rules apply to you. . . . Julie, how lovely to see you, and how lovely of you to be here at all."

"The Admiral came down to congratulate you, so I thought I'd come too."

"I didn't see you on the quay."

"I was hiding behind a crane. My congratulations are different." Suddenly she put her arms tight round his neck, and said: "Oh darling, I'm so glad you're back."

457

He could not remember that she had ever called him "darling" before, and as his arms closed round her he felt weak with surprise, and with emotional reaction. How incredible to come back to this. . . . He said: "I'm afraid I'm rather bristly," but he kissed her none the less, and her lips met his warmly. Then he pushed her away with gentle hands, so that he could look at her face, and he said: "Are you really Julie?"

She laughed, giving him a complicated, confederate look, and said: "Well, anyway the uniform is the same."

"You seem different—you even feel different. What have you been doing?"

"Waiting for you—watching the plot—wondering what was going to happen next. . . . Oh darling," she said again, "what an awful convoy! Those aircraft all the time—and the destroyers—I thought you'd never get there. And then the weather on the way back, and that U-boat to finish up with. We must find you a shore job after this," she said, suddenly grave. "I can't go through all that again."

Now what is this, thought Lockhart—but he did not really want to know: the wonderful change was enough. To have Julie in his arms cured all his tiredness, and made the bare cabin unbelievably warm and bright: to have Julie in his arms, renewing the sweet past so willingly and adding so much to it, was a moment already overflowing. He kissed her again, and this time it was not a short kiss; and presently she turned in his arms and began to murmur into his ear:

"I didn't know anything about loving anyone, until a little time ago. I didn't relate things like parting or danger to you at all. The war was just the war, a convoy was just a collection of ships. You were you—everything was separate and manageable. . . . It was when I read your signal: 'Engaging enemy destroyers,' that I started to know all about it, and you and I were suddenly right in the middle of the pattern, and you were in frightful danger from it. I've never felt involved before, but from that moment I was terribly involved, and it was all you—you were the convoy, you were everything." She pressed him closely to her, rubbing and

458

smoothing the rough surface of the duffle coat. "You suddenly became very precious to me," she went on, in a low,
gentle voice, "and I knew I couldn't bear it if anything happened to you, and after that there was just the endless waiting for you to come back—four weeks, nearly five. . . ."
She smiled. "You see?—the uniform may be the same, but
inside, inside . . ."

"You're sweet," he said, "and I love you. What happens
now?"

"Anything you say—anything you want."

"Are you really Julie?" he asked again.

"New model," she answered. Her face looked especially
lovely as she said this, her eyes were full of a tender readiness. "I feel like a woman now, and it's totally new, and I
don't mind who knows it or what it involves. Say what you
want us to do."

"I'm due for leave," he said, hesitating.

"When?"

"As soon as I've got things clewed up here—in about four
days."

"Where will you go?"

"Anywhere."

"Somewhere with me," she said.

A shaft of sunlight, traversing the open porthole, moved
gently on the cabin floor; but they did not see it. For now
they were looking at each other, and their looks were no
longer complicated, but charged with a simple need, a simple
relief. He said: "I love you, Julie," and she answered: "That
is now a very two-sided arrangement," and held up her
mouth to be kissed.

[7]

It was a cottage, lent to them by a school-friend of Julie's
whose work had taken her to London. It was a cottage not
without drawbacks.

459

It lay deep in the wilds of lowland Scotland, at the foot of a glen near Loch Fyne: it was served by a single daily bus, and there were no shops nearer to it than five miles away. The place was old, stone-built, draughty: its wood fires smoked, its oil lamps, romantically dim, gave to every room a profound reek of paraffin. The roof over the kitchen leaked, and the kitchen itself boasted a villainous old cooking-range, from which food emerged either crisped to a cinder or stone cold. There were low, head-cracking beams in all the passages, and a staircase well designed for the twisting and wrenching of legs and ankles. The plumbing was primitive, the hot water system uncertain and often mutinous. It was damp. There were clearly mice. There was no one to look after them.

It was wonderful.

It was not wonderful all at once, but it became so within a little while, as soon as the main astonishing margin of their meeting had been crossed. When they got off the village bus, self-conscious with their suitcases, it was still early afternoon; before them was a half-mile walk up the deserted glen, and the half mile seemed to take them deep into constraint and uncertainty. "It will be all right as soon as I kiss her," Lockhart thought, opening the garden gate and standing aside for Julie to enter; "everything will come out straight, she will be just as she was in the cabin." But why then was this not a kissing moment? . . . When they started to explore the house, they did so almost in silence: Julie mounted the stairway alone, while Lockhart, listening to her footsteps and knowing that she was entering what was perhaps to be their bedroom, stood below and wondered if, after all, this was going to be a success.

Presently he heard her coming down the stairs again, and then she was standing in the doorway, watching him, gauging his mood. Then she said:

"What next?"

After a moment he answered: "It's damp. I'm going to light lots of fires."

"Do that. . . ." Then she smiled, equally at herself and at

their joint embarrassment, and crossed nearer to him, and said: "We can't expect to step into this all at once," and then, more certainly: "You can take it for granted that I *do* want to be here with you"; and after that it was, for the next few hours, all right.

But there was still the evening, and then the night.

Darkness came early on that November day; soon after sunset, the glen filled with shadows, the small house merged gradually with its background, and the frosty night descended, holding them hidden in its firm hand. They ate, they talked, they listened to music on the old battery radio; the house was now warm, their setting seemed private and unassailable. But to Lockhart, the darkness brought back with it straightway the constraint of the afternoon. It was new and moving to be with her alone, in this enclosed world on which he had been fixing all his thoughts: she looked lovely— her hair loosely bound, her eyes dark and large in the lamplight: she wore a housecoat so feminine, so gracefully accented to her body, that it made her seem another person altogether. But against the implication of desire, there was tension between them, the sweet defeating tension of uncertainty: perhaps she had caught it from him, perhaps hers was of her own making, but on his side it sprang from a doubt as to whether, even now, they were to be lovers. Certainly, the right true end of love was there for them, but he could not decide whether they were due to reach it, or whether it was something she did not really want.

He sensed in her the same continued change that had brought them together—not dependence, but a readiness to give the lead into his hands: he sensed it, he could see it often in her glance and hear it in her voice, and he was mortally afraid of misusing it, of crossing too soon or too robustly the frontiers of her will and compliance. Worse things than diffidence sprang from this fear. Perhaps he had even made the whole thing up, he thought, with something like panic lest he should commit himself upon false ground: perhaps she had never meant that they should be lovers, but just that they should spend their leave together. Perhaps he did not deserve so beautiful a woman, perhaps he would be no good anyway.

It was she who cured the foolish moment of uncertainty, and she cured it with a single swift stroke that recalled, on the instant, the old Julie, the capable and competent person who disposed decisively of ships and people, and always looked round for more. Though this disposing was on a somewhat different plane. . . . They had been listening to the radio, he standing by the fire, she lying back on the sofa; and seemingly on an impulse she got up and walked across and kissed him. It seemed natural now that, as they stood clasped gently together, still listening to the music, the beating of their hearts should begin to overlay it. . . . A woman's voice on the radio sang a song with the phrase: "To hold you close to my eager breast," and at the words he felt Julie's body stir under the thin material of her dress, and then she lifted her head and said softly:

"Did you hear that?—that's exactly what it feels like."

Lockhart said: "That is what it feels like to me, too," and she smiled lovingly, and as if to explain beyond question the urgency that now began to flow from all her body, she answered: "I think I am wooing you," and after that it came all right once more, and it came all right for ever.

Perhaps it was the contrast that was most moving: the tender refuge after strife and slaughter, the softness welcoming his hard body. It was, indeed, a contrast for both of them: he had come from the rough demanding school of war, she from her astringent dedication in the same field. They had been preoccupied, and therefore celibate; it had suited them until they met, and then it suited them no longer. But the surrender of this celibacy was overwhelming: it did all things: it astonished by its sweetness, it drowned in sensual fervour, it cleared magically the brow. . . . There had been nothing in their previous meeting, nothing indeed in their lives so far, that had promised or pointed to such a tempest of feeling and such a relief thereafter.

Lockhart awoke some time before dawn on that first night,

after the deep drugged slumber that had claimed them both; and when he felt her stir near him, and heard her murmur: "You should be still asleep," he answered: "There are other times for sleep," and he struck a match and lit the candle by the bedside, for the pleasure and comfort of seeing her again. What he now found in her was as moving as all the offering of the previous night, all the ready tumult. Her face on the pillow was tenderly relaxed, framed by the dark wayward crown of hair: her eyes, large and soft, now regarded him as if he were a beloved child that had done something especially pleasing, especially to be rewarded. Her eyes had been lovely before, on a cool plane of perfection: now, having seen and answered his ardour, and then softened to release and sleep, they had a residual contentment that caressed him and the air between them with grateful recognition, with warmth and a happy languor she need not deny.

She reached out both arms in greeting, uncovering for him her bared breast; and as he slipped within her embrace, and they continued to stare at each other, her look as for a beloved child changed into a look of a different sort—welcoming, acquiescent, humble, and assertive within the same fervent pattern.

He took her in an intent trembling silence that neither wished to break.

After that they did not sleep: it was as if their second love-making, unravelling the sweet, strange fact of the first, released them now to enjoy all the rest of what they could give each other. They talked, unhurriedly, till morning, while the grey light, filling the glen again, seeped gently into their room: of all the countless dawns of the war, thought Lockhart, this was the first tranquil one, the first one when nothing could harm him, the first one with the lovely label "Julie." . . . They talked of many things: of loving and being loved, of what attracted them in each other, of their nervousness the previous evening: the process of bringing themselves and each other up-to-date within their small corner of history was easeful and exciting by turns, and deeply healing to all past fears and ordeals. "I have won her," thought Lockhart, looking beyond Julie to the window-square of light that announced the day: "I must keep her also—it is not just those eyes, and the body that is cool and hot at the same time, pure and shameless, her own and then mine, by quick turns, as I wish it and as she wishes it: this is the *person* for me—she makes sense of it all. . . ." He turned on his elbow, looking down lovingly at her, and she met his glance with clear pleasure, and said:

"You are pale. . . . What are we going to do today?"

"Well—this," said Lockhart, with little hesitation.

"It has my vote also." She eyed the ceiling speculatively. "But wasn't there some talk, a long time ago, of your being a Puritan?"

"That I am," he answered determinedly. "Who are you to doubt it?"

"I am a girl to whom a lot of nice things have been happening, almost continuously. . . . What is your brand of Puritanism, and why do you tell me all these terrible lies?"

"They aren't lies," he said, with seriousness. "I'm not a sensual person at all, really. You make me so, but then you are you. . . . There's been nothing like this in the war for me—nor ever, for that matter. It's a complete change, a complete break."

"A break with what?"

"With reality, I suppose."

"Look," she said decisively, "I do not like to be in that category."

"I mean," he said, floundering a little, "that there's the war—you've come as a lovely surprise in the middle of it—I wish to God you could alter it for ever—but it's still there—"

"And you'll just go back to it afterwards?"

"I can't go back the same, but I have to go back. We both have. Julie," he said, seeing in the half-light the hint of a smile on her face, "you don't have to try to put me in the wrong. I do it quite well myself. . . ."

"My Puritan," she murmured, "how can I make you love me?"

"There are three ways," he said with energy, steering

away from the doubtful ground. "You must look as you do now, you must feel as you did a couple of hours ago, you must talk as you do always. Even separately, they are irresistible. Together—" he stopped.

"Was it really two hours ago?" she asked innocently.

"Yes."

"Puritanism indeed. . . ."

"I refuse to be put in the wrong over *that*. . . ." Attracted by a new and delicate sound, he turned towards the window. "Do you know," he asked after a pause, "that it is snowing?"

She raised herself to look out of the window, showing her breast and shoulders a warm glowing white against the coarse sheets. "How lovely!" she exclaimed. "Now no one can reach us for days. . . ."

"For ever," he said. "Snow on—we have eggs, we have many things in tins, we have a large ham from Canada. . . ." The isolation that had threatened to be an embarrassment, on the previous night, now seemed the prime blessing of their lives. "Snow on, snow us up completely. Leave us here in peace."

"And your war?"

"*The* war," he corrected, "need never reach Loch Fyne, and we need never see it again. . . . My darling," he said, lying back once more, "it is now seven o'clock, it is snowing hard. You said: 'What shall we do today?' and I said— what did I say?"

She leaned over him, confidingly close again, swiftly warm and alive, as if what she had heard in his voice were linked to something deep within her. "I seem to remember," she murmured, "that you said: 'This.' "

"What is 'this'?"

"This."

She had beckoned him sensually, that first night, and she never ceased to do so, whether it was by a smile or a look or a movement, whether by a motionless ecstasy or some candid intonation of her voice—as when she said, stroking the

smooth skin of his chest: "You must light lots of fires again—
I can't tell you how few clothes I'm going to wear, during
the next nine days. . . ." For it had a deep, an astonishing
strength for her, too. Occasionally she would surprise him
by her wildness in love-making, the tender and tormented
clenching of her body. "My storm," he would whisper at the
end—and as if that were a signal, he would feel the en-
gulfing wave of her passion begin to break under him, and as
if *that* were a signal, his own would break with hers, surging
together upon the shore of their delight.

During all those days and nights, the dream-like haze in
which they moved seemed to grow deeper, transfixing, sub-
merging them both. Her eyes, her voice, her cordial body all
ravished him; and she also, guiding and submitting at the
same time, seemed able to make of his body a weapon for an
extreme private rapture.

They often became, for each other, special people not alive
before.

[*8*]

When, back on the Clyde, they had to part—Julie to her
austere office, Lockhart to sea again—he wrote her in farewell a letter of love and deep gratitude, marked here and
there by a tender reminiscent carnality—the sort of thoughts
he was bound to have, after so moving an interlude. It ended:

> *I don't think there is anything more to write except that you
> have become incalculably dear to me, and that the things it is
> grounded in are the things I want above all others. They are
> NOT all centred round that region of your body for which I am
> sure there is some startling piece of Wrens' slang; but it's idle
> to deny that they include it, as closely and as happily as it,
> last night, included me. I now adore you.*

PART SIX

1944: *Winning*

[*1*]

The ship worked for some months of the new year, the fifth in the dreary succession of the war; and then, for *Saltash* and her crew, there came a strange and sudden holiday. They were at St. John's, Newfoundland, waiting between convoys, when the news reached them; the brief signal told them that they were to have a refit, with the long leave that went with it. But they were not to return home for the occasion; they were to dock on the opposite side of the Atlantic, in the Brooklyn Navy Yard in the heart of lower New York, and there enjoy a two-months' rest.

"New York!" said Lockhart, when Ericson showed him the signal. "What's wrong with the Clyde?"

"Too crowded, probably," answered Ericson. Then he smiled. "You can't have all the luck all the time, you know."

Lockhart met the smile, ruefully acknowledging what had been in his mind. "I won't see her for ages," he said glumly.

"War is hell," said Ericson, with cheerful conviction. He welcomed the prospect of the refit, wherever it was to take place, and the news that they were to spend it in novel and attractive surroundings had put him in a holiday mood already.

"America," grumbled Lockhart again, frowning down at the signal. "Never heard of the place. What do they know about repairing ships?"

But that criticism, at least, did not survive their arrival,

467

four days later, off Long Island Sound, and their sailing past the Statue of Liberty, up to the fabulous skyline of New York and the entrance to the East River, and into the teeming maw of the Brooklyn Navy Yard. Not less than anyone on board, Lockhart found himself reacting to the first impact of America. The country might, from the English point of view, be rather a long way from the centre of affairs; but, judging by the evidence so far, going by size and noise alone, these people *must* be able to do things. . . . The impression of efficiency was presently confirmed, when *Saltash* came alongside and was invaded by a horde of quick-moving, entirely silent men who paid no attention to anyone on board, but simply set to work tearing things to bits.

"Now just you take a rest, Commander," said one of the dockyard officials, when Lockhart asked some question about shore-lighting. "We'll fix your ship up real pretty. . . . Know what I'd do, if I was you?" he added, with no alteration of his expression. "I'd get to hell out, and come back around six weeks from now."

"It's so difficult," said Lockhart later to Scott-Brown. "You don't even know whether they're being rude or not. . . ."

"It works both ways," said Scott-Brown judicially. "*They* don't know whether our feelings are hurt."

As soon as they were docked, and before any shore leave was granted, Ericson addressed his crew on the quarterdeck.

"We're here," he began, "primarily because the shipyards at home are too busy to take us for refit, but that doesn't mean that we'll do badly out of the exchange. I'm quite sure that this shipyard will look after us just as well as one on the Clyde or at Liverpool—and if anyone thinks otherwise, I want him to keep it to himself. There are two or three things," he went on, "that I want to say about our stay here. First is that, as soon as we go ashore, we are guests of this country—and guests have to behave themselves especially well, they have to fit into their host's house and into his habits, even though they don't find it easy. Anything else is bad manners—and don't forget that people here will judge

England by the way you behave. If you are noisy and rude, that means that England will get the same reputation. . . . Secondly, no matter how differently things are done here, don't criticize them out loud—and above all don't laugh at them until you're quite sure that Americans are prepared to laugh at them too. It's even possible that they do some things better here than they do in England—and even if that's not true, it doesn't do any good to make comparisons about different methods and different standards." He paused. "The other thing I want to mention is your own personal behaviour. I hope you'll make lots of friends. But don't try to overdo it, especially where women are concerned. Just because you're in a foreign country, that doesn't mean that every woman you meet is a potential prostitute, and that you can treat her like one. Treat women as you would at home—because they *are* the same as the women at home: there are the good ones and the bad ones, and they're in exactly the same proportion as they are in London or Glasgow. You'll find," he ended, "that the beer here is rather weak, but the whisky's rather strong—and cheap. If you want to get drunk, do it in private. Don't fall flat on your face in Fifth Avenue, because that's liable to get into the newspapers, and—" he became briefly stern, "no one in Royal Naval uniform, and especially no one from this ship, is going to get into the newspapers, in that connection or in any other."

[2]

The radio building was large, shiny, and bustling: the studio where Lockhart was being interviewed resembled an aquarium, through whose glass walls other men and women, ridiculously silent, moved their mouths like suppliant fish.

"Just a short talk," said the program organizer, a grey man with a look about him of secret and permanent torture. "But plenty of action, of course. Let's see, now. . . . Have you sunk a lot of submarines?"

"Only two," said Lockhart.

"Gee, that's too bad. But we'll think of something. . . . Have you worked with the U. S. Navy at all?"

"We've run across one or two of your destroyers. We haven't worked in a group with them."

"It'll come, it'll come," said the other man, with a faint flicker of encouragement. "Just as soon as you get yourselves organized. . . . How long have you been on combat duty?"

Lockhart hesitated. "What do you mean by combat duty, exactly?"

The radio man stared. "Gee, Commander, you're out of touch, aren't you?"

"Yes," said Lockhart, "I'm terribly out of touch."

"Well, I want to do this program, anyway. It's a cinch from the Allied solidarity angle. And they said you gave them a right smart talk yesterday, at—where was it?"

"Women's Section of the Bundles for Britain organization."

"Sounds like Mother's Day in hell. . . . Well, let's get something down on paper."

In a corner of the huge popular restaurant on Times Square, Scott-Brown, the doctor—correct, austere, self-sufficient—was enjoying a singularly tender steak. At his side the waitress, a buxom young woman dressed in frilly apple-green, watched him intently, hand on hip. Each time he conveyed anything to his mouth, her interest seemed to reach a new crescendo.

When he became aware of the scrutiny, Scott-Brown turned and smiled. The waitress answered the smile, with a ready twist of shoulders and hips.

"You a Limey?" she asked, after a pause.

"Yes," said Scott-Brown politely, "I'm from England."

The waitress nodded, enormously pleased. "I can tell you boys a mile away, just as soon as you start on the meat dish. Know why?"

"No," said Scott-Brown. "How do you recognize us?"

The waitress pointed at his left hand, then at his right.

"Knife and fork stuff," she answered. "Both hands together, like you was driving a team or something. No one else does that. Kills me every time."

Midshipman Holt stepped into the automatic elevator behind a large tough-looking woman with blue-white hair. They were alone in the elevator, and there was silence as it began its descent. Then the woman, who had been eying the two white patches and the twisted braid, denoting his rank, that marked Holt's lapels, said suddenly:

"Say, can you tell me something?"

"Certainly, madam," said the midshipman, who had dined well for his age.

"It's those things on your jacket." She pointed to the white collar-patches. "What's it mean?"

"I'm not really allowed to tell anyone," said the midshipman.

"No kidding?" said the woman. "I think you English are the cutest things."

"But I'll tell *you*," said the midshipman, with an alarming leer. "It means the secret service—M.I.5."

"No kidding?" said the woman again. She beamed at him. "So young, too."

Ericson stood on the bridge of the new American destroyer, saying nothing, watching how they did it all. He was very glad to be on board, making the trip down the Sound as a guest on one of the ship's working-up exercises; a day at sea, after he had been so long tied to the land, was exactly what he wanted.

The American captain bent to one of the voice-pipes. "What are you steering?" he asked his quartermaster below.

"Two hundred degrees, sir," came the answer, in a ripe New Jersey accent.

The American captain turned to Ericson, smiling in a vague and friendly way. "Fine day," he said. "Glad you came along. . . ." Then, forgetful, he bent to the voice-pipe again. "What are you steering down there?"

"Jesus, Captain!" came the same voice in answer. "I just told you."

"They're not a bit like us," said Johnson, the engineer-officer, looking round the wardroom dinner table, reproof in his voice. "No discipline at all."

[3]

My darling one [Julie wrote] *I'm starting a baby—at least I think I am, and the frogs will say yes or no tomorrow. I'm sorry. I thought of not telling you, and then I thought how close we've become, and so I'm telling you after all. But even so it is nothing to worry you with. It hasn't happened before, because we haven't been lovers before, but it isn't the end of the world: I'll take a quick trip to London, where (you once told me in a lordly sort of way) they understand these things. You are not to worry.*

But come back soon: it is lonely, it is dull, it is a little ache of missing you, all the time. New York women may have everything else to commend them (you must make me a list of what they have) but they haven't got this heart that beats and warms for you. I will show you what I mean as soon as we are together again; and please make that as soon as possible.

Lockhart held the letter for a long time, without moving; it was as if her heart were lying in his hand. Swift pictures of her multiplied, just behind his eyes: feelings of shock and of tenderness strove within him, making him guilty and deeply loving at the same time.

The letter was so exactly like her. There was no panic, no reproach, no query of any sort: she had accepted the situation, and was about to deal with it competently. Perhaps she had done so already. In any case she seemed in no doubt that he would agree to what she had in mind.

Her ready acceptance, her competent planning, hurt something deep within him. She was accepting the situation, taking for granted her next step and his endorsement of it, because of his own clumsy manœuvring: because he had said, or implied, many times, that they could not think of marriage until the war was finished with, that their love and their loving had been "a break with reality."

He remembered the crass words with shame and disgust.

He knew now that they were not true. She was the person he must have, not some time in the future, but now: he needed her—to love and be loved by, to salve the dreary war, to keep intact the bright warm promise that lay between them, whether they were together or apart.

The child would be the occasion of their marriage, not the reason for it. That reason was something deeper, stronger, more moving altogether. They had found it when they became lovers—perhaps a moment before—and it was not to be lost again. Not by his act, not by hers.

The simple fact was that she had become a precious part of his life, always to be cherished and now to be made sure of; and behind this need of her loomed his huge regret, and the hideous idea of her body being tampered with.

He cabled: "Have it," and then sat down to write to her all that was in his heart.

[4]

"It's an absolute fact," Scott-Brown told them, wonder still lingering in his voice. "There were these two people sitting at the next table to mine: an old chap with white hair, the kind you see in *Esquire*, and a young person with all the bosom in the world, and a mink coat to match it. They were talking of this and that—I couldn't help overhearing—and then suddenly the old chap leaned across—it was lunch time, mind you, and bright sunshine as well—and he said, in a very respectful way: 'Little lady, I sure would like to po-sess you.' "

"What was the answer?"

"She said—" and here Scott-Brown's voice reached an extreme pitch of disbelief "—she said: 'Honey, I'm just brushing and combing my hormones.' "

"Of course," said the man in the bar, "we Americans take a different view of women altogether, from what you folks do."

"I understand that is so," said Raikes, the navigator, who had been in the bar longer than most people.

"Yes, sir," said the other man, who had been there almost as long. "We put them right high up on a pedestal."

"Very wise," said Raikes. "Best way of seeing their legs."

"And then," said the man, who wasn't listening, "we bring them tributes of candy and flowers, and we respect them."

"That ought to do the trick," said Raikes.

"That's why," said the man, "America is the only country in the world where women are one-hundred-per-cent safe all the time. Our young American girls," he went on, developing his theme with relish, "are clean and decent, without a wrong thought in their heads—and that's particularly so in the State of Missouri, where I come from. Our American homes are sacred, our American mothers are honoured throughout the land, and our American womanhood is universally held to be the purest in the world."

"Good show," said Raikes.

"Did you say something about legs, Captain?" asked the man presently.

"Yes," said Raikes.

"I'm a tit man myself."

"It was between dances," said Raikes modestly. "We went out into the garden, and she said: 'You're welcome,' and I was."

474

"I noticed that it didn't seem to take you long," said Scott-Brown austerely.

"She seemed to have some sort of quick-release gear round her waist. No trouble at all."

"As long as it doesn't harm Anglo-American relations."

"Huh!" Raikes snorted. "It's nothing to what the Yanks are doing to ours."

"They're not a bit like us," said Johnson severely. "No morals at all."

[5]

Lockhart wrote to Julie, from the New York hotel where he was spending a week's leave:

I've been playing poker most of the night, with some news-paper men. What good company they are—and how grand all the Americans have been to us; and, after nearly two months, how I long to get back to you! Now it is Sunday, Sunday dawn: the birds are tweeting, the cards fall from the nerveless hands, the Regency scene dissolves. I love and think of you, even in this cold un-tender hour on the fourteenth floor of a New York hotel: I think of being married to you soon, I think of the child you are guarding for me.

But are you with me, in this dawn? Are you sleeping, are you restless, do you think and dream of me also? Is our cottage, where we first were lovers, in your dream? Are there seagulls crying, is there wet heather to walk through, do we hold hands, is there a stirring somewhere in both our bodies: does love live, does it grow, does it move for us? What are your eyes like, your trembling lips, your breast that stroked my own? What is there for us in your dream, in your waking?

No, the hour is not cold, not un-tender: you are ever wanted, ever missed: you are Julie always, my sensual sister and child

475

*and loved one. I reach out for you now: we have shared many
dawns, we said good-bye on one, many weeks ago: we share
this one again, horribly divided—but the same birds sing, the
town stirs, the light comes through the curtain, I touch you and
hope you will wake. Wake, sweetheart: that was a kiss, that
was a hand on your shoulder. But how warm you are. What
were you dreaming of? Was it of this?*

*Oh sweet, dawns are still like that, even masculine ones
when the room is wrecked by empty glasses and cigar-ends
and smoke and stale water in the ice-bucket. Perhaps it is bad to
write like this, bad to send it to you; but it is no cruel reminder
—these things are there for both of us, all the time, and soon,
very soon, we will find them again. And now, in this belated
dawn, you are kissed and bidden farewell.*

[6]

"Halt!" said Chief Petty Officer Barnard. "Off caps!
Signalman Blake, sir."

"What's the charge, coxswain?"

"Did leave a piece of chewing-gum adhering to the signal-
projector, sir."

"Oh. . . . You must keep your equipment clean, Blake,
whether we're likely to go to sea or not. Otherwise you'll
get into trouble. Caution!"

"Caution, sir. On caps! About turn! Double march!"

"Chewing-gum, coxswain? How revolting!"

"We've been here too long, sir."

"Don't come down to breakfast," Ericson's host had said,
when wishing him good-night. "We none of us do on Sun-
days. Get your sleep, and I'll have it sent up to you."

Now, lying in bed on a bright Sunday morning, listening to
a far-off radio and to some vague farm-noises below, Ericson
waited for the promised breakfast. Physically he was at

ease, but his thoughts did not match his body; this bed, this comfortable and cheerful room, this kindly welcome should have been all that he wanted, but they were not—they had a sour taste of guilt about them, which he could not dismiss.

It was the fault of the war, of course, the war they were escaping. *Saltash* had now been out of action for two months, and she would not be ready to go for another fortnight or even three weeks: though the Brooklyn Navy Yard had proved efficient and co-operative, the delay was due to engine-room spares that could not be conjured out of the air.

Ordinarily, nothing would have been more pleasant than this lazy holiday. But the times were not ordinary, and the holiday could not be accepted save shamefacedly: while they lived on the fat of the land, the war went on, and other people carried it, people who had not had breakfast in bed for five years, and who usually had a rotten breakfast anyway. . . . In their welcome, the Americans had been kindness itself—witness the present invitation, a surprise approach by a complete stranger; but Ericson and his ship's company had been in debt to that kindness for too many weeks, and it was sapping and destroying all the hard, built-up training of the war. The waiting had put everything out of gear—men as well as machinery: *Saltash* now seemed to him a useless run-down hulk, shirking the battle; and her crew, strangers to the sea, were becoming in the process strangers to all but the most negative aspects of discipline.

The plain answer was that they had been there too long, and there was no cure except to go away and start being serious again, and that was still out of his hands.

There was a knock on the door, and a pretty child of ten or eleven, wearing bright red dungarees, came in, bearing a piled-up tray.

"Good morning, Commander," she said, with the utmost self-possession. "How did you sleep?"

"Very well, thank you."

"I'll bring you the funnies just as soon as I can, but—" she explained seriously, "in this family it's very hard to get hold of them before noontime."

"There's really no hurry."

"Dad says, eat a good breakfast, and then maybe you'd feel like playing a little golf."

"I haven't played for a long time," said Ericson, "but I'd like to walk round."

"That's fine. . . . Dad also said," she went on, eying him gravely, "that I wasn't to say anything about your accent. But it sure is cute."

"Thank you. What's your name?"

"Ariane. For my grandmother. It's kind of French." She looked down at the tray. "Here's breakfast. Is it enough?"

Ericson's eyes followed hers. Breakfast consisted, besides coffee, of three large oval-shaped dishes; and on them, neatly arranged, was a composite meal that was difficult to take in at a single glance. Its basic items were bacon, sausages, two eggs, some kedgeree, a piece of fish, four things that looked like scones, mustard, marmalade, a tomato, a fried banana, three slices of toast, and a waffle with a load of maple syrup.

"It's enough," said Ericson. "But stay and talk to me."

"I'd like to. I mustn't stay long, though—I've got work to do."

Disputes, sometimes small, sometimes big. Disagreements about how to do things, how to run countries, how to win wars. Arguments with workmen on board, with waiters ashore, with men in bars and women in bed. Slow grumbling in the mess-decks, quick flare-ups at parties: stately or sulky anger when other people would *not* see the point of view. Leave-breaking, coming aboard drunk: a row with a dock policeman, a complaint about molesting that came near to rape. Recollection of what things were like in England; resentment against comfort in the midst of war.

Remembering, sometimes mentioning, those first two years of neutrality, while Britain took it and bled and went broke. Fights, arguments, futile comparisons, bitterness, boredom. All part of the stagnation period, the waiting to get on with it.

"Sounds to me like you British are kinda burned up because

Patton's troops are going ahead, and yours are stuck down somewhere."

"It isn't that. It's just that we don't like noisy generals."

"The trouble with these people," said Lockhart, "is that you can't help liking them, even though you know you oughtn't to. . . . Do you remember what it was like, back in the middle Thirties? They lectured us for years on end, about stopping Mussolini, stopping Franco, stopping Hitler: it was a pretty safe lecture to give, three thousand miles away across the Atlantic. When war did break out, they waited over two years before they came into it: waited while we were Dunkirked and bombed to hell and lost nearly two thousand ships and Christ knows how many men: while we bankrupted ourselves, while we gave them almost all our overseas investments to buy arms, while we signed away British possessions like Bermuda and Antigua, in exchange for fifty destroyers that were never out of the repair dock. Then they did decide to come in themselves. With a rush? Like hell. . . . They came in because they were attacked by the Japanese, and for no other reason: if it weren't for that attack, we'd still be waiting—and so would Hitler. If ever there's another war," he said dreamily, "I shall stay out of it for at least two and a half years; in the meantime, I'd send plenty of instructions on being brave and standing firm, and I *might* start an organization called 'Bundles for Both Sides'— it would depend on how nice people were to me. . . . But when this one is over, the thing to be will be an American. They'll be running the world, because we'll be broke and exhausted: they'll be in charge of everything—these charming dunderheaded children who can't see round the very first corner of history, these products of a crapulous chauvinism—"

"Steady!" said Allingham. "Fighting words. What do they mean?"

"They mean that I still like the Yanks, but I miss my soapbox. Have a rum 'n coke, bud."

. . .

479

"The trouble with these people," said Johnson gloomily, "is that they've no common sense. They're not a bit like us."

[7]

He began to read it again, without understanding it at all—the terrible letter from a friend.

> *You will have heard about Julie Hallam, [it said] horribly sad, and the worst luck in the world. She would never have been in the picket-boat at all if she hadn't been standing in for another girl who was ill. I gather it wasn't anybody's fault: they were making the long trip back from Hunter's Quay, late at night, and a bad squall blew up which no one could warn them about. Perhaps the engine failed as well. None of us here knew anything about it for hours, and then a man rang up to say he'd seen the picket-boat's lights disappear, and was it important? . . . By that time, even if they'd been able to swim round at all, they couldn't have survived the cold long enough to get ashore. We got all the bodies in the end—seventeen, mostly libertymen, but four Wrens among them. I thought you'd like some details, as I knew you were a friend of hers. We miss her here very much. When do you and Saltash get back to the war?*

Better, perhaps, to hear like this—almost accidentally, from a man who thought you knew already, a man not fumbling for the first foolish phrases. But drowning. . . . The fearful images slipped readily before Lockhart's eyes, because he knew Julie so well, because he knew drowning by heart: he saw the spread hair round her lolling head, the murky river rolling her over, the embryo child growing cold under her breast. Ophelia, he thought immediately: something about "poor wretch"; and with sick apprehension he recalled the exact phrase—"and dragged the poor wretch down to muddy death." Mud in Julie's eyes and nostrils, mud clogging her livid throat: icy cold attacking her, and then the sucking currents where the river met salt water.

It was like *Compass Rose* again, though this time it was a single sword. But the same enemy had robbed him: a small wave of the cruel sea had taken her for ever.

Better to hear like this, pierced unawares as by an ill-chancing thrust in the dark. But drowning, Julie, drowning. . . .

He was walking alone among tall buildings, buildings that crowded in but failed to crush him, leaving the top of his brain fatally free to think and feel. "Men have never cried on this street," he thought: "no tears on Eighth Avenue"— but what did the rules matter, when every rule in earth and heaven had been broken at one stroke? He had lost the immediate pictures of Julie dead: now it was the ache, the grip of bereavement, and the wild self-reproaches that went with it—how he should never have left her, how he should have married her straight away, how perhaps he had killed her, by betraying his dedication, and hers. . . . She had even been dead when he sent his last letter: he had been writing to a wraith, a spirit, a poor pale Julie who, when he tried to reach her, could only whisper and fade and leave him cold and alone, as he was now: stricken and shivering, among the crowds and the traffic and the buildings that would not fall.

Suddenly, up the street, he saw her coming toward him: Julie herself, with her dark hair piled up, Julie walking with that odd economical gait which was still the most feminine thing about her. Weak with shock and with longing, he waited for her to reach him: it *was* she—no one else walked like that, no one else had that lovely hair, that shape of head. It was she: the letter must have been wrong; even the countries had got mixed up.

When she had only a few more steps to go, he reached out an uncertain hand, and with it the crazy spell broke and his brain cleared agonizingly.

The stranger passed him, staring.

Something about "another country," he thought. Some man from the grave once more sharing the shroud of his thoughts. Julie had died to such thoughts, such words, such mournings. . . . "But that was in another country, and besides, the wench is dead."

Now it was not the vile image of death, nor the ache of loneliness: now it was a wild desire to be away, to work, to do something to kill time and memory.

Up on the fo'c's'le, coiling down a wire, a man had made a clumsy job of it. "Look," Lockhart began, in mild rebuke, and then he had remembered, and turned away, unable to finish the sentence, leaving the man puzzled and relieved. But "Look" had been Julie's phrase, whenever she wanted to claim his attention. "Look," she had said, "you don't know what love is," and: "Look—if you want *anything* from a woman, it is to be from me." To stumble thus upon the word "Look," upon the very voice and touch of her wrapped in an innocent phrase, was enough to destroy him; it seemed that it might do so utterly, unless he could somehow exorcize the past. For now, pinioned by misery, he was the target of every stray dream, every longing that before had been thankfully referred to her.

"Dry sorrow drinks our blood," he had thought; and presently, down in Ericson's cabin, appealing almost wildly: "Can't we get away? Can't we start?"

"Soon," answered Ericson, watching him with compassion that was very nearly love. "Just as soon as we can. You know I'll do my best."

[*8*]

It was, cruelly, a good time to be dedicated, a good time to flog the body and the brain; for when *Saltash* did return, it was to a wonderful moment—the beginning of winning.

It was not yet victory: the enemy still had snapping teeth,

and still used them when he could; but it seemed that success could now be sighted, far away at the end of the enormous tunnel of the years, and that *Saltash* was returning to a conqueror's ocean. They had been away only two and a half months, but already it had happened, already the wonderful change was apparent, Another colour seemed to have been added to the Atlantic, another blue to the sky; at night, the stars pricked a heaven full of the balm of victory. For after four and a half years of deadly struggle, when both sides, locked in combat, had stung themselves to a vicious and mortal fury, the enemy had begun to crack.

It showed itself in small things, it showed itself in big. It showed in the number of U-boat sinkings—ninety were sent to the bottom during the first five months of the year: a single escort group on a single twenty-day cruise accounted for six at one stroke. It showed in the huge convoys that went unharmed across the Atlantic, pouring the stuff in for the last assault; in March, for example, only one merchant ship was sunk, out of the enormous total that crossed and re-crossed the ocean. It showed in U-boat tactics, which had become a pale shadow of what they had been in the past: now, cautious and indecisive, they broke off the battle as soon as resistance was met, and they exhibited no sort of readiness to come back for more.

It showed in an ignominious surrender at sea, with the U-boat captain the first to start swimming toward the ship that had attacked him. It showed in a signal that came from *Rose Arbour*, one of the corvettes, when *Saltash* rejoined and took over command of the group.

"Glad to see you back," ran the message. "We were afraid you'd miss the last act."

May, 1944, was not *quite* the last act, but it was near enough for the signal to make cheerful sense. The lights were brightening for the final scenes: there could not be many of them, and the play was now too far advanced for there to be any chance of a surprise ending.

But before that ending could be reached, the soldiers had one more thing to do.

[*9*]

On the bright and awful morning of D-day, *Saltash* found herself, for the first time in many months, in unfamiliar waters. She was one of a number of support groups, patrolling in a wide ring across the mouth of the English Channel: they were there to intercept any U-boats that might be tempted to leave the dubious shelter of the Atlantic and make for the invasion beaches. They were, in fact, on guard at the back door, and Ericson, for one, felt very glad that he was doing a job connected, however loosely, with the main fabulous assault. On June 6, 1944, there was only one piece of land and water worth concentrating on; and any soldier, sailor, or airman who could not join in was missing an irretrievable moment of history.

Stretching far out of sight on either side of them, the lines of destroyers and frigates and corvettes wove a search pattern that covered five hundred miles of water. It needed patience, that endless patrol—with the news coming over the wireless every half hour, with the knowledge that, one step beyond the horizon, the huge armada had just delivered its first thrust. Viewing the battle from afar, knowing what was involved, they could only hope and pray: the men in the escort ships stood on guard at a distance, but others, fighting and dying as *Saltash* circled peacefully, were making this the most solemn and moving moment of the war, in which an outsider must take a truly humble part.

"I'm glad we got as near as this, anyway," said Ericson, standing on the bridge and watching out of the corner of his eye the rest of his group turning at the limit of their search area. "It's not exactly spectacular, but at least we're part of the main operation."

"I wish we could have gone across with them," said Lockhart wistfully. "*Some* frigates did. . . ." He looked outboard, where far away to the northeast the outline of Land's

End and the Scilly Isles lay like a purple shadow on the horizon. "It's funny that, in all these years, this is the only time we've ever been anywhere near the Channel."

"Good moment to make the trip," said Allingham, who was also up on the bridge, drawn there by the feeling they all shared—that this was not a day for being alone, or shut off from one's friends. He looked at his watch. "Midday already. Wonder how it's going."

"It's *got* to be all right!" said Lockhart, almost violently. "This is the whole point of the war. . . . It's just our luck to be on the wrong side of the wall."

It was the first time any one of them had felt involved in any theatre of war except their own. But on this day, the great Atlantic was nothing: all the sea war and all the land had shrunk down to a few miles of beach, a few yards of shallow water, and nothing else counted at all.

Saltash guarded the back door. Northward to Land's End, eastward up the Channel to Plymouth Sound, southwest toward Brest—the area altered daily, but the intention and the drill were the same. As a safety measure, the patrol proved well worth while; the U-boats *were* leaving the Atlantic, to try (as they thought) the rich and easy pickings waiting for them off the Normandy coast, and the dozens of escorts that barred their way were in a position to score decisively. The U-boats never did get through, save in negligible strength, and they never came to grips with any of the cross-Channel convoys: in trying to do so, they suffered losses as heavy, proportionately to their numbers, as any of the war.

Saltash herself, with *Streamer* in attendance, added one to the quota of loss: she cornered her quarry close inshore, off Start Point on the Devon coast, and blew it to the surface with astonishingly little trouble. But it was odd, and faintly alarming, to be hunting a U-boat to its death and at the same time keeping a sharp eye on the depth of water under their keel, and the rocks lying off-shore: it was the first time they had ever had to worry about lack of sea-room, and it seemed as if they had left their proper element altogether and were splashing about, naughtily chasing goldfish in a pond. The crowds of people waving to them from the nearest headland were the final disturbing item. This was not the Atlantic pattern at all. . . .

But it was good to justify their existence at such a time, when others were doing so in such brutal and bloody measure. Otherwise, thought Ericson, they hardly counted in the main tide of war at all: they remained on the outside looking in. Even his own son was more closely involved. *His* ship had gone in on D plus 3. . . .

Back, soon, to their Atlantic beat, which now seemed like patrolling the streets of a dead town that everyone had deserted in favour of something more interesting. Now it was, in truth, a victorious ocean: scarcely a U-boat was to be seen, and huge convoys—one of them a record one of 167 ships—made the journey unmolested, bearing the vital supplies that the expanding battlefields of France must have. Some of *Saltash's* charges were now routed direct to Cherbourg—a strange turn of fate, compared with the old days, when they had, with enormous difficulty, under constant air and sea attack, crept mouse-like into Liverpool Bay. . . . But that was the way of it now, and so it continued to the end of the year: the U-boats, denied their bases in the Bay of Biscay, were being pushed back to Norway and even to the Baltic—and the Baltic was a very different matter, when it came to trying to keep up the pressure in the Western Approaches.

There was plenty for the Navy to do, because the needs of the cross-Channel shuttle service meant that there was a chronic shortage of escorts; and there was always a chance that German strategy might change, and try to strangle the supply-line at the Atlantic end. But it was mostly hard, monotonous sea-time, with nothing to brighten it and no crises to cope with: it was rather like the first months of the war, when there were not enough U-boats to make a show, and what few there were had not yet worked out a plan of campaign.

1944: *Winning*

Now they had had their campaign, and it was five years later, and for all the good it had done them, they might have saved themselves the trouble, and spared many ships and men.

But perhaps it had to be proved, thought Ericson, bringing *Saltash* up, for the twentieth time, alongside the quay at St. John's, Newfoundland, with a featureless fourteen-day crossing behind her, and the ship needing nothing except fresh stores and a lick of paint. Perhaps it had to be proved, and there was no other way of doing it, no other way of sleeping peacefully in their beds, save at the fearful cost that lay in their wake.

[*10*]

Christmas in home waters, Christmas at anchor in the Clyde.

They all felt that it was the last Christmas of the war, but the thought was never phrased aloud, for fear of reprisals from history. They had a wardroom party, but it was just like other wardroom parties: they drank a lot, Ericson joined them and then left at a discreet moment, the stewards got mildly drunk and upset the brandy-butter sauce on the turkey. At the head of the table, Lockhart presided, observing custom automatically: this was like last Christmas, and the Christmas before that—part of the war, part of the job that never ended. Last year there had been Julie, this year there was not: it was sad if you thought about it, so you didn't think about it: you ate and drank and chaffed the midshipman about *his* girl. . . .

That afternoon, while the ship slept, he had paid a visit to the hideous mass grave where she lay. But there was no special feeling, even about that; it was just a cold day, and an ache inside him, and being alone instead of being together. The usual empty thoughts, the usual hunger and wretchedness.

"Number One!"

"Sorry." He jerked to attention. "What did you say, Mid?"

"I've got the bachelor's button out of the pudding."

He made an appropriate comment.

Presumably things would get better, after a time.

PART SEVEN

1945: *The Prize*

[*1*]

A nd that is why," said Vincent, plodding to the end of his
lecture, "it was absolutely essential to go to war in the
first place, and why it's even more important to make sure
that we do a proper job of winning it now."

He shut his notebook with an unconvincing snap, and put
on top of it the *Army Bureau of Current Affairs* booklet, on
which his lecture had been based. Then he looked up, facing
uncertainly *Saltash's* lower mess-deck, and the rows of stolid
men who were his audience. The serried eyes looked back
at him unblinkingly, with very little discernible expression:
a few of them were bored, a few hostile, most of them were
sunk in a warm stupor: they were the eyes of men attending
a compulsory lecture on British War Aims. As on so many
previous occasions, thought Vincent, the heady magic of
ABCA had not worked. . . . He cleared his throat, sick
of the whole thing, knowing only one way to play out time.

"Any questions?"

There was a pause, while silence settled again; many of
the eyes dropped or turned aside, as if fearful of establishing
contact with Vincent at this crucial moment of demand. The
dynamos hummed loudly; *Saltash* swung a point to her anchor, and the shaft of sunlight through the porthole moved
across the deck and over the feet of the men in the front row.

A man at the back cleared his throat, and spoke at last.
"Sir?"

"Yes, Woods?" It was bound to be Signalman Woods: Woods always asked the first question, sometimes the only one. Woods was hoping for a recommendation for Leading Signalman, and Vincent was the only man who could give it to him.

"Sir, if we get rid of all the Nazis, who'll run the country? Germany, I mean. Who'll be the government?"

"I should really encourage him," thought Vincent, "I should say: 'Now that's a very interesting question.' But it's not, it's a bloody silly one, because it means he simply hasn't been listening at all."

"*As I mentioned,*" he said, with just enough emphasis to make the point, "we are quite sure that there are enough non-Nazis in Germany to form a proper government. All they have to do is come forward, and—" he finished lamely "—that is what will happen."

"Thank you, sir," said Woods politely, his effort accomplished. "I just wanted to be sure."

Silence settled again. "This should be a brisk and lively discussion," thought Vincent sadly, "but it isn't working; there ought to be a quick series of questions, a little argument, a fresh approach by some highly intelligent sailor, a great upsurge of speculation on this crucial question. . . ." Most of the failure was his own fault, he realized; the matter interested him, but he had not been able to communicate that interest to any of them; it had been just another lecture period, filling in the time between Stand-Easy and Hands to Dinner—preferable to gun-drill or painting ship, not as interesting as playing tombola or doing nothing.

But here was someone else with a question, one of the stokers for a change. "Sir," said the man haltingly, "when you said about fighting for a better world. . . ." But had the phrase sounded as appalling as it did now? "Did you mean the League of Nations, like? No more war?"

A better world, thought Vincent—now how could he sum it up in terms that would mean something to a second-class stoker who had been a boilermaker's apprentice before the war? He knew in his own mind what it involved—the Four

Freedoms, the rule of law, an end to tyranny, the overthrow of evil; but he had listed all these things in the course of his lecture, and explained them as best he could, and gone into detail whenever detail was worth while—and clearly it had meant absolutely nothing to his questioner, it hadn't made a single ripple. . . . "I can't go through it all again," he thought despondently, "there isn't time, and there's no point either, if the words and phrases that mean so much to me are meaningless to this man, this roomful of men like him."

"The League of Nations, or something of the same sort," he said, "will certainly be part of the postwar world. One of the things we've been fighting for is that international law should become strong again—that is, if one nation wants to start a war, the rest of the world really will combine to stop them. But when I talked about a 'better world,'" he swallowed, "I meant a better world for everyone—freedom from fear, no big unemployment, security, fair wages—all those sort of things."

Silence again. Had his words meant anything to them, Vincent wondered: did they kindle any spark?—was there indeed a spark to be kindled?

Another man spoke, simply, doubtfully. "Is it all going to be different, then?"

What was the answer to that? I hope so. "I hope so," he said.

A third man spoke, scornfully, out of some personal political copy-book he carried forever in his head. "There'll always be the bosses. Stands to reason."

"That's outside this discussion," thought Vincent—"and yet, should *anything* be outside this discussion? If this man has been fighting for a world without 'bosses,' why shouldn't he say so? If he thinks that his particular fight has been a failure, why shouldn't he say that as well? But it isn't really a fight about bosses—not in the sense he means; and I very much doubt whether he gave that aspect of it a single thought when he enlisted, or was conscripted." Yet "bosses" or "no bosses" *was* a postwar problem: it could even be true that the war, obscurely, was being fought to end the whole range of boss-tyranny—big bosses like Hitler, little

491

bosses like the foreman with the rough tongue. If that were true, then it was a dangerous subject: the pamphlet hadn't said anything about the master-and-man relationship, it had treated with oppression at the international level only. . . . And that was what he had failed to interest them in— the large-scale pattern, the moral issue: those things had rung no bell at all.

He was about to answer non-committally when Signalman Woods came through again, this time in prim reproof.

"It's got nothing to do with the bosses. That's a lot of talk. It's war aims—what to do when we've won."

At that there was a final, blanketing silence: the moment of spontaneity was lost for ever. Last week's lecture had been so much better, thought Vincent; but then, that had been on venereal disease. . . . He cast about him for some phrase that might stimulate further questions, and found none; the subject had been dealt with, the potent leaven distributed, and the result now confronted him, unalterable, totally defeating. Then, far away, came the sound of a pipe: the audience brightened and shuffled: the pipe came nearer, and with it the quartermaster's voice: "Hands to dinner!" There was movement at the back of the mess-deck, a stirring, a heightened receptivity toward the first attractive idea of the morning. Vincent picked up his papers.

"That's all," he said. "You can carry on."

Back in the wardroom, Allingham looked up when he came in.

"What's the matter, Vin? Brassed off?"

"Yes," said Vincent. He went to the sideboard and poured himself a drink. "I don't think these lectures of mine are much use."

"What was it this time?"

"War aims—postwar prospects. . . ." He swung round. "It ought to be interesting. It *is* interesting, to me. But it doesn't seem to raise a single spark, for anyone else."

"For some of them, surely," said Allingham helpfully.

Vincent shook his head. "No. . . . It's so difficult to make it sound convincing, or even to explain it properly. And morally speaking, people shouldn't really be called upon to fight, if they don't understand the real issues and wouldn't believe in them if they did." He looked at Allingham with curiosity. "Do *you* think it matters?"

"That we should explain—dress the war up a bit, make it a matter of conviction?"

"Yes."

Allingham considered, frowning. "I used to. I started the war like that, anyway. Now I'm not so sure. We've got to win the bloody thing, whatever material we use—willing or not. . . . Perhaps it doesn't make a hell of a lot of difference, either way, when it comes to action—fighting, danger. Able Seaman Snooks doesn't shout: 'Another blow for democracy!' when he looses off a couple of rounds at an aircraft: he says: 'Got the bastard!' if he hits, and: '—— it!' if he misses. He just doesn't want to get killed, and he doesn't need any special inspiration or moral uplift for that."

"But you feel the need for it yourself?"

"I don't even know that. I came a long way to fight this war, and I thought it was some sort of crusade then—but maybe I'd have come anyway. . . ." He smiled, and rose, and came towards the sideboard and the gin bottle. "No good being left out, you know, even if you're an Australian."

"But if it's just a *war*," said Vincent despondently, "it's not worth winning, it's not worth all the trouble."

"It's even less worth losing," said Allingham, with conviction. "That's one thing sure. . . ." He raised his glass, and drank deep, as if toasting the prospect of victory and survival. Then he smiled again. "Cheer up, kid! It's too late to worry about it now, anyway."

[2]

Now there was a lull—but it seemed a friendly, not a foreboding lull: this was the pause before going on holiday, not the halt on the edge of the grave. The transatlantic convoys went on, unceasingly, but convoys were different now—once again, they were like the convoys at the very beginning of the war: ships and men occasionally ran into trouble, but they were always other ships, other men— strangers who had had bad luck, amateurs who had probably made some silly mistake. . . . For the most part, the U-boats held off, for a variety of reasons which could only be guessed at: it might be fear, it might be insufficient numbers, re-organization, the saving of strength for some huge final effort. Whatever it was, the spring of that year gave them what all springs should give—ease, hope, and promise, in abundant measure.

For Ericson, it was a lull that he needed—he and *Saltash* together. One could perhaps divine more of the past history of strain from looking at *Saltash* than from looking at Ericson; but that did not mean that Ericson was not feeling it just as strongly. . . . His men had become used to his grey hair, his gruff manner, his stern face which looked with an equal indifference upon a sinking ship, a dead man, a defaulter with a foolish excuse, a pretty visitor to the wardroom. This mask hid his tiredness; *Saltash* had no such camouflage. She had now been running for over two years, hard-driven years with little respite from the weather or the enemy: she was battered, salt-streaked, dented here and there—a typical Western Approaches escort, telling her whole story at a single glance. Ericson, surveying his ship as he put off in the motorboat, sometimes found himself wondering what *Compass Rose* would have looked like, if she had still been alive and afloat. Not as pretty as he remembered her, certainly; for some of the original corvettes, which had seen it through in the Atlantic since 1939—*Trefoil*, *Campanula*, their own *Petal*—looked like tough and battered old women who had been streetwalking too long. "So do I, by God!" thought Ericson grimly. It was his fiftieth year, and he looked and felt every hour of it.

"I'm thirty-two," Lockhart told him on one occasion, in answer to his question. "The best years of my life have vanished. . . ." But that was not really true, Lockhart

494

knew well enough: for him, they were not lost years, in spite of the futility and wastefulness of war. He had grown up fast in the meantime, he was a different person from the twenty-seven-year-old, goal-less, motive-less, not very good journalist who had joined up in 1939. War had given him something, and the personal cost was not a whit too high: he had missed five years of writing and travel, but he had gained in every other way—in self-discipline, in responsibility, in simple confidence and the rout of fear. . . . "I should be all right after the war," he told himself sometimes: "because they can't muck me about any more, and I can't muck myself about, either."

For him as well as for Ericson, the lull in action was welcome, the more so since he saw it as an appropriate part of the pattern: it was the way things ought to be going, at that stage, to ensure that they would have the hoped-for outcome. "If I were writing the story of this contest," he thought, "this is where the book would tail off, because we've reached the moment when nothing happens—we're just winning the war, and that's all there is to say." That would be the whole point of the story, really—that in the end nothing happened, and it petered out into silence. The petering out was their victory.

" 'And enterprises of great pith and moment,' " he quoted to himself vaguely, "de dah, de dah, de dah: 'and lose the name of action.' " But thank God the enterprises had done so: thank God for being alive on a fine spring morning in 1945, when he had never really expected to be, and when lots of people, who for five years had been trying to kill him, were dead themselves. Now in truth nothing was happening, and nothing was just what they had been aiming at, all along.

If only Julie had been alive as well, to share the moment with him, to give it warmth and happiness as well as its cold satisfaction.

[*3*]

April. . . . April, in the Atlantic, brought the last few
strokes of their war; and one of them, involving a homeward-
bound convoy that *Saltash* was taking in to Liverpool, gave
them the most unpleasant surprise they had had for many
months. After the lull, the recent weeks had been startlingly
and dangerously active: the enemy still had about seventy
U-boats able to keep at sea, and though the brief and violent
flare-up cost thirty-three of them sunk, it cost many merchant ships as well. On one of these occasions, *Saltash* lost a
ship on the very front doorstep—inside the Irish Sea, within
sight of home. The ship was hit close to the bows, and she
sank slowly, with little likelihood that any lives would be
lost; but even so, the sudden mischance, at that late hour of
the convoy and the war, had an evil element of shock.

They watched *Streamer* counter-attacking, on the other
side of the convoy, but they could still scarcely believe that
it had happened: it was the end of the war, the U-boats were
virtually defeated—*and no U-boats operated in home waters
anyway*. They had been aware that April was proving a bad
month at sea, and that the enemy seemed to be making a last
vicious effort to avert defeat; but it had never been brought
so close to them, they had never seen it proved in so violent
a fashion. It induced a sense of discomfort, a nervous foreboding, which lasted long after the situation had been set to
rights. If this sort of thing could still happen, it not only restored the wicked past—it threatened, in an extreme degree,
the promised future as well.

"You silly bastards!" said Raikes, aloud, when the flurry
was over—the U-boat neatly dispatched by *Streamer*, the
merchant-seamen rescued from the water: "You silly bastards—you might have killed some of us." He echoed all
their thoughts at that moment: their hopes of staying alive,
their prickling haste to get the thing over before they ran
into any more danger or took any more chances. In the

whole of the rest of the war, there might only be two or three more convoys for them to escort: in the whole of the rest of the war, it was possible that only one more escort ship was going to be sunk. "Make it not us," they thought —"not at this stage, not so late in the day when we have very nearly finished, very nearly survived. . . ."

Raikes, up on the bridge, had spoken for all of them; and later, in the wardroom, they returned to the subject, with a readiness that showed how deep an impression the torpedoing had made on everyone in the ship.

"It gave me the shock of my life!" said Allingham, downing one drink very quickly and reaching out for the next one. "U-boats in the Irish Sea—at this stage? They must be stark staring crazy!"

"Crazy or not," said Scott-Brown, "it happened, and it can happen again. Particularly if it's their last chance, and they know that it is. They'll go all out, and they won't care what happens as long as they do some kind of damage. That was a suicidal attack, this afternoon—but they made it, all the same. We've probably got to expect that sort of thing, and worse, in the future."

"All I hope is that we don't get in the way of the next one," said Raikes. "I haven't lived as long as this, just to stop a torpedo when we're nearly home and dried."

"It would certainly spoil my war aim," said the midshipman, with decision.

"But it's the end of the fighting!" said Allingham, violent emphasis in his voice. "We're over the Rhine, we've nearly joined up with the Russians, Hitler himself may be dead by now. What do they hope to gain by it?"

"Perhaps nothing." Vincent, who had been sitting quietly by the stove, spoke suddenly. "They're just going on fighting, that's all. . . . If it were we who were near defeat, wouldn't we do the same thing, however hopeless it looked?"

He glanced round the wardroom, waiting for an answer.

"I should do exactly what I was told," said the midshipman modestly. "But I don't think I'd volunteer for anything special. . . ."

"But if it were really hopeless—" Allingham began, and then stopped. After a moment he smiled at Vincent. "You're right, Vin—it *is* the only thing for them to do, and I hope we would do the same. They've got bags of guts, you know—you've got to hand it to them."

"They can have any sort of testimonial they like," said Scott-Brown, "as long as they don't try to earn it by sinking *Saltash*."

Raikes nodded. "That's just what I thought this afternoon. It may sound a bit selfish—but this is such a bloody silly time to be killed."

[4]

May—and now, surely, now at last nothing could go wrong, nothing could steal their victory, nor take their lives.

Saltash, divorced from the rest of her group, had been on independent passage from Iceland when she received the unusual signal: "Remain on patrol in vicinity of Rockall"; and there she now was, steaming in a five-mile square round the isolated, inexplicable pinpoint of rock which was really the tip of a mountain in mid-ocean—Rockall, rising from the depths of the Atlantic to break surface, by a few feet only, 300 miles from land: Rockall, the unlighted, shunned graveyard of countless ships, countless U-boats. But, Ericson wondered, why Rockall?—unless their Lordships wished to place a finger on *Saltash* in case of need; and why "on patrol"? —unless she were waiting for something that did not require an escort group, something that one single ship could do.

"I think this is the end of it," said Ericson privately to Johnson, when they were discussing the fuel situation. "How much oil have you got in hand, Chief?"

"About two hundred tons, sir. Say, fourteen days' steaming, at normal speed."

"I don't think we'll be moving very fast. We're just hanging around, at the moment."

Johnson looked at him curiously. "How long for, sir?"

"I don't know, Chief. Till the bell strikes."

Saltash steamed her slow circle. There were no ships to be seen, there were no convoys in her area: it was just a stretch of grey, flat-calm sea, with the gaunt rock in the middle, the horizon round them, the dull sky overhead. The radar screen was blank, the asdic probed an endless empty sea: *Saltash* turned ninety degrees to port every half hour, and in between times traced an uneven zigzag course, in case anyone were watching them. "We've done this before," thought Ericson—"in this ship, and in *Compass Rose* as well: once when we were hove-to with a damaged merchantman, once when we did a box-search for survivors, once when we were too early at a rendezvous." It had always been the same sort of exercise—waiting patiently, searching endlessly, keeping on the move in case of surprises. Now they waited, in the same way, but this time not knowing what it was they waited or searched for. They turned their ordained circles, first under a grey sky, then under a black, then under a grey again; they sweated out the successive watches, steaming at a steady ten knots and getting nowhere, doing what they were told and hoping the answer would come soon, before something went wrong, before this simple merry-go-round turned to wicked witchcraft, on the authentic Atlantic pattern.

Ericson told no one what it was about, because he did not know himself and there was therefore nothing to tell; there was just the bare signal-log, which anyone could see, and the order: "Remain on patrol." In his private mind, he knew that they were waiting for the end of the war—but that was guesswork, not to be shared because it had no backing from authority. The signal-log, the last explicit order from the Admiralty, was all they had to go on.

Once Raikes, when he was Officer-of-the-Watch, said:

"I hope they don't try any tricks. It's a rotten time to be killed."

Ericson frowned. "That hadn't struck me," he said, somewhat coldly. "But it'll be a rotten time for anyone who tries to kill *us*."

The expected signal came at dawn, on a dull calm morning that saw *Saltash* still circling the rock, still occasionally weaving a cunning variation of her course, still plodding along as ordered, and serving three meals a day, and remaining keyed up for any danger, any last attack.

"Hostilities terminated," it said. "All U-boats have been ordered to surrender by German High Command. The surrender signal is a large black flag. You should take appropriate precautions against individual enterprise. The two U-boats that are presumed to be still in your immediate area should be escorted to Loch Ewe."

"Immediate area?" said Ericson. "It's a libel. . . . We'll wait for them to show up."

The beaten foe emerged.

All over the broad Atlantic, wherever they had been working or lying hid, the U-boats surfaced, confessing the war's end. A few of them, prompted by determination or struck by guilt, scuttled or destroyed themselves, or ran for shelter, not knowing that there was none; but mostly they did what they had been told to do, mostly they hoisted their black surrender flags, and said where they were, and waited for orders.

They rose, dripping and silent, in the Irish Sea, and at the mouth of the Clyde, and off the Lizard in the English Channel, and at the top of the Minches where the tides raced: they rose near Iceland, where *Compass Rose* was sunk, and off the northwest tip of Ireland, and close to the Faeroes, and on the Gibraltar run where the sunk ships lay so thick, and near St. John's and Halifax, and in the deep of the Atlantic, with three thousand fathoms of water beneath their keels.

They surfaced in secret places, betraying themselves and their frustrated plans: they rose within sight of land, they rose far away in mortal waters where, on the map of the battle, the crosses that were sunken ships were etched so many and so close that the ink ran together. They surfaced above their handiwork, in hatred or in fear: sometimes snarling their continued rage, sometimes accepting thankfully a truce they had never offered to other ships, other sailors.

They rose, and lay wherever they were on the battlefield, waiting for the victors to claim their victory.

Two rose to *Saltash*, off Rockall.

They saw them on the horizon: the two hard shapes topping the sea level stood out like squat battlements: they could only be U-boats—the hated and longed-for targets that were now part of the rubbish of defeat.

"Two submarines in sight, sir," said the starboard lookout, stolidly submitting the most unusual report of the war; and *Saltash* began to speed towards the meeting, coming to Action Stations as she did so. "Keep her weaving, coxswain!" Ericson called down to Barnard, and *Saltash* listed sharply as the wheel was put hard over, and the ship began to trace a swaying corkscrew pattern—the precaution Ericson had decided on, as soon as the present occasion arose. No desperate last-minute torpedoes for him. . . . When they drew near, they saw that the two U-boats were side by side, and stationary: their black flags dropped at the masthead, their decks were crowded with men—as were *Saltash's* own. *Saltash* swept round them, moving at twenty-two knots in a tight, high-speed circle, listing heavily, following the U-boats with all her guns; the frigate's solid wash set the smaller craft rocking, and the men on the decks clung on as best they could, and occasionally shook their fists.

"What do we say to them?" said Ericson, who was clearly enjoying himself.

"Herr Doktor Livingstone, I presume," said Lockhart.

"How about a warning shot, sir?" suggested Allingham hopefully.

Ericson laughed. "I know your finger's itching, Guns, but I don't think there's anything to warn them about." He considered. "Perhaps a depth charge would be a good plan, though—not too near, not too far away—just close enough to shake them. I want them to behave properly on the way home. Tell Vincent the idea—one charge only. He can drop it whenever he's ready."

The depth charge exploded at about the same distance from *Saltash* as from the U-boats; there was thus no possibility of damaging the latter's pressure-hulls. But the single heavy charge, detonating with a crash somewhere near the surface of the sea, had a marked effect on all concerned. The mountain of water that shot upward cast a dark shadow over the U-boats: the fine spray, falling slowly back, moved across them like a damp and drifting curtain. When it cleared, it was as if those on board had been through some sort of moral shower-bath as well: most of them raised their hands over their heads, there was some confused shouting on a querulous note, and a man climbed up the mast and spread out the black flag, so that it could be better seen.

"They've got the idea," said Lockhart, who was watching through his binoculars.

"Glad they can take a hint." Ericson picked up the loud-hailer microphone, and spoke through it. "Can you understand English?"

Affirmative waves and nods came from both U-boats.

"University types," said Raikes.

Ericson raised the hailer again. "That was a depth charge," he said hardly. "I have nearly ninety more of them. . . . You give no trouble, otherwise—" he gestured ferociously "—*donner und blitzen!*"

"Damned good, sir," said Lockhart. "Make 'em sweat."

"Could you spell it, sir?" asked the hard-pressed signalman whose duty it was to write out whatever messages left the bridge.

"We are going to Loch Ewe in Scotland," continued Ericson, making it sound like a father's unalterable curse. "What is your speed on the surface?"

Faintly across the water came an answering hail: "Ten."

"It'll take us about two days," said Ericson aside to Lockhart. "I think we'd better steam in line abreast—I don't

want these bastards pointing themselves at me, however subdued they're feeling. . . ." He spoke into the hailer once
more. "Get your men below decks. Form up one on each
side of me. The course is one-oh-five degrees—one hundred
and five. . . . Do you understand?

More waving, more acquiescent nods.

"Off we go, then," said Ericson. "Do not alter your course
for any reason. Do not signal to each other. Burn navigation
lights at night. And don't forget those depth charges."

"Isn't this a mistake, sir?" asked Holt later that afternoon. He pointed to something on the signal-log. "This signal addressed to the Admiralty. 'I have collected two Ewe-
boats'—spelled E—W—E."

"We're taking them in to Loch Ewe," explained Ericson.
"It's a joke."

After a moment the midshipman said: "It's a jolly good
one, sir."

"All right, Mid," said Ericson, looking at him. "I won't
make any more."

But the curious convoy was not to have a quiet run home;
their holiday mood suffered a last disturbance, and the jovial
toughness that had prompted Ericson to give the U-boats the
full benefit of *Saltash's* wash, and then to shake them up with
a depth charge, was brought into action once more, this time
with crude anger to back it up.

It happened on the afternoon of the second day, when they
were nearing the Butt of Lewis, the northernmost tip of the
Outer Hebrides, which marked the entrance to the Minches
—the front drive to their home. The two U-boats had behaved themselves with perfect propriety during the past
thirty hours: their courses could not have been straighter,
their navigation lights at night had been models of brilliance.
As a matter of precaution, however, Ericson had kept his
asdic-operators at work, though there seemed little chance
that they would have anything to report; when in fact they

did get a contact, and a strong one at that, dead ahead of *Saltash*, the resulting flurry cancelled the whole end-of-the-war feeling at the first shrilling of the alarm bell.

Ericson brought his ship immediately to Action Stations: whatever the echo was, he was taking no chances, and if it were in truth a U-boat that was disobeying the order to surface, it was either still fighting the war or else playing the fool. He felt in the mood to punish both those things. . . . He signalled to his two prisoners: "Stop instantly, and stay where you are," and as the U-boats obeyed, and their way fell off, *Saltash* increased to Full Ahead and went in, prepared to attack. Lockhart said: "It feels like a U-boat, sir, on the same course as us," and Ericson answered: "We'll drop a pattern, Number One. They may not have heard the news."

The "Stand by to drop!" warning had already gone to the depth-charge crews aft, when the U-boat rose a hundred yards ahead of them, breaking surface in a sluggish, take-it-or-leave-it manner that seemed designed to indicate that it was only doing so because it chose to.

"Stop both!" ordered Ericson. "Port twenty!" *Saltash*, losing speed, came round in a circle under the U-boat's quarter, while Ericson looked at the wet grey hull through his binoculars. "I suppose," he said grimly, "this is meant to show that they haven't really been beaten. It would serve them right if—"

He did not finish the sentence, but within his own mind he found that he was wrestling with a violent temptation. He wanted above all else to continue with the attack—the absence of the black surrender-flag gave him legitimate excuse; he wanted to ram, or to shoot it out, or to toss a depth charge right alongside the target: he wanted to show them that the war *was* over and the U-boats defeated, and that a British frigate could send them to the bottom, any time she felt like it. He wanted, at this last moment, to prove how easy it was, by increasing his total war-score from three U-boats to four. . . . He stood stock-still in the centre of his bridge, recalling an old anger—the way he had felt when the U-boat captain, down in his cabin, had started throwing his weight about. Bloody Germans . . . Now a man in a high-peaked cap appeared in the conning tower of the U-boat, looked about him with leisurely care, and then stared through his glasses at *Saltash*. Another man climbed up by his side and stood there, doing nothing in an unconcerned sort of way.

"Still playing the fool," grunted Ericson. "Guns!"

"Sir?" said Allingham, from his place at the gun-control microphone.

"Fire a shot over his conning tower. As close as you like."

Allingham spoke his orders: B-gun roared: the shot fell with a great tawny spout of water, fifty yards beyond the U-boat.

"That must have just about parted his hair," said Holt.

It seemed that it might well be the last shot of the long war. The two men lost their air of indifference on the instant, and waved energetically; others began to climb alongside them into the conning tower, and then to overflow onto the fore-deck. A black flag jerked upward on the short ensign-staff, and a signal-lamp started to wink with frenzied speed.

"Signal, sir," said *Saltash's* yeoman presently. " 'I will not fight you.' "

"I don't mind if you do," said Ericson, in prompt and stentorian tones over the hailer. He waited for an answer to the challenge, but none came. Some more men, leaving the conning tower, now ran along the deck of the U-boat, their hands high above their heads.

"That's more like it," said Ericson. And over the hailer, crisply, finally: "Take station with the others, and follow me."

[5]

So their battle ended, and so, all over the Atlantic, the fighting died—a strangely tame finish, after five and a half years of bitter struggle. There was no eleventh-hour, death-or-glory assault on shipping, no individual attempt at piracy after the surrender date: the vicious war petered out in bubbles, blown tanks, a sulky yielding, and the laconic order: "Follow me." But no anti-climax, no quiet end, could obscure the triumph and the pride inherent in this victory, with its huge cost—thirty thousand seamen killed, three thousand ships sent to the bottom in this one ocean—and its huge toll of seven hundred and eighty U-boats sunk, to even the balance.

It would live in history, because of its length and its unremitting ferocity: it would live in men's minds for what it did to themselves and to their friends, and to the ships they often loved. Above all, it would live in naval tradition, and become legend, because of its crucial service to an island at war, its price in sailors' lives, and its golden prize—the uncut lifeline to the sustaining outer world.

[6]

Their U-boats had been taken under guard, by a trio of bristling motor-gunboats, which shot out of Loch Ewe and came snarling towards them at approximately forty knots. The newcomers had turned in a welter of foam and spray, loosed off a burst of machine-gun fire for absolutely no reason at all, and then settled down ahead and astern of the prisoners, with the contented air of men who had done the whole thing themselves. Their only signal had been: "We have them."

Saltash, feeling as if she had been rescued in the nick of time, was free to go to her anchorage.

The big frigate moved up the quiet sheltered waters of the loch towards the collection of shipping that lay at its head. It was past sunset, and cold: home from the sea, they were still muffled with strange caps and helmets, still duffle-coated, still stamping feet that were heavy with sea boots and thick grease-wool stockings. A strange quiet lay over *Saltash*, though her decks were crowded: there must have been a hundred and fifty men on the upper deck, lining the rails or sitting inboard on ammunition lockers and hatches, but they watched in silence the calm water round them, the lovely hills still orange-tipped by the sun, the white cottages on the fringe of the loch, and the anchorage they were making for. It was the end of their day, and of the battle; but it was a sub-dued moment all the same: at such a time a man could not easily speak, he could best stand and stare.

As they drew nearer to the ships ahead, they saw that with the exception of a corvette, an oiler, and some small craft, all the rest were U-boats—sixteen of them, moored in a compact group under the eye of a battered trawler.

There was a murmur at that, and then silence again. The men of *Saltash* edged slowly across to the port rail of their ship, and gazed down on the surrendered U-boats as they steamed past them. They saw that the U-boats were already empty grey shells—their crews taken off, their guns shrouded: they lay silent and useless—but they were still the enemy, still the things that *Saltash* and the others had fought and defeated. There was about them much to look at, much to note, but the single detail that drew every man's eye was the big white "U" on each conning tower. The captive letter, repellent symbol of a hated warfare, now summed up the whole struggle for them: they had been chasing that "U" for years on end, and now here it was, fought to a standstill and safe under guard—U for unsuccessful, U for undone, U for everything that meant victory for one side, final defeat for the other.

Saltash moved on past them: Ericson rang for Dead Slow: Raikes busied himself taking cross-bearings from the shore. On the fo'c's'le, the windlass clanked and hissed as the first shackle of cable was run out: Allingham, standing in the eyes of the ship, faced the bridge and waited for the signal to let go the anchor.

Raikes called out: "Coming on the bearing now, sir."

"Stop both!" said Ericson. While *Saltash* drifted to a standstill, he glanced round him. It was a good anchorage, the best they could wish for—sheltered, no shallow water near by, no other ships to crowd him if *Saltash* started swinging. And the U-boats were within sight. . . .

"On, sir!" said Raikes.

"Slow astern, both!" Ericson called out, and then, as *Saltash* gathered gentle sternway, enough to lay out the cable in a straight line on the sea bottom, he said: "Stop both. . . . Let go!"

Allingham raised his hand in acknowledgment, and repeated the order to his leading hand. There was a clunk! as the stopper was knocked off, and the anchor plunged down with a rattle and a roar, waking the echoes all round them, making the sea-birds chatter and cry. The ripples spread, and faded: *Saltash* came to a stop, tugging gently.

"Got her cable, sir!" Allingham called out to the bridge.

Ericson drew a deep breath, stretching a little under his duffle coat. That was all. . . . Over his shoulder he said: "Ring off main engines."

[7]

Though the rest of the upper deck had long been deserted, Lockhart was not surprised to find Ericson up on the bridge: the big figure, looming suddenly out of the darkness, did not startle him at all. He might have guessed where the Captain would be, at this closing hour. . . . Ericson turned when he heard his step, and said: "Hello, Number One," as if he too were unsurprised. They stood side by side in the cold darkness, saying nothing for a space, sharing the moment of relaxation and the grateful calm round them.

It was still early evening, but by now it was almost dark; the moon was already entangled in the rigging, and one by one the shore lights were coming on—the stars of peace, the first lights since the beginning of the war. The edge of the loch could be seen, and the shadowy hills above it: astern of them, the clutch of U-boats lay silent and immovable—solid black patches on the restless water. Outside their sheltered haven the wind moaned, as if still greedy for *Saltash*, and in the far distance the cruel sea beat and thrashed at the entrance to the loch.

Lockhart knew why they were standing there together, leaning against the side of the bridge under the frosty open sky, though he was not sure that the moment could be adequately honoured. They were there because it was the last day of the war they had shared: the Atlantic battle was done with, and secretly they wanted to review it, even if it were by vague allusion only, even if no word were spoken. It was a time to draw the threads together—but perhaps, thought Lockhart, there were too many threads to this story: perhaps there was too much to be said, and to say it would entail a foolish babbling that the moment did not deserve. . . . But then this man, for whom he had such enormous affection, would not babble, would not cheapen.

"Five years, it's taken," said Ericson suddenly. "Getting on for six. . . . I wonder how far we've steamed."

"I added it up for *Compass Rose*," said Lockhart, grateful for the lead. "Ninety-eight thousand miles. . . . But I never did it for *Saltash*. It seemed to be unlucky."

The noises of the ship rose vaguely to them: as was usual in harbour, somewhere a radio was playing, somewhere a small wave curled and broke against their hull, somewhere a heavy-stepping quartermaster made his rounds. Now the U-boats, the black shadows with no more fear in them, were caught in the track of the moon, and held there for their pleasure.

"I wish some of the others could have seen this," said Lockhart presently. "John Morell. Ferraby."

Ericson nodded. "Yes, they deserved it."

Lockhart, drawing some lost names from the shadows of his mind, murmured aloud: "Tallow. Leading Seaman Phillips. Wells."

"Who was Wells?" asked Ericson.

"The yeoman in *Compass Rose*."

"Oh yes. . . ."

"He used to say to his signalmen: 'If you get worried, just sing out and I'll be up straight away.' "

"This is the time that you miss them."

"M'm. . . . But perhaps there are really too many people, to remember them properly. The names are just labels, in the end. Young Baker. Rose. Tonbridge, Carslake. All those chaps in *Sorrel*. And the Wrens we lost, on that bad Gibraltar convoy."

"Julie Hallam," said Ericson suddenly, trying it for the first time.

"Yes, Julie. . . ." For Lockhart's surprised heart, a twinge, and then nothing again. Perhaps, after a year, she really slept now, and he as well. It had been much the same with *Compass Rose*: there must be a special kind of war-memory—showing mercy in fading quickly, drowning for-ever under the weight of sorrow.

"You didn't get any medals," said Ericson inconsequently. "But I did my best for you."

Lockhart smiled in the darkness. "I can bear it."

"You deserved something, Number One."

"I can still bear it. . . . Remember when we had that lunch in London, and I said I wanted to stay with you in *Saltash*?"

"Yes. Made a lot of difference to me."

"Same here."

One thread, at least, was tied: one of the things they had not been going to say was happily said after all.

Ericson sighed again. "And we only sank three U-boats. Three, in five years."

"We worked hard enough for them, God knows."

"Yes." Ericson brooded, leaning heavily against a corner of the bridge where he must have spent many hundreds of hours. Out of the deep dusk he said—and after sixty-eight months it was still a shock to hear him use the words:

"I must say I'm damned tired."

A NOTE ON THE TYPE

This book was set on the Monotype in Janson, a recutting made direct from the type cast from matrices made by Anton Janson some time between 1660 and 1687.

Of Janson's origin nothing is known. He may have been a relative of Justus Janson, a printer of Danish birth who practiced in Leipzig from 1614 to 1635. Some time between 1657 and 1668 Anton Janson, a punch-cutter and type-founder, bought from the Leipzig printer Johann Erich Hahn the type-foundry that had formerly been a part of the printing house of M. Friedrich Lankisch. Janson's types were first shown in a specimen sheet issued at Leipzig about 1675.

Composed, printed, and bound by KINGSPORT PRESS, INC., *Kingsport, Tenn. The typographic scheme and the binding design are by* WARREN CHAPPELL.